Chris Niles was born in New Zealand. After ten years in London, she recently moved to New York City where she was lucky enough to find an apartment after only three and a half months of looking. She lives with her husband and a small dog in a 5th floor walkup and often entertains desperate schemes to pay the rent.

She is also the author of a series of crime mysteries featuring radio reporter Sam Ridley: *Spike It*, *Run Time* and *Crossing Live* (all available in Pan Books).

**By the same author**

Spike It

Run Time

Crossing Live

**Praise for Chris Niles and the Sam Ridley novels**

'Refreshingly assured . . . I can't wait for her next book.' Simon Brett

'A light touch and sparkling dialogue make this the most promising first for some time.' *Irish Independent*

'Sharp and funny portrait of life in a low-rent radio station.' *Daily Mail*

'An excellent debut, with hopefully more in a similar vein to follow.' *Crime Time*

'A good, engrossing tale which should keep its readers turning the pages.' *Oxford Mail*

'A slick and cheeky debut.' Val McDermid, *Manchester Evening News*

'An excellent first novel . . . Stylish, witty and making convincing use of its West London locations, this is a highly accomplished debut.' *The Hill*

'No airport reading would be complete without a terrific thriller, and *Run Time* is just that . . . The thrill factor doesn't slacken for a second.' *Cosmopolitan*

'Chris Niles' novel is brilliant.' *Eva*

# Chris Niles

# Hell's Kitchen

PAN BOOKS

First published 2001 by Pan Books

an imprint of Macmillan Publishers Ltd
25 Eccleston Place, London SW1W 9NF
Basingstoke and Oxford
Associated companies throughout the world
www.macmillan.co.uk

ISBN 0 330 48292 0

1 3 5 7 9 8 6 4 2

A CIP catalogue record for this book is available from
the British Library.

Typeset by SetSystems Ltd, Saffron Walden, Essex
Printed and bound in Great Britain by
Mackays of Chatham plc, Chatham, Kent

This is for the Epsteins:

Jack, Joseph, Martha, Randi, Stuart & Charlie.

The author wishes to thank:

Sam Maser and Jack Lechner for their constant
support in sickness, in health and in apartment-
hunting. Jamie Lehrer, John O'Brien and Kate, Luke
and Ian, for providing sanctuary.
And Roderick, for everything.

# Prologue

He hit thirty like a race-car driver hits a brick wall.

It was like he woke up one day and found 'This Must Change!!' tattooed on the inside of his head. The 'this' being his life.

Sometimes he even imagined he'd heard it out loud, but that couldn't have been right. He didn't go in for mystic mumbo-jumbo. He was a modern man.

His revelation – he'd decided to call it that – was this: here we are, stuck on a rock, light years from anyplace. Sure it's pretty and we're evolving as fast as we can and everything but basically it's the ass-end of the universe – did anyone ever stop to think that the reason nobody has visited is not because they didn't have the spaceships or technology, but because they didn't give a damn?

So here we are, on Earth, talking among ourselves. And if every single person, fish, tree and single-celled amoeba died, and the planet frizzled up into a congealed ball of carbon, who would even notice besides us?

But even though we are clearly unimportant, we're still obeying the Big Plan of the universe. We've still got gravity and tides and we revolve around a star, just like every place else. Big or small, we're part of it. Like fractals – one millimetre of coastline looks exactly the same as one kilometre.

Once Cyrus looked at the big picture, he started to think differently about himself. He could imagine cutting a smooth swathe, like a planet's trajectory. Confident. In charge. Composed. Grooving right along with the cosmos.

Up till then – through his teens and twenties – his life had really suffered for not knowing this. He'd despised who he was and didn't trust any decision he made, so he tried to make no decisions at all. He had drifted with no goals and no drive.

He hadn't even known himself. He saw his reflection in the mirror every day, but who that person was – his values, his hopes, his fears – he didn't have a clear idea. The information was mixed, like a radio that was tuned to a weak, far-away signal. One day it was rock and the next, heavy metal. Totally confusing.

His parents were no help whatsoever. In fact, he firmly believed that many of his problems stemmed from them. He was a result of their failure to be human beings. He was the only child of a socially ambitious couple who had wanted their son to be as driven as they were – a biological mirror to their own successful but shallow lives.

This hadn't happened. How could any kid have lived up to what they wanted?

Not that they had given up easily. Once they figured out he didn't have the raw material, they tried to buy success for him: the best boarding schools, the best nannies for his educational vacations, the best private tutors and psychotherapists. Cyrus had visited a grey-haired Freudian analyst on Park Avenue from the time he was old enough to understand the concept of the superego.

Oh, well.

He had emerged from the family cocoon not a vibrant butterfly but a miserable worm, crushed by the sense of his own inferiority. Little that had happened since had tempted him to change his mind.

His personal life really sucked. He had tried with women. God, how he loved women! Too much, probably. He didn't know how to hold back, to be mysterious. He was like one of those dumb clucks who spill their whole life story right after they've been introduced. He just couldn't hold it in, even though he knew it was social suicide to blab, blab, blab. And there was no way he could keep his poor sense of self out of the picture. He'd tried, skipping over the glamorous details of his so-called privileged life. But somehow they always knew. It was scary how they knew. Did they have some kind of radar? Like bats? He couldn't figure it out. Sure, some of them responded to him. He wasn't bad-looking, he kept himself neat, he wasn't a total schmuck. But even the most sympathetic ones gave up after a few weeks. He really wished he knew what drove them away.

There wasn't much else to keep his mind occupied. He didn't have a job, didn't need one. His family had plenty of money. There was no need to park himself in some cubicle every day just to pay the rent, processing words so fast that it sent darts of pain up his arms. He had bank accounts and trust funds, and a tax-sheltered Individual Retirement Account.

Most people would have called him lucky, but he didn't see it that way. Having money freed him from the burden of making a living, but presented a much greater challenge – how to fill those relentlessly empty hours that rolled around every day.

There were few hobbies that he could get excited about. His parents' well-funded attempts to make him accomplished had only made them poorer. Despite years of lessons he couldn't ski, ride, cook, sail or dance the merengue. A five-year-old had once beat him at chess.

In short, he was a failure in a society that valued success over every other quality.

Somehow, in his twenties he'd kind of limped by. It had been bad, but not too bad. Back then, to be a slacker was kind of fashionable. But in his thirties he knew that wouldn't work. He needed something. Not just for appearances' sake or to find a woman, but for him.

And it was amazing the way things worked out, because pretty soon after he'd started to think like that the answer had come.

He found the Master Motivator. And the Master Motivator began showing him the way.

# PART ONE

PART ONE

# Chapter One

After three months in Manhattan, Tye Fisher had decided Upper West Siders didn't deserve New York.

It was a question of attitude. The city had everything one could want. Any perversion or passion could be catered to, at any time, in any place. Pleasure – or pain – could be ferreted out in a dungeon in the Lower East Side, in the foot-fetish bars of the Village, in the dance clubs of Harlem, in obscure ethnic restaurants in the Garment District. New York was the cultural capital of the modern world, the most influential city in the most influential country on earth – the new Imperial Rome. And it was the beginning of a new century.

But this news had not reached the busy burghers west of Central Park, who thought they were living in the suburbs.

In the city that never slept, they dined early – in stodgy, overpriced chain restaurants with bad service and worse food. Then they were home and tucked up by ten because one's personal trainer came at six.

It was a style desert. The women looked as though their outfits had been pieced together in the aftermath of an explosion at a craft fair. Matrons who clogged the pavements with triple jog-strollers and golden retrievers wore cutely embroidered jumpers, blouses with flouncy collars and chunky, woven overcoats in variegated shades of sludge brown. Men wore shoes with tassels and talked incessantly about golf.

Tye had expected so much more. Americans had invented the twentieth century and everything that made it stylish, then turned their backs on it.

Not that she had tired of the city, far from it. It suited her just fine. She liked the way it made her feel. You could be anybody here; just jettison the old persona like a spent fuel chamber and speed off with a streamlined new one.

As far as she was concerned, the booster rockets had dropped and stage two had begun.

Tye had had high hopes of Adrian, whom she'd met at a party in London and had followed across the Atlantic on a vaguely articulated whim.

Adrian was an artist. He was good-looking in a Daniel Day-Lewis verging-on-a-nervous-breakdown sort of way and he liked to make barnyard noises during sex. This was no problem at all for Tye, who, possessing many faults of her own, considered they made her ill-qualified to judge others.

But there was no denying Adrian could be difficult. He was moody, overbearing, pompous and ill-informed. He had only a spasmodic interest in personal hygiene and was, by most educated standards, a terrible artist. This, too, was perfectly fine by her. Tye could see past the surface and appreciate Adrian for an attribute more true and lasting – three thousand square feet of Art Deco duplex on Riverside Drive.

It was a beautiful apartment, possessing all the right real-estate buzzwords – spacious, sunny, south-facing balcony. It was obscenely, fatly large. People gasped with admiration and envy when they walked into it. Tye, who'd initially only planned to stay for a few weeks, had known Adrian was the man for her the minute she laid eyes on it.

But now, it appeared, Adrian was kicking her out.

'My wife is coming to visit,' he mumbled one morning over breakfast.

'Precious, you didn't tell me you were married,' she said sweetly. Not that it would have mattered one jot.

'I am.'

'Congratulations. And how long is your wife staying?' Tye was thinking she'd take a short holiday. Perhaps a little spa in the desert. On Adrian's money, of course. If he was going to inconvenience her, he'd have to pay. She'd act put out, just so he wouldn't get the idea she was a complete pushover, then skip off to Arizona and bury herself in expensive mud. Bliss.

'For good.'

'For good.' Tye repeated it calmly. It couldn't be as bad as it sounded. There had to be a way round this. Perhaps Adrian would set her up in her own apartment. She began mentally shopping for furniture. Fifties, perhaps, or modern. She could never decide. Perhaps a classy mixture of both – yes, that was it. Eclectic. She didn't want to be pinned down. None of his art, of course. Not while she had eyes in her head.

'She has been living in France, but she is tired of France.'

'It can so easily happen, if one isn't careful,' Tye said sympathetically.

'Lyon is so provincial.'

'I'm very sorry to hear that.'

She pursed her lips as if to stop the question that was poised to emerge from them . No time for niceties. If Adrian was disinclined to give her an explanation for the wife-in-absentia, then she wasn't going to drag it out of him. Not her style at all.

The radio played softly in the background. NPR, with news of wars, taxes and police killings. Adrian busied himself with his croissant. Tye took a thoughtful sip from her coffee. The china cup clinked lightly against the saucer. He really is a shit, she thought. But she didn't dwell on it. No point.

She had the gift of thinking fast. One of her best traits, even early in the morning. She walked around to where Adrian sat, casually letting her bathrobe fall open, exposing her lean, flat stomach and more besides. She slowly unzipped his pants and caressed his dick, casual like, as though nothing could be more natural. It sprang to attention, just as it had that first night in the potting shed at the party in Crouch End. No matter what their intellectual incompatibilities, there were never any problems when it came to sex.

She massaged him teasingly, until she was sure she had his complete attention. Adrian squeaked softly as Tye lowered himself down on him. Her concentration on Adrian was total. There was a lot riding on this, in more ways than one.

He bleated as Tye's rhythm got faster. A signal for her to slow down, ease off the clutch a bit. Usually, he liked what Tye thought of as teenage sex – rough, fast and semi-clothed, up against a wall somewhere. Nought to sixty in thirty seconds. Usually she obliged him.

But it wasn't going to be quick this time. She had to give him something to think about. Something that would make him reconsider his precipitous decision.

It was easy to string him along. There were no prizes for guessing when he was about to come because he always started grunting like a pig due for slaughter. She'd keep him just off the boil the whole morning if need be. Why not? She didn't have any more pressing engagements. She eased herself gently down on him.

But her plans for a lingering seduction went awry. Adrian grabbed her, jiggled her up and down a couple of times and then yelled, 'Wonderful,' thus transferring the remains of his croissant from his mouth to her face.

It happened so fast she didn't have time to feign ecstatic pleasure.

'She comes here next week. You have to leave.' He said, lifting her off and dusting the croissant crumbs from his lap. Then he picked up the newspaper.

'But where will I go?'

Adrian shrugged. 'Wherever you like.'

Not back to London, that was for sure. Too many burned bridges in old London town. Besides, she liked New York. It was flash and brash and not nearly as important and sophisticated as it liked to think. She could admire that kind of attitude.

The problem was finding a place to stay. She had

no real money of her own and no friends here. She needed a kind and preferably rich stranger to take her in – that would be the quickest, easiest way out of her problem.

She began a mental checklist of Adrian's friends. Boring businessmen, mostly. Boring didn't matter, of course. Rich was the only qualification. But who was rich enough? Most of the people Tye had met through Adrian were either married, with their wives firmly in residence, or probably didn't have the kinds of funds needed to keep her separately in a style that made her feel relaxed.

But Lonzo Parker might be a possibility. A chunky guy who did something in mergers. He'd given her the eye at a cocktail party only last week. Poor old Lonzo. He played squash, never drank anything stronger than caffeine-free Diet Pepsi and thought his red braces the last word in sophistication. Still, he *had* mentioned a loft in Soho.

Tye had a weakness for lofts.

As she packed, she selected a pair of her tartiest knickers, crotchless black with purple bows, and put them at the back of a drawer in the walk-in closet. They'd been a gift from Adrian. She was sure Mrs Adrian laboured under no illusions about her husband, but the knickers would at least remove the agony of doubt. She sprayed some of her strongest perfume – one that she knew Adrian didn't like – onto the hanging, fabric sweater-holders and tipped some more into the fabric-conditioner compartment in the washing machine. It would linger long enough for wifey to get the message.

Three hours later she was done. Her life packed in two suitcases and ready to go downtown. She smiled as she stepped out onto the street and inhaled deeply.

It was a brand new day.

# Chapter Two

Gus and Susie Neidermeyer knew that finding an apartment in New York was going to be tough.

They'd read the articles in the *New York Times* about walk-in closets in the Village renting for two grand a month. Two grand! They'd heard the horror stories from people they knew who'd lived there – the cockroaches, the sleazy landlords, the greedy doormen, the bribes. But they were mentally prepared. Gus and Susie had never done anything without careful research. That's what had made them honour students at school back in Michigan. And it was going to stand them in good stead for the rest of their well-thought-out lives. So when the Big World called, they answered gladly, but a little cautiously. Planning, research, groundwork: their motto and their mantra.

Gus had a job at a respectable insurance company where he'd be starting in a couple of weeks. Susie had had a poem and two short stories published in a Michigan magazine. She planned to work in publishing. Her first task though, was to look for an apartment. Gus had wanted to go to New York ahead of her and get everything lined up, but Susie said no. In the three months they'd been married, they'd never been in separate towns, not even for a night. Besides, even though she loved her husband, she doubted that he'd be able to pick out the kind of place she'd be happy living in. Gus's taste was basic dorm stuff. Finding their first apartment in the city was going to be an adventure. Choosing the furniture, exploring the stores in the neighbourhood. Setting up their home. She wanted to be part of it from the beginning.

When they arrived at Penn Station they took the subway to a Catholic hostel in Chelsea, which their research told them was the cheapest place to stay in Manhattan. At sixty dollars a night it was still expensive, but they indulged themselves a little. They were grown-ups now, not college students.

They had sex, then went out to a Mexican restaurant in the Village, drank a couple of beers and rubbernecked a crowd they didn't yet recognize as B and T: the Bridge and Tunnel people, the suburbanites in town for a good time. They made it back to the hostel before the midnight curfew.

The next day they picked up copies of the *New York Times* and the *Village Voice* and started looking at the classifieds. They knew better than to go through a real estate broker. Brokers were expensive and would want all sorts of things they didn't have yet, like a track record of full-time work or lots of money in their bank accounts.

It was cheaper and easier to find someone who had an apartment but was going out of town and wanted to sublet.

They took the papers back to the hostel and started circling the ads for places they could afford. There weren't that many. But it was the middle of the week. There were bound to be more at the weekend. In the meantime, they'd beat the bushes a little. Find out what was out there.

They called a few numbers. Most of the apartments had already gone, even though it was still early. They arranged to see one apartment that afternoon, just off Avenue A. To kill time they took a walk in Central Park, admiring the rollerbladers. For lunch, they sat on a bench and brown-bagged it – bagels and cream cheese with an apple each to finish it off. Last night's dinner had been an indulgence. They had to keep a watch on their money till Gus got paid.

The apartment was crowded when they arrived – at least ten people were ahead of them. It was in a basement the size of Susie's bedroom back in Lansing, Michigan. The walls were painted a sickly purple and there were only two windows in the whole place. A woman, an NYU grad student, was telling the current tenant about her educational accomplishments. She did it nervously, as if she were taking a test. She had bank statements clutched in one hand, references in the other. She also had her chequebook open and ready. The tenant was taking her information down on a clipboard. He looked disapproving, as if there wasn't anything she could say that would impress him. Maybe there wasn't, Susie thought. She could see there were at least twenty other names on that list. The apartment wasn't even that great. For one thing, it smelled like burned food and old laundry. It felt chilly, too, even though the evening was warm.

Susie felt depressed. We're totally unprepared for

this, she thought. We haven't even opened a bank account in New York yet. She pulled Gus. 'C'mon,' she said. 'Let's go.'

'You don't wanna put our names on that list?'

'He's never gonna call us,' Susie said. 'Besides, look at this place. Would you really want to live here?'

Gus shrugged. 'It's New York.' But he followed his wife back up the rickety steps.

Susie walked fast through the crowded streets. She needed to get some air in her lungs. Suddenly she regretted leaving their safe place in Lansing, where they had friends and family. Gus caught up with her. Made her stop and sit down on a bench. He stroked her hand and tried to comfort her. She was so cute! He still couldn't believe she'd married him instead of Joe Sorenson. He didn't want to ever give her a reason to doubt her decision. Gus knew Susie was the only woman for him. He was going to make her happy.

'It'll work out,' he said softly into her ear. 'Everybody says this is the toughest real-estate market in the world. One per cent vacancy rate – it's the most demeaning, degrading experience known to man.'

'I thought that was bikini shopping.'

'Are you kidding? That's for women. Bikini shopping is great for men.' He kissed her. They relaxed. It was okay; they'd only just started. And they had each other.

The next day Susie made more calls. Mostly she got answering machines. Sometimes a rude person on the other end would bark that the apartment was already let. Rudeness in any form distressed Susie, who placed a high value on civility. But she pressed on.

Gus hired a pager so they could be reached.

They saw three apartments the next day. The last was a group showing of a studio in Hell's Kitchen. Come between six and eight, the person on the other end of the phone said. Gus and Susie debated whether it was better to go first and make a good impression, or go last, by which time the other candidates would have merged into a blur. They decided on seven thirty. Susie paid special attention to her hair and Gus wore his new chinos and a red plaid shirt. They had matching sweaters which were a little warm for the October weather, but they still had the Michigan habit of dressing warmly, in case the weather 'turned'. They were both nervous.

'I feel like I'm going on a first date or something.'

'You blew me away on our first date.' Gus caught her from behind and smelt her hair, thinking as always, he was lucky, lucky, lucky. 'You can do it again.'

Susie didn't honestly think so but she put on a cheerful smile. Marriage was so new to her she was still learning when to be honest and when to dissemble. She had Gus to think about now, not just herself. No use throwing a hysterical hissy fit, which was what she really wanted to do, that would only make Gus feel worse.

'Oh well,' she said lightly. 'Nothing ventured, nothing gained.'

The viewing was as bad as they feared. And so was the one after that, and the one after that. They trooped through cellars, attics, corridors. Any kind of interior space that had a front door attached was called an apartment. The tenant always wanted some laughable amount of money and ten or fifteen people would have killed to get it. Most of the time when she walked into these places, Susie really did feel like laughing. Some didn't even have windows. Not that it mattered; no one ever called them back. No one ever chose them.

It was like dating in hell.

'What are we doing wrong?' Susie asked.

Gus, who was hunched over his calculator, shook his head. 'It takes time,' he said. 'We'll get there.'

Susie was hand washing some underwear in the sink when Gus's beeper went off. Gus had gone out for a bagel. Bagels were their staple food these days, that and hot dogs. She grabbed some change and went to the pay phone across the street from the hostel.

'Mrs Neidermeyer?' The voice was educated, with a slight accent. Susie couldn't figure out what the accent was. 'I'm returning your call about the apartment in the Village. My name's Cyrus.'

Susie's hand raced down the list of places she'd called. Beside each one she had written 'left message' in her precise handwriting. Here it was: studio flat to sublet for six months. Sunny, spacious. NO FEE. Which meant no greedy broker.

'Hello, Mr Cyrus,' she said, glad to be talking with someone who had good manners for a change. 'Thank you for calling back.' She was excited. She had a feeling about this one. Here – maybe – was a civilized person they could do business with.

'My brother has to leave the city for six months, and I'm looking for someone to take care of his place.'

'Oh,' Susie said. 'My husband and I are very responsible.' She stopped herself. She was gushing. She didn't want to gush. She had the feeling this man would not appreciate it.

'It's pretty small, but it's cosy. And it's just been renovated. Would you like to see it?'

'We'd love to see it.'

'Excellent. How does eight o'clock tonight sound?'

'We'll be there,' Susie said. When she put the phone down she did a little dance. Then she realized she hadn't asked what the price was. Oh no, it was going to be way too expensive. She slumped onto the bed, studied her reflection in the mirror. Damn. Maybe she should call him right back, so no more time was wasted. But she didn't. She had a good feeling about this one. Perhaps he'd like them so much – and would see right away that they were careful and responsible – that he'd agree to give them a good deal.

She was singing when Gus came back from the deli.

# Chapter Three

William Quinn found himself abruptly homeless when the landlord of his place in Chinatown died. The fatality occurred after a dispute with a rival businessman that left the landlord with parts of his body pierced in an unfashionable way. Quinn came home to find his building surrounded by cops and ambulances and blood sprayed up the walls of the take-out food joint that occupied the ground floor. After that he had had to leave. It wasn't the bloodshed that discouraged him; it would take more than murder to pry a New Yorker from a good, cheap apartment, but a couple of days after the landlord was zipped into his body bag, his son came by and let the tenants know that things were going to be different. He had found a convenient loophole through which to force a two hundred per cent rent increase.

Quinn was more than a little irritated by this turn of events, but not as much as his brother Malcolm, to whom he'd immediately turned for succour and shelter.

'Two weeks, no more,' was his brother's welcoming salutation.

'Nice to see you too, Mal,' Quinn said wearily, having schlepped his two suitcases and a laptop computer several blocks. He dumped his bags in the living room.

'You're sleeping on the sofa.'

'You mean we're not having conjugal relations?'

'I mean don't get any ideas about the spare room. I've got all my computer stuff in there and it's not moving. It's really delicate.'

'Unlike me,' Quinn said, stretching his shoulders. His bags had been heavy. 'Love a cup of coffee.'

'You know where it is. You're here often enough.' Malcolm crossed his arms to emphasize that he wouldn't be running around after his brother. He watched while Quinn found the coffee in the fridge and the plunger in the right-hand drawer above the sink, and put some water onto boil.

'Go easy with that, it's expensive,' he said as Quinn ladled several spoonfuls into the plunger. Quinn checked the packet: Dean and DeLuca – strained through the nose hair of a Mongolian goat, no doubt. That was the only way the outrageous price could have possibly been justified. Mal was such a yuppie. He would make the front page of the *Times* the day he bought something that didn't have a fancy-schmancy label.

'Strong is the whole point of coffee,' he said mildly, pouring the boiling water over the grounds. 'Besides, I've had a hard week.'

'Sure. Working your fingers to the bone. What's the occupation du jour? Busboy? Doorman?'

'I have a writing job, as a matter of fact.' It was true. Quinn sipped his coffee contentedly. Shelter, work and caffeine – what more did a guy need? The pay was crap, naturally. But it was worth it to be able to contradict his brother.

'I thought you were supposed to be blocked. Mom told me not to expect the Great American Novel this year.'

Quinn stifled his irritation. Deep down, his brother was a sweetheart. Trouble was, it'd take a diving bell to get deep enough. No point in expecting him to change. 'I never said that. I never said I was blocked. Anyway, the creative process is a mystery. It depends on the whims of the Muse,' he said airily.

'The goddamn Muse,' Mal snorted. 'You're a bum. And in ten years' time you're still going to be a bum.'

'Don't worry, it's not contagious.' There were times when he wondered how he and Mal could have come swimming out of the same gene pool. 'Hey, we'll have fun, eh? Go out, have a few brewskis?'

'This isn't college, Quinn. Some of us have grown up.'

Quinn sighed. 'Where should I put my stuff?'

Writing aphorisms for fortune cookies was not something he was going to be able to brag about at fancy parties, but it was work and it got him sitting at his laptop every day. Or, rather, it got him hunched over Mal's kitchen table with his computer perched between the Alessi mug rack and the exotic fruit that Malcolm displayed on a shiny platter but never seemed to eat. Mornings were the best time. Mal left for his job on

Wall Street early and Quinn got to hang around the apartment, pretending it was his.

Quinn sometimes had to admit that working on Wall Street had its advantages, and a sunny apartment in the Village was one of them. The problem for poor Mal was that he had no time to enjoy it.

*You will graduate from business school and buy a house in the Hamptons,* he typed. Reassuring but not very original. He was supposed to come up with something with a little more zing. He deleted and started again. *Your house will burn down but you will rediscover the joys of living.*

Too specific. He chugged some coffee. No brain work got done before three cups, at least.

*Good things are in store for you and your extended family.* It had a vague but modern ring to it. He poured himself another cup of coffee and went to the window. It was fall, but the summer temperatures were still hanging on. The sun blazed and people were showing skin. It was much too nice to be inside. The thought of going out to the Italian bakery around the corner was tempting. He could take his laptop and watch the world go by, get inspiration from the ebb and flow of human life. But he wouldn't, he knew it. He'd get inspiration from the toasted pannetone and five shots of espresso. He forced himself back to the computer. He needed the money. He needed the discipline. He breathed deeply, willing his creative mind into action, flexed his fingers and began to type.

*You will never be killed in a freak accident.* He erased it. Started again. Think loose. Let the ideas spring up from the subconscious.

*The wise man does not shop at Bloomingdales on Christmas Eve.*

Quinn deleted everything he had just written. This wasn't working out. Perhaps he wasn't equipped to hold down a job, least of all a writing job. Perhaps he was using up all the creative energy that he should have been directing to his book. For a minute he thought about calling his friend Mark, an out-of-work actor who managed a Starbucks in midtown. He could get a job as a latte jockey. No thinking involved there. Then he imagined the legions of uptight bastards who'd yell at him from daylight to dark because their mochaccinos weren't mocha enough and it was a symbol of everything that was wrong with their lives. He decided he could live without it.

He sighed and went back to his computer. Started typing.

*Perseverance always pays off . . .*

# Chapter Four

Cyrus hadn't ever imagined that he would find the point to his life in a cut-price bookshop on West Broadway. He had always thought that the answers to the great secrets lay in inaccessible places, such as the tops of mountains, or someplace you had to make an effort to get to. But there it was. Waiting for him one day when he had been so deep in the dark spirals that it had taken all of his energy just to get out of bed.

He'd got up, hadn't even showered, run his hands through his hair and pulled on yesterday's clothes. He'd bought coffee and a doughnut from the Armenian street vendor, an indomitably cheerful guy who always wanted to chat about the weather.

'Hello! Yes. Good day, no?'

'Sure,' Cyrus mumbled. Tried to smile. He didn't mind the guy, he just couldn't figure out why he was always in exactly the same mood.

'Good day, today. No rain.' The man beamed as he handed over Cyrus's order. Cyrus nodded.

It had been a warm day, late spring or early summer and the streets were crowded. The tourists had begun their annual migration to the city. Cyrus walked slowly, sipping his coffee and breaking bits off the doughnut which was sitting in his pocket. He had no destination in mind, he was just walking. Sometimes it made him feel better, sometimes it didn't, it depended on how deep in the dark spirals he was.

There were drugs that could coax him out of these phases, and quite efficiently, but Cyrus didn't like taking drugs. His parents were 'Great Believers' in drugs for everything. Cyrus wasn't. Besides, there was a part of him, and he hadn't known it then, that was striving for the answer to his predicament – he didn't like to call it a sickness although he knew that others did – and the solution wasn't a tablet that masked the symptoms. The solution was something 'out there'. Cyrus liked to think of it as a helping hand. He'd had faith – and there was another old-fashioned word – that it would come. Eventually, it had.

If he had to sum up in one word the difference the Master, and his book, had made in his life, it would be this word: purpose. He had thought about it a lot, imagining himself being interviewed on *Larry King* or *Oprah*, with them asking him the secret of his success. And he'd lean back in his chair, one leg folded lightly over the other, fingertips touching and he'd say, 'Well, Oprah. If I had to sum it up in one word, it'd be –' and he'd pause to emphasize it – 'it'd be purpose.' And then he'd tap his fingers together.

For a while he'd thought the word he would choose was 'focus', because it was also true that the Master had helped him to do that, but in the end he'd decided on purpose. Focus was too much of a buzzword these days. It had lost its meaning. Purpose, on the other hand, felt weighty. It had *gravitas*.

'Because, Oprah, you know, as Martina Navratilova once said: "Going after what you want is easy, once you know what it is."'

He imagined he'd get a little laugh from the audience with that line. Or at least they would smile and nod their heads at the truth of the statement.

The dark spirals hadn't gone away when he found the Master, but they had become manageable. He no longer spent days in the apartment marinating in his own sweat, eating frozen food because he couldn't muster the energy to put the TV dinner in the oven. He no longer let the place get so messy that you couldn't see the floor, or let crusty dishes pile up. He had a routine now, just like any regular guy. He got up at seven thirty. He showered and dressed in clean clothes. Sometimes he went out for breakfast, sometimes he ate in, depending on what he was feeling like. He read the *Times*. He shopped for fresh food at the farmers' market. He bought a couple of recipe books and started making simple meals at home. He kept his place clean and on Friday afternoons he went to an art museum. Not big changes necessarily, but for him, profound. An outward manifestation of the Master's inner work.

The bookshop was one of those bargain-basement places with harsh strip lighting and linoleum floors. Cyrus would not normally have gone in at all, but he did. On impulse. Other people might have called it destiny, but not him. Destiny was another of those words that got bandied around way too much, in his opinion.

The woman behind the counter was reading the

*Village Voice.* She didn't even look up as Cyrus came in. If she had, she would have seen he was holding his coffee and she would have told him to leave. The sign outside read: No pets/blades/boards/unofficial solicitation/food/beverages. Cyrus put the coffee cup in his jacket pocket. It was cold now, anyway.

The books weren't even categorized. Some of the covers had been damaged because they had been thrown into big cardboard bins that wobbled if you touched them. Cyrus's eyes ranged over the titles, daring one of them to snag his interest. Classical literature, wonder diets. Books about how to navigate the Internet, how to decipher your software programme. How to speak a foreign language in three weeks.

He picked up a book on bonsai gardening but put it down quickly. He could hear his mother's voice, wheedling him to get a hobby, show some interest in something for God's sake, for once in your life. Hobbies were for nerds.

He was drawn to the other book first because of the cover. It was canary yellow. It had a picture on the front of a smiling man. He was kind of handsome, although a bit jowly. He had a suntan, grey eyes and a thick crop of hair. Cyrus instinctively put his hand to his forehead. His own hair had begun to desert him, slowly, and he felt betrayed by the loss.

The guy in the photo had his finger and thumb resting on his chin and he was looking pensively into the distance. Cyrus flipped the book over to read the author's biography. Dr Chance M. Finkelziz, MD. Same guy, in shirt sleeves this time, sitting backwards on a chair. Respected physician . . . Successful practice . . .

Adviser to the stars ... divides his time ... Cyrus decided not to read any more. It sounded too much like his own father for one thing. He started to put the book back.

Looking back on it, he was forced to concede the panhandler who came in on Rollerblades was like a force of fate or something. The panhandler was a big guy, unkempt, with a throbbing stereo clamped to his ears. Cyrus could hear a dull thrashing sound leaking from the earphones.

'Spare some change?' The big guy zoomed right up to him and planted himself in front of Cyrus, a cup held out. Cyrus looked at the woman behind the counter. It was then that he realized that she too had a stereo plugged into her ears.

'No.'

The guy didn't move. Cyrus went to step around him. The guy moved sideways too. The threat was implicit.

'Can't you read? The sign says no rollerbladers or panhandlers. You shouldn't be in here.'

The guy couldn't hear him. He went on shaking his cup with a couple of quarters in it. Sighing, Cyrus pulled some change from his pocket. Gave the guy fifty cents. The guy didn't move. Cup didn't stop shaking. Cyrus looked at the sales woman, but if she had noticed, she didn't care.

Cyrus put two dollars in the cup. The panhandler spun on his wheels and left the store waving the cup in the air like a victory banner.

It wasn't as if he had deliberately decided to steal

the book, so that made it okay. What happened was this: he left the shop quickly, shaking with fury because he felt so powerless. What he'd really wanted to do was tell the fucker to get lost and stop bothering innocent people and what he'd done instead was totally cave in. And while he was going over in his mind all the things he should have done and would do the very next time something like that happened, he realized he still had the book.

He was maybe half a block from the store. He could easily have gone back and explained what had happened. But he was kind of confused right then. Angry at the bookstore person and the panhandler and the stupid guy on the cover who reminded him of his father. He decided to keep it. To show everyone. And when he decided that, the very next thing he realized was that the dark spirals had disappeared. He felt clear-headed and light as though his own personal storm cloud had been blasted into a million insignificant vapour drops. It had been like waking up on the first day of summer vacation.

'I bet he's an academic or something,' Susie said as she and Gus walked over to the apartment. A busy Friday night crowd jostled them. New Yorkers barging impatiently, even on the weekend. Gus put his arm over her shoulders. Her hair was held back with butter-fly clips and smelled like lemons. 'He's probably going off to Europe or someplace.' Susie said, grabbing the hand that draped her. 'Florence or Berlin. And I bet the apartment's really neat, with books and kilim rugs and lots of souvenirs from his travels. I bet he's been everywhere.'

'I thought you said it was his brother's.'

'Same thing,' Susie said. 'He's a traveller, I can tell.'

'I bet he's got three incontinent cats and you've gotta wear a gas mask to get past the door,' Gus said. 'I bet there's mould halfway up the walls and it only sees the sun for three minutes in August. In the winter it's an icebox, and in the summer it's so hot you can cook an egg on the floor.'

'Always the optimist.' Susie let go of his hand in mock disapproval. He looped a skein of her hair lightly round his fingers.

They walked a block or so in silence, enjoying the rhythm of the city, and the still-new feeling of being together all the time.

'How much is it?' Gus said suddenly. 'How much does he want?'

'I forgot to ask,' Susie said. 'And the ad didn't say.'

They were silent once more. Susie berated herself again. Why hadn't she remembered to ask? Why hadn't she called him back? Unless the apartment was the size of a luggage locker, they wouldn't be able to afford it. Not in the Village.

'Maybe he'll give us a deal,' she said eventually, 'if he likes us. It is his brother's home after all.'

'Always the optimist,' Gus teased.

'We'll just have to charm him.' Susie tossed her hair. 'Leave everything to me.'

\*

'You've come about the apartment?' A tall, thin man, hands thrust in the pockets of a black overcoat, approached Gus and Susie as they checked the street number against the address that Susie had written down next to the *Village Voice* ad.

'I'm Cyrus,' he said, putting his hand out to shake theirs. 'Thanks for coming on such short notice.' He had long, greying hair pulled back in a ponytail, black jeans and black Converse hi-tops. A well-thumbed paperback book jutted from his pocket. Susie wondered idly what it was he was reading. She made a note to ask him later, before they got down to specifics about price. She loved to talk about books.

'We haven't got anything else to do,' Gus said. 'Finding a place is the priority.'

'You're from out of town, right?' Cyrus produced the key from his pocket, jiggled it in the lock. 'How long have you been here?'

'A week or so.' Susie smiled winningly at Cyrus as he stood back to let her through first. She was right. He was a gentleman.

'Not so long. And how are you finding our fair city?'

'About as much fun as a root canal,' Gus said. Susie shot him a look. She wanted to keep everything light and upbeat. Besides Cyrus had addressed the question to her. She wanted to seize the chance to dazzle him. Susie knew she had a certain effect on men, but she only used it when she had to. Cyrus was looking at her appreciatively. For a minute Susie wondered whether it had been a mistake to bring Gus.

But Cyrus laughed. 'A root canal, yes. What an apt analogy. Painful and expensive. An experience that calls for artificial stimulants.' He grinned, showing good, white teeth.

Susie decided then to stay out of it. Maybe Gus was going to be the one to bond with him after all.

'I realized after we talked on the phone that we hadn't discussed the price,' Cyrus said as he unlocked the door to the apartment. 'And you saw the ad in the *Voice*, yes? Where they forgot to put in the price. The *Times* remembered. I took out two ads.' He ushered them into a tiny corridor. 'So why don't you look around and tell me what you think, and if you like it, then we'll discuss money.'

The apartment didn't take long to look over. It was small. A living room, a kitchen that opened out onto it, and a small bathroom and bedroom. It was unfurnished, but it was clean and bright, despite being in a basement. After a whispered conference in the bedroom, Gus and Susie emerged, eyes shining. 'We like it,' they said, almost in unison. 'How much?'

'Twenty-five hundred,' Cyrus said. Susie could tell from his voice that it wasn't negotiable. She cursed herself for being a fool. She was a stupid, naïve country girl whose values had no place in this city. She felt teary and brushed a hand across her eyes to compose herself.

'Oh,' she said. 'That's way too much.'

Cyrus, leaning on the radiator, arms crossed, regarded them sympathetically. 'That's too bad. But look, you seem like nice people. Are you interested in another proposition, perhaps?'

# Chapter Five

Prior to the evening she spent with Lonzo Parker, Tye had been under the illusion that she had been on some boring dates in her life. After two hours in Lonzo's company, she realized that the men whom she'd previously thought of as tedious low-life tossers were – by comparison – statesmen and scholars.

They had arranged to meet at a restaurant. When Tye first rang to set up the date he tried the Manhattan version of the mating dance which goes 'I'm too busy and you're not important enough to waste a whole evening on'. He'd suggested slotting her in for twenty-five minutes sometime between seven fifteen and seven forty on an evening two or three weeks in the future. Tye, who knew from Adrian that Cistercian monks had racier social lives than Lonzo, insisted on dinner. It's a quaint custom from the old world, she said. Humour me. Lonzo snorted and harrumphed; he'd have to do some re-arranging. Tye gave him half an hour to consult his virtual schedule, then called back. He caved in, but seemed embarrassed to admit that he was available at short notice and blustered to cover it.

'I'm on a very strict diet,' he said. 'I'm lactose and

wheat intolerant. I only eat organic and I never go above Lincoln Center.'

Tye, who wasn't much interested in diets or geography, didn't quibble on any of those points, and agreed to a place he recommended in Tribeca.

It was fantastically expensive. Even Tye, who had thought herself inured to the casual extravagances of the rich, was shocked. The main courses started at fifty dollars and climbed steeply. And it was air food. Spun organic tofu, shredded Swiss chard reared on the sunny side of some holy mountain in Nepal, peas that had been hand-picked by Vestal virgins. The menu was unstinting in its verbiage. The actual food, even when placed in front of the puzzled diner, couldn't be found without a search party.

Tye stared at her plate in disbelief, then listlessly picked up a fork. She would have killed for haddock and greasy chips with gobs of tomato ketchup from her old chippie in London. Instead, she ordered a second Martini. There'd be some sustenance in the olive, at least.

Her order gave the barman something to do. Everyone else except she and Lonzo were drinking vertiginously priced Peruvian glacier water out of what looked like milk bottles.

Lonzo was attacking his third cola. It didn't fit the picture, Tye thought as she studied him, watching his larynx bobbing. He was clearly desperate to control his appetites but the craving for coloured sugar water indicated some deeper conflict. She wondered what he did when nobody was looking. Perhaps guilty lunchtime trips to McDonalds, ducking in like a bloke in a dirty raincoat sneaking into a sex shop.

Lonzo finished gulping and delicately wiped his mouth with the starched white napkin. A definite closet McDonald's freak, she decided.

Tye considered herself good with men, and it wasn't just because God had been carelessly generous with her physical attributes. She had straight black hair, long limbs and the sullen good looks of a super-model. Her perfectly angled face – wide-spaced, grey eyes, nose with a hint of a bump, delicately arching brows – gave absolutely no hint of what was going on inside. Which was good, because most men assumed nothing, and that put her one up on them. She knew she was a man-magnet, but when she thought of her looks at all it was in a dispassionate rather than narcis-sistic way. She didn't go to the gym, she wasn't particu-larly interested in fashion or manicures. She did the minimum of upkeep but in the way one would main-tain a rare vintage car. She had no fear of growing old or losing her looks; her genes were good. Her parents, despite their present troubles, looked almost as youth-ful and clear-eyed as they had done at her age. They were tall and slender and didn't yet need glasses or false teeth or plastic hips.

So Tye knew that because of her surface qualities, life would be kind. But it was only recently that she'd started to think about how she could maximize her advantages.

It had started in London. She had had an epiphany. Actually, she had been at the hairdresser, thumbing through a copy of one of the newspapers that was weary with the effort of pretending it was anything more than a society gossip sheet when she realized, reading an account of some pitifully minor celebrities who were grinning their faces off over inferior champagne at a posh party, that there had to be more enjoyable ways of making a living than her present occupation.

Tye had worked in the family business for some years, but had grown tired of it. And in London, it seemed, after the traditional British restraint and modesty had been ripped out by the roots, a victim of years of political 'modernizing', a lot of people who lacked her advantages were making an awful lot doing not very much at all. The media was full of their social exploits. In the new Britain, the less you did and more you boasted about it, the faster you got on.

It had taken her some time to act on this because her work ethic was so deeply ingrained. But eventually she conceded that the work ethic was about as useful as a stone flint on a spacecraft. Tye reasoned that if girls called Fenella and Sasha could forge careers out of trilling around celebrity parties in sluttish dresses then she could, too. It wasn't cheap and degrading, it was a post-modern career option. As with soap powder, it was just a matter of positioning oneself correctly in the marketplace.

'So,' she smiled at Lonzo over the gin-slippery rim of her glass. 'Tell me about yourself.'

*

One hour and twenty minutes later, she waved the metaphorical flag of defeat. In a city where to be boring, spoiled and overpaid were social advantages, Lonzo stood head and shoulders above the crowd. A giant among pedants. Lonzo didn't live in his own world; that would have been much too constricting for a man of his talents and opinions. He was the centre of his own finite, yet unbounded universe.

First, although the restaurant had been his choice, it was clear the food offered was never going to reach his exacting standards unless he guided the staff, step by step, in its preparation. If the menu suggested the Chilean sea bass be steamed, Lonzo demanded it poached. If the chef had constructed a salad dressing from ten-year-old Modena balsamic vinegar, Lonzo wanted fifteen. He went through the ingredients on each dish point by point, like a lawyer haggling over a millionaire's pre-nuptial contract. Occasionally he would look over at Tye and roll his eyes, inviting her into the circle of his displeasure. She stared back at him blandly. A single finger tapping lightly on the tablecloth was the only indication of her thoughts.

Lonzo didn't know it, but that evening he was lucky to leave the restaurant with his life. While he carved out bold new definitions of the word 'unbearable', Tye had the strongest urge to gently clean off her knife and plunge it into his throat. She imagined the blood spurting over his Armani suit, his little eyes bulging in horror as he slowly comprehended what had happened. She imagined the restaurant staff applauding.

'Jesus Christ, what is this?' Lonzo exploded as a plate was laid before him. The waiter stepped smartly to attention, his neutral professional mask carefully in place.

'Yes, sir?' he murmured.

'I told you I didn't want the yucca wrapped in banana leaves. I'm allergic to goddamn banana leaves.'

'They're palm leaves, sir.' The waiter stayed way back. Wise, thought Tye. There was going to be blood when she'd finished. Perhaps she'd just kill him right now, in front of witnesses. Apart from the satisfaction, it would also solve her accommodation problems.

'Who wraps anything in goddamn palm leaves?'

'We do, sir. Baby palm leaves, hand carried from Vanuatu.'

'Vanuatu? Where the hell is that?'

'It's a South Pacific island sir, known for its—'

'I know where it is,' Lonzo snapped. 'It was a metaphorical question. I thought you understood. I don't just eat anything.'

'No sir.' The waiter slid the plate away.

'This place has gone downhill.' Lonzo whistled at a passing waiter. 'No fucking idea, I mean, come on. Hey, you! Another Pepsi over here!'


Of course he had haggled over the bill, making Tye pay extra because her two Martinis cost more than his four colas. Of course he under-tipped the waiter, mumbling again, for the fifteenth time, that service had declined. Tye slipped back to put another twenty on the plate while Lonzo was threatening to call the manager because of the lack of respect with which his cashmere coat had been hung.

Outside she breathed the fresh air, pulled her wrap around her. She had intended to walk back to her hotel, to conserve her dangerously low funds, but now she would have given her last dollar to get away from him.

'I don't sleep with people on the first date.' Lonzo shuffled to the kerb, inspecting the sleeves of his coat for imaginary lint. 'I'm really not free till next month. And I'm going to need to see a full medical history. Why don't you drop it off with my secretary. You don't have a drinking problem, do you?'

'I don't think so.'

'Either you know or you don't. You did have two Martinis.'

'Yes, I did. When I say I don't think so, I mean there won't be a second date.'

Lonzo gaped. He shouldn't gape, Tye thought irrelevantly. It showed off his double chin.

'Why not?' A whine crept into his voice.

Tye stared at him. He really had no idea. Should she tell him the truth?

A taxi pulled up.

'I have a terminal disease,' she said. 'I'll be dead by Tuesday.' She put a hand on his shoulder. 'And did I mention? It's contagious.'

# Chapter Six

He'd never stolen anything before, not even a packet of gum. So the book became a trophy. He put it on his bookshelf with the cover facing out and every time he looked at it, he'd get a little jolt – part thrill, part guilt. It was like, 'I did that!' then: 'I did *that*?'

For days he fretted. The cops would show up at his door with a search warrant. He'd be arrested and there'd be a horrible, sneering story about him in the newspaper. Not because of who he was, or what he had done, but because of his parents. He would face ridicule and infamy.

But nobody came. After a week or so had passed he even went back to the bookstore carrying the stolen book with him, in case the assistant suddenly realized what had happened and he could pretend he was bringing it back, but she didn't. He carried the book out of the store a second time, his face burning. His groin tingling with excitement.

And it was weird, but even before he'd opened it, the book seemed really to fit in at his apartment. It was like having a friend there or someone coming over that you knew you had to make it nice for, like a girl. Almost the first thing he did when he got home was clean his place inside out. Then he washed himself and went out and bought groceries and flowers. That night he ate dinner sitting at the table with a napkin and place mat. He selected a bottle of Cabernet Sauvignon at the wine store and decanted it correctly. He even bought a dessert from the Hungarian pastry shop up the street and ate it off a china plate.

Only people who suffered from the dark spirals knew what kind of achievement that day represented. The couple who came to his apartment certainly wouldn't, as he could tell from a single glance. They were as sunny and wholesome as a breakfast cereal commercial.

But he was getting ahead of himself.

The Master had spoken to him. That was how it had started. He had been chosen, like a disciple. How else could he explain what happened in the bookstore? But the Master wasn't a guru or a god or anything, he wasn't running an ashram in the Catskills. He didn't have a gold Rolls Royce or hundreds of women lining up to sleep with him. The Master was someone you created, like a trainer or a spiritual cheerleader. He couldn't run the race for you, but he could make sure you were in peak condition. Actually, a Rubik's cube was a better analogy, now that he thought about it, with Cyrus as the cube. The bits and pieces were all there, the Master lined them up in regular order, made a pattern out of chaos.

The race? Well, you chose that for yourself, of course. You selected your goal and you worked towards it. The Master suggested visual images to help you choose but the decision part, that was all done by you.

It was important to be relaxed, Cyrus had found. He'd got into the habit of sitting quietly in his bedroom once a day for about thirty minutes. He'd felt silly at first, repeating the 'self-actualizing power mantra' while imagining himself bathed in the pink possibility light, but after a while he stopped thinking about it that way. And once that happened, he started to feel the power.

About two weeks later he got the first inkling of his purpose. Like all inspiration, it had stolen up quietly, taking him by surprise. He hadn't done anything with the knowledge – not acted on it or anything. He'd just let it sit there, as though by his inactivity he was testing the strength of it. It hadn't gone away. He had asked the Master to take it away if it wasn't right but it had stayed put, like a stray dog. Eventually he'd started feeding that idea, the way you start feeding a mutt simply because it hangs around the house.

Accepting his decision had two side effects. The first was no dark spirals. He no longer greeted the day with dread, running a timid mental check-up to see whether or not he would have to trudge through a swamp of despair, summoning every atom of energy just to clean his teeth or leave the apartment.

The second thing – and this was easily the best part – was confidence. He felt damn good about himself. First time ever. When he looked in the mirror he smiled at what he saw. He *liked* what he saw. He started to build a picture of his life. He could imagine himself asking women out on dates, shooting the breeze with them, telling jokes, them laughing. He could see himself doing normal things: meeting friends for dinner at a restaurant or playing ball in the park. He was suddenly in focus in his own head.

The focus wasn't always sharp, that was the problem. There were days when it got a bit fuzzy. Which was how the situation with the two out-of-towners came about.

Cyrus was easy and free. He was in no hurry. He had a few plans, but they were loose plans. Like an artist's cartoon that only vaguely prefigured the finished work. He was sketching in his head, that was all, just playing with ideas. He didn't want to commit himself to anything firm. He didn't have to, he had all the time in the world.

It was the guy's fault. If only he hadn't looked so much like a jock. And if only his wife hadn't had that hair. Falling gold.

It was the look that really got to him. Cyrus had opened the door to the apartment thinking these two would be for rehearsal, like actors blocking out a play. But it'd all gone a little crazy. He'd stepped back to let the woman in first. He'd been able to smell her hair. It smelt like lemons. Cyrus had wanted to go in next, but the guy brushed past him, almost pushed him to one side – and in his own home! Then he stood there with his arm around her shoulder, touching that hair, grinning, as if to say, 'I'm sleeping with her and you're not.'

It was the smirk that made Cyrus realize they both had to die. So what if his plan hadn't been specifically for them? He'd make do.

He'd taken them to his other apartment. He had two. Obscene really, in a city where space was the most valuable commodity, but there you go. He took them there. Told the girl to check out the bathroom while he'd taken the guy into the kitchen.

He was going to drug the kid with curare, which would slow him down in a big way. He had questioned his father about it some time ago and got a thumbnail sketch of dosages and so on. The plan was to jab him with a needle that was sitting waiting near the bread box. Then he was going to pretend that the guy had collapsed all of a sudden and when she came to check it out, he was going to whack her over the head with the baseball bat. He knew that wasn't the most efficient way to do it, but he had this picture in his head of him striking someone with a bat, and he thought maybe it was some kind of sign and it'd be a shame to waste the bat, since he'd bought it specially, so he decided to go with it. Then he'd finish her off while the other one watched, tied up and gagged. Drugged, but perhaps still able to comprehend what was happening.

He really wanted to do it that way. It appealed to his sense of theatre. He wanted to kill the girl while her husband sat there, helpless. Melodramatic it was, like a silent film or a soap opera. He had been so pleased when he'd thought of it.

But the girl came back. Saw her husband collapsed on the floor. And she knew. Cyrus had a story all ready, but he didn't get time to say any of it. Then he realized he had the syringe in his hand.

She kicked him hard in the jaw. The shock of surprise was almost as bad as the pain. The Master hadn't prepared him for this. He staggered, lost his grip on the syringe. What the hell was going on here? How did she get her foot up to his face so fast?

The girl was trying to get her husband to stand up. He was groggy. There was blood. Both Cyrus and the guy were bleeding. He was glad he remembered to put the plastic painter's dropcloth down on the floor – blood was hell to get out of parquet.

He picked up the fallen baseball bat, fingering his tender jaw. He was probably going to lose a tooth.

'Don't come near us,' the girl warned. She straightened up but stood over the guy, lightly balanced on the balls of her feet, skinny arms flexed in front of her. This was not the way he'd envisioned it. This wasn't what he'd seen in the pink possibility light. Why hadn't the Master prepared him for more eventualities? Had he deliberately set him up to fail? Perhaps this was some awful test – and if so, what would happen if he *did* fail?

Cyrus held the baseball bat in front of him. The girl danced in that small space. She was terrified, her eyes wide and wild, but she wasn't going to cave in. He noticed, too late, that she had a lean and well-trained body.

What would the Master do here? What was *he* supposed to do?

He squeezed his eyes shut and lunged, poking the bat at her like a fencing foil. The girl grabbed the bat, feinted to one side and kicked him swiftly in the kidneys. That hurt too. But she didn't get the bat away from him. He gripped hard.

The boy groaned, tried to get up. The girl's eyes went to him. Her attention was divided. Cyrus lunged again, swinging the bat this time. He cracked her on the shoulder. A direct hit! She crumpled. She was wounded but stayed on her feet, swaying a little now because of the pain. One arm still up. The other, injured, flopping down at her side.

This was so messy! Not at all as he'd pictured it. What was the problem here? Perhaps his mental preparation had not been stringent enough. Or maybe the Master was teaching him a lesson about improvisation. Yes, that must be it. After all, what was creativity without spontaneity?

The girl pulled at her husband, making for the door. That, at least, he had taken care of.

'You can't get out. You have to stay here with me. That's the way it is.' He said it gently, not in anger. Trying to make her understand she was part of a larger plan. To submit was the only option.

'I'll kill you first,' she snarled.

She tried to get her husband to his feet, but the last of the drugs had invaded his bloodstream. He was 250 pounds of blubber.

She screamed then, in pain, frustration and anger. She'd been trained to fight, but not while her husband lay at her feet and not with a broken collarbone. He'd bet anything it was broken, and he knew a bit about these things. Her eyes searched the room, looking for weapons. There were none.

Cyrus understood then; it was a battle of wills, like any competition. If he was going to overpower her, he had to break her concentration and her spirit first.

He thanked the Master and received the lesson.

\*

Tye went to Fanelli's for an omelette and fries. She sat at the bar, ate quickly and silently and thought about her position. She couldn't afford to stay at the hotel for much longer.

She extracted Adrian's contact book from her bag. It was one of two souvenirs she'd taken from the apartment of her former lover.

Peter Glick. Adrian's dealer. He ran a small but well-respected gallery on the Upper East Side. Reportedly made a fortune in the seventies representing some abstract impressionist who'd conveniently died young, hiking up the prices of his work.

Definitely a possibility. Peter was no Adonis: his skin bore the marks of the habitual excesses he'd shared with his artists in the days before needle-sharing became really deadly, and his health was shaky from an extended romance with heroin. But he knew everybody, and his parties were legendary. Tye could make contacts at his parties.

'Get you another one of those?' The barman pointed at Tye's empty coffee cup. 'Or something more interesting?' There was invitation implicit in his remarks. Tye clocked him. Tall, lean, sandy blond hair. Football-player pecs. Cute Dennis Quaid-style grin.

She shook her head. 'Just the check.'

She'd had it with American men for tonight.


God, it was always awful doing something for the first time, before familiarity smoothed and guided your hand. Cyrus had had a dread of it since childhood when his parents, in their desperate attempt to find an activity he had an affinity for, constantly urged him to try new things. He had hated each one because he was always clumsy, stupid, unknowing. As an adult, he had consistently avoided the unfamiliar and as a consequence – until he met the Master – his life had been shrinking. Now that he knew himself a little more, he was learning the thrill of the challenge: to rise, to embrace it and to grow.

Still, it was tough. Even with the will to do it, you couldn't unlearn entrenched habits overnight.

Part of the problem was that he was now in a bad mood. The girl had hurt his jaw and the pain made it difficult to concentrate. It was hard even to remember his plan, let alone execute it with any sort of style.

And he'd had to kill the boy first, which was a major bummer. He'd wanted to keep him alive while he killed the girl, his wife. That had been his fantasy. That was when he saw himself powerful and in control.

Killing the girl had been easy. Her will had slipped away with her husband's consciousness. She'd surrendered to him with a horrified inevitability. But preparing her body after death hadn't given him the pleasure he'd anticipated, until he had the idea. He propped up the boy so he looked like he was sitting. He had to get a chair from the back room, drape one arm over it to stop him from slumping forward. Then he got masking tape and fixed his hair against the wall so his head wouldn't fall forward. Not bad. Not bad at all.

He propped up the girl straight across the room – gave her husband a clear view. Then he took the scissors and cut off her hair. He cut off her clothes – her cheap denims and her cotton polo-neck sweater. Her well-worn running shoes and socks. Using a cut-throat razor, he shaved every part of her body. Her slim legs, her pudenda, her underarms. Scrape, scrape. The sound of sharp blade on dry skin. He made a pile of the hair on the floor. Long, golden locks, short curly, pale downy – from all over her body. He absorbed the sensations of the act, at one with the moment. To give him a sense of power and purpose he pretended the husband's lifeless eyes were watching, that there was still a vital connection to his soul. It wasn't such a big leap – he'd been alive moments ago, his body was still warm. All that was missing was his essence. And what was that? Nearly three thousand years of civilization, and philosophers still couldn't agree, so why should he quibble over a few minutes?

He whistled a little song as he carefully packed the hair in a Ziploc bag. It would stay yellow, he thought. He could keep it forever.

# Chapter Seven

Searching for a sublet did two things for Quinn. It prevented him and his brother from fighting, and it kept him away from his computer.

Quinn had made a career out of being a writer who didn't write. He had conscientiously avoided a 'real' job because he needed time to devote to his art. Half-written outlines for a handful of novels languished on computer disks and he talked through his themes at parties. He owned a stack of books in the 'how to' vein. He drank lots of black coffee and in the winter wore a beret. The only thing he never did was write.

Quinn acknowledged this failing, at length and often. Hell, he joked about it. It was part of his charm, part of the thing that women went wild for. That and the soft, low, almost Dublin accent, the black Irish looks – in a dim light he could almost pass for Jay McInerney – the professed weakness for Guinness, the love of the good yarn. Quinn liked to think of himself – spiritually at least – as having descended from a long line of distinguished Celtic men of letters. And this would have been true, except for the letters part.

But he would write, eventually. He fully intended to. Each day he was confident that he'd be favoured with A Bloody Great Idea that would make him a sensation. He imagined his name on the *Times* bestseller list, people talking about him, writing articles, asking his opinion, shooting pictures of him in trendy clothes for magazine layouts and so on. It'd be like winning the lottery, only he'd have artistic and financial credibility.

Up until now though, he had got more satisfaction from talking about the decreasing relevance of the novel as an art form than in doing anything concrete to arrest its decline. The talking was not only easier than the doing, it gave you more time to pursue women. Women loved writers; they had all the wrong ideas about them, which was how Quinn had blagged his way into Rhonda's bed.

Rhonda was strident, sexy, and a New Yorker down to the tips of her French manicured nails. Tall, blonde, coiffured to within an inch of her life. She had, Quinn considered, the brain of a gerbil – no intellectual interests or aspirations whatsoever. But she loved sex. They had been sweatily wrestling each other within two hours of meeting.

Another plus for Quinn was that Rhonda, after the initial, imperative enquiry about his occupation had decided she wasn't interested in his writing or lack thereof. Rhonda was the kind of girl who read one Danielle Steel novel a year, at the beach. Quinn liked that they didn't talk about it. He hadn't admitted it to himself yet, but he was growing bored with discussing his 'work'. These days he avoided looking too closely at the discrepancy between what he said and what he did. Somewhere, buried in the back of his brain was a bog patch of dread. Seething in that damp, dark space were all of Quinn's fears of failure. They hadn't seen daylight yet, but they were itching to, and on a subconscious level Quinn was working very hard to keep them covered.

He and Rhonda would go out once or twice a week, eat cheap Mexican, take on board a couple of margaritas and go back to her place for an hour or two of athletic fun. Quinn always left happy.

'Know anybody who's got a sublet, babe?' Quinn said idly, sipping his drink, thinking about her thighs, which were magnificent thanks to her gym-dedicated hours. If they kept to their timetable, and they usually did – Rhonda was a very focused girl who ran her life at a pace that would make a sergeant major blanch – they be in bed in fifty-five minutes. Quinn savoured the thought.

'I'm thinking of having a nose job,' Rhonda said, frowning into her make-up mirror. 'I've got a bump, it looks silly in profile.'

'You look great,' Quinn said. 'Don't have a nose job. Have another margarita.'

'I want to. I'm not happy with the way I look.' Rhonda pouted, snapping her compact shut. Quinn stifled a spurt of annoyance. He'd never met anybody who worried so much about appearance, and for so little reason.

'Be happy. And don't do it. Rhinoplasty – even the word sounds awful. Imagine how much worse the operation is.'

'Kathy had one. She says it changed her life.' Kathy

was a friend of Rhonda's who worked at the same marketing firm. She had even less going on upstairs than Rhonda and the two women competed fiercely.

Their food arrived; same order every week. A salad for Rhonda and a chicken burrito for Quinn. He applied a dollop of green sauce. 'That's not saying much about Kathy. She hasn't had a date since 1995.' Quinn hoped the anti-Kathy jibe would make Rhonda laugh and get her off the subject. Normally it was a sure thing.

Only fifty minutes and change to go. He attacked his meal. Just thinking about sex gave him an appetite. Rhonda picked at her salad, frowning. 'Kathy's dating an analyst.'

'A shrink?'

'An investment analyst. His speciality is leisure resorts. He bought her a Gucci watch for their third-week anniversary.'

'In this town, three weeks is some achievement.'

Rhonda shrugged and moved some food around her plate.

'Food no good?' Quinn said after a few minutes' silence. This was new. Dead quiet wasn't her style at all.

'Can we talk about us?' Rhonda said.

Us? Quinn thought – fear stabbing him. There is no us! he wanted to say instinctively. He didn't. Because there was an us – for four sweet hours, twice a week. 'Sure, babe. What about us?' He smiled lazily, although his heart was doing the three-minute mile. Not the commitment speech, please God, not that. There was no better way to put a damper on great sex.

'I'm twenty-nine, Quinn.' Rhonda picked up a slice of pepper on her fork, examined it and placed it to the side of her plate.

Oh, shit! I've forgotten her birthday. He flicked through his mental calendar. But she was March, he was certain of it. Pisces, yes. March, definitely. Safe on that count, then, March was months away. 'You don't look a day over thirty,' he said, smiling with relief. Rhonda rolled her eyes and consigned another piece of greenery to the side of her plate.

'And I'm not getting any younger . . .'

Did she want a baby? Quinn gulped a lump of unchewed burrito and nearly choked. Surely not, that would entirely ruin her figure. Somehow he couldn't see her with the 'Strollercise' moms in Central Park.

'. . . so I think it's time to make some decisions.'

Another joke nearly tripped off Quinn's tongue but he silenced it. Decisions for Rhonda probably didn't mean black beans versus pinto. Time to concentrate. He put his fork down. He felt sick. She wanted commitment and he was going to have to let her down so gently that she'd still invite him back to her place. This was going to be tricky. Quinn said a silent prayer to his grandfather, Pierce Mallon Quinn. Pierce had once told Quinn that he'd talked more than fifty women into the sack, an admirable total for any man, but in post-war Catholic Ireland a certifiable miracle.

'I guess what I'm trying to say is – I don't think we should see each other any more.'

Now Quinn was really shocked. This sort of thing didn't happen to him. He grew tired of women, not the other way around.

'You're a great guy. I really do like you, but I'm looking for someone with more drive.' Rhonda looked him straight in the eye. 'I couldn't marry you, Quinn.'

'Nobody's talking about marriage,' Quinn said faintly.

'If we're not, then where is this going?'

'Back to your place, twice a week.' Quinn grinned, trusting the old black Irish magic. 'Think of it like the gym, only more fun.'

But a sense of humour was not Rhonda's strong suit. She shook her head. 'You don't have a job. You're not going anywhere. How do you expect to be able to support a wife and family?'

'Marry money?'

Rhonda pulled a face as though she was tired of his jokes. 'I know what I want out of life, and it's a house and kids and a car and a couple of vacations a year, Paris maybe, a place in the Hamptons. I know where I want to be in ten years.'

'Ah,' said Quinn. He was thinking about Kathy and the leisure-resort analyst. Damn her.

'I know you think you're so smart and everything, and so artistic, but not everybody lives the way you do. And those aren't bad things, those things I want.'

'No, they're not.'

'And you're never going to be able to provide them. I'd be supporting you, more likely.'

'Probably true. But I look good in a frilly apron.'

Rhonda brushed this aside. 'You can see my point, then.'

'Can't we just fool around in the meantime? Till Mr Right comes along?'

Rhonda shook her head. 'Haven't you learned any-thing from me?' she said sadly. 'That's, like, such bad karma. I have to set sail on the course I want to take. The universe will not respond to me if I'm not open to the chance.'

'Yeah, it will. Men are like buses, didn't your mom ever tell you? They only come in bunches.' He reached out to take her hand. She withdrew it.

'I'm sorry, Quinn. Don't take it personally.' Rhonda threw a twenty on the table, leant over and kissed him on the cheek.

When she was gone he ordered another margarita. Women – who could ever figure out where they were coming from?

# Chapter Eight

Afterwards, when he'd put the bodies away, he felt smooth and clean and in control. Sure, it hadn't worked out exactly to plan, but he had got there in the end. He, Cyrus, had roused himself from his passivity, reversed the downward spiral of his life. Sure, he would do it differently next time, but there was no use beating himself up over that, it was part of the learning process. As he cleaned up, he realized he was content, the dark spirals sure were gone now and he was in charge.

He rubbed down the plastic he'd laid on the floor and rinsed it off in the shower. He sponged down the walls – the light paint showed up every trace of blood, but that was what he'd intended. He could see it then, and clean it off. No point in having other people come by and say, 'Hey! Where'd that blood on the walls come from?'

No point at all.

The plan he'd come up with to cover his trail was a good one. And he could take credit for it. It was not something the Master had helped him with; it had been his own idea. He'd rented a small apartment around the corner from where he lived. That made the trail between him and his new 'friends' impossible to follow.

He'd invited them to the first apartment, which they couldn't afford. So then he just happened to mention the second place, his real place. He'd told them a little story about his being a realtor, so they wouldn't be suspicious. The apartment was just around the corner, small but a steal at twelve hundred a month. Would they like to see it right away? Of course they would. Who would ever turn down a deal like that? And so he lured them to his trap. Even if they'd told somebody where they started out – left a message or the phone number from the ad – nobody would know where they ended up.

Neat.

He cleaned around the light switches and the door jambs and all the little corners. He used firm, even strokes with the old-fashioned scrubbing brush. It had a sturdy wooden handle and harsh bristles. He cleaned all the walls with great, sweeping strokes, relishing the physicality of it. He was warm all over, almost sweating. It wasn't long before the water in his plastic bucket was black.

He thought he'd finished until he looked up and realized some blood had even got on the ceiling. He fetched a ladder and another mop, with a long handle. When there were no dark spirals, he didn't mind cleaning. Before they had started, when he was a little boy it had always relaxed him. He'd kept his room clean and dusted, all his toys arranged according to size and his books alphabetized.

He let his mind roam as he scrubbed and polished.

He knew the Master would be pleased with him. He was pleased with himself, for sure. He'd done a good job.

Before he left the apartment, he checked the bodies in their hiding place. They were safe as could be. He'd have to get rid of them eventually, but there was no hurry. He didn't want to dump them in a place where a hapless dog-walker or jogger would find them; that was too dumb. He wanted to finish the job as neatly as he could. And he knew the Master had something special in mind. He would wait to figure out what it was.

In the meantime, he was going to kick back and enjoy this new feeling he had about himself.

It was still early. As he locked the apartment, he inhaled the chilly air with its shy promise of winter and smiled. He had an appetite; he'd find somewhere nice to eat. As he strode towards Seventh Avenue, he fingered the paperback book in his pocket. He never went anywhere without it now. It was the source of all his power.


Quinn woke to the sound of his brother's espresso machine. Still not used to waking on a strange sofa bed, he was confused at first. What the hell was that God-awful sound?

The mystery was solved when a cup of coffee appeared above him. It was connected to a hand, an arm, a college T-shirt and Mal. He was dressed for the gym.

'Hey brother.' Quinn rubbed his eyes, sat up. Remembered Rhonda. 'Shit,' he said.

The cup jiggled impatiently, Quinn took it. 'Shit,' he said again. 'Do you think I'm a bum?'

'Does the Pope wear a dress?' Mal was in a rare good mood today. He'd had the Quinn sense of humour once, but he used it so rarely his brother thought he'd donated it to the Goodwill. 'You're a disgrace to the venerable Quinn name.'

'Except that we come from a long line of peasants and drunks.' Quinn sipped the coffee. God, did he need it. 'I think, looking at it that way, you're the disgrace.'

'To be sure that was because of Cromwell – and the bastard English who kept us down.' Mal did a good imitation of their maternal grandmother, Molly, who had emigrated with the family when the boys were in their teens. Molly had declined to live with her daughter and son-in-law in the new land and had instead run off with a plumber from Queens who was twenty years her junior. She'd married her plumber and now spent the winters in Las Vegas, making money at the tables. The luck of the Irish – well, Molly had that, to be sure.

'Rhonda left me,' Quinn said.

'Who's Rhonda?'

'This girl I was seeing. She said I was a bum. Well, she didn't exactly say I was a bum, she implied it.'

'You are a bum.'

'Thanks for your support.'

'You don't need any support, Quinn.' Mal put the cup in the sink and turned the water on it. 'You live a charmed life. You don't do a lick of work, you cruise around telling people you're a fucking writer, you've never written even a shopping list, far as I can tell. People love you, and you always get your own way. Our parents think the sun shines out of your goddamned rectum.

'I'm the one who works seventy hours a week. I'm the one with the postgraduate degree. I'm the one with the investment plan. Do you think it makes any difference in our family? They don't give a toss about me. It's only ever been about you, baby brother.'

Sun and silence filled the apartment. Quinn was shocked.

'Oh,' he said. 'I didn't realize.' He had known though, somehow. He had known and taken it as his due.

'Yeah, well what does it matter? I'm going to be able to retire when I'm forty-five, right?'

'I'm sorry, Mal.'

'Don't be. It's a fact, is all. I've got to go. My spinning class starts in twenty minutes.'

'You've taken up crafts?'

'Very funny. By the way, this guy called for you – it's about a sublet.' Mal threw a card on top of Quinn's sleeping bag. 'He actually called yesterday afternoon, but since you can't be bothered to learn how the answering machine works, you didn't get it. It's probably already been taken.'

'Manned space flight is less complicated than that stupid machine,' Quinn said indignantly, but Mal had gone, slamming the door behind him.

Quinn looked at the card. *Call Cyrus*, Mal had written in his untidy hand, followed by the number.

He'd call anyway. Perhaps Cyrus was waiting for the right person to come along and sublet his apartment. Perhaps he liked writers and would give him a deal.

Yeah, right.

# Chapter Nine

Tye waited till mid-morning to call Peter Glick, the art dealer. She didn't want to seem too desperate and wondered if Adrian had already told him that they were no longer an item. Adrian and Peter had known each other for years, but whether they liked each other was another matter. Artists had such fraught relationships, it was often hard to tell. Adrian wasn't above making bitchy remarks about Peter, but he was so insecure, he bitched about everyone.

Tye knew that now was not the time to shrink. She had to get New York in a headlock before it trampled all over her. She didn't want to have to go home in disgrace.

'Peter. It's Tye Fisher.'

'Tye? Oh, Tye, darling. How are you? I hear the Mrs is back in town. Has His Nibs got you stashed somewhere?'

'Not exactly.'

'Oh.' A delicate pause. Peter sensed gossip and there was nothing he loved more.

'It's over. More or less. Well, more, more than less.'

'That bites.'

'Not any longer,' Tye said. She thought of Adrian in bed and stifled a giggle.

'Not pining, then?'

'I have more pressing problems,' Tye said. She sensed Peter would appreciate frankness. 'Housing.'

'Don't tell me. It's hell in this town.'

'I thought you might have some pointers.' Tye came straight to the point.

'Ask everybody you know.'

'I don't know that many.'

'Then you must come to my place and meet a few people. Perhaps someone who's going out of town, someone who knows someone. What price range are you looking in? I'm afraid everything is insanely expensive.'

Tye, who had no idea how she would even pay for something that was cheap, ignored the panicky feeling in her breast. If there was one thing working in the family business had taught her, it was that there was no point in worrying about trouble before it happened. Sufficient unto the day was the evil thereof, as her dad was fond of saying.

'I hadn't thought much about price,' she said. 'I'm afraid I can't afford to be fussy.'

'I'm having a few people over tonight. Come at eight. And don't worry, darling. These things always seem hopeless but they rarely are.'


Quinn made himself a second cup of coffee before calling the number Mal had left. *Small apartment in the Village*, he'd written, which meant it was probably the size of Mal's second bedroom. He looked in Mal's second bedroom. It was small, and crammed with high-tech gadgets, but he could fit everything he owned in there. He wondered if he could make Mal an offer for it. It would be so much more congenial than the cattle call that was subletting. Perhaps the two brothers could learn to get along. Quinn didn't think Mal resented him as much as this morning's outburst suggested; it was just a calculated ploy to make him feel guilty. Money was Mal's measure of success. He liked it and the things it bought, and he always had. When they were kids, Mal had put his allowance in interest-bearing accounts while Quinn had blown his on games and candy. Quinn had always had the flashy, cheap toy of the moment and Mal would save steadily until he could afford something really cool and expensive. He'd been a label freak even then.

But at this point in his life, Quinn was beginning to see the logic of Mal's position. He could not keep trading on his loveable-loser credentials for much longer. He would have to do something. He shuddered. Real work – even the idea gave him chills. Besides, what was he trained for? A big, fat nothing.

But first things first. He needed a place to live. He picked up the phone.


Tye started preparing for her date early. She had to make an impression, and fast. That meant hair and nails, everything. She studied her wardrobe – it wasn't vast, but every item had been carefully chosen to convey the impression that she was an idle rich girl. It was Tye's experience that the rich attracted each other by subliminal signals that the rest of the population didn't understand – rather like dogs hearing high-pitched sound.

It would be an art party, so everyone would be in black. She therefore needed colour. She picked out a pale-green Gucci dress that had holes scooped down both sides, held together by big gold rings. It was a bare-flesh fiesta. She wriggled into it.

Blah. It had looked great in summer. Tye didn't believe in suntans – she thought they looked cheap – but summer skin had a different lustre than winter, and now she looked like a blanched sardine. She threw the dress on the bed, and picked out a mauve lace and velvet slip from Voyage. Very nouveau-peasant – it had cost a fortune and still the seams weren't straight. Great for a lunch date, perhaps, when she had time to make an impression, but no good for tonight. T and A, as the Americans called it – that was what she needed: Tits and Ass.

There was a red dress scrunched in the back of her suitcase. A tight, stretch number, not a designer but a very good rip-off. Her father's tailor had put her onto a woman in Whitechapel who could make dresses that would fool a Paris couturier. This one, or its original, had first been seen on the catwalk at the Herve Leger show a season before. Tye had hers run up for a hundred and seventy quid. She eased into it. The fabric was stiffer than an elastic bandage and it felt like wearing a whole body corset. It pushed her breasts up and out, and her stomach in. A miracle. Tye pulled her hair back, smiled and was dazzled by her reflection. In this dress, she could be booked for speeding.

Cyrus was busy in the apartment when the phone rang. He was cleaning up his breakfast things before he went to the gym – he had an appointment with a man who was going to help him work out. He was going to get on a treadmill and have his heart rate monitored and be checked out for high blood pressure and other things. Cyrus knew he was in reasonable shape, he knew how to take his own blood pressure and sometimes did, but he was getting to the stage in life where a little extra effort was needed. Perhaps some changes in diet, too. Fact of life – the older you got the less you could take things for granted.

Exercise had always been a struggle for him, he wasn't very co-ordinated and had never understood his country's obsession with games. But it was time to pay more attention to staying in shape. People often lost it in their thirties, he was surprised at how some could look forty or even fifty just because of a careless gut. He didn't intend for that to happen to him.

Cyrus packed his brand new gym clothes and rounded up his keys and wallet, picked up his paperback book and put it in his pocket. Always the right pocket, never the left. He stroked the cover once, twice, his touch reverential. He had a lot to thank that book for. It was great the way help always came from the most unlikely places. Who would have thought a bunch of paper and ink could have had such a profound impact on his life?

He locked the apartment after checking that all the lights were off. It was a complicated process. When you lived in a basement you couldn't be too careful.

His cellphone rang as he took the key out of the lock. Another 'friend', probably. Another poor, desperate person looking for walls and a roof. The city had an endless supply, it seemed.

And who knew who it might be? He realized he'd left the phone in the kitchen. He unlocked the door and went to answer it.

# Chapter Ten

Quinn had felt cranky and depressed all day, which was unusual for him. He was down about not finding an apartment and angry at Rhonda and his brother for pointing out his shortcomings. It didn't help that he was starting to get an even stronger inkling that he wasn't the head writer on the script of his life, that other, more malevolent forces were ready to assign him something other than the wildly successful happy ending he had assumed for himself.

He'd rung the number Mal had left. The guy had been snidely rude, saying the apartment had already been taken by a lovely young couple who were very happy with it and he should have called earlier. Didn't he realize these things went quickly? The man on the phone had taken pleasure in rubbing Quinn's nose in his misery. That was the trouble with this town: people always trying to tell you your own business.

What had been his problem? Everybody knew what hell it was to find an apartment in the city. It was the one thing that could draw tears of sympathy from the most battle-scarred New Yorker. It was as unifying as war, because they'd all been through it. They might kick you down in the street and walk on your face, but if you were apartment hunting, that drew instant, 'Hey buddy, go get 'em' support. Quinn briefly thought of trying to get Rhonda back by playing up the homeless angle. But no: if she wanted a corporate slave, she wouldn't be bowled over by hearing he didn't even have a place to live. Besides, she was right. If they didn't love each other, there was probably no point in wasting time.

This novel, noble thought immediately made Quinn feel better about himself. Perhaps he wasn't a sex slut after all. Perhaps he was a sensitive human being with deep, genuine feelings. And perhaps these experiences were preparing him for the time when he could write. Yes, that must be it; he was embarking on a writer's voyage. After all, there was no great art without suffering. And if that were the case, it followed that it was best not to write anything just now. Better to wait until he knew where his suffering would lead him.

He picked up the *New York Times*, along with a new book he'd found. It was called, *Breaking the Block: Writers Talk Shop*. Then he went to the cheap Italian on Carmine.

Tye paused outside the Glick Gallery, mustering her composure. Normally it came effortlessly, but tonight she felt shaky. Her experience with the odious Lonzo had reinforced the fact that she wasn't on her home turf. These people didn't play by the same rules. They were strangers.

It was eight thirty, and a knot of people were chattering over wine. The gallery seemed too bright, and as Tye looked in, she recognized that what she was feeling was loneliness. I can't do this, she thought. I really can't, this isn't me.

But then the alternatives reared in front of her. Call her parents for money – and they had their own problems right now – or go home in ignominy, failed after only two months, all her friends assuming she hadn't been able to hack it. She couldn't do that.

She sucked her stomach in and pushed her chest out, then remembered the dress was doing all the work for her. She went inside.

'Tye, gorgeous.' Peter slipped a glass of champagne into her hand and stood back, arms apart. 'My!' he said, looking her up and down. 'Let's get you circulating.'

'Who's the artist?' Tye asked, as Peter guided her through the crowd. The canvasses strung around the walls had matchboxes, condoms and what looked like human hair clinging to them. They were, Tye thought, startlingly ugly. Most already had discreet red dots beside them. The prices, she didn't doubt, were exquisitely expensive. An artist could urinate on yesterday's newspaper and Peter Glick would flog it for twenty grand.

Peter guided her to a cluster of partygoers. Two men, two women. They stopped their conversation, looked her up and down – the women with an imperceptible tightening of the corners of their mouths, as though each had just bitten on a very small lemon – the men with a slight widening of the eyes.

'I want you to meet Tye Fisher,' Peter said with a bitchy smile. 'Be nice to her. She's just off the boat.'

Nobody at the Chelsea hostel worried when Gus and Susie Neidermeyer failed to make the curfew on Friday night. The hostel was cheap and nearly always full, and the two elderly men who ran the desk at nights were busy. They only noticed if people knocked at two in the morning demanding to be let in, not if they didn't come in at all.

In Lansing, Michigan, Marion Neidermeyer wondered why her son hadn't called her on Friday as he'd promised in the postcard he'd sent that week. He'd included the number of the telephone pager where he could be reached, but Marion decided not to call it just yet. Gus was her eldest child and the first to leave home. She didn't want him to feel pressured because she knew he had lots on his mind and a fussing mom was not what he needed. Even though she did worry about him – almost every minute of the day – she did her best to hide that from him.

Instead she loaded her thirteen-year-old twins, Antonia and Grace, into the Toyota and took them to the mall for a burger. They bickered all the way there, all during the meal, and all the way back, and Marion wondered for the millionth time why, when everybody said that twins were supposed to have a special bond, she'd had two who fought like weasels in a sack.

She got home exhausted, poured herself a glass of

wine and marked a few English test papers. She'd call Gus tomorrow and get caught up on his news.

The party was dull. Crowded and dull. Tye had been introduced to several people – men – who'd ogled her breasts and even her face, but she was no closer to her goal. And now that she was here in this warm room that reeked of money, she wondered why she had even thought her plan would work. She wasn't going to meet someone who'd invite her to stay or need an apartment sitter. These things took ages. Perhaps it really was time to go home. Then she thought of England and realized she couldn't conjure up a picture of it. It seemed diffuse and vague, except for the weather – she remembered that all right. Just thinking about its dampness made her shiver. Perhaps she should try Hong Kong or Sydney. There at least it was still possible to get by on the right accent and a few old-school connections.

She looked around the room for Peter so she could make her apologies and go, when a man in a blue blazer and chinos squeezed through the crowd, making straight for her.

'I'm Rich,' he said.

'How nice for you.'

Rich was thirty-odd, balding, slicked-back hair, beginnings of a paunch. Cheeks flushed from the heat and the Scotch he held in his other hand. Tye noted the gold Rolex and the Gucci loafers. Emerging markets, she'd bet her bottom dollar.

'What do you do?' she asked, because that was how he no doubt expected the conversation to begin.

'Emerging markets.'

Bingo. Was there anybody at all in this town who didn't work in emerging markets? And what did that mean, anyway? She decided not to ask. She was bored enough as it was.

'You must be obscenely rich, Rich.' An Englishman would have slapped her face for that. Rich just shrugged. 'It depends what you mean by rich.'

Tye suddenly felt very good indeed. People who were truly rich always qualified it. Sure they had ten million, but they were really just getting by. Tye bestowed her dazzling smile on him and was pleased to see his face become redder. Just when she'd thought it hopeless, a lifeline. He wasn't wearing a wedding ring.

'You haven't told me your name,' Rich said, putting out a warm, damp hand. She stretched her thin, pale one out to meet his.

'It's . . .'

'Tye!' The voice rose over the chattering swell of the party. Tye swivelled; the accent was unmistakable.

Oh, shit, she thought.

Adrian was bearing down on her like the *Bismark*.

# Chapter Eleven

Adrian kissed Tye two times, roughly. He smelt of her perfume. The laundry-dispenser trick had worked.

'Cherie,' he murmured.

'Darling. So nice to see you,' Tye said stiffly. 'It's been so long. And how is your lovely wife?'

Adrian ignored Tye's comments. He slung one arm over her shoulders with a proprietorial air, and looked Rich up and down. 'Who is your friend?'

'Rich Long.' Rich put out his hand, Adrian ignored it.

'Did you buy something?'

'Not yet.'

'But you might?'

'Maybe.'

'You collect?'

'Sure.'

Rich looked from Tye to Adrian, trying to figure out what was going on. Tye tried to get out from under Adrian's arm but it was firmly clamped about her shoulders. She couldn't move it without making a scene. She wanted to hit Adrian, hard.

'Do you have a nice place?' Adrian asked Rich.

'Excuse me?'

'Do you have a nice place?' Adrian repeated the words slowly, as though talking to a child.

'Yeah.' A small frown line appeared above Rich's fleshy nose. 'What's that got to do with anything?'

'She likes a big apartment, preferably with a doorman. She has very specific taste – in men,' Adrian continued, clamping Tye's shoulder even more firmly. She really began to hate him. 'She only goes for the ones with money. I hope you have lots of money. She likes the theatre, restaurants, clothes.'

'Oh, he is *such* a kidder.' Tye laughed lightly. 'It's a good thing we're such old friends. From London, you know.'

'Oh, I can tell you about London.' Adrian smirked. 'This woman has a very interesting history. She could tell you some stories about herself. Very entertaining, if you could ever get her to tell the truth.'

'Really, darling, shouldn't you be looking at the paintings, trying to pick up some tips?' Tye said, teeth gritted. 'Your work has been suffering since the accident.'

'This woman looks like an angel, but the truth is very, very different.' He said it with a dramatic flourish that made Tye feel as though she was about to be unmasked as the villain in an Agatha Christie book. 'Keep your hand on your wallet, my friend. That is all I can say.'

'Darling, what did I say about drinking too much? What are you going to tell your friends at AA?' Tye made another futile attempt to get out from under his grip.

'Yeah, well, nice talking with you folks,' Rich said.

He shot a quick, puzzled glance at Tye before he merged back into the crowd.

'Oh, dear. We have scared him off.' Adrian slapped Tye on the backside and beamed at her.

'You arsehole,' she hissed. 'How dare you?'

'Never mind,' he said. 'There are always others.' He strolled off, smirking.

Tye didn't stay long after that. She decided it would be a waste of time looking for a patron in Adrian's crowd, since he would undoubtedly try the same trick again. Perhaps the tarty knickers in the back of the drawer had been a mistake.

There were a couple of tasks to take care of before she left. One was to visit the bathroom to copy down the number and expiry date of Adrian's American Express card, which she'd lifted from his back pocket while he'd had his arm around her. The other was to slip it back without him noticing.

It wasn't too hard. It was a crowded room and she knew a little about these things.


Cyrus didn't usually go out on weekend nights. He didn't know anybody he could call and ask out and the phone never rang so it was sometimes painful for him to watch others having a good time. He had always felt awkward and out of place sitting in a bar or restaurant alone, and feared the manager would come up and insist that he leave because he wasn't a real customer. But now he knew he was a valid person, whether he was with someone or not.

He actually rang a place – a nice restaurant – in

Murray Hill and made a reservation. He'd read about it in a magazine. The critics agreed it was expensive but worth it.

He chose what he was going to wear carefully. After all, you never knew – he might even meet a woman. He laid out a plain black suit, blue shirt, red tie and a new pair of wing-tips which he'd had hand-made by an Italian in Port Chester. Expensive, but his feet were long and thin and his arches were a bit flat so it was the only way he'd been able to get shoes he could walk in.

He'd washed and brushed his hair and tied it back. He'd shaved carefully. Now that the hair on his face was beginning to go grey, he didn't want to end up looking like a grumpy old grandfather. Premature grey-ness ran in his family. He'd noticed the first signs when he was in college, and had considered dye. Until the Master, that is. Now he knew that vitality came from within, not out of a box.

He liked the distinguished image he saw in the mirror and gave himself a mental pat on the back. He was getting into the habit of praising himself. Now he walked with his shoulders pulled up straight, and a slight smile on his face. Instead of being defensive, he was open. He worried less about the dark spirals lying in wait to ambush him. He was growing into a whole new person.

The French restaurant was panelled in wood and brass, like the places he'd been to on endless European trips with his parents – those little jaunts that were supposed to bring them closer together. Not that he'd spent any more time with his parents on those trips than at home; they had so many social and work obligations. But there was always a nanny.

This restaurant reminded him of a place in Brussels. He'd had a steak so rare it sat in a pool of blood. What was that nanny's name? Alfreda? Constanza?

'Something to drink, sir?'

He was seated at a small table at the back, not too close to the kitchen. Usually the staff of a fancy place like this would take one look at him and think, 'poor schmuck'. There was no sign that was happening tonight. That was good.

'Yes, I'll have something to drink. I'll have champagne, please. A half bottle.'

Why not? He had something to celebrate.

It was Constanza, he remembered. The nanny had been called Constanza. In one of his parents' futile attempts to get him to learn another language, Constanza had been hired from Castile, for the purity of her accent. She spoke only Spanish.

Constanza hadn't lasted. None of them had.

# Chapter Twelve

Quinn ordered a beer at a bar in the East Village and worried at his break-up with Rhonda like a loose tooth. The more he thought about it, the more irritated he became. She had had no right to say those things about him. It wasn't as if she were a high flyer; she had some crummy job in marketing, and talked endlessly about boring meetings and presentations. She had no love of art, and her general knowledge was appalling. She believed everything she read in glossy magazines.

Quinn stared gloomily at his beer. He, Quinn, had been dumped. How dare she? Now he had nothing to do on weekends.

A tall, rangy man wearing a stockman's overcoat slid onto the empty stool next to Quinn's, signalled to the barman. Ted O'Reilly.

'Quinn, wha's up?' he said, slapping him hard on the back.

It was amazing, Quinn thought. He must have some kind of in-built distress beacon, because whenever he was at a low ebb or feeling disgruntled about the way his life was shaping up, there was Ted. Without fail he would breeze in, grinning inanely – back-slapping, cliché-spouting Ted. Full of frigging good cheer.

'Ted. How ya doin'?'

'Great, buddy. Just great. Never been better. Things are going so well I can hardly fucking believe it. Everything's falling into place, y'know. It's like I got a lucky angel or something.'

You would, Quinn thought bitterly. He and Ted were friends by dint of the fact that they'd known each other too long. They were too much alike to share any genuine feelings. Ted loved to talk about himself and his accomplishments and could do so for hours, regardless of whether he received any encouragement. The thing which stuck in Quinn's craw was that Ted's life always seemed to have an inverse relationship to his own. Quinn went down, Ted went up. Except these days. Quinn never seemed to go up.

They had known each other since college. Ted had decided then that the two had a spiritual bond because of their common Irish ancestry. Their common ability to smoke dope, more like. They'd hung out a lot, stoned.

Things became rocky when Quinn had stolen one of Ted's girlfriends. It was something Quinn suspected Ted had never forgotten or quite forgiven. Now Ted was always popping up like a deranged jack-in-the-box, and Quinn had come to realize that he would always be on the fringes of his life. Even if he migrated to Argentina, Ted would find him. Years from now, sitting in the old folks' home in Otter Creek, Florida, Ted would come hobbling up on his walker, demanding to know whether he'd sold a book or not.

'Buy you a beer?' Ted asked. 'Then we can get caught up. Where've you been anyway?'

It was no use fighting, Ted was a fact of life, like taxes and tornadoes. Besides, his glass was nearly empty.

'Oh, around,' he said. 'Bud, please.'

The bar had suddenly grown noisy and crowded with the arrival of a bunch of NYU students. Ted and Quinn checked them out. Quinn knew the conversation would come around to Ted's good fortune so he might as well get it over with. He took a sip of beer to fortify himself.

'What's the good news?'

'Sold a screenplay.' Ted couldn't contain his smugness. It was leaking out of every pore.

'That's great.' Quinn's spirits plummeted. God, how he hated it when talentless hacks did well. Scratch that; he hated it when anybody did well.

'Good money. Very good money.' Ted said. 'Close on a million.'

Quinn felt sick. Christ, he really did. He was going to vomit. 'Todd Rachenbach.' Ted named one of the new, young Hollywood directors. Critically and commercially successful.

'Todd Rachenbach, well done. I shoulda ordered champagne,' Quinn said, stretching his mouth into a smile, praying that his envy didn't show. He hated being a sore loser, but Ted! Anybody but him. Was God trying to punish him?

'He says I have a rare and startling talent. I've captured the voice of post-Generation X-ers with verve and wit,' Ted said complacently.

'All those things? Todd Rachenbach said all those things?' He really was going to throw up. This was it, the absolute last straw. The universe was mocking him. He'd never write another word. He was fucked. Double fucked. Might as well wrap him in chains, chuck him in a coffin and throw it into the East River. 'He said all those things and a million dollars? How about that?'

'Nearly a mill. But I'll get more for the next one. They're very interested in another idea I've pitched.' Ted winked at a girl further down the bar and raised his voice so that she could hear. 'I've put in an offer on a loft. Deal should be signed any day now. I beat them down on the price. You can do that with cash.'

It was on the tip of Quinn's tongue to ask him if he needed a roommate. He checked himself. A week full time with Ted and he'd be jumping off the nearest bridge. Correction: he'd be flinging Ted feet first, with a concrete tyre, for peace of mind.

Quinn closed his eyes briefly. It was an anxiety dream, he was sure of it. A mind-fuck. But he opened his eyes and Ted was still there. He drank his beer faster. Ted wouldn't mind if he didn't reciprocate on a round. His one good point was his absent-minded generosity. Status was the thing that mattered to Ted; everything else was loose change.

'How about you? How's the writing going?'

Quinn saw his jealousy as a rat, feeding on his insides. He was tempted to lie, sorely tempted. Instead he shrugged.

'You know,' he said. 'Great work takes time.'

Ted shook his head. 'You gotta get into a rhythm,' he said. 'Just start. Once you do that, you'll be done in no time.'

Quinn did not consider himself a violent person but he was strongly tempted to deck the bastard.

Tye didn't go straight to her room when she got back to her hotel. The thought of it made her feel trapped.

She sat in the lobby in an exquisitely uncomfortable imitation Eames chair. The hotel was small and had about as many decorative flourishes as a prison. It was the last word in millennial chic. It was also rather expensive.

She was screwed.

An elderly woman came into the lobby wearing a thick overcoat, although it was not cold. Behind her trailed the concierge, carrying two expensive suitcases.

Tye watched her sign in. She radiated the cool composure of money. The bags looked heavy, but the concierge was beaming the smile of a man who expects a respectable tip. He guided the woman into the elevator. The doors hummed shut and they disappeared.

'Can I get you something, ma'am?'

'Sorry?' Tye roused herself from her reverie. The receptionist was standing in front of her, hands clasped, arrogant and submissive in equal amounts. Her first, panicked thought was he was going to kick her out.

'Oh, no thanks . . . actually, yes you can. I would love a cup of tea.'

'I'll have it sent over.'

When the tea came it was surprisingly good. Tye felt better just looking at the tray with its tiny silver pot, delicate china and even a little plate of Hobnobs – they must get lots of English customers. She wasn't hungry, but she had one anyway, thinking it would induce an unbearable nostalgia that would make her want to run home. It didn't.

If she wanted to stay in New York, she needed an idea and she needed it fast. She thought for the hundredth time of calling her father. He was a good lateral thinker. It was something he'd trained his daughter to be, too. But lately it hadn't been working for her. Maybe she was losing her touch. Or maybe the decision not to work had softened her brain.

Tye was still sitting in the lobby, holding a cold cup of tea when the concierge returned.

'Evening, Miss Fisher,' he called cheerily.

'Hi, Enrico.'

'You don't look so good. You doin' okay?'

'I'm fine, thank you.'

'You sure don' look fine. Anything I can do?'

Tye smiled, shook her head. Enrico was a typical immigrant, working his arse off and probably supporting six or eight people back home in Guatemala with the money he made in wages and tips. The city was full of people like him, working as busboys, waiters and cleaners, doing the shit jobs that nobody else would touch. Yet she never saw Enrico without a smile on his face. He was doing all right. He was in America. Enrico hovered.

'Are you well? You need something?'

Tye swirled the cold tea in her cup, put it to her lips reflexively. Paused. She was an immigrant, after all. Maybe she should ask another immigrant how it was done.

She put the cup down.

'There is one question,' she said. 'Perhaps you do know the answer to this.'

# Chapter Thirteen

Cyrus walked home from the restaurant enjoying the mild evening air and the pleasant feeling of a good meal. It had been simple – green salad, steak frite and cream caramel, accompanied by an excellent Burgundy and an espresso to finish. Not fashionable, but Cyrus preferred it that way. He didn't see the point of fusion cooking. He thought it was dumb to force different countries' foods together, like a shotgun wedding. He was kind of traditional in that respect.

It was late but the streets were filled – walkers, skaters, lovers, bulky bunches of tourists. Cyrus walked slowly, his hands in his pockets, checking out the girls, but subtle, not leering or anything. He wasn't a pervert.

The women in the city were clinging to summer's last breath. Stretchy camisoles showed off still-tanned shoulders and, in many cases, tattoos. Painted toes peeked out of thin strapped sandals. Whimsical bags were slung round slim hips, off shoulders. It was a good crop, this year's. But then he thought that most years.

He smiled at a cute woman as she walked past. She smiled back. Cyrus got a jolt out of that. He looked at his reflection in a shop window. He didn't look too bad.

A little formal, perhaps, when you compared him to most average guys, but then he wasn't most guys.

He stopped to slip some change into a panhandler's outstretched hand. Then, on impulse, he gave the guy – who was dragging a mangy dog behind him – twenty bucks.

'Hey thanks, man.' The homeless guy looked up in surprise when he saw how big the bill was.

Cyrus smiled. He walked on briskly, buoyed up by the guy's amazed gratitude. His parents had given thousands of dollars to charity over the years, but he wondered if they had ever derived as much pleasure from their largesse as he had from that one modest act. He didn't feel he'd patronized the homeless guy; he'd handed him a green bill – a meaningless thing except that the deluded society they lived in chose to invest it with value. When you thought about it, Cyrus was the one who had gained more from the transaction. After all, it was a beggar who had brought him to the Master. Considered in that light, it should have been him thanking the beggar, not the other way around.

He let himself in the front door and checked his messages. None. Good. Then he stood in the dark, sniffing the air. Cyrus had a very highly developed olfactory sense and he believed that smells left imprints, like psychic auras. But the apartment smelt normal; there was no hint of anything, except perhaps a trace of the coffee he'd bought that morning.

There are many odd living spaces in New York City, but Cyrus's apartment was that way by design. Although it occupied the whole basement floor of a large brownstone, the interior was actually two separate spaces. It had originally been two apartments and although Cyrus now owned them both, he had kept the configuration. He'd only made a couple of small changes. The first was to extend the front apartment into the hallway, so when you walked in your impression was that it was now one apartment. The second was the secret door.

It was something he'd dreamed about for a while. As a child, he'd been obsessed by secret spaces, spy-holes and concealed exits. The only foreign holidays he'd enjoyed were the trips to English stately homes where he could see for himself how eccentric aristo-crats had indulged their architectural whims. Secret staircases, secret rooms, sometimes even whole wings of houses were concealed behind panels and hidden doors to make intrigue, sex, adventure, easier.

The only way to get from the front to the back apartment was through the concealed door in the bed-room. The door looked like a bookcase – it was a bookcase. But it had two very special features. You pressed a button and the shelves opened to reveal a second storage container behind. You pressed another button – with a catch hidden in the skirting board and the entire thing swung back to reveal the other two rooms.

It had cost a fortune, that door. The cabinet maker hadn't asked any questions about its use, but he'd been excited by the task – kept telling Cyrus it was the first time he'd ever done anything like it.

He'd done a superb job.

Cyrus went through the open door. He had to bend to get through because he was tall, but not by much.

There were two rooms, one behind the other. It was spacious, but a little dark as only the back room got any natural light. The middle room was sparsely furnished with a futon, a side table, and a lamp, a free-standing armoire and a tall metal cabinet. Cyrus sometimes slept in there.

The second room was tiled in Tuscan terracotta. His parents had shipped the tiles back, at eye-watering expense, after a vacation in Siena. This was at a time when they expected their son would leave home and find a job, a partner and a life of his own. They'd laid the big, expensive slabs to have the ground floor thinking this would be a nice place to sit and look out at the gardener tending their back yard. That plan had gone away, receding as fast as their expectations for their only child.

That room, although it got some oblique light, could not now be called relaxing. There was a sink, because this had been the kitchen of the second flat, but apart from that, it had only two pieces of furniture; a metal table and a large, walk-in freezer.

Cyrus went to the cabinet and selected the tools he'd need for his evening's work – a butcher's apron, a pair of rubber gloves and a small saw – the type surgeons use for breaking open skulls and ribcages. He hummed as he laid out his tools, pleased with himself, being in the moment, taking care in the smallest details, as the Master had taught him. Although it was late, he wasn't tired, which was good. There was a lot of work to do.

He put his precious book in the metal cabinet so it wouldn't get messed up. He was eager to begin.

# Chapter Fourteen

'*Si*, Miss Fisher, is very difficult.' Enrico shook his head sadly from side to side, his hands thrust firmly in his pockets. 'Very difficult. There is so many people who want to live here and so little buildings for them. So many rich people with big, big houses and then – the rest of us.' He shrugged his shoulders.

'All my friend needs is a base.'

'She need somewhere to stay soon?' Enrico wasn't stupid, he knew they were talking about her, but Tye was grateful he didn't show it.

'Pretty soon.'

'She have no family or friend to stay with?'

'No, not really.'

'She is not legal, yes?'

Tye shook her head. She wondered where Enrico lived. A cube in Bensonhurst or Flatbush, probably. Maybe Jersey City. Were there a wife and kids? Tye stifled an impulse to ask him. He knew his place, as they said in England, and she had a feeling he wouldn't appreciate personal questions.

'She need a sublet,' Enrico said. 'Is the only way.'

Tye had a vague idea what a sublet was. Someone went out of town and another person took over the lease. It was a less formal process than renting, and in some cases quite illegal, but everybody did it. Apartment space was just too valuable to give up once you got your hands on it.

'How do – how does she find a sublet?' she asked.

'One moment.' Enrico dashed outside. At first, Tye thought a guest must be arriving at the hotel, but Enrico walked out through the front doors and down the street. In a few minutes he was back, clutching a copy of the *Village Voice*, a give-away paper that Tye had seen but hadn't been bothered to read.

'Is in here,' Enrico said, holding it out to her, 'everything you need, you find it in here.'


Marion Neidermeyer woke at five in the morning with a certain sense that something was wrong. She sat up, turned on her bedside lamp and groped for the post-card that Gus had sent her. She read it through again, clutching at comfort from the spidery words on the small piece of cardboard that had a picture of the Statue of Liberty.

Gus and Susie were fine. She was the one who needed help. She was transferring her own anxieties about New York to them. She was terrified of the place and hadn't wanted them to go there. Wanted them to stay near her. She reflected on the irony of it; she'd worked all her life to give Gus everything he needed – a stable home, a good education, and her reward for those years of labour – he collects his college degree and takes the first plane out of town.

It hurt like hell. It still surprised her how much.

She hadn't felt this bad when her husband had left her to go and live in Florida with that condominium saleswoman. She'd got through that, even with the kids fighting and in pain as much as she was, somehow they'd inched out the other side into the light. She'd taken a job, paid the mortgage, kept the kids in clothes and school. Apart from pride in her own achievement, Marion had taken comfort from knowing that nothing would ever be as bad again. Charles's leaving had been her boot camp, the badge of pain that made her as tough as piano wire. She wasn't just a dull suburban mom with nothing on her mind except knitting and bake sales. She was a fighter.

She got up, went to the bathroom for a glass of water. The house was quiet and warm – too warm. Perhaps that was what woke her. Yes, that must have been it. She turned the central heating down a few degrees and climbed back into bed. She wouldn't sleep, but she intended to lie with her eyes closed for another hour, until it was time to get up.

She'd call Gus as soon as she could. Just to set her mind at rest.


'Are you going to look for a sublet or what?' Mal said to Quinn the next morning. 'I'm not running a hotel.'

'I'm looking,' Quinn said. Mal was starting to get on his nerves. 'I've made some very promising contacts.'

'That's why you stink of beer.' Mal was sitting drinking coffee. It was nine thirty and he was glowing from his run.

'It's the weekend,' Quinn said patiently. He wasn't

going to let Mal get under his skin. 'Anyway, I was talking to a guy who might have a place in Williamsburg.'

This wasn't precisely true, but it would do for the meantime. Ted had said he'd look out for him and Ted had a lot of friends. There was bound to be someone who knew something. That was the way things always happened for Quinn – through contacts and acquaintances. He would lie in wait for opportunities, like he was tracking a small woodland animal.

'Rhonda Rupnick called for you,' Mal said, changing the subject. Perhaps he wasn't in the mood for a fight this morning either. 'I thought you broke up.'

'Rhonda?' Quinn sat up in surprise. 'I thought we did too. Perhaps she's missing me.'

'She said call her.' Mal got up to make a second cup of coffee. Quinn wondered whether there was anyone in his brother's life. He'd never mentioned it, but that did not necessarily mean he was celibate. Mal was secretive by nature. Quinn loved to talk about himself but friends of Mal's who'd known him for years always claimed they were finding out things about him.

Did yuppies even have sex? Quinn wondered as he headed for the shower. Perhaps they only read about it in glossy magazines. Or perhaps they scheduled it between personal training sessions and power breakfasts. Half an hour of designer passion, with clothes carefully folded on Bauhaus sofas.

The shower blasted needle-sharp and Quinn drenched himself, letting last night's cigarette and beer aura wash away. Rhonda missed him! He had known she would. He pictured her in her Calvin Klein sports underwear – functional but sexy at the same time, a bit like Rhonda herself. She did have a great body, he missed it a lot. Nevertheless he decided not to call her right away. He didn't want her to think he was going to come panting back just because she said so. He'd make her wait an hour or two. Give her some time to think about the consequences of what she'd done.

Fifteen minutes later he called.

'Hey babe,' he said, cocky from Mal's Nicaraguan espresso and the thought of what he and Rhonda would soon be doing. A light Sunday afternoon tussle – what better way to ease oneself into the week? – and who knew, he might even get some writing done afterwards. Sex always helped him to relax and relaxation was the best frame of mind for writing.

'Quinn. You left some things here,' Rhonda said. 'A book of Brendan Behan poems,' she pronounced it Bee-han.

'Be-an, babe.'

'Whatever. There's a jumbo sized box of condoms, and your Swiss Army knife.'

'Oh.'

'You wanna meet somewhere or shall I bring them over to you?'

'Why don't I drop by?'

'No, Quinn.'

'C'mon, what harm can there be in me stopping by?'

'Plenty of harm. You'll be making the moves as soon as you get in the door.'

'I won't. Scouts' honour.'

'You have no honour, Quinn. Don't try and hide behind kids in uniform. Now give me your new address and I'll leave them off on my way to the gym.'

Quinn sighed. He hated it when women knew their own minds.

'Don't bother with the condoms,' he said. 'I'm joining the Marist brothers.'


Gus always got up early, Marion knew, so nine o'clock was not an unreasonable time to call. She tried to keep herself busy all morning, not to rush it. Several times Marion decided to hell with it, just call. Even though it was early, Gus wouldn't mind. He'd understand if she told him about her sense. Once, when Gus was a teenager, Marion had read a story in the newspaper about a Russian Cold War experiment in telepathy. The Russians were convinced there was a mental bond between a mother and her children and they used a bunch of rabbits to try and quantify it. They took the babies on a submarine deep into an icy northern sea and they kept the mom at home, her brain wired up to a machine. Marion had read that one by one they killed those rabbit babies and each time they did so, the mommy rabbit, back in Moscow or wherever, registered extreme mental anguish. Even though her children were hundreds or even thousands of miles away, she knew.

Gus had scoffed at this but he had been fourteen or so, he scoffed at everything. Maybe the mother just missed her kids, he said.

Maybe he was right, Marion reflected. After all, that rabbit had had no way of knowing if her babies would ever come back. To her, separation was as good as death.

The twins had gone out, in a rare moment of friendship, to play basketball. Both girls were tall and fast and could have made good teams but they preferred fooling around with kids in the neighbourhood on a Sunday. Marion fixed herself another cup of coffee and looked vacantly around her large, empty kitchen at the breakfast mess they had left. The difficult age; what a host of horrors that phrase concealed. The twins had been 'difficult' since birth. Before, even. Not like Gus, her first-born, her friend.

The clock hands inched forward. Ten o'clock wasn't too early, not even for newly weds. Besides, it wasn't as if he had to pick up the phone, she'd leave a message on his voice mail pager and he'd retrieve it when he could. The message would be light and sunny. She wouldn't say she'd been in agony. She'd say: 'Hi, darling, it's just your mom calling to see how you are. Love to hear from you.'

That's all. Not whining or pushy, but light and chatty.

Hands shaking, she picked up the phone.

# Chapter Fifteen

Tye picked up Adrian's address book again and leafed through it. She knew many of the names, even though she'd only been in New York a couple of months. Adrian was an inveterate party-giver and kept a large circle of friends and contacts in continual orbit around him.

The *Village Voice* that Enrico had found for her lay open on the bed. She had considered the solution he proposed. It seemed so awful to move into a complete stranger's house, sometimes with their furniture. Borrowed furniture did not appeal to Tye at all. When it came to decor, she was a purist.

She was also reluctant to give up her original idea. It was simple. She knew lots of rich people who had guest bedrooms. What could be easier than moving in? No bother to them whatsoever. She would be a decorative asset, someone to impress their friends with. If they wanted sex, so be it. If not, she was cool with that too.

On the other hand, if she had to strike out on her own at this stage, the complications would be enormous. She was new and she didn't know enough about how the city worked. She had no job and no verifiable source of income.

The *Village Voice* was for when things got dire. She opened the book to the 'Bs'.

Randall Buckford IV. Bucky to his friends. The family owned an estate – not just a huge house, but a goodly swatch of land around it – on the waterfront in Greenwich. Tye had been to a party there with Adrian in the summer. Champagne, canapés. Boats bobbing on the bay, braying girls in hairbands, sunburned men so obtuse it seemed incredible to Tye that any university had admitted them, let alone the distinguished establishments that they boasted of in their conversation.

Bucky was divorced. Tania, his first wife, had run off to Beverly Hills to live with her hairdresser-turned-soap-star. Dreadfully bad form, Bucky's set agreed, especially as Bucky had just bought her new breasts to celebrate their fifth anniversary.

Bucky was alone now, rattling round his cavernous apartment on Park Avenue, toddling off to work at the brokerage firm his great-grandfather had founded, knowing on some level that the younger, brighter, less WASP-like people wheeling and dealing in his name were the true inheritors of his ancestor's smarts.

But for the meantime he had other things to console him. Naturally there were millions of women vying for him. He was probably getting his end away more in a week than the whole five years he'd been married. Every time Tye had seen him, always with a different woman, his laugh had been louder, the lines around his eyes more pronounced. Lack of sleep, she was sure of it. He was bonking all night, every night, like a wind-up toy.

But no one was in residence, Tye knew that from Adrian's gossip. Bucky was not the sharpest blade in the drawer, but he wasn't stupid. He could see the potential second wives – as numerous and as determined as Mongolian hordes – coming a mile off and he was determined to delay the inevitable as long as possible. He freely admitted that marriage to Tania had met very few of his expectations and he did not want to go back down that road for a while yet.

So he was bound to have a room or so to spare.

Tye tossed the *Village Voice* into the waste basket.


Cyrus slept soundly after his night's work and woke rested and refreshed. The bodies had been processed. Cut up neatly into manageable sizes and placed back in the freezer in Ziploc bags. His freezer now looked like a supermarket compartment with its labelled, neatly stacked bags of frozen flesh.

Only the process hadn't been neat, it'd been hell. He'd had no idea how difficult it was to cut through bone and frozen fresh and the saw hadn't been sharp enough. While he was wrestling with some of the bigger bones, the bodies had become unfrozen, slippery. They'd dived off the table and onto the terracotta floor. He'd had to chase after them. It had been a struggle and a test of his new-found calm. Sometimes he had wanted to just give up, walk away, but the Master helped him. He was new to this; he had to cut himself some slack.

So Cyrus had persevered, sawing, hacking, goresplattered, chopping into the night. He knew he wasn't going to win any butchery prizes, but in the end, he'd been pleased.

Soon he would dispose of them, but not now. There was no rush, the plastic packages were safe. Nobody was coming looking.

In the meantime he had a session scheduled with the Master.

These encounters had fallen into a pleasing, comforting pattern and Cyrus had become used to the ritual. He started first thing, before he'd had any stimulants and while the morning was calm and still. He selected a Japanese robe and light cotton slippers from his wardrobe – the look was important. He put them on and sat at the foot of his futon on a Turkmeni rug, cross-legged, hands resting lightly in his lap. The room was dark and this pose made Cyrus feel spiritual and relaxed.

He sat for a couple of minutes enjoying the sensation one has when one is doing the right thing. Despite some stiffness in his joints from the night's unaccustomed activity, his body felt serene, warm. Outside, the garbage trucks were rumbling, but it was a distant stimulus here in his inner chamber.

He shut his eyes, concentrated. The pink light filled his mind.

On the edge of his consciousness, a sound intruded.

At first Cyrus thought he could just ignore it. He was sufficiently advanced with the Master to be able to focus on only him. He thought of the pink light, bathing him in calm, transporting him to a new plane.

The sound persisted. Telephone? But there was no telephone back here.

It got bigger and bigger. Something about the pitch made him want to scream. He nearly did, then checked himself. A moderate response was called for. He downgraded his anger to irritation. Nothing interrupted his sessions with the Master. Nothing. He shut his eyes more tightly, attempted to block out the electronic pinprick. Focused hard on the pink light.

'I am a valued and important person. I have a right to be here. I am accomplished and clever and worthy of respect.' Cyrus mumbled the mantra.

Beep, beep.

'I accept my mistakes and my achievements together. I forgive my mistakes and respect my achievements.'

Beep, beep.

A trilling mockery of his private time. God, was it not possible to get any peace at all in this city?

'I am continually growing and becoming the person I am intended to be. I am worthy of love and—'

Beep, beep.

It was the last straw. Cyrus leapt up.

'I don't fucking believe it!' he roared, stomping his foot.

'Beep, beep.'

Cyrus stayed still, legs askance, arms out, listening. There were very few places it could be. He would find it and get back to the Master. He prowled the room, one hand cocked behind his ear.

Beep, beep.

The cabinet.

He opened the metal door gingerly.

# Chapter Sixteen

Neat plastic packets lay in piles. Clothes, shoes, trousers. Hair. The beeping got louder. Cyrus picked up each of the packages and held them to his ear.

Beep, beep.

He ripped open the bag containing the boy's jeans. His hands flew through the pockets until they found a plastic beeper.

Cyrus tossed the bag and the jeans back in the cabinet, forgetting that an aware person took pleasure in the mundane tasks of tidiness. He stared at the beeper as though he'd never seen one in his life.

It was a sign. Nothing happened by accident, this he knew. Everything was for a purpose and that purpose was ultimate good. Was this electronic pager then a sign from the Master? Perhaps they were taking their communication to a new level? But if so, what could it mean?

He pressed the button on the beeper but it didn't tell him anything more than its own phone number. He pressed it again. The pager stubbornly refused to divulge its information. He went to the phone, dialled the number. A recorded voice told him pleasantly to key in his four-digit code. What was the code? He had no idea about any code. He pressed four digits at random. The voice told him to try again. He pressed another four numbers. No luck.

He went back to the cabinet to see if the boy had carried the code with him. He searched their pockets, her backpack. Nothing. There was no way he could retrieve the message.

He threw the pager to the corner of the room.

In Michigan, Marion Neidermeyer put the phone down, and absently started clearing the twins' breakfast debris. Doing something had made her feel better.

She finished the last of her coffee and put the mug in the dishwasher. Everything was fine. Gus would call and they'd laugh about it. She'd remember from this not to worry so much.

Quinn spent a lot of time thinking about how Rhonda would find him when she came to deliver his things. What kind of tableau should he present? The heart-broken writer? The carefree man about town? Mal had a cross-country ski machine in his bedroom. Perhaps he should start working out, maybe that would win her around. He would greet her at the door with a towel around his neck and a sheen of perspiration and she'd fall into his arms. Working out was Rhonda's religion and he always suspected she didn't trust him because he swore no allegiance to a health club. When Rhonda wasn't at the gym she was reading magazines that advertised things like 'Perfect Abs – with no crunches!'

and 'Change your whole body in twenty minutes.' There was a stack of such magazines at her apartment that was at least three feet high. Quinn had once tried to persuade her to spread them out on the floor and have sex on them but Rhonda had been shocked – you didn't defile things like that.

All these women working out, it was getting scary, Quinn thought. Not just aerobics but kick-boxing and boxing and arcane martial arts. Soon he wouldn't be able to approach a woman in this town for fear that she'd repel him with a right hook.

Perhaps he should go back to Ireland, where it was imperative for writers to hang about in pubs, jawing and not doing terribly much. He'd heard Dublin was rocking these days. Yeah, maybe he just would.

'Are you going to kill those eggs?' Mal asked impatiently. Quinn looked at the bowl in his hand. He was beating eggs for a breakfast omelette. Mal called it brunch but Quinn's breakfasts never took place till after eleven, it was breakfast to him. Such loving brothers, they couldn't even agree on what to call their meal.

'Just making sure they're dead.' Quinn lit the gas flame and manoeuvred one of Mal's heavy cast-iron pans onto the stove. It had been a battle even to get Mal to agree to eat a yolk or two. He'd wanted an omelette with just the white but Quinn refused. That was not food, that was affectation. Mal had caved in pretty quick and Quinn could see the lascivious way he was looking at the bowl. He was starved, poor chap, that was his problem. He was irritable because he wasn't getting enough saturated fats.

Cooking came easily to Quinn. He had a natural affinity and respect for food. Surprising when you considered he'd come from a family where soggy cabbage and grey meat was about as fancy as it got. His mother was a culinary felon and she knew it. She got to the stage, like a lot of immigrants, where she abandoned the cooking of her own country and would only eat American fast food. Quinn remembered his first decent meal – his father had brought him into Manhattan to see a game and afterwards they'd gone to Chinatown for dumplings. He'd been twelve years old and his father had let him go to the front of the restaurant and watch the chefs working. He'd had to be dragged back to his plate to eat his meal – but what a meal! Quinn had never been the same. He'd devoured duck and crab and rice and chilli and had come away with the revelation that food didn't have to be some dead thing that lay on your plate, a punishment to be chewed through before you could go back out and play football.

After that he'd started cooking at home, to his mother's horror – she thought it meant he was homosexual. She regarded the piles of cookery books in his bedroom with as much enthusiasm as if they'd been S & M manuals.

Mal had a state-of-the-art kitchen which he never used. Quinn whistled a jaunty air as he coaxed the eggs around the pan, added ham and mushrooms and cheese – he slipped in the last when Mal wasn't watching, otherwise he'd have a heart attack. Well, not literally, of course. Quinn flipped the omelette onto a plate. He hadn't cooked for a while, he realized. A true sign that his life was out of whack.

The doorbell rang.

'It's for you. A woman,' Mal said as he pressed the button to open the door.

'Who? Rhonda?' Why was she here early, damn it? He hadn't had time to prepare. He wasn't even properly dressed and there was egg on his T-shirt. 'Don't let her come up.'

'Too late,' Malcolm said gleefully.

Quinn dived into his backpack to try and find something respectable to put on but everything was wrinkled or dirty. He went into Mal's room, yanked open the wardrobe. 'Where are your T-shirts?'

'What are you doing? Don't go messing up my closet.'

'One clean T-shirt – that's all I'm asking.'

'She's at the door.'

Mal was right. Quinn could hear her knocking. He turned his T-shirt inside out and put it back on. Went to answer the door.

'Hey, babe, come on in.' He leaned to kiss her, she turned her cheek.

Rhonda was in pink sweats and her hair was tied up in a ponytail high on her head. Poised on tiptoes nearly, ready for flight. Or fight.

She held out a Macy's bag. 'I can't st—' then she got a proper look at the apartment in all its architecturally inspired glory. She stepped in. 'Wow. This is nice.'

'Hi,' Mal said. 'I'm Malcolm, Quinn's brother.'

'Oh, hi.' Rhonda put a hand up to her breast. 'I didn't even know he had a brother.'

'He got the looks but I got the brains. Won't you stay for coffee?'

'She doesn't drink coff—' Quinn began, but Rhonda nudged him aside, nearly flattening him. God, that girl was strong. 'Love to,' she said.

I don't fucking believe this, Quinn thought as Rhonda and Mal perched on the sofa, knees pointed towards each other, Mal's omelette forgotten.

'This is your place?' Rhonda asked, breathy, taking in the space, the sheer exuberant size of it. 'It's so big!'

'The bank's and mine.' Mal was as nonchalant as a lizard in the sun. He leaned one arm over the sofa behind her.

Quinn eyed them both. Bastard, he thought.

'You have neat taste.'

'He had a decorator,' Quinn said scornfully.

'A decorator! Cool.'

'You know, I'm so busy. Not much time to shop. You work out?'

'A little.' Rhonda brushed a non-existent hair out of her eyes.

You big, aerobically conditioned liar. Quinn could see where this was going. His own brother hitting on his girlfriend – with him less than twelve feet away. Was there no honour in the world?

'She had to mortgage her eyeballs to pay for the Reebok Club.' Quinn tried to get a foothold in the conversation. 'Miss one of those payments and – bingo! Stevie Wonder glasses for her.'

'You belong to the Reebok Club? I belong to the Reebok Club!'

'Isn't that incredible?' Rhonda giggled.

'Un-be-fucking-lievable,' Quinn said. 'Of all the gym joints in all the world.'

But they weren't listening. His eyes strayed to the omelette. Mal clearly wasn't interested, he might as well have it.

Damn, it was good! As he attacked his food, his thoughts were already turning this experience around in his mind – as a bar anecdote, they didn't come much better. Maybe even a short story. Perhaps that was the key. Start short, work up to long.

*I was sitting at home with my brother, minding my own business, when in walks* . . . It could work. With a twist at the end.

# Chapter Seventeen

On Sunday nights Bucky liked to take the evening train from Greenwich to the city. Same train every week, his routine never varied.

It wasn't that he didn't have a car – he had two – but he preferred to keep the Jeep Cherokee in the country and the Mercedes in town. The train was a habit he'd got into when Tania had first left him – she would never have stooped to public transport and he took a perverse thrill in hoisting his monogrammed weekend bag into the luggage rack of the local commuter. He'd always been fascinated by trains. He told people he used the time to catch up on his reading, but in truth he mostly dozed or stared out the window. He found the syncopated monotony of the journey restful. There was no pressure to do anything or talk to anyone. He could relax and let his mind drift.

So he wasn't happy when he heard somebody call out his name.

'Bucky? I thought it was you. Goodness, what a coincidence! Have you been at your estate?'

'Er . . .' Bucky hoisted his glasses further up his nose and peered upwards at Tye.

'Tye Fisher. We first met at your party in the

summer,' Tye said, flustered and embarrassed. 'You probably don't remember me . . . I'm sorry, I've disturbed you . . .' She made as if to go, knowing centuries of breeding would not allow Bucky to turn her away.

'Wait . . . I remember you now. You're Adrian's . . .' he poised, searching for the noun.

'Exactly.' Tye beamed. 'Is this seat taken?'

'Well, actually . . .'

'I'm sorry, you want to be left alone. How insensitive of me. One can be such a clod.'

'No . . . no . . . it's okay, really. Please, sit.' Bucky moved the newspaper from the seat. Tye slid in beside him, beaming. She was wearing Capri pants, boat shoes and a blue Oxford shirt buttoned a millimetre or two above her red push-up bra. Bucky wouldn't have to lean too far forward to see it. She had a violet sweater knotted casually around her neck and her hair was tied back with a chiffon scarf. The look she was aiming for was Audrey Hepburn meets the Long Island Lolita.

The train moved off and the conductor came weaving down the aisles.

'I popped up to see some old family friends,' she said, searching in her bag for her ticket. 'Lord and Lady Mountley have taken a house. Quite amazing. Normally nothing can induce them to leave Buckinghamshire, but dear Bernie is to marry an American, so that brought them scurrying over. Had to check out the in-laws, eh what?' Tye adopted a gruff old colonel's accent, and said a small prayer of thanks for the society pages. She'd always been an inveterate reader of them. And Americans, for all their talk of egalitarianism, were just as fascinated by toffs as the Brits were.

Bucky stared at her, his eyes slid down to her breasts and he'd drag them back up again. 'Didn't I meet you also at the Martin party? You were wearing yellow.'

'Oh, that dreadful thing! It simply would *not* stay up. I can't think why I allowed the salesperson to talk me into it. You know she actually said to me, "only one out of ten women could wear a dress like that," and I went and fell for it. The oldest line in the book.' Tye shook her head regretfully as if chastened by her youthful folly. 'And Adrian was absolutely no help. Never take fashion advice from an Englishman. If it's not wearing a saddle they don't know one end from the other.'

'How is Adrian?'

'Oh – I –' Tye paused, reached for a handkerchief and dabbed her eyes. A slight, ever so lady-like sniffle escaped her.

'Is everything okay?' Bucky placed a tentative hand on her shoulder.

'I'm so sorry,' Tye said, stifling a tiny sob. 'It's been over a week and I still can't quite believe it. Adrian and me . . . well, we're having a few problems.'

'I'm sorry to hear that.'

'Yes. Yes, it's simply frightful. He's married, did you know that? I couldn't believe it when he told me – the lies! I feel so cheap, so used.' Tye sobbed a little more.

'I had no idea.'

'Nobody did. But that's not all, it gets worse. His wife is in town, but he says he still loves me. So he's told me to get out of the flat and just hang around waiting till wifey goes home.'

'And are you?'

'I don't know, I don't know.' Tye buried her head in her hands. 'I just don't know what to do.'

'It seems a little much to ask,' Bucky said hesitantly.

'Oh, I'm so glad you agree!' Tye laid a hand on his arm, raised her tear-stained face to his. 'It's not me, is it? I mean, he's put me up in a nice hotel and every-thing. But he expects me to be around for . . . assigna-tions . . . it's so demeaning. This is not the way I was raised. I'd like to strike out on my own but I don't know where to turn. I asked Daddy for help, but he's so cross with me for coming to America in the first place. Some days I think he wants to starve me into coming home. But I really don't want to, I'm so happy here for the first time ever. My life hasn't been easy you know. You might look at me and think it has, but it hasn't. I know I shouldn't grumble, and I'm really not, but it's all got on top of me. I'm so sorry. I didn't mean to burden you with my worries, it's just that, I feel like you know what I'm saying.'

Bucky nodded mutely.

'It would all be so much easier if I had my own place. I could think . . . clearly. Get a little perspective . . . decide what my future is to be. Oh, it's such a mess!' She bent over her handkerchief, weeping gently without sound, almost. She knew that too much emotion would embarrass him.

'Hey, don't cry. There has to be something you can do.'

'Yes, if only I could think of what it is.'

'Don't be silly. There's got to be a really simple

solution and we're going to figure out what it is,' Bucky said briskly. 'Now, what can I do to help you out of this mess?'

Quinn thought that this Sunday was the worst he'd ever suffered. And he wasn't predisposed to liking them anyway. No matter how lapsed a Catholic you were, there was always the tremor of guilt associated with hanging out and having fun when your atavistic memory said you should be in a dark dank place listening to a priest mumbling ritual and waving incense.

The speed at which Mal and Rhonda had latched onto each other was indecent, and under his very nose. After thirty minutes in the apartment, they'd gone off to the gym to 'work out' together, Mal conveniently forgetting he'd already run five miles that day.

Quinn had decided to use his pain as a spur to prose. He opened up his laptop and perched it on the breakfast bar. He pressed the 'on' button. He was suffering, spurned by the woman he quite liked.

Damn, it just didn't have the right feel to it. Spurned by a beautiful woman who had nipped the bud of their relationship off before it had time to flower.

That sounded better.

As the computer hummed to life, Quinn felt low-level dread like an old friend. He couldn't do it. He had nothing to say. He was a useless, miserable speck of gobshite who had no right to harbour any artistic pretensions.

He squashed it. He was a writer, that's who he was. He'd told everybody, therefore it must be so. He placed the cursor on the start button. Ran it up to programs. To accessories. To games.

An hour later, having lost fifteen straight rounds of FreeCell, he folded the laptop shut and went out.

The twins came back at two and found Marion on her knees scrubbing the kitchen floor. She'd decided cleaning was a good way to not think about why Gus hadn't called. But down on her knees, the prayer position almost, she found herself running through the reasons like a liturgy. Perhaps he'd gone out of town for the weekend, or lost his pager. Perhaps he hadn't even got the message, maybe the company had screwed up in some way. Perhaps he just didn't feel like calling back just yet. She didn't want to call again. But still, but still, he hadn't called when he'd said he would, and he never did that. He always called, no matter where he was. If he said he'd call, he called.

Marion threw the sponge down and stood up.

'What's for lunch? I'm starving,' whined Grace, picking at a hole in her sweatshirt.

'Anything you feel like making,' her mother said. She'd had enough. She was going to call the hostel.

At Grand Central Station, Tye leaned on Bucky's arm like an invalid. She had been humbled by his invitation to stay on Park Avenue until she 'found her feet'. Such sweetness, such gallantry. Was he sure it would be no problem? None whatsoever, he assured her, he had plenty of space. In fact, he was just thinking the other week how very much too large it was for one person. It needed to be filled. Tye promised she would cook. Her cordon-bleu training was nothing really, a little dabbling, but she'd had a year after college and daddy had suggested she spend it in Paris improving her French. Well, she couldn't just sit around in cafes doing nothing, could she? So she'd taken a wee course or two. Did Bucky like to give dinner parties? Hardly ever? Well, there was always a first time. Not that she'd be there long enough to get settled in, oh no. She'd have made other arrangements before you could say 'lodger'.

They strolled through the concourse almost like lovers. Walking slowly, Tye gazing around her with unfeigned admiration at what she considered one of the great interior spaces ever designed. So big and yet so intimate. It was like being in a grand salon, she remarked to Bucky. He agreed that he never tired of it. They had the warm feeling of people who were fast finding common ground.

Tye was working hard to conceal her elation. She'd pulled it off. She had just enough money left to pay her hotel bill. She'd have to think of another source of cash later – for the meantime she was in the clear.

'Bucky?' The woman's voice cut through the hum of human traffic in the terminal.

Bucky traced the source of the noise. Swallowed visibly, dropped Tye's arm. 'Oh, Natasha,' he said faintly, 'I didn't expect to see you here.'

'Obviously.' The well-groomed, underfed woman

planted herself in front of them, hands on hips. 'Although I did tell you I'd meet you. Maybe it slipped your mind.' She glared at Bucky, then at Tye. 'And who the hell are you?'

# Chapter Eighteen

The apartment was quiet when Quinn returned. He'd been on the Staten Island ferry. He'd sat at the bow of the boat watching lower Manhattan recede and reflected that it really did look as though it was floating. Sometimes, usually after a few beers, he felt like that himself. Not floating exactly, but treading water. Wondering if the next wave to break over his head would be the one that drowned him. When he got that way he would head for the ferry. Getting off the rock always helped to clear his head. It was hard to stay down for long out here, smelling salt and watching the gulls glide by. He was miffed at Rhonda and Mal hitting it off, he reminded himself. His heart wasn't broken, only his pride had suffered. Besides, it wasn't as if they were dating or anything, they'd only gone to the gym together.

Quinn settled down to read the *Times*. He was deep into a depressing story about a young writer – two years younger than he – who was being feted for a small but perfect novella written about his experience as a banana picker in Ecuador. Never mind Rhonda – now that really did hurt.

Quinn glanced over at his computer. Perhaps there

was something to be written about his experience concocting Chinese fortune-cookie aphorisms. Novels with Chinese subjects were big these days; why couldn't he cash in on that? He was roughing out a structure in his head when he realized there was sound coming from Mal's bedroom. Giggling. Two people giggling.

He put the paper down, frowned slightly. More giggling. The muffled heavy thump of furniture falling over. Quinn turned his attention back to the paper. Tried to concentrate. The words blurred. He could hear a woman's voice, recognized the cadence of her moan.

Rhonda!

'Oh, Jesus.' Quinn put his head in his hands. His brother and Rhonda? Was he trapped in a designer nightmare of Mal's?

The sound got louder, as if they were fighting. Quinn knew Rhonda's routine. She wasn't a passive girl. No lying back waiting for things to happen. She liked to be in there, taking control.

More laughter. Bodies bumping against walls. Tripping, stumbling, falling.

Quinn got up. He knew what was going on and he didn't want to hear any more.

He had his hand on the door handle when Mal came out, towel wrapped lightly around his waist.

'Hey,' he said, shocked, a little embarrassed.

'Hey.'

'Didn't think you'd be back so soon.'

'Obviously.'

'Sorry, but it is my apartment.'

'So you've said.' Quinn hefted his keys. He needed the comfort of a Guinness.

'Quinn?'

He turned, regarded his brother, his straight dark hair, smoky brown eyes, shoulders pulled back sternly like a military man. The cheek of the guy, who would have thought? The things you didn't know about the people closest to you.

'She says there's some . . .' Mal fidgeted, eyes darting over the room. Quinn said nothing. Let him squirm, the bastard.

'. . . some . . . in the bag of stuff she brought back.'

The Macy's bag lay on the sofa. Through the thin plastic Quinn could see his Brendan Behan book and a box of Trojans. Extra sensitive. Unlike his brother.

'Help yourself,' he said. 'To everything.'


Jim Johnson and Mike Schwab worked together on the desk at the Chelsea hostel. They were genial guys in their mid-sixties, old friends. Both had seen hard times but come through and now considered themselves to be doing okay. They had work, they had a place, they had people around them they liked. There was a little money left over for recreation, in Jim's case, be-bop music and in Mike's a modest bi-weekly stake on the horses.

The phone had rung at five. Mike spoke to the woman from Michigan and when he put the receiver down he was frowning. Mike always took the calls. Jim's speech was a little slow because of a stroke last fall.

'Got pr . . . problems?' Jim said.

'Maybe.' Mike took the set of master keys from its hook. 'Remember those kids from Michigan? You see them lately?'

Jim shook his head. These days he didn't speak unless it was necessary. Hated the clumsy way the words came out.

'Me neither. The boy's mom was just on the phone. She ain't heard from him. He was supposed to call and he didn't. She wants me to check it out.' Mike ambled towards the elevator.

'Think they . . . ran out?'

'Didn't seem like the type.' Mike pressed the elevator button, waited for the car to return to the lobby. He really hoped nothing was wrong. The woman on the phone had sounded tense, apologetic, words tumbling out. She'd had time to get worked into a stew. Mike had tried to calm her. New York was a safe place these days, safest place in the world. That bad old image was way out of date. Place was safe as a theme park. Hell, it *was* a theme park.

He knocked several times on the door to the Neidermeyer's room before he unlocked it.

It was neat, clean. Everything folded. Bed made. A photo of the couple – their wedding picture – sat on the side table. Mike bent to get a closer look. Her veil had been caught by a gust of wind, wafting it upwards. She was laughing, delighted, her husband's arm around her waist. His eyes locked on her. He clearly adored her. It was a sunny day in that photo.

Mike sighed, checked the bathroom. Again, as neat as a pin. Cosmetics, shaving things lined up above the basin. Towels folded over the shower rail. If only all their guests were this tidy. Some of the stories the cleaners told him, you didn't want to believe it.

He stood in the bedroom trying to get a sense of things. The woman, the boy's mother, had said she would call back. What would he tell her? He didn't know.

Damn it, where were they?

Tye collapsed on her bed in the hotel, ripped off her sweater and kicked the shoes viciously into the corner of the room. For once, the careful luxury of the room didn't please her. 'Shit, shit, shit,' she said loudly. She'd been so close. Damn that bitch Natasha, Bucky's new squeeze. She was no fool. She knew the score and had repelled Tye as if she were a contagious disease. Made him choose, right there in the terminal. What was he going to do? He apologized to Tye, hands outspread. She graciously accepted, the brave heroine. Walked slowly away, back straight, shoulders quivering. Towards God knew what.

Marion Neidermeyer sat in the kitchen biting her knuckle. The twins were in the den watching television, sound turned up too loud. Electronic squawks punctuated the soundtrack. Marion barely heard them. She sat still, upright. Frozen. Praying with her whole body that this awful thing would go. The hostel concierge had said that Gus and Susie hadn't been seen for two days, but that couldn't be right. They must be there. Perhaps they were so involved in apartment hunting that they were coming in late and leaving early. Any minute now Gus and Susie would walk back into the hostel, call her and say everything was okay.

Let this cup pass from me. A long-forgotten fragment of a prayer she'd learned in Sunday school, rose unbidden. Jesus the night before his crucifixion, wasn't it? Even the son of God had pleaded with his father.

Why? Hadn't she had enough crap in her life? A divorce, a cancer scare. Now this. A sob rose inside her. She wanted to smash everything in the kitchen. Her beautiful kitchen, where she'd cooked and cleaned and fed her kids for twenty years. The first and probably only house she would ever own.

She didn't smash so much as a glass. She clenched her fist, banged it hard a couple of times on the bench and stood up.

There were things to do.


The message on the pager had ruined Cyrus's sensed of enlightened calmness. Not only had his session with the Master been interrupted – and that had had an unsettling effect – but he still hadn't figured out how to retrieve the message. What if it was important? All day he couldn't help feeling that the message was a test that called for an ingenious response and that he was supposed to think what it was. He felt wanting somehow.

He called the pager company and told them he'd forgotten the code, could they just give him the message anyway? No, had been the polite response. Could he change the code then (he was thinking of possible future messages). It had to be done in writing, the woman on the phone told him. It would take several days.

He was stymied. And that made him mad. It also set him back, made him forget all the things he'd recently learned. Anger was not conducive to a calm, ordered state of being. It didn't help him to think well of himself. He just felt shitty and worthless, that old thing coming back. The dark spirals. The hopeless feeling that closed around him, suffocating him.

He tried another session with the Master. He tried chanting, imagining himself bathed in the pink light, imagined his achievements, his dreams. It didn't work. The Master wasn't speaking to him. He was cold and distant. He felt like a failure. He wanted to cry.

He had to find out how to get that message.

# Chapter Nineteen

The next morning Tye woke with a headache. Her head felt as though a cheese wire had been threaded between her ears. It was a sharp, nasty little pain that was aggravated by the slightest movement. Perhaps Adrian had a voodoo doll of her. It wasn't enough to make her homeless and humiliate her, he had to make her sick as well. She lay on her bed with a flannel pressed to her temples, waiting for the Advil to kick in.

Damn Adrian. Damn him. Somehow she was going to make him pay. She rolled over in bed, the movement making her groan. Lying on her side she spotted the *Village Voice* poking out of the rubbish bin.

'Not that,' she mumbled. 'Anything but that.'

But even as she said the words, she realized she was fast approaching the place where she had no choice.

Susie Neidermeyer was an orphan. Both parents had been killed years before in a car crash and Susie had been raised by her elderly aunt Margaret who was now suffering from Parkinson's disease. Marion had been going to call her but decided it would be easier to speak to her in person. She didn't live far away, a ten-minute drive. Gus and Susie had known each other since they were children, had played together in elementary school, been friends in high school, but not special friends. Only got together in college, and in the final year, at that. Susie had blossomed that year. She got tall and her skin cleared up and she started doing well. Boys noticed her.

Marion wouldn't have chosen a better wife for her son. Susie was gutsy and strong, didn't take any crap. She'd been thrilled when Gus had said that he'd met the woman he wanted to marry and she lived in the same town. She thought that meant he wouldn't be going anywhere soon.

How wrong.

As she drove, she rehearsed what she would say to Margaret. Gus and Susie were missing. The police had been contacted. She was going to New York to find out what was going on. She hated the thought of being the one to break such awful news to a woman who was so fragile. Margaret's body had given up but her mind was as sharp as ever. Marion wondered how she would feel if someone lay such a thing on her shoulders and she was not able to do anything except sit and wait.

Maybe she should call her ex-husband, Marion thought, although she didn't want to. Chuck had abdicated his responsibilities years ago. He had more kids now, she'd heard. Toddlers. Her children had been dropped, sacrificed in Chuck's rush to rejuvenate his life. She imagined him driving a Harley and wearing an earring – the small-town accountant who hit forty and yearned to be cool. She snorted with contempt and then realized what she was doing. This was no time to be stoking up old bitterness. She had more important things to think about.

Quinn was up and out of Mal's place early. He had apartment-hunting fever, was sick with it. He grabbed a New World coffee, double espresso, and took the subway to Brooklyn.

It was a crisp, clear day, the light was stingingly bright and the bohemians of Williamsburg were going about their business. Williamsburg had the buzz these days. All the artists and writers and bicycle couriers who said they were artists or writers had moved across the river and turned a lot of old warehouses into lofts and performance spaces.

Quinn walked a couple of streets, looking for laundromats and coffee shops which was where the notices of apartments to let would be found. Most were for shares. He didn't feel like sharing, he was too old to share. He could afford a modest place on his own. Mal didn't know it, but Quinn had a secret source of funds. Molly the gambling granny sent her favourite grandson a cheque each time she won at the tables, which was quite often. Quinn knew he shouldn't rely on it, Molly sometimes had bad streaks, but for a while now the cheques had been regular, which meant he had a small cache – not huge, but enough for the deposit on a place and a couple of month's rent. Molly never referred to this money, always brushed aside any thanks. He'd worked out that it wasn't something to be proud of, that his grandmother didn't think that he, a grown man, could support himself.

But what the hell. One day when his literary, yet incredibly popular novel was at the top of the best-seller list and had Hollywood producers fighting for the right to have Johnny Depp star in it, then he'd be able to pay her back with interest. A trip to Monte Carlo, perhaps. He pictured Molly and him driving on the Corniche from Nice to Monaco. Yeah, that'd be the first thing he'd spring for.

'Quinn! 'Sup man?'

It was Ted. Sitting at a street corner cafe in front of a plate of bacon and waffles. The beginnings of a goatee beard. Wearing a ridiculous oversized Kangol cap backwards.

Quinn swallowed the horror, which was his instinctive reaction to Ted, and raised a hand in greeting. Ted was going to help him find a place, he was a necessary evil.

'Join me. Food's good here.'

'Thanks.' He hadn't eaten properly yet, no sense in starving oneself. The cafe was filled with cosmopolites wearing black who picked at fruit salads. Quinn ordered pancakes. Having some starch in his stomach would at least make Ted easier to bear.

'Getting any writing done?' Ted asked casually.


Detective John Abruzzo went to the hostel in Chelsea. More missing kids. He hated these ones, there was so little they could do. The world was big and most people who wanted to disappear could just pick up and go. If somebody wanted them out of the picture, well, that was easy too. Especially in New York. Families didn't stay together any more, that was the problem. People lived alone. It was too, too easy. In his twenty years on the force he'd seen it done a hundred different ways.

He interviewed the two guys on the front desk, Jim and Mike and took the name of the manager too. Mike told him the mother was flying up from Michigan. No point in calling her and telling her to let cops do cop work, John Abruzzo thought. He'd give her a call anyway, when he got back to the station, just before he filed his report, just in case they turned up. You never knew. Perhaps they'd just got sick of New York City, thousands did every day. Perhaps they got scared and freaked out and would turn up weeks later, shame-faced for the trouble they'd caused. Sometimes these cases ended like that. The ones he preferred did.

But he didn't think this was going to be one of them. Looking around the room, it seemed wrong. They were neat people, or one of them was. Neat people didn't up and leave – they packed, paid their bill, let people know where they were going. They tidied up the loose ends.

He took the photo, the wedding picture, in its frame. He'd need to get familiar with these kids' faces.


Tye's headache abated. She went out to a cafe, picked at a light, late breakfast and scanned the *Times*. It didn't take long, American affairs meant nothing to her, and she wasn't one for keeping up with the news.

She felt listless, paralysed by the enormity of the task in front of her.

Fumbling in her purse, she found Adrian's American Express number, the one she'd scribbled on the back of a postcard. What with everything else that had happened, she'd forgotten she'd lifted it. She memorized the numbers, as a precaution against losing it, an old habit. On her way back to the hotel, she stopped at a phone booth, dialled information and got the number of Balducci's, the city's premier food store. Then she dialled the number and ordered fifteen large turkeys to be sent to Adrian's wife. Thanksgiving was a few days away, and the store was busy. They took the order, named a price which almost made Tye drop the phone in shock. She could have bought a car for the same amount.

'Actually, did I say fifteen? I meant twenty.'

'Twenty turkeys, ma'am?' The clerk sounded surprised. Even by Balducci's standards, that was probably pushing it.

'It's a very big family reunion,' Tye cooed, thinking of the expression on Adrian's face when he saw them. He didn't even eat turkey. When asked how she'd be paying, she recited Adrian's American Express number and the expiry date on the card. Thank God he had a unisex name. She hung up the phone feeling better.

She was broke. She was going to have to hunt for a miserable sublet. The person who put her in this position was going to be sorry.

# Chapter Twenty

Cyrus could laugh now, looking back on his paranoia, his panic. Of course it had been a test. The Master did not communicate by pager. What a dumb idea. He'd woken in the night and it had been as clear as glass: don't get distracted by peripheral stuff. Focus on your vision and see it through to the end.

He walked over to the East Village. By now he'd completely forgotten about the pager. The dark spirals had gone. Even his mother calling had failed to bring them back. She was staying away from home as she frequently did. Too much money, Cyrus reflected. It had spoiled her and she had tried to use it to spoil him. But he wasn't buying into that any longer, no sir. He had his own standards now.

They'd had a brief, but for them, remarkably pleasant conversation. His mother said she'd be coming home in a week or so, along with his father. The maid would come first and open the house. She didn't ask how he was or what he was up to, she didn't care about him at all, he realized. And he no longer cared that she didn't ask. He was hearty and civil. Great, he'd said, he was looking forward to seeing her. His mother no longer intimidated him. From now on they would be dealing on his terms only. Let her just see how much he'd changed. Let both of them see!

New York University students were gathering for the coming semester. Hopeful out-of-towners, clutching books and forms, lost, dazzled by the glamour of the big city. Young kids, so young! Cyrus strolled around Washington Square. He remembered his first day at college. His parents had selected a very expensive school and backed up his humble SAT scores with a great dollop of money to smooth the progress of a new science library. Cyrus had entered the portals of the respected institution with great joy. He was away from his family – removed from their power to hurt him.

He'd done okay, not too bad, considering. Looking back, he realized he'd been too young and hadn't made the right choices. If he had that chance again, he'd do it differently. He wasn't stupid, he just didn't fit the plan his parents had drawn up.

Four generations of doctors. Respectable, intelligent, dedicated doctors. World famous, some of them, leaders in their fields. Then him. He didn't want to let them down. Part of him hoped he'd be effortlessly brilliant at medicine, that against all his experience, he'd find the place where he could shine.

As if.

Undergraduate school had been okay, but undergraduate school was nothing in his family. He'd had to go on to medical school. He'd only lasted two years because he'd failed his National Board exam. Majorly embarrassing. The flunk-out rate at his medical school was very low. Cyrus had to put up with the pity of his

fellow students. Their surface kindness meant something else underneath – that he wasn't good enough.
He couldn't cut it.

His whole adult life, Cyrus had not been able to
think about that without a sickening pain in his
stomach. But that was behind him now. The Master
had taught him to consider it another way. He hadn't
failed – he'd eliminated an option. All along he'd been
edging towards his true purpose without realizing it.


It was a curiously murky phenomenon, the open house
arrangement for subletting, Tye thought. One put an
ad in the paper, invited complete strangers into one's
home and tried to assess their suitability for taking
over one's lease on the basis of a ten-minute meeting.
In New York, of all places, where a good fifty per cent
of the population were certifiably wacko.

And God, these people were desperate. Standing
around nervously, laughing too loudly, humour and
smiles forced. Like the party of the socially damned.
She really wasn't cut out for schmoozing in these
situations. She didn't mind it one on one with people
who could be useful to her, but these were of a lower
calibre – defensive, sad little creatures. They were
valiantly trying to pretend that New York wasn't getting them right in the gut and twisting so hard it hurt.
Tye could see it etched in their faces. They were
running upwards on a down escalator.

The one with the apartment was a particular case.
Adam somebody or other. A gnomish little chap with a
facial tick. He didn't speak, he barked, staccato soprano.

'So,' he said to Tye, standing in front of her, arms crossed, legs akimbo. 'So. What can you give me?'

'Give you?'

'How much do you make?'

'Well, that's—' *none of your Goddamned business*, Tye was going to say, but Adam wouldn't let her finish.

'Lemme see your references. Where are your bank accounts? I need to see bank accounts.' His little hand flicked out flapping as fast as his mouth.

'What do we do if something breaks?' a woman interrupted, pushing Tye out of the way.

'I'll give the super a cover story. Tell him you're my cousin.' The little guy had the jerky movements of an animated cartoon character.

'You mean this is illegal?' Tye said innocently. She felt like goading him.

'Who wants to know?' He jerked and twitched a couple of times. His head seemed to be vibrating of its own accord.

'Just asking,' Tye said as she strolled into the kitchen. She poked the tap, it swayed and clanked. The place was tiny, a damp little dump but it was in Murray Hill and Adam thought $2,300 a month was a fair price. Tye wondered how much he was paying, half that probably.

'What's the security?' a beefy guy in a check shirt asked.

'Four months rent,' Adam said as if defying the guy to contradict him. He didn't. He nodded as though that's what he had expected.

Nice, thought Tye, doing a few sums.

The bathroom had an interesting tracery of mildew

on the tiles, it smelt of old socks. She returned to the living room. Six people in there and it was crowded. Adam stood almost preening in the centre. He hadn't had this many people clustered about him since the day he was born. Some had their cheque books out and were waving them like supplicants. The smell of burnt fat from the kebab restaurant downstairs was sweet and sticky.

Tye began to move towards the door.

'Hey,' Adam barked, reminding Tye of a hyperactive chihuahua. 'Are you interested?'

'I think you can count me out,' she said flashing her devastating smile. Adam twitched as though he'd been electrocuted. 'But I want to thank you so much for the experience. It's been extremely informative.'

'Have a nice day,' he yapped. It sounded like 'go fuck yourself'.

Tye skipped lightly down the rickety stairs. She felt as light as air.

At last, an idea.

# Chapter Twenty-One

She wasn't cut out to be kept, she reflected as she ordered a triple latte. Her blood was fizzing. Only a really good plan could make her feel this way.

It had been an interesting experience, had given her an insight into how others lived, but she was a working girl. It was the way she was raised. Her father worked, her mother worked. Her whole family worked. And she would again too. The thought made her happy.

Quinn spent the morning pacing out his rage in Williamsburg. Nominally he was looking for an apartment but really he was roiling inside. His girlfriend and Mal? How could they? Had they no respect for his feelings? What kind of world was it where people did this to one another? His own brother, the person whom he'd known all his life. He had no apartment, no girlfriend, no job – worse, no novel, not even a screenplay. Then there was Ted O'Reilly. Frigging Ted selling a screenplay for all that money.

Meanwhile, he was knocking on doors, stopping

people in the streets, asking if they knew of any spare space, any space at all. He checked every bulletin board in a twenty-block radius. He spoke to shop-keepers, garbage collectors, school children and mailmen.

He found nothing. He was exhausted and empty-handed except for an invite to a party at Ted's new apartment. A party that was bound to be the most excruciating social torture he'd ever endured. He'd already decided not to go.

A travel agent seemed to Tye the obvious place to begin.

She walked around Murray Hill, looking for a suit-able candidate. She found three or four. Most were small operations, two or three people, scruffy carpet, peeling faded posters promising sun, beaches, beautiful companions, advanced skiing ability.

She eventually settled on Custom Elite Travel because she liked the look of the harassed guy who sat behind a shabby desk. Ink on his fingers, thick hair plastered down in front but poking up defiantly at the back, clutching a cappuccino that had dried milk froth caked on the sides. A blackboard outside offered trips to 'Johannesberg' and Tye wondered if travellers could trust an agency to get them to a place they couldn't even spell.

'Leon Falk?' She read the name from the chipped enamel sign perched on his desk.

'Yes, ma'am.' He looked up from his computer, fingers shaking from too much coffee.

'I wonder if you can help me,' Tye said, sliding into a chair.


Marion went straight from the airport to the hostel in Chelsea where Gus and Susie had stayed. It took her ages to get there. She couldn't work out the subway system, kept getting on the wrong lines. Her overnight bag grew heavier and heavier. Finally she took a taxi at huge expense because the traffic was so slow. She found out she could have walked there faster.

The guys at the hostel couldn't have been nicer. They gave her a room. She was told to drop her bags off, get freshened up before she went to talk to the cops. Mike told her not to worry, there was bound to be an explanation. They would work it all out soon.

What explanation? Marion wanted to scream at him. My reliable, responsible eldest child is missing. There can't be any 'explanation' apart from disaster.

But she knew he was only trying to help.

She hadn't told her twins the full story, not yet. She'd bailed them off to her pal Jonie, and told them she had to go to New York to get something sorted out concerning Gus. She wasn't sure if they believed her, but they were docile for once, sensing she was not in the mood to be crossed. She'd told Jonie the truth, sitting in her sunny kitchen, drinking coffee and looking out over the vast lawn that Jonie's husband Rick tended with religious devotion. She had to tell someone.

Her oldest friend knew not to offer false words of

comfort. She heard Marion out in silence, then she went to the cookie jar, dug her hand in and pulled out a roll of twenty-dollar bills.

'You're gonna need this,' she said. 'Don't argue with me, just take it.'

Now here she was. The big, bad apple. Even the smell she didn't like. There was no air, just a swirling stickiness. Impossible to get a good lungful, not that you'd want to.

She hadn't wanted to 'freshen up'. What a ridiculous notion. Her son missing and who cared whether she was ripe or stale, but once in her room she turned on the shower without thinking, took her clothes off and stepped in. Let the icy water beat down.

When she looked in the mirror, she discovered she was crying.


'I need a vacation,' Tye said, smiling brightly.

Leon nodded glumly then clocked a good look and perked up. Men were seldom indifferent to Tye. 'But I can't decide where.'

'Hot or cold?'

'Hot . . . I think. Or maybe cold.'

'A sports vacation? A resting vacation?'

'Oh, definitely resting. On the other hand . . . maybe not. Culture would be nice. I need the choice of culture, the thought of culture, without having to partake necessarily. You know what I mean?'

Leon nodded.

'Culture is all very well if you're in the mood for it,

absolutely fabulous if you're in the mood, but it should be a love match, not a forced marriage, do you see what I'm saying?'

'Europe?'

'Last year.'

'Asia.'

'Oh but that's so passé.' Tye shuddered. 'I want something stimulating, yet restful. Cultural, yet mindless. Perhaps rafting.'

'We have a deal on—'

'No, what am I saying? It's much too cold for rafting.'

'Down under?'

'Did I mention my mother will be accompanying me? She's confined to a wheelchair. And she has a small dog, a Pomeranian I believe, or at least that's what the breeder told us. Frankly, between you and me, I think she was sold a pup.' Tye tittered.

Leon stared at her, dazed. One hand poised over the coffee, the other at his computer keyboard. Looking as though he wished he were somewhere else, despite her beauty and her legs.

'Don't worry,' Tye leaned over the desk, patted his arm, 'we'll sort something out in no time at all.'


Marion told Detective John Abruzzo of Missing Persons everything she knew, which was not much, she reflected bitterly. The precinct house had been just what she'd expected. Government buildings were the same shade of grey everywhere. This one was shabby, disorganized, overcrowded. She perched on a metal chair in the corner of a tiny office and told John Abruzzo about her son. She tried to keep the emotion out of her voice, to give him only the facts. To give him a sense of who Gus was and why this was so very wrong. The cop regarded her steadily, wrote in a little notebook. Asking her the expected questions – were there any problems? Any drugs?

No, Marion said quickly. Nothing like that. Any problems in the marriage? No. They were newly weds. Violence? No. Not that you know of, John Abruzzo corrected. Financial problems? There wasn't a lot of money, they'd just finished school, they had loans to pay off but they had a little cash in reserve. They'd both had summer jobs.

Abruzzo scratched away at his notebook.

'Is there anything else you can think of?' he asked, finally. Marion shook her head, mute now from the strain of talking about her loved ones to strangers.

John Abruzzo snapped the dog-eared notebook shut. Slipping it into his shirt pocket. He had the shape of a pear, Marion thought irrelevantly. A big, brown pear.

'What are you going to do now?' she asked, pushing down her anger, fear, uncertainty, panic.

'Everything in our power, ma'am,' John Abruzzo said wearily. 'Everything in our power.'

# Chapter Twenty-Two

Quinn stared at his computer screen. He wanted to write, but he couldn't shake the lurking premonition of failure.

He had always thought that he had approached society on his terms. Staying outside its prescribed career rules had been his choice. But what if Malcolm was right, what if he really was just a lazy bum?

Quinn ran a hand through his hair, shaking his head as if he were dismissing the argument. He had to stop thinking like that. What did success mean anyway? More things? He, Quinn was happier with a different path – the less he owned, the more successful he was. His art was his sole priority.

And there was the problem. His art.

His idea for a semi-autobiographical novel about a young man growing up between Ireland and New York had been kicking around since college. He had an outline, one or two chapters roughed out. But he wasn't happy with it. The voice in his head was so much smoother and more complex than what came out on paper. In his head he was fluid, insightful, in control. On paper, well, he wasn't anything on paper.

After university Quinn had lived for a couple of

years in Dublin. It had been a happy time, he'd been able to elaborate on plans for his literary life in smoky bars without the inconvenience of having to do anything about them. The fair-skinned, dark-haired girls who had invariably accompanied him on those occasions lapped up his talk, his theories about the novel, the exotic air conferred on him by his years in the United States. They were used to such stories. Lots of people in Ireland considered themselves writers. Nobody expected that you would necessarily do anything about it. Here was different. It was what you did that counted, not who you were or said you were. Americans didn't appreciate the value of blag, that was the problem. They were so goddamned goal-orientated.

Mal and Rhonda burst into the room giggling. Mal carried a bottle of Krug by the neck. Rhonda had a bag full of food.

'Hey.' They both stopped short when they saw Quinn. Pulled their smiles down to neutral expressions. Mal's hand slipped down from behind Rhonda's back.

'Don't worry, I'm going out,' Quinn said, snapping the lid of his computer shut too fast so it squealed in protest. He grabbed his coat, checked for wallet and keys. This was the absolute end. He tried to catch Rhonda's eye as he went past but she looked studiously at the parquet floor. There were a few things he'd like to say to her.

Quinn walked fast when he got outside, thinking of his options. The situation had to change fast. Perhaps he should just use Molly's money for a one-way ticket to Dublin. Perhaps that was where he belonged –

perhaps he was just too artistic for New York. Then he thought of the Irish winters. The country was so god-damned cold and damp it was a wonder it wasn't choked in mould. All right if you were used to it, but he had never been able to banish the chill from his bones, no matter how many pints of Guinness he sank. Quinn knew that an artist's inner life should not be affected by such prosaic concerns, but he was used to warmth and solid food and strong water pressure. He was an American, after all. Even if only by adoption.

An ad for a sublet posted on a telephone pole caught his eye. Wickedly expensive and only for three months, but in Chelsea. He thought of the Irish winter and ripped off one of the numbers.

It was time to get real.


'Leon, fancy meeting you here.' Tye snagged the stool next to him from under the nose of a woman in a camel-hair coat. The woman started to complain but Tye cut her off. Smiled at her in a way that suggested she should not even think about trying to cross her.

'Hi,' he said, embarrassed, flustered. He was hunched over a cappuccino, hands shaking impercep-tibly, hair standing up in clumps. Perhaps the caffeine had gone to his follicles, Tye thought. She hitched up her skirt a little, a gesture not lost on Leon. He closed his book. He was reading a horror novel which had a screaming woman on the jacket.

'It's Michelle,' she said. 'Remember? At your office today?'

Leon nodded glumly, his face now flushed from more than just the effect of the caffeine.

'What an interesting job you must have,' Tye said gaily. 'Catering to people's fantasies. Giving them their dreams! What a privilege.'

'It's just a job.'

'Ah.' Tye shook her finger at him. 'You are far too modest. Think about it: because of you people get two weeks of every year in absolute bliss. Now, how many other people can say that about their work?'

Leon looked doubtful.

'You are filling a valuable need, so don't sell yourself short.' Tye stirred sugar into her coffee. Although she normally never took it, she'd notice the empty sugar sachets scattered about Leon. 'God, I've got to kick this habit sometime.' She sighed.

Leon nodded, comforted by the acknowledgement of a shared vice. He turned his body to face Tye's.

When Marion got back to the hotel room she lay down on her bed and breathed deeply. The insurance firm where Gus had been about to start work hadn't been much help. She'd spoken to a cold-voiced woman in personnel who said Gus hadn't been in. They had no idea where he was.

She had been out all day with Gus and Susie's photos, stopping people in the streets, asking store-keepers, talking to anyone who would listen. Had they seen her son and his wife? Most people pushed past as though she was crazy. New Yorkers didn't speak to each other. You had to have lost a grip on your sanity to stand in the middle of the street and stop strangers. Only panhandlers and salesmen did that. But Marion was beyond caring what people thought. She had to do something. Sitting in her tiny room all day would make her crazy. She'd called John Abruzzo in the afternoon, just checking in. He'd told her again in his weary, sad voice that everything they could do was being done. There was nothing she could do either.

But there must be something. Every cell in her body screamed against inaction. She had given life to her boy, it was because of her that he existed. She wasn't going to stand around. She couldn't.

She'd brought all Gus's postcards, wrapped in an envelope. She took them out and re-read them for clues. Gus's comments had been perfunctory. Dinners eaten, sights seen. She packed them up and put them away. She'd wait till later and go out checking neighbourhood restaurants, when the night shift came on.

Somebody might recognize her son.

Leon didn't demur when Tye had suggested a bar that served good burgers. He was probably lonely, Tye thought. Like everyone else here. The bar was near Leon's office. That too was planned.

God, I love America, Tye thought, surveying the menu. Meat, cheese, cake, ice cream. 'Wine?'

'I don't?'

'Course you do.' Tye summoned the waitress. Ordered a bottle of French Sauvignon Blanc.

The bar was softly lit, quiet. Some people clustered

on bar stools, some already eating at tables. An English pub at this hour would have been crowded, noisy and smoky, people drinking like automatons so they could chuck it up on the pavement later. Tye had rarely gone to pubs in London. She couldn't stand the noise or the crush.

The bottle arrived. The waiter poured a couple of inches into each glass.

'My father makes wine,' she said. 'He has a small estate in the Loire. Jean-Louis is one of his old friends.' She pointed to the label on the bottle. 'He'd be so insulted if you didn't try some. He's particularly proud of this vintage.' She pushed the glass across the table.

Leon looked at it as though it might explode in his face.

'Go on. Take a sip. You don't have to swallow if you don't want to. I sometimes don't.' She wagged her eyebrows lasciviously.

Leon's hand reached out, his lips pursed. Raised the glass to his lips.


Quinn called the sublet number he'd taken off the telephone pole.

'Like, come on over,' said the woman on the other end.

'Great. Now?'

'Sure.' She gave him the address. Then she told him to wait outside and she'd throw down the key. The front-door buzzer wasn't working.

At seven thirty, Quinn hit his mark. Right on time a head poked out the window.

'Quinn?'

'Yeah.'

'I'm Jolly. Third floor.' She moved her arm and a key landed with a tinkle on the pavement beside his feet. Such trust, Quinn thought, as he picked it up and unlocked the front door. I could be the next Ted Bundy and she's inviting me into her apartment at night.

Then again, she could be the next Ted Bundy, he countered as he arrived at the third-floor landing. He knocked, oddly excited by the thought.

# Chapter Twenty-Three

Leon wasn't used to drinking. He took a little kosher wine at Passover, but no more than a sip. And religious wine wasn't that great. It was sweet and sticky. This stuff was quite different. Tye looked at the label. She'd never tried this one before and it was very average. A little too bland for her liking, but if it knocked Leon's socks off then it was okay by her. She refilled his glass as they finished their burgers. By her calculation he'd drunk three quarters of a bottle and it was starting to show.

'Tell me about your work,' she said, leaning across the table so he could get the full benefit of her cleavage.

'It's just a job.'

'You're too modest.'

'It's the truth. I punch buttons on a computer all day. People come in, they give me money, they go away. If they had a terrible time they come and yell at me, if they had a great time I never hear from them. It's no way to make a living.'

'Why do you do it then?'

Leon shrugged. 'Habit.'

'I think you're being too hard on yourself. Travel is a noble calling.'

'Some calling. I send fat Americans out into the world so they can insult the locals by speaking English at them loudly. So everybody thinks America's full of schmucks. It's a wonder the Environmental Protection Agency hasn't closed me down.'

Tye suddenly didn't want to have to do anything bad to Leon. She was beginning to like him.

'What are you doing here?' The wine had made Leon honest. 'What's a babe like you doing here?'

'I like you,' Tye said. 'You've got a brain.'

Leon giggled.

'You're honest, you're smart. Not many in this town like that.'

'You wouldn't sleep with me though,' he said, emboldened by booze. Tye thought of all that unaccustomed alcohol racing around his bloodstream, delivering silliness to his organs. She laughed. Took his hand. There were calluses on his thumb. 'For that, you'll have to wait and find out.'

She called the waiter for another bottle of wine.

'Come on in.' Jolly was wearing combat pants and a florescent orange shirt. Her short hair was dyed green. The Red Hot Chili Peppers were cranked up loud.

Quinn's first thought was that he had entered a lumber yard. The main room was maybe fifteen by fifteen feet, the ceilings were high and there was wood stacked haphazardly next to the walls. It was a studio that had been chopped up by an amateur home-improvement specialist. A wooden shell had been constructed near the ceiling to give the apartment a second-floor platform. The sound of banging was coming from the kitchen. Quinn looked in to see a bare-chested man hammering nails into a plank supported by sawhorses.

'Nice,' Quinn said. 'A fixer-upper.'

Jolly looked at him blankly. 'This is the second bedroom,' she said.

Half of the main floor had been sectioned off with plywood to make a sliver of a room perhaps five feet wide. There was a mattress on the floor and two people entwined on top of it. A huge dog slumbered in the corner.

'Hi!' Quinn said. A single finger emerged from the blanket.

'Wanna go upstairs?'

Quinn looked at the staircase. Shook the banister. It wobbled wildly under his light touch. Years of labouring on building sites during school vacations had given him a rudimentary knowledge of carpentry, and he knew he shouldn't trust his weight to this rococo edifice. But then again, what the hell. He might get something out of it he could write about.

'Sure,' he said. 'Let's go up.'

The upstairs room contained a mattress on the floor and a small shrine. Rotting fruit lay around a centrepiece which looked to Quinn's eyes like a bell jar with ashes inside.

'Cool,' Jolly said as she noticed Quinn looking at the ashes.

'Cool?'

'It's my last boyfriend. Cool.'

'His name?'

'Yeah. And his attitude.'

'How'd he . . .'

'Pass on?' Jolly gnawed at a black-painted finger-nail, which made her speech even more difficult to understand.

'Fell. Off the mezzanine. Utilities are included.' Jolly crouched at the shrine and tweaked the photo of a bearded man, rearranged the incense sticks so all the colours were grouped in like bunches.

'Utilities.' Quinn peered over the mezzanine.

'Gas, water. Nineteen hundred a month. I'll need three months up front.'

The apartment, Quinn realized. 'Oh, right.'

'I'm moving out on the third. Taking Cool to Arizona. He likes it there.' Jolly stroked the cheek of the man in the photo. 'I like it too. I'll get composed, you know. Deal with my grief.'

'You'll compose, he'll decompose.' The words were out before he could stop them, but Jolly appeared not to have heard. 'Grand,' Quinn said, a little louder, backing towards the stairs. Time to be leaving Kooksville.

'I can't let this place to just anyone. It's special. We lived here together.' Jolly leant towards the photo, whispering to it. 'He's with me. I hear him. We still have sex. Only it's psychic, you know?'

'Is that good?'

'Sure.' Jolly grinned. She was quite attractive, Quinn thought, if you discounted the multiple piercings. Perhaps . . . Quinn put another foot backwards and realized there was no solid floor beneath him. As he pitched backwards into empty space he immediately recalled a long-forgotten prayer to the Virgin Mary.

Leon didn't take much persuading to go back to the office. Normally, he told Tye, he wouldn't have had a key. But his uncle owned the business and he was on vacation, so Leon was in charge.

'Where do travel agents go on holiday?' Tye asked, keeping a grip on Leon lest he stumble under the weight of the wine. Keeping his mind off the fact that he was too drunk to be making decisions.

'He never leaves New York,' Leon said, mournfully. Even the booze couldn't make him cheerful. 'He was born and raised here. He wants a break, he goes to Long Island. Sag Harbor. That's his idea of exotic. He's got a place there.'

He fumbled with the keys, opened the doors, got to the alarm system.

I'm in! Tye thought. Sometimes it was too easy.

Quinn had his arm set at the emergency room at St Vincent's Hospital by a harassed young doctor who he decided was utterly gorgeous. Her blonde hair was tied back in a ponytail and the dark circles under her eyes contrasted sharply with her translucent skin.

Quinn became hypnotized by her pale, long-fingered hands. The sleeve of a pink blouse poked out from the hem of her hospital coat. She smelled of pine and wore no rings on her left hand. It was time for the old Quinn moves.

'What's your name?' he said as she prepared his arm for the cast.

'Doctor Forelli.'

'Don't you have a first name?'

'Doctor.'

'Funny first name.'

'My parents were very ambitious for me. Stay still, please.' She began applying the plaster to Quinn's arm.

'You know I've never broken anything before?' The plaster felt cold. 'Thirty-three. Remarkable really, when you consider all those years as a covert operative in South America. Top-secret tasks, of course. For your eyes only, highest level. And then there was the time I climbed Mont Blanc without oxygen. Not even a scratch. Not to mention travelling with the circus. High wire. Fell once, twenty feet. Landed on my tippy-toes. It's all in how you land. Relaxing is the key. Ask any cat.'

Dr Forelli worked fast. She said nothing.

'Say, do they ever let you out of here? Do doctors do dinner? Dancing?'

'I've been up since Friday,' the beautiful doctor snapped. 'The exit's that way.'


When Quinn got home, he was thankful that Rhonda had left. His brother was sitting in front of a televised football game, sound turned down, a sex–induced smirk on his face.

Quinn pulled a beer from the fridge. Plonked himself on the sofa. Tussled with the pop-top one handed.

Stared at the Broncos and the Jets on Astro Turf, his mind on something else.

'What happened to you?' Mal's smirk changed to a slight frown when he saw Quinn's arm.

'It's just a scratch.'

'What happened?'

'I fell backwards down some jerry-built stairs that it seems had already claimed the life of one innocent man.' Quinn took a dramatic swig from his beer can. 'I am the victim of a society that doesn't give a stuff.'

Mal's shoulders raised in a slow-motion shrug. 'You okay?'

'Yeah.'

'Why?' Quinn asked finally. 'Why'd you do it, Mal?'

'It's chemistry.'

'That's a reason?'

'D'you know how hard it is to meet single women in this town?'

'About as hard as picking daffodils in spring.'

'They're all lunatics.'

'Rhonda's a lunatic.'

'She's sweet.'

'She's got great tits and legs.'

'So? You didn't think she was chopped liver.'

'I didn't steal her from my own brother.'

'You'd broken up.'

'The ink wasn't dry on the agreement!'

'You were finished.'

'We were not.' But Quinn slumped back in the chair, his righteous anger forgotten. He had meant to have it out with Mal, man to man. He pictured them fighting to the death. But now he couldn't muster the energy. And his arm hurt. He was having difficulty even remembering Rhonda's face.

Sometimes it was a curse being so easy-going. Grudges slipped through his fingers like wet soap. What did it matter? What did any of it matter?


Marion was a reserved woman and going into crowded restaurants, dark bars, striking up conversations with complete strangers was a difficult thing for her to do. But she'd learned a trick when her husband left her for the condo saleswoman, and that was to narrow her mind. Marion considered a narrow mind a useful thing in times of extreme stress. She did it by shutting down her deductive processes. The part of her brain that fed the 'what if' questions became sealed off. She was blank the night she went to those places where people congregated to escape from whatever kinds of lives they led. She went up to people regardless of the looks they gave her. She ignored the pity or contempt in their eyes. If they cold-shouldered her, she pressed on. This wasn't about her, it was about Gus and Susie. And anything was better than sitting alone in her room.

'Have you seen this couple?' She must have asked the question a hundred times. Most people shrugged and turned away. Some shook their heads in pity. Some ignored her completely.

'Have you seen my son? Or his wife?'

Nobody had. They had vanished.

*

'So I come into your office to book my holiday and you do what?' Tye and Leon were close together, sharing a single swivel chair as Leon fumbled with the buttons on his computer. It refused to start.

'Damn it!' Leon said, he slid off the chair.

'Hey!' Tye laughingly reached down to grab him.

'It's the plug, it always falls out,' Leon said, muffled under the desk.

'Oh, for a minute there . . .' Tye crossed her legs. She heard a bang as Leon's head met the underside of the desk. She pressed one of the computer keys. The screen stayed dark.

'Hang on a minute,' Leon said.

'Need a canary?' She bent down. All she could see was Leon's rear end, it wasn't too bad, considering his desk-bound life.

'Got it. Any second now. Damn, where's that plug?'

The computer screen jerked to life, a thin horizontal line expanded as though exploding.

'Every day it falls out. Keep meaning to get a new one.' Leon scrambled to his feet, patting his hair into place unsuccessfully. He looked Tye over and his eyes gleamed.

'Come and show me what it's all about.' There was no mistaking what she meant.

# Chapter Twenty-Four

Now that he'd conquered his fear of self-expression, Cyrus reckoned it was time to make a statement with the bodies. All he had to figure out was what that statement should be.

He spent hours lulling himself into a relaxed frame of mind, seeking inspiration. When that failed, he took to walking the streets in the hope that the city, his home town, would give him his answer. He'd even considered chanting, had found a chant written on a scrap of paper in the bottom of a pocket, a souvenir from a disastrous foray into yoga. But he'd felt stupid chanting words he didn't understand.

All he'd come up with so far was a big, fat zero.

But he wasn't too worried. He didn't need to think about it right away. And he knew that an idea would occur when he least expected it. On the treadmill at the gym maybe, or waiting for the subway. He didn't need to decide everything right this minute. The important thing was to keep focused on his goal. And when the time came, everything would fall into place.

Still, he couldn't help yearning for the answer. He was excited about the changes he was experiencing and felt as though he were about to enter a new stage.

He was looking forward to that: he wanted the feeling. The ease that comes with familiarity, the flair. He wanted flair.

Meanwhile the Master was patiently guiding him. Preparation was the most important part of his plan. Cyrus was pleased with the ideas he'd come up with so far. Like the one where he asked people to come to one address and then took them to another afterwards. That had been his very own. The cellphone number he used was assigned to the name Reginald John. Cyrus liked the way he'd thought of cleverly combining Elton John's real and stage names. He'd gone to the phone company with his false information and the name had just popped into his head. He'd always been a fan although he hadn't liked the way Elton butchered one of his old classics for Princess Diana's funeral. That seemed cheap. He should have composed an entirely new song for her. Cyrus would have done that if Diana had been his friend. She had such beautiful hair.

Leon had opened the computer database. It was a Windows programme. Tye didn't doubt it wouldn't take her long to find her way around it now that Leon had logged on and typed in the password – four letters and four numbers. The four letters were Leon's name. The four numbers were 1-2-3-4. Among the computer's other features, it contained what Leon drunkenly explained was the 'back office booking system' which kept track of all his clients' itineraries.

Tye put her hand on Leon's shoulder, caressed the

short hairs at the back of his neck. He stopped typing, turned to her.

'Let's forget about that silly stuff, shall we?'

Leon nodded mutely as Tye led him towards the couch.

He dozed afterwards, unaccustomed to the excitement, the alcohol. Tye returned to the computer. She went into the customer bookings file and located several names and addresses of people who were planning vacations starting in the next couple of weeks. She copied the names, addresses and phone numbers into a small black notebook.

She left Leon sleeping. But not before writing a note which said. 'I had fun. Let's do it again – Michelle.'

# Chapter Twenty-Five

Early next morning she began her research. She felt as though a dense fog had lifted. She was energized, refreshed and ready to get to work.

She put on jeans, a sweatshirt and trainers and spent the morning checking out buildings. Whom she chose would depend entirely on where they lived. The building couldn't be so small that people would notice a stranger coming and going and it couldn't have a doorman who'd be asking questions. That ruled out more than three-quarters of her list.

But there was one on the Upper East Side that she had a good feeling about. Juliana Franklin lived there. According to Leon's records, she was taking a hiking trip out west.

When Tye saw the apartment building, on East 88th Street she knew that it was the one. It was in a brownstone, five stories tall with two apartments on each floor. The names on the doorbells showed that Juliana Franklin lived on the second floor in the east apartment.

Tye went to a flower shop on Lexington and ordered Juliana Franklin a bunch of flowers, wrote *Bon Voyage* on a note and scrawled an illegible signature.

Then she called Juliana's number to check that she was home. When she answered the phone, Tye explained that she had dialled a wrong number. She had the flowers sent over immediately.

Tye was fumbling in her handbag at the front door of the brownstone when the delivery boy arrived. Juliana Franklin buzzed him in. Tye followed the delivery up the stairs. The building had no elevator.

She waited until the delivery boy had knocked on Juliana Franklin's door.

'Oh, they're lovely,' the young woman exclaimed. She had red curly hair and was dressed in a long velvet skirt and high lace-up boots. She wore a blue sleeveless T-shirt and her upper arm was tattooed.

She tipped the delivery guy and shut the door. Tye climbed up to the next floor for appearance's sake, and then went to a coffee shop for a latte.

In all the years she'd worked for her father, Tye had picked up some useful skills. One of these was pickpocketing. She'd started young, practising on her dad's pockets. Him laughing with amusement as her ten-year-old fingers tried to get into his double-breasted suit jacket. He didn't encourage her in this endeavour, he considered pickpocketing a waste of time.

'If you're going to rob, think big,' he used to say. 'You know Machiavelli? The Italian geezer? He knew a thing or two. He said men will forgive a huge wrong but not a small one.'

Tye had not heard of Machiavelli, but she knew that her dad knew things other people didn't, which was why they lived in such a big house and she went to a school where there were only girls. And Tye knew instinctively that her daddy's line of work was different from other girls. When people asked her what her father did, she would say 'he makes money'.

Her father adored her. Long before the state had institutionalized 'take your daughter to work' days, Tye had been hanging around him, picking up stuff: quite literally. Practising her pickpocketing.

She grew older and she learned. When other girls her age were obsessed with teeny-bop stars and glitter nail polish, Tye refined her skills. Her hands had stayed thin, which helped. She'd go with Ronnie, one of her dad's 'fixers', to Oxford Circus or Leicester Square on a Saturday and relieve the tourists of the crap they'd been overcharged for in the first place.

But eventually she grew tired of it. It wasn't very difficult and there was no real need. Her parents provided everything. Eventually, too, she'd come round to her dad's way of thinking – if anything was worth doing, it was worth doing properly.

She wished she could talk to her dad now. They were extremely close, but if she called him, he would know immediately that something was wrong and it would kill him that he wouldn't be able to do anything about it. His parole hearing wasn't for another eight months.

She had to tackle this one on her own.


Cyrus hung out in a coffee shop near NYU for most of the morning. He had his sacred book in his pocket as usual, but for appearance's sake he was reading an obscure but well-regarded literary magazine. He'd decided to become a professor of literature for a few hours.

He'd taken extra care with his appearance that morning. His clothes were freshly laundered and he'd washed his hair and tied it back with a ribbon instead of the usual rubber band. He looked every inch the academic, he thought, as he checked his reflection in the cafe mirror. He'd practised his story. He was taking a sabbatical at UCLA and he needed someone to care for his apartment while he was away. Water the plants, that sort of thing. He needed somebody quiet and responsible, the neighbours didn't like a lot of noise. It could be for six months, maybe longer.

A young woman yelped as she dropped her coffee cup, spraying milky liquid everywhere. Some of it landed on Cyrus's newly cleaned shirt.

'Shit, shit, shit,' she said. Scrambling to mop the liquid before it reached her sociology text books.

'Let me help you.' Cyrus grabbed a wad of paper tissues and began blotting with her.

'Thanks,' she said. 'God, this is not my day.'

Cyrus got a fresh supply of paper napkins. He knew this woman was the one. He could feel it. The Master had given her to him. He didn't have to do anything; she would come to him. The thought made him a little reckless.

'Let me get you another coffee.'

'Oh . . .' A confused expression crossed the woman's face. She looked wary but then she saw the way Cyrus was mopping and she relaxed. 'Sure, thank you. That'd be great.'

Her English was flawless, but there was a European

accent underlying it. German or Scandinavian, Cyrus guessed. Her books looked new.

'How do you like New York?' he said, when he brought another cappuccino to her table. She was blotting the last of her books, spreading them out on the table so they'd dry.

'Oh, I like it fine,' she said. She groped in her handbag for cigarettes and then saw the sign that forbade smoking. 'Except for your strange laws. In Europe we are not so uptight.'

Cyrus, who couldn't abide smoking, nodded sympathetically.

'You are American, no?' Her fingers drummed the cigarette packet.

'Born and bred right here in New York City.'

She held out a smooth, brown hand. 'I am Anna.'

# Chapter Twenty-Six

Cyrus should have been more surprised when Anna told him her accommodation had fallen through unexpectedly. But the circumstances seemed weirdly right.

The university was trying to find her student housing, but she wasn't hopeful because the academic year had started. She was getting desperate.

She looked as though she could afford to spend the money if she had to. Her clothes were casual but Cyrus noticed she wore a Cartier watch and carried an expensive leather backpack. Her glossy blonde hair was expertly cut and coloured. Dark and light gold. Some of it looked almost red, but the overall effect wasn't cheap. She ran her fingers through it now and again, after she'd reached for the cigarette packet which still lay out on the table. Addiction was a terrible thing, Cyrus thought. He was glad he'd never started smoking.

According to Leon's records, Juliana Franklin was booked to fly out of La Guardia airport in two days' time for a walking holiday in Nevada.

The computer hadn't recorded what Juliana did for

a living but whatever it was, she didn't go to an office. Tye followed her to a luggage shop where she bought a new backpack, and from there on to Bloomingdales where she stocked up on other things for her trip. She met a friend for coffee on Columbus Avenue in the afternoon and got her hair trimmed at a small hairdressing salon nearby. She went to a bookshop on Madison and bought a novel then went home. Tye was fairly sure that she lived alone. She tried her number a few times when Juliana was out. The answering machine did not mention a second person and nobody else picked up the phone.

She had thought of stealing her keys outright but had dismissed that, firstly because Juliana would immediately get her locks changed, and secondly because they were the sorts of keys that could not be duplicated. In London this wouldn't have been a problem, but in New York, where she didn't have any contacts, it would be harder to pull off. So she decided to borrow the keys instead. It would be time-consuming, but better in the long run.

Juliana Franklin went out that night. She took the subway to the Bowery where she met a dark-haired man with a beard. They went to a bar where they each drank a Martini and picked at a salad. They were home by ten. He went up to her place for half an hour or so then left. The lights in the apartment went out soon after.

Tye was pleased with her day's work and wanted to celebrate her impending solvency. She went to a French restaurant in SoHo, a bistro famous for its Eurotrash crowd, and ate a steak at the bar.

The crowded restaurant was noisy. People were smoking and drinking, shouting to be heard over the crowd. Having fun. Tye felt a stab of loneliness. She shook it off.

'Tye! Tye Fisher. Is it really you?'

Tye turned. A tall blonde man approached her. He wore a tweed jacket, cravat and cavalry twill trousers. He was holding out his arms as though he meant to hug her.

'I thought it was. My God, what are you doing in New York, dear girl?'

For the life of her, Tye couldn't think of the man's name.

'It's Dickie. Dickie Porter.' He wrapped his arms around her and plopped a big kiss on both cheeks. His breath smelt of whisky. 'Don't you remember?'

She did now. Dickie was a minor aristocrat with loads of cash who had hung around on the fringes of Tye's London crowd. She'd seen him at Cheltenham a few times. He drank Krug from the bottle and bet amounts that many would have considered a respectable annual salary on horses that seldom distinguished themselves.

'Of course,' she said. 'Dickie. What brings you to New York?'

'Pictures, dear girl. I'm in pictures now.' Dickie kept his hand casually draped over her shoulder. 'Just popped in from LA to try and buy a rather smashing script. Listen do come and join me. Just ordered a bottle of bubbly. Shame to drink it on one's own. And you must tell me all about yourself. What have you been up to since we last met?'

Tye was tempted to make an excuse. Dickie and she had not been close. But he was company and she was yearning for proper conversation, not just the stark trading of career facts that seemed to pass for it in this town.

Tye folded her napkin. Collected her bag. 'Oh, you know. This and that.'


Cyrus didn't go out that evening at all. He didn't feel like cooking, so he called the local Chinese and ordered in. It gave him a thrill to go to the door, cash in hand and a big tip ready for the delivery person, with Anna tied up so close. There was nothing she could do. He'd taped her arms and legs tightly and covered her mouth as well. The best she could achieve in the way of protest was a dull thumping sound with her legs.

The delivery person didn't suspect a thing. He accepted the recklessly generous tip and went away. Cyrus carried the food back through the door in the bookcase to the middle room. Anna was on the floor.

'Chicken with black bean and salted chilli squid?' he asked.

She glared at him, terrified, but angry too.

'I admire your spirit,' Cyrus said. 'Following a strange man to an apartment. What were you thinking? And you could be pleading for your life, but you're not.'

Anna's eyes screwed up in pain. Her whole body squirmed in agitation.

'Oh, you *are* pleading,' Cyrus said. 'Sorry, my mistake.' He set the containers down. He hadn't really intended to eat just yet, he just wanted the thrill of someone coming to the house. Anyway, he could always zap them in the microwave later, if he felt hungry.

He crouched down beside Anna. A stifled sob shook her whole body.

'Don't cry.' He reached out a hand to wipe her tears away and then smelt something warm and acidic. There was a puddle on the floor. It would leave a stain.

The surge of rage that he felt surprised him. He would not have thought he was capable of such anger. It burned him.

He kicked the girl in the head, about the body, in the crotch. Again and again. She couldn't protect herself; she couldn't move. She was a soft, sitting target. It was not a fair fight. But he didn't think about any of those things because the sound in his head was like a wave breaking over him.

He kicked her until he couldn't hear her cry. He only stopped when there was no resistance left in her slender body. His new shoes were covered in blood and gore and he was exhausted from the effort. He had no idea how much time had passed.

# Chapter Twenty-Seven

'One moved to Los Angeles three months ago and one hasn't looked back,' Dickie drawled, emptying the last of the champagne into Tye's glass. 'It's the only place to live. Sunshine, fabulous food. One has one's own production company, you know. Coronet Films. Yanks love it. Anything to do with royalty.' Dickie slid his pinkie ring off, inspected it, frowning and put it back on. 'And what brings you to New York, dear girl?'

'Love,' Tye said. 'At least it did. It's over.'

Dickie's eyes flicked lazily over her. No interest there, Tye thought. Two days ago, before she had her own plans, she might have pushed her luck – there were a lot of things worse than hanging out with a movie producer. Tye was fascinated by the movies. She devoured the gossip columns about Hollywood stars and she loved to see films with glamorous locations and beautiful people.

She was a little tipsy as she walked back to her hotel. Dickie had made sure they traded addresses. He was in town for a week or so, he said. They must get together again, he said. Tye agreed. She was ready for diversion.

She was anxious to get home. She walked quickly,

thinking about Adrian for the first time in days. Perhaps she should really thank him for putting her in this position. Her life was taking unexpected turns – who knew where it would end up? Somewhere good, if she was lucky.

It was recycling night. New Yorkers had laid out their waste in orderly piles. Cans, bottles, newspapers. Tye noticed a Victoria's Secret lingerie catalogue inserted into a pile of papers. She took it out, flicked through it, getting ideas. A lot of the stuff was only a step above soft porn. She stopped when she found a purple and black leopard-skin-print teddy, trimmed in crimson synthetic lace. She ordered five of them in a size sixteen when she got back to the hotel room, using Adrian's American Express. She had them gift wrapped and sent special delivery to his wife. The card read, 'Because you're special'.

Tye didn't know anything at all about her ex-boyfriend's wife, but it was safe to assume that the bourgeois Frenchwoman would be unimpressed.

She made herself a cup of tea and drank it sitting up in bed, thinking the single life had much to recommend it. Then she turned out the light and was asleep in minutes.


Marion Neidermeyer got up at two that morning and went out. She couldn't sleep – hadn't done so in days. She thought walking might help.

It was strangely warm. In Michigan, winter was bearing down, but New York had still not entirely chased off the sultry sleepiness of summer. Marion took off her sweatshirt and tied it around her waist. She wasn't afraid of being on her own at night. She no longer feared anything this city could do to her. As the days went by she had begun to think the worst had already happened.

A gust of wind blew a stray newspaper around her feet. She kicked it away impatiently. It clung to her sneakers. The harder she kicked, the more it stayed. She reached down to flick it away. As she did, she thought of a new line of attack.


Cyrus had a lot of cleaning up to do after Anna. He worked into the night scrubbing and mopping. It was an expensive mistake – the shoes had cost a fortune and he'd only worn them a few times.

He took Anna to the back room and put her in the freezer with the other two. There was more room there now that he had chopped up the bodies. They were wrapped in plastic bags and stored neatly in wire baskets.

Cyrus had more trouble trying to wedge Anna into the space. She flopped over him, refusing to stay propped up. Several times he tried to shut the door on her, but she'd fall out. In the end, he was grunting with exertion and a little bit frustrated. It was like she was trying to ruin his good mood. Cleaning up relaxed him. He worked smoothly, the radio tuned to a jazz station. He was done by about three. He'd check the place over again in the morning but it looked okay for the moment. Her clothes, her handbag and that expensive watch were stored in the secret compartment in the bookcase. Anyway, it wasn't as if he was expecting any visitors.

He heated up the Chinese food in the microwave and ate it sitting on the floor, happy.


Marion downed a cup of take-out coffee and packed a couple of photos of Gus and Susie into the side pocket of her handbag. She'd even put on make-up. It couldn't hurt. She'd been attractive once, she remembered. Before all this.

She called the number of a local television news station found in the phone book.

'WKLP, all news all the time, how may I direct your call?'

'Hello, I'd like the name of the person who assigns news stories please.'

'That'd be Eric Atlas, ma'am.'

Marion wrote the name in her diary.

She walked the twenty or so blocks to the station because it was still early and she wanted to kill time. It was a bright day and the streets were beginning to get crowded. Marion watched people with shoulders hunched, briefcases clamped to their sides, frowning as they made their way to work. If only they knew how lucky they were, she thought. Normal, boring everyday days. She found she couldn't remember what they were supposed to be like. She'd had a routine, but she couldn't recall what it was. Even the faces of her twins were unclear to her now.

She felt sick. She breathed deeply, and concentrated on putting one foot in front of the other. Purposely she didn't think about anything except the rhythm of her steps and the half-fresh morning smell of the city.

'I'd like to see Mr Atlas, please,' Marion asked the security guard at the front desk of the television station.

'Do you have an appointment?'

'Yes, I do.' Marion lied.

'What's your name?'

'Marion Neidermeyer.'

'The reception area's on the twenty-fifth floor,' the security guard said, writing her name in a book.

Marion told the same story to the receptionist.

'I'll see if he's available, ma'am,' she said. 'What's this concerning?'

'I'm here to be interviewed. It's about a news story.' Marion tried to sound as confident as she could. Her insides were quaking.

The receptionist dialled and Marion watched the silent images on the bank of televisions suspended above her. The screens were filled with happy, bright, well-groomed people with improbably large smiles.

'He's not at his desk right now. Can you wait?' The receptionist gestured to the chairs lined up by the television screens.

'Uh, sure.' Marion sat, clutching her handbag. Her hands shook.

'Would you like some coffee or something?' The receptionist's voice was kind. She moved out from behind her desk.

'I'd love some. Thanks.'

'This place is not so bad, you know. It looks scary but it really isn't. My first day here, I was scared half to death. But after a while you realize they're no better than you or me. They put their pants on one leg at a time, just like the rest of us.'

Marion nodded, her eyes bright with tears.

'I'll get you that coffee.' The woman patted her shoulder. 'Girl, you look like you could use it.'

# Chapter Twenty-Eight

Tye spent the morning watching Juliana Franklin's apartment from the betting shop across the road. She placed a couple of bets on races she knew nothing about just for the hell of it, and even won a couple of dollars. Maybe it was a good omen.

She'd taken precautions to appear inconspicuous. She was dressed casually in jeans and a sweater from Gap that she'd picked up cheap from a thrift shop. She wore clear, unflattering glasses and had her hair pulled up inside a baseball cap. There were a million young women in the city dressed exactly like her.

Juliana didn't do much that day. She went out in the morning for coffee, collected some groceries from Gristedes and returned to the apartment. Then she left dressed in her gym clothes. She came back about an hour later, again via the coffee shop. Tye joined her in the queue. She ordered tea and a muffin and counted the change very carefully.

Marion had been waiting for forty-five minutes when a nervous young girl came out. She was wearing a very short skirt and a practically see-through blouse, Marion noted disapprovingly.

'You're waiting for Eric . . . ah . . . Mr Atlas?' The girl blushed. She didn't look much older than Marion's twins. If she were her daughter Marion would have sent her home to get dressed properly.

'Yes,' Marion said. She clutched her handbag tightly. She was going to get the bum's rush.

'He's, like, tied up in a meeting right now. Why don't you come through?'

Marion could scarcely believe what she was hearing.

'Sure,' she said, gathering her bag and her coat.


Being the head of the intern programme sure had its advantages, Eric Atlas thought as he screwed Freya Leith on his desk. Freya was a peach. Sweet, tight and willing to do absolutely anything he wanted. At the moment she was bent forwards, hands gripping the desk, ass pointed skywards. She moaned softly as he busily pumped away. God, he loved having sex in the morning, in his office with the executive editor not fifty feet away. Stuffy old Gerald Long, prep school, Columbia, Yale, never had a fun day in his life. Didn't understand what drove men like Eric.

Atlas boasted of having grown up in a trailer park in South Carolina. He used to be ashamed of this fact, but now that his management career was secure he'd become proud of it. He told people it gave him special insights into the great unwashed and what they wanted to see on their television screens. The other, unspoken implication was that he was smarter than the rest of them because he'd overcome more obstacles than the guys who'd had success handed to them with a side order of fries. Nobody had given Eric Atlas anything. Until now, of course. Perky young things were throwing themselves at him.

'Ah, ah, Eric. You're so good . . . so hot!'

'Spare me the porno lines, Peaches.' Eric gasped, although he was secretly pleased. He reached past Freya's smooth, rhythmically-pulsing butt to the computer keyboard. Last week his stockbroker had cut him in on a slice of an Internet IPO, and today it was trading on the NASDAQ. His hand stroked the pad lightly, the screen flashed up. Rising. Good. Everything was going his way.

Freya's moaning became louder, high-pitched. She was squeaking, in fact. Like one of his kids' plastic toys. God, she was a good actor, Eric thought. Or maybe he really was doing it for her, but he doubted it. Nor did he particularly care. Freya wanted to get on air without having to put in several dreary years in Moose Tit, Michigan, and he wanted to poke young flesh. They both understood old-fashioned values. Not that he had any intention of giving her a job, but he'd string her along for a few weeks. She'd find out, eventually. And she'd have learned a valuable life lesson in the meantime. He should be charging her for this kind of education – you couldn't get it at some fancy private school.

Climax. His stock hit a hundred dollars. He slid out of her. Bent and bit her hard on the butt. She tasted good. She was sweating, flushed. She slumped on the desk and rolled lazily over, pulling her skirt down playfully. Then she wet her fingers in her panties and put them in his mouth while she kissed him. That alone was good for a three month extension on her internship, Eric thought.

Freya Leith left the office demurely. Eric whistled as he hitched up his pants. God, he loved his work.


Marion followed the young woman into the newsroom and was hit by a wall of sound. People were screaming at each other, rushing places, a dozen television monitors pulsing out different programmes. The room was also the studio set, with cameras and lights posted at various stations. She wondered if she was going to end up on television just by walking across the room.

'. . . when did you first notice you had leprosy . . .'

'. . . the President this afternoon said . . .'

'. . . troops to the former Yugoslav . . .'

'. . . fifteen out of twenty people interviewed . . .'

'. . . government sources say the toll is expected . . .'

'I'm sorry you've been kept waiting,'

Marion started. 'Sorry,' she said.

'I'm sorry you've had to wait,' the girl repeated. 'Eric's not free yet but I thought I'd bring you in. He's pretty busy, you know.'

'Thank you,' Marion said faintly. She was beginning to wonder if she'd overstepped the mark. What was she going to say to this man to convince him that he should do a news story about Gus and Susie?

'You can sit here,' the girl said, pointing to a small couch tucked away in the corner of the room, next to a coffee table with three or four newspapers strewn across it. The activity in the room didn't let up. Marion wondered how people could work in such a frenetic atmosphere, how they could think above the noise. She regretted now that she hadn't gone to a newspaper, which had been her first idea. She had changed her mind because she thought television could reach more people. Nobody read anymore. As a school teacher she knew that better than anyone.

A pugnacious little guy with a barrel chest strutted across the room, tucking his shirt into his pants. He had big hands, Marion noted idly. Too big for his frame. He had a bony nose and his hair was in retreat at the temples. His stomach stuck out, his feet were splayed and he was sniffing the air like an animal.

The intern approached him, nervous. Marion could tell what was going on by their body language. The girl's was supplicatory, his confident. He planted himself in front of her, feet apart. Displaying himself like an ape in the jungle, Marion thought.

The young woman pointed in Marion's direction. The man looked over, puzzled. Looked back at her. He had no appointment, he didn't know who she was. The intern looked confused. She thought . . . The boss frowned. His face darkened. The girl's crumpled. She'd done the wrong thing and now she was in trouble. She was about Gus's age, Marion reckoned. Just out of college, she didn't know that one wasn't supposed to let complete strangers into the newsroom. They could be anybody: terrorists, lunatics, heartbroken mothers.

She walked over to the couple.

'Excuse me,' she said.

'Who are you?' The boss turned on her.

'My name's Marion Neidermeyer.' She stuck out her hand seeming more confident than she felt. She couldn't let this man sense she was scared. The look in his eyes showed he fed on others' fear.

He ignored her hand. 'And?'

'I have a news story.'

'Send me a fax,' Eric Atlas said, turning.

'But I'm here right now.'

'I haven't got time to deal with it.'

'I don't have a fax. Won't you at least—'

'Eric, we need you to go over this live shot for lunch time.' A young woman wearing a headset and clutching a sheaf of papers pushed between Eric and Marion.

'Sure,' Eric said. He nodded at the intern. 'Show Mrs Neiman out, will ya?'

The intern, red-faced, began to usher Marion towards the door. Eric walked off in the other direction with the headset woman.

The kid had on the same fragrance as Susie. Marion registered the sweet citrus smell. Calvin Klein or something like that, all the young girls were wearing it. It brought memories in a rush. She stopped. Turned. Summoned her voice like she was yelling at the twins. Or her pupils.

'Mr Atlas. Turn around, you jerk.'

There was a sort of silence in the newsroom. Everybody stopped what they were doing.

'What did you say?' Eric Atlas turned slowly, incredulous.

'You heard me.'

Marion knew every ear in the place was on her.

Eric Atlas couldn't resist the challenge. He walked back towards her cockily. He reminded her of her ex Marion decided. She had his number. The world was full of men like him.

'I ask that you give me five minutes of your time. I do not expect to be treated in such an unprofessional manner.'

'Unprofessional!' Eric Atlas mugged incredulity. He looked around the room for support. People stared back blankly. Some were hiding smiles. The intern jiggled from one foot to another, nervous as a deer.

'When someone comes to see you, you shouldn't turn your back on them and walk away. No matter who you think you are.' She'd gone too far, Marion knew, but the stress, confusion and fear of the last few days had finally found an outlet.

'You shouldn't even have gotten in here, lady.'

'But I did.'

'I don't have to talk to you.'

'I need ten minutes of your time. That's all.'

Once more Eric Atlas scanned the room for support. Then he noticed an older man standing in the corner, arms folded. Wearing a baggy cardigan, glasses falling down his nose. Gerald Long. The boss. He was a boring old fart whom Eric Atlas was sure wasn't going to survive a looming management shake-up but in the meantime, it didn't hurt to humour the old imbecile who, for all Eric knew, would land a really great job after he was sacked.

'All right then . . . my office.'

# Chapter Twenty-Nine

'This better be good.' Eric slammed the door. God, he hated pushy women. He didn't ask her to sit down but she did so anyway. She took a deep breath. She had to get this right.

'My son and his wife are missing. They came to New York to live and they've disappeared. Nobody's seen them for over a week.'

Eric pulled his chair into his desk, one hand straying to the computer mouse.

'What do you want me to do about it?'

'A news story.'

Eric pulled up RealTick – checked his stock. Holding steady. He smiled, turned back to Marion, shook his head. 'Look, lady . . .'

'Mrs Neidermeyer.'

'Whatever. That's not news.'

'Two people who just vanish into thin air?'

'There are millions of people in this city. And to be brutally frank, the fate of two of them doesn't matter. Not enough to get on my show. Besides, they'll turn up. Kids always do.'

'It matters to me.'

'Sure it does. All I'm doing is showing it to you from my point of view. The big picture.'

'But you do news about the city.'

'Of course. Our news is up to the minute and relevant.' Eric scanned RealTick. His other buy of the week – a speculative stock in the small software company was doing okay. He'd bought them on a whisper that they were about to be taken over by Microsoft.

'When I was waiting in the lobby you ran a story about a dog that Rollerblades.'

Eric Atlas kept his eyes on the computer screen long enough for Marion to realize she was being snubbed. 'That's a human-interest story,' he said eventually. 'News doesn't have to be all hard facts, you know. People like to be amused.'

'You're interested in dogs but not people? What's relevant about a dog on wheels?'

'Look, lady – I don't have to explain my news judgement to you. My station has perfect faith in it. My managers have perfect faith in me. I'm real sorry about your kids, but that's the way it is.'

He didn't sound the slightest bit sorry, Marion thought. She breathed deeply but it didn't seem to be helping. The odious little gnome smirked at her across his desk, not even bothering to conceal the fact that he was looking at his computer screen. How did people get so far with so few manners?

'It would be such a help,' she said, 'if we could get some publicity – if I could. I've been searching for them for days . . .'

'It's not my job to give you free publicity. If you want publicity, why don't you buy an ad?'

'Don't you care that it's possible for two people to vanish into thin air? Don't you think people who live here want to know that sort of thing goes on?'

'Of course it goes on. Nobody's safe here. In this town, poor suckers get shot by cops – the people who are supposed to protect them. Anything's possible in New York, lady.'

'It's Mrs Neidermeyer.'

Eric shrugged. 'That's what makes it the greatest city in the world.'

'I don't see that that's anything to be proud of.' Marion gathered her things. She'd wasted too much time already.

'Besides, there are no pictures.'

'Excuse me?'

'No pictures. Look, I'm very sorry about your son and everything, but it's not a television story, understand? There are no pictures.'

'I have a picture.' Marion took the wedding photo from her handbag. Eric didn't even look at it. 'I have several.'

'Moving pictures,' he said, not bothering to hide his impatience. 'If there are no moving pictures, there's no story.'


Tye had agreed to meet Dickie for dinner at the Gotham Bar and Grill. She'd spent the whole day staking out Juliana's apartment. Juliana had taken out the trash and Tye went through it. There was no evidence of a pet – a good sign. She'd thought of calling her pretending to do a household survey, but people were wise to that now. There was too much solicitation by phone.

She'd have to play it by ear. She had a rough plan for how to get the key from Juliana. It depended on many variables: how she was getting to the airport; whether anybody was staying in her apartment while she was gone; how her answering machine was configured. But it was worth a punt. No plan was ever perfect. The key lay in locating the weak spots and not getting complacent.

Dickie had cracked open a bottle of champagne by the time she arrived. Tye had taken a long bath at the hotel to soak off the grime of the city. She felt refreshed but jittery, the way she always did on the eve of a job. She wished she could have spoken to her dad. Too bad it wasn't possible.

'Dear girl,' Dickie said, kissing her on both cheeks. 'You look ravishing.' He handed her a glass of bubbly. She downed it almost in one, more nervous than she'd thought. She'd been out of the game for a while.

The restaurant was crowded with beautiful people. Tye had heard that it was almost impossible to get a reservation here, and she wondered how Dickie did these things. He was the best-connected person she had ever met, and she'd known a few. If the country had been plunged into war, Dickie would have been the one with the stash of silk stockings, cigarettes and whisky.

'What are you up to these days, dear girl?' Dickie asked.

'Shopping. Hanging out,' Tye murmured. 'There's so much to do in this city.'

'Isn't it the best? New York is the epitome of civilization. LA is a large garden suburb. Fabulous, of course, but New York is the place that rocks.' Dickie lifted an eyebrow. 'Anything is possible here,' he waved his champagne in one hand, 'anything at all. But you know that, of course. So tell me, dear girl, which version of the American dream are you pursuing?' He looked at her shrewdly. Tye had a sudden panic spasm. Did he know anything about her?

'No particular one.'

'Have you thought of acting?' Dickie put his glass down and looked at her intently, one eye half shut as though he were appraising a painting.

'I . . . No.'

'Ever had any experience? Amateur dramatics, that sort of thing?'

Not anything that could be put on a CV, Tye thought. She shook her head. Though now that she thought about it, acting was almost all she did.

'Dear girl, you must. You're a natural. Those bones.'

Tye was flattered. She murmured something inconsequential, but her heart was leaping. Acting, of course. Fun, well paid. No risk of going to jail. Why hadn't she thought of it before?

'If I can nail this script – and drum up the finance – you must come out to LA and read for a part.' Dickie cupped her jaw in his hand, turning it this way and that. 'The camera would love you.'

'Dickie! If it isn't old Dickie Porter.' A tall, swarthy guy wearing an Australian stockman's coat pushed his way through the throng at the bar.

'Ted – you mean they let you in here?'

Ted faked a punch at Dickie's jaw. Then he saw Tye and straightened his shoulders, awaiting the introduction. Dickie supplied it.

'Ted O'Reilly, scribe – Tye Fisher . . . what exactly is it you do Tye?'

'I act,' Tye said, holding out her hand. Might as well start somewhere.

# Chapter Thirty

Man, this city really kicks you when you're down, Quinn thought as he sat at his laptop. Writing aphorisms was now more complicated because of his plaster-cast arm, but he was determined to master it. He could type with two fingers. Trouble was, he couldn't think of anything optimistic to say. And fortune cookies were no good without banal optimism.

A pal of Quinn's had given him the job because he was trying to establish a market in fortune cookies that had advertising on the back. This particular batch were to go with some that promoted a popular brand of household cleaner. He had told Quinn that people needed to feel good about themselves and their household cleaner. All Quinn could think about was deceit and bad fortune.

Relations with Malcolm were getting worse. Mal was giving him an increasingly harder time about not finding a place.

'Get out there, ask people. Talk to doormen. Make contacts,' he said, tying his bow tie expertly in front of the mirror. He and Rhonda were going to the opera.

'You know she thinks a libretto is a type of pasta,' Quinn said.

'Isn't there something more important you should be thinking about?'

'I do. I am.'

Mal fished in his suit trousers, came out with a Post-it. 'Got this guy's name from someone at work whose sister knows a person in her building, an old woman who's on the verge of death. She's got that really gross cancer that kills you in like, days. Have a word with the super, you might get in first.'

Paddy McNally lived in a basement off First Avenue. Quinn knocked hard several times before the door creaked open and a ruddy face peered out. Suspiciously ruddy, Quinn thought. Another of his countrymen who'd succumbed to the national stereotype.

'I'm William Quinn. I heard there might be an apartment coming free soon.' Quinn overdid the Irish accent, hoping it would help.

'Come in, me boy.'

When he got inside he realized that Paddy's face was red, not from drinking, but because he was sitting next to a wood stove that was belting out heat at blast-furnace temperature. The room was small, dark and cluttered with broken furniture, the sort that most people put out for the garbage. Books and magazines were scattered in piles around the floor. They too looked as though they'd been recovered from somebody's recycling pile. Quinn stepped around them carefully.

'Would ya be havin' a cup of tea?'

'Sure,' Quinn said. Paddy shuffled over to the sink

which looked to be not connected to the wall securely. He ran some rust-coloured water into a dented kettle, shuffled back over to the stove and put it on. The kettle sizzled. Quinn was starting to get overheated, too. And his eyes were itchy. He blinked a couple of times, but his lids still felt as though they were coated with sandpaper.

'Where would you be from then?' Paddy asked.

'Long Island – I mean, Dublin.' He was beginning to regret his decision to say yes to tea.

'I hear it's grand. Never been to the city meself. A Cork man.' Paddy fished some teabags out of a sock that was hanging on a hook above the two-ring gas stove. A huge ginger cat uncurled itself from near a pile of broken table legs and stalked towards Quinn.

'Cork is grand, too,' Quinn said although he'd never been there. Still, how different from the rest of the country could it be? The whole place was the size of Connecticut.

The cat stared at him. Cats did that to Quinn. He was allergic as hell. He only had to see a picture of one in a book to make him break out. This was why he had itchy eyeballs. He sneezed once, twice, three times.

'God bless you, son. Three times, that'll be a disappointment you're in for. How will you be taking your tea then?' Paddy assembled two chipped mugs advertising the services of a pest control firm. The milk sat, unrefrigerated, on the windowsill.

'Black,' Quinn said hastily. 'I hear there's an apartment coming free soon?' He didn't want to appear to be rushing things, but the cat gave him no choice. He had to get out of there fast.

'Aye, old Mrs Donohue. It's a terrible shame.' Paddy stamped a foot. 'Get away off with yer!' he shouted.

'Pardon?'

'Blasted mice,' Paddy said. 'They're the bane of me existence.'

'Mice?'

'Aye. We've been fighting them for years. Worthy opponents, the little buggers. Cunning, quick-witted. Tried everything, we have. Poison, traps, bacon grease. Everything except boiling oil and they're still with us. Built up a healthy respect over the years.'

Quinn's attention was distracted for just a second and the cat leapt onto his lap, leering. Quinn never was quite sure how they knew, but they always did. They always made a beeline for him.

'Strange,' Paddy said. 'He's never done that to anyone else. Usually keeps himself to himself, does Gerry Adams.'

A second cat detached itself from an old Chesterfield chair in another corner of the room. It, too, seemed eager not to miss out on the allergy action. Quinn eyed it nervously.

'Who's this one then? Martin McGuinness?'

'No, that one's a girl. We call her Bernadette Devlin.' The kettle boiled. Paddy edged nimbly through the rubble on the floor to claim it. It sizzled and popped all the way back to the bench. Quinn fully expected it to burst open and scald them both.

'About the apartment.' Quinn swatted Gerry Adams away. His eyeballs felt as though they were bursting. If he stayed much longer, he'd be blind.

'Aye, the apartment. Mrs Donohue has to go into

hospice. There's not much hope for the poor dear. A crying shame. She's only young, fifty-five last birthday. But she'll be needing someone to sublet her place. Her nephew owns it, lives in Westchester. Someone responsible, he says.' Paddy picked some cat hair out of the mugs and poured in the water. 'I can tell ye're the responsible type, just be looking at ye.'

Quinn tried to look as responsible as he could.

'Because we're going to need someone who is not a flibbertigibbet. Mrs Donohue's babies are going to need a great deal of care.'

Quinn felt another sneeze coming on. He pinched his nose, hoping it'd go away.

'Babies?'

'Aye, babies. She's got thirteen.'

'She's got thirteen children?'

'No, no, no. Cats. Started out with just three, but then the mice . . . And they're going to need a great deal of care. That's the only condition for the sublet. One of the reasons it's so reasonably priced.'

'Ahhhh, ahhhh . . .' and Quinn sneezed. A bellowing explosion that felt as though his guts were being pulled out through his nose.


Cyrus waited until Anna was frozen through, and then he laid her out on the metal table and divided her neatly. He sawed off her limbs and divided the torso into halves, quarters and eighths. He'd bought supermarket bags to store the pieces in, although some of the larger ones had to be placed in garbage sacks. They were all laid out and ready to go. He'd even purchased a small pump to suck the air out, as he'd sometimes seen his mother's cook do when freezing food.

It was only when he was nearly through that he realized he'd forgotten to shave her hair off. He was so angry with himself that he cursed loudly and threw several instruments across the floor and kicked the wall for good measure. He'd ruined everything! His artistic statement counted for nothing. He considered doing it now, but it was impossible. He couldn't shave her legs; they were in three pieces. Her hair was a stiff white mess. It had been freezing for hours and some had broken off when he'd pulled her out of the freezer because it was stuck to the wall. There was no point in doing it now.

Damn, damn, damn. That was just plain stupid. He couldn't be a serial killer if he didn't have a method, any schoolkid would tell you that. But it was too late. He made a note to be more careful of the details in future. They were what mattered.


Marion had a drink in a bar that night. In Michigan, her usual custom after she got home from work and had made sure the twins weren't going to kill each other was to have a glass of wine. It helped her unwind.

Tonight she would have given anything for the just-controlled chaos of her normal life. Instead, she sat at the bar and imagined Eric Atlas dying an ugly, horrifying death. She loathed that man, his smugness, his arrogance. He had become the symbol of everything she hated about the city.

'The guys at the hostel told me you were here.'

John Abruzzo, the cop, slumped wearily into the stool beside her. 'Can I get you another?'

She nodded and pushed her empty glass towards the attentive barkeeper. Normally she didn't have a second, but tonight she could do with brain numbing.

'Is there anything?'

John Abruzzo shook his head. 'Whatcha been up to?'

'Asking around.'

'We are working on it, you know. You don't have to do this.'

'I tried to get a television station interested . . .' Marion trailed off. Shook her head.

'They only want sex and showbiz. News don't matter.'

'Yeah.' Marion took a sip of her wine. 'So I found out.'

Abruzzo ordered a beer. His big butt couldn't fit on the stool, so he propped himself against it with one leg. He was wearing black, which made him look younger.

'You got kids?' Marion asked.

'Nah. No kids, no wife. Haven't met the one yet.'

'You will.'

'Yeah. I'm such a great catch.' Abruzzo laughed. 'Gotta play the field a bit, right?'

'Damn straight.'

They lapsed into silence. The juke box played an old Elvis song. Marion stared at her wine. The second glass was almost empty and she couldn't remember drinking it. The pain was the same.

Abruzzo finished his beer, threw some notes on the

bar. 'I wish there was something else . . .' He offered her his hand.

'Thank you.' Marion put her small hand in his huge one, shaking it. 'So do I.'

The problem in this town, New York City, was you lived your life on show whether you wanted to or not. Cameras were everywhere – on street corners, in stores, theatres, parking lots. There were no private moments. They had gone away for good.

It was important to choose the right place, so Cyrus tried to think of a way around the camera problem.

At first he'd considered the twenty-four-hour delis on almost every street. He'd go in wearing a broad-brimmed hat, perhaps a false moustache or beard, and keep his head down. But the more he thought about that, the more he realized it was a bit seedy. What he had in mind needed a bigger canvas. If he was going to take a risk, why not an extravagant one?

It was late, but the Village crowd was just getting going. The tourists had gone, leaving the place to the regulars, although regular was hardly the word to describe the transvestites, clubbers, goths and mutant boys that hung out looking for God knew what kind of action. Even though he'd lived in the Village for years, Cyrus didn't think he'd ever get used to the many strange people who were his neighbours. Sometimes they scared him. He couldn't imagine what their kinky, nocturnal lives were like, but he knew they didn't live like normal, respectable folk.

Two transvestites were arguing over someone called Darcy. They were both tall, and wore three- or four-inch platform soles. One had on a green lamé ball gown split to the thigh. This didn't stop her throwing a punch at the other, dressed as a Swiss mountain maid in embroidered dress with puff sleeves and yellow blonde wig. The punch missed, but the Swiss maid grabbed the other's arm and expertly twisted it so she was off-balance. She fell to the sidewalk, losing her wig. In a trice she was up again, pummelling away at her companion. A crowd gathered to cheer them on. Nobody noticed Cyrus bend down, swipe the wig and put it under his raincoat.

Almost without him having to do anything, a plan was taking shape.

Food Phantasmagoria sold produce found in most other places in the city, but its retail hook appeared to be that you paid two or three times more for the privilege of shopping while classical music played much too loud over a tinny stereo system. Cyrus didn't go in very often, but when he did he was always appalled by the choice of tracks: *The Four Seasons*, Ravel's *Bolero*. This was music for morons who thought that any classical music meant you were cultured.

They were playing the 'Hallelujah Chorus' that night. Which only strengthened his resolve. The place was an aural health hazard. It deserved to be shut down. He had half a mind to come back that very night. Teach them a lesson. But he didn't. He checked the place out, and then went home and put the wig in his wardrobe and cleaned up the apartment some. Now that he was 'going public' he needed to be very careful.

This was a whole new game and it had to be played with the utmost planning and thought.

Soon everybody in the city – the whole country, even – was going to know his work. Yeah, he had to do it right.

# Chapter Thirty-One

Tye overslept – too many glasses of Dickie's champagne. She woke with a start at 9.15 and realized she would miss Juliana Franklin if she didn't hurry. She found a taxi and told the driver to take her to the airport.

The journey was intolerably slow. They inched through the Queens mid-town tunnel. On the Long Island expressway they sped up briefly but went back to a crawl on the Brooklyn Queens expressway. Tye clutched her now cold coffee and hoped that Juliana had been subject to the same delays. If not, it'd take days to find another mark and do the set-up and she didn't have days.

At last, the airport. There was a line of taxis snaking out from the departures terminal. Tye threw some money at the driver and sprinted to the building.

Inside was jam packed, which was good. She needed a crowd to work in. She scanned the departures boards for the airline and flight number. It wasn't yet boarding. Tye took a deep breath, squared her shoulders and plunged into the crowd looking for a tall, red-headed woman.

Juliana was standing at the check-in desk when Tye spotted her. Passport in one hand, shoulder bag gaping open behind her. Tye could have wept. The crowd was like an angry sea. Several planes had been delayed. There were families, business people, skiers, tourists all jostling for floor space, irritated that their plans were skewered on the whims of weather and air traffic control.

Juliana got her boarding pass and patiently picked her way through the crowd. She had a small carry-on and a leather shoulder bag that she still hadn't bothered to close. Tye pushed politely through the crowd, flexing her fingers. Praying that she hadn't lost her touch.

She was gaining on Juliana, close enough to reach into her bag when Juliana clutched it to her and zipped it shut.

Someone elbowed Tye in the ribs. A bratty kid who grinned at her and held a large, pump-action water gun to her chest. She ducked out of his way, resisting the temptation to swipe him. Juliana went into a magazine store. Juliana's flight had started boarding but she didn't appear to be in a hurry.

Tye merged with the crowd while Juliana browsed. Again she flexed her fingers, stretched them out one by one. She also kept her head down, didn't so much as glance in the direction of the security cameras.

Juliana bought three or four magazines and a thick paperback novel. She left the shop with her purchases in a plastic bag, this time heading straight for the departure gates. The crowd was thinner around here, but still workable. Tye threaded patiently behind Juliana, waiting for her moment.

She was getting ready to strike when Juliana stopped. Grabbed her bag and rummaged frantically through it. Her face broke out in a smile of relief when she saw what it was she thought she had lost or left behind. She started walking again.

Fast was the key. In and out. Trouble was, that worked well for wallets and purses which were generally bulky items, but keys were another matter. They usually slid to the bottom of the bag, got snagged in other things. It was going to be tricky, and Tye hadn't done any serious work of this kind since she was a teenager on Oxford Street. She'd been good back then, partly because it had been a game for her. She had done it for the challenge. You had to focus on the task or you were lost. You needed guts, speed and skill. Sometimes too, you needed luck.

Now was different. She needed those keys.

Juliana dipped into her bag again, pulled out her boarding pass. The zipper stayed open. Tye saw her moment to strike.

She pushed, not too gently, past two middle-aged men and walked into Juliana. Bang.

'Oh, I'm so sorry,' she said in a nasal, mid-western accent. 'I am such a klutz. Are you okay?'

'Fine, thank you.'

'Are you sure?' Tye gripped her arm lightly.

'Sure. Don't worry about it.'

'You have a good vacation, then.' One hand patted her reassuringly while the other grasped what it sought.

She disappeared into the crowd, feeling sixteen years old.

Tye called twice and rang the buzzer before she went into the apartment. No reply. The answering machine had a generic message. That didn't exclude the possibility of a house sitter, but it did make Tye feel slightly more comfortable about entering.

She'd never broken into someone's house before, it gave her a spooky feeling, like she was walking on a grave.

The space still smelled of its owner, a faint combination of herbs, soap and patchouli. It was small. One bedroom, a tiny living room and an eat-in kitchen. It faced north–south and the morning sun was streaming in, showing the spots where the dust had collected.

She checked the kitchen and bathroom. No pet bowls, no kitty litter. The only house plant was a tiny succulent on the mantelpiece, which probably meant no friend would be stopping by to take care of the greenery. It was looking better all the time, even though she had a story prepared if anybody showed up. She was the lost cousin from England. She'd met Juliana by chance and had been offered the keys to her flat. It wasn't a brilliant story. What if that person who showed was a family member who knew every leaf and branch of the family tree? No, better that no one show up.

Juliana's furniture was hippy eclectic. A bronze Buddha reclined in the ornamental fireplace and a large mandala took up almost one wall. The books on the shelves advised on how to find oneself through Eastern religions. An old-fashioned Macintosh computer rested in a corner.

The answering machine was thankfully old-fashioned too. Juliana was certainly no techno-geek and Tye blessed her for it. She took out the micro-cassette and inserted one she'd bought at the Wiz and re-recorded the message so that it said, 'Hi, leave a number, I'll call you back.'

Tye started to relax. She had the good feeling she got when jobs were going her way. This one was all hers. She locked up carefully and went to a phone booth to put an ad in the *Village Voice*. She figured the apartment was worth $1,800 a month, easy.

# Chapter Thirty-Two

The *Voice* ad was placed on-line and there were calls within hours. Tye scheduled the appointments forty-five minutes apart.

She spent the afternoon getting ready. Fortunately there were lots of thrift shops in the neighbourhood. Tye bought a maroon skirt with a flounce around the bottom, a cardigan with embroidery and a pair of sensible black shoes. She checked her reflection in the mirror at the store. In clothes like these, she could move to the Upper West Side.

She'd bought an auburn wig cut in a bob and a pair of clear glasses. She went to a photo booth and had some pictures taken without make-up. She pinned them to the notice board in Juliana's kitchen. She spent an hour or so familiarizing herself with the apartment, locating the fuse box, the power points. The laundry room was in the basement. Tye unlocked the door using another of the keys on the ring. There were two washers, two dryers. The machines took six quarters. She climbed the steps to the apartment, dying for a cup of coffee. She looked through the cupboards and in the freezer. There was only decaf, which Tye hated. She went out to a coffee shop on Lexington, bought a half pound and came back and brewed it. It had the corollary of making the apartment smell nice, not that she'd need any selling points. This baby was going to fly right out the window.

Quinn was still in the throes of his cat allergy when Mal arrived home from work. He looked at his brother lying on the sofa, skipping through the cable channels, and his eyes narrowed.

'Cats,' Quinn said and sneezed. 'I've never known any thing like it. Gerry Adams, Bernadette Devlin.'

'What?' Mal reached in the fridge for a beer.

'Hated me . . . could see it in their eyes.'

'Because you supported the referendum?'

'Cats . . . the size of groundhogs. Radioactive.'

'Quinn, we need to talk.' Mal sat on the edge of the sofa and took the remote control from his brother's hands. 'Rhonda . . . I've asked her to move in.'

'What?' Quinn shot up and almost knocked himself out with his concrete arm. 'How can you do this to me?'

'It's what we want,' Mal said. 'We both feel it, it's important.'

'Oh, really.'

'It's not like I haven't given you a chance. You've been here for weeks.'

'Not that many weeks.'

'Long enough. You can't sponge off your family forever. And I can't put my life on hold for you.'

'Like I'm an imposition now?'

'If you want to put it like that.'

Quinn said nothing, he stared angrily at his brother.

'You haven't even been looking for a place.'

'How do you think I got this?' Quinn pointed to his swollen eyes, his arm in a cast.

'Try harder,' Mal said, getting up. 'I mean it.'


'What's the water pressure like?' A sullen, pale woman with lank hair stood accusingly in the apartment. Her boyfriend was poking in the cupboards.

'Good.' Tye smiled. Why was everybody so sour in this town? Wasn't it supposed to be the greatest city in the world?

'What are you taking?' the guy asked.

'Clothes. I'll clean out the storage areas. The rest stays.'

'And how long will you be gone for?'

How about forever, Tye thought. 'Six months but could be longer. My girlfriend's moving to Arizona to start a restaurant. Look, if you're interested, I can pretty much tell you it's yours. I've seen a lot of people and frankly, most of them I wouldn't want in my home. But you guys, you seem right.'

The girl, Debbie, smiled tightly. The guy, John, leered at Tye, thinking what a goddamn waste it was she was a dyke and what she really needed was a great, big . . .

'Cheque,' Tye said in answer to Debbie's question about payment. 'The usual, three months up front. I hope that's okay.'

It wasn't, but they wanted to live in Manhattan more than money. They looked at each other.

'If you're not interested . . .' Tye began.

'We are.' They said it in unison. They'd told Tye they had a week to find somewhere.

'When can we move in?'

'One week from today.'

That did it. Debbie wrote in careful cursive five thousand, four hundred dollars made out to Sandy Lee. Tye had opened four accounts with four different banks using the three false passports that had been a gift to her from her parents on the occasion of her eighteenth birthday. Once again she blessed their foresight. The other girls at her exclusive and academically demanding private school may have had trust funds and Porches but Tye's parents knew the value of gifts that kept on giving.

'Call me if you have any questions,' Tye said. 'You know where I am.'

Tye put the cheque with the two others she'd collected. Candy from babies. Not everybody had wanted to hand over the money. They'd talked about escrow accounts or only putting a couple hundred up front. Tye, who didn't even know what an escrow account was, had politely told them she'd let them know. But the suspicious ones were in the minority. Desperation did that to people, she supposed.

The phone rang. She waited to confirm that the call was for her before picking up.

'Hi, my name's William Quinn and I'm calling about the apartment . . .'

'Hi,' she said. 'I'm Kathleen Terry.'

'It's probably gone, right?' He had a soft, Irish edge to his accent. It was a sexy voice. Baritone.

'Wrong. Still interviewing. Want to come over and see it?'

'Sure.'

'Nine thirty?'

'It'll be my pleasure, Kathleen.'

She got the junior accountant out the door by nine twenty and put his cheque alongside the others in her handbag. It was appalling that this system operated on blind trust of complete strangers. What kind of society was it that allowed abuses like these?

'It's a nice place,' Quinn said after he'd looked around. He was about her height, with black hair and grey eyes. There were spurts of grey in his hair too. He was well built. He wore a soft grey T-shirt and faded Levis, and his arms were muscled and brown. At least, one was. The other was in a cast.

'Where are you going?'

'To Vermont. My mother has a tree farm, she's had a fall and needs help. I'll be gone for six months.'

'And the city will be poorer,' Quinn said. Tye smiled. She admired that he wasn't leaving anything to chance.

'I wasn't going to go but my boyfriend left me and took the miniature pinscher and life hasn't felt the same.'

'You miss the dog that much?'

'Like crazy.'

Quinn nodded sympathetically. 'I can see how a dog would be happy here.' He grinned – a lopsided expression which, surprisingly, did funny things to her stomach.

'What do you do, Mr Quinn?'

'It's just Quinn. I'm a screenwriter. Extremely solvent.' Quinn strolled over to the bookshelf and perused the titles. 'You like self-help?'

'Since the boyfriend . . .' Tye realized she didn't have a clue what was in the books. 'Well, since the dog left . . . I went crazy and bought a few but I haven't read them yet. To tell you the truth, they all seem pretty much the same. I think I wasted my money.'

'Poor man's wisdom.' Quinn selected a book, opened it and frowned. 'You'd do better with some good fiction. Everything I know about life I learned from Mark Twain.' He grinned again. He was devastating, Tye thought. And he knew it.

'Are you interested in the apartment or not?' The conversation was straying. She wanted to get back to the hotel. 'If you are I'll need three months rent up front.'

'I'm your man,' Quinn said, pulling a chequebook from his pocket. 'And I need somewhere sooner rather than later.' He wrote with a fountain pen, and in green ink. Typical, thought Tye. A show-off. 'When will you be moving out?'

'I'll have to . . .' Tye liked this guy, and suddenly had a twinge about taking his money.

'Have to what?'

'I'll have to let you know. Within the next week, definitely.' Business was business, she told herself. You get sentimental, you get screwed.

She took the cheque and gave him a receipt.

'You're not going to run out now?' Quinn said cheerfully as he accepted it.

She laughed.

# Chapter Thirty-Three

Cyrus spent the day preparing his costume. The transvestites had given him the idea of disguising himself as
a woman. He went to a chain store and bought a cheap
dress in dark blue and then to a thrift store for a pair
of medium-heeled shoes. Since it was the Village,
nobody gave a second thought to a man buying
women's clothes. Then he went upstairs to his parents'
part of the house and raided his mother's wardrobe for
accessories. His mother loved clothes. She had a collection of haute couture dating back thirty years or more.
There were museums that coveted this collection, and
his mother spent a lot of time trying to figure out who
was going to get it after she died.

The house was dark and quite empty. His folks
travelled a lot. A cleaning woman came once a week
to dust but, apart from her, Cyrus was the house's sole
occupant.

There was something about the place that wasn't
right. Cyrus had never been able to nail down the
feeling he got when he entered. It was as if somebody
was standing over his shoulder. Like a ghost or something. His mother didn't like to stay there on her own

and he didn't blame her. This part of the house wasn't like his apartment, which was cosy.

His mother's dressing room took up almost all of the fourth floor. Everything was neatly stored. Hats in one corner, scarves, jewellery, shoes all stacked in custom-made cedar containers. The hats alone took up half a wall. Many were still in their boxes, never worn. Cyrus's mother shopped with a compulsiveness that left most of her friends, who considered themselves nifty around a store, gasping. She was adored by the city's top saleswomen. At Christmas and on her birthday the house was flooded with rare and expensive flowers. As a child Cyrus had thought they were ugly and wondered why the stores couldn't have sent his mom something nice, like daisies. Now he knew the blooms cost hundreds of dollars.

These sales women knew more about Cyrus's mother than her husband and son. They kept little books that recorded her every like and dislike. Even though they never came to her house, they knew the contents of her wardrobe intimately. Once Cyrus had been with his mother when she chose a blouse and the saleswoman had murmured that it would go perfectly with the San Laurent trousers she had bought six months ago. And the San Laurent trousers had been bought at another store.

Cyrus started going through the piles of boxes. He wanted a hat. His mother had loads of them. Few of them were suitable for Cyrus's purposes. They were either too extravagant, festooned with feathers and bows, or they were too tiny. After he'd opened about twenty boxes Cyrus began to think perhaps he didn't need a hat. Nobody wore hats like this any more, except to weddings. He'd only draw attention to himself. And he had the wig. He'd make do with that. He started putting the hats back in their homes, carefully replacing the tissue paper because his mother was particular about such things. She'd been very upset with him one day when, as a kid, he'd got in her wardrobe and drawn on the boxes with a red crayon. She and his father were getting ready to go on one of their trips and she had been so angry she'd left without saying goodbye. Cyrus waited for two weeks before he heard any word from her and then it was a terse postcard from Palma de Majorca telling him to make sure he did his homework, otherwise he'd never get into a good college. He had been five years old.

Cyrus could laugh at it now. The Master had taught him how to stop old hurts from contaminating his life. His parents' power to wound him had gone. He felt sorry for them with their trivial concerns and their shallow, materialistic lives. They didn't mean any more to him than the man who delivered his dry cleaning.

He'd packed up the last box when he saw it: a vintage Christian Dior day dress. A fitted bodice with a shawl neck and a flared skirt. It was one of a kind. His mother loved that dress, even though it didn't fit her. She had bought it second-hand, meaning to have it altered. But she'd never done it because she didn't want to interfere with workmanship of that quality. It was nearly fifty years old and still exquisite. The medium-blue colour as lustrous as ever.

Cyrus picked it off the hanger and placed it tenta-

215

tively around his waist. To his surprise, it fitted. He pulled the sleeves out and placed his arm alongside. A little short, but not too bad, considering. He held the shoulder seams across his shoulders. Damn, it was close enough.

Tye's original plan had been to move on from Juliana's immediately, but she decided another day couldn't hurt. Besides, there were bound to be people who got cold feet and cancelled their cheques. She couldn't count on any of this money until it had cleared.

To celebrate success she ordered a meal to be sent to her room and she ate it in bed, watching an old episode of Seinfeld. Then she called a florist and had them send a hundred dollars worth of blue carnations and dried, pink eucalyptus to Adrian's wife. Poor Adrian, she thought. Men could seldom handle having two women in their lives. This episode would teach him that, if nothing else.

Marion gave in and called her ex-husband in Fort Lauderdale. It was late and he wasn't pleased.

'What the hell,' he spluttered when she explained who was calling. He sounded tight.

'Gus is missing, Chuck. And I need your help to try and find him.'

'Missing? God, Marion, what do you mean?' In the background she could hear the noisy bonhomie of an over-liquored crowd. She hoped his second wife loved parties as much as Chuck did.

'In New York. He's missing in New York'

'What the hell was he doing there?'

'Finding work.'

'Finding work?'

'He's graduated from college, Chuck. He's married. Please don't repeat everything I say.'

'Gus is married?'

'You know very well he's married. Look, I don't expect you to come up here, but I do need some money. I wouldn't be asking if I wasn't desperate. And I'm not asking for me. He's your son.'

'What kind of money?'

'I want to take out an ad. I don't know what it'll cost. A couple of thousand maybe.'

'He can't be missing. He's probably just taken off for a few days.'

'He hasn't, Chuck.' Marion gritted her teeth. She was close to tears. Her ex was so dense. 'He's missing. The cops are involved.'

'Well, if the cops are involved then there's nothing you can do. Look, Marion, you're overreacting. He'll turn up in a couple of days. Why don't you—'

But Marion didn't want to hear any more of his pompous advice. She slammed the phone down and walked angrily back to the hostel. There were days when she thought less of herself for ever falling in love with such a jerk.

The dress was a little tight across the back, so Cyrus slit the side seams and patched in a couple of panels using the dress from the thrift store. He didn't know how to sew, so he used a staple gun and masking tape. It wasn't too bad a match as long as he kept his arms down at his sides. At night it'd be especially easy to get away with it. He shaved carefully and put on some of his mother's make-up: foundation, mascara, a little pink lipstick. The wig looked a little silly, so he cut it shorter.

He was unprepared for the reaction on the street.

'Hey, bitch, dig those rags,' a sassy young guy in a leather sheath dress called out softly. 'You got some time to spare, baby?'

Others were more direct. Hissing, making gestures. Cyrus hurried on, clutching his shopping bag to his chest, disgusted at these people. How dare they? What kind of freaks were they, anyway? Why wasn't the mayor doing more to keep creeps like that away from decent people?

The store was quiet. There was hardly anyone around to suffer the eardrum-popping rendition of the *William Tell Overture*. Cyrus grabbed a cart and walked up and down the aisles a couple of times. The Hispanic staff took one look at his eccentric attire and shrugged. Crazy Americans.

The freezer was at the back. It was filled with gourmet frozen dinners and the ice cream crafted by artisans.

Cyrus walked past a couple of times. There was space to put his little 'gift'. He detoured into another aisle and put a hunk of parmesan cheese in his trolley. Suddenly he was nervous. What if somebody recognized him? But that was impossible. His own mother wouldn't recognize him dolled up like this. On the other hand, she probably would, because of the dress. Damn, he should never have worn the dress. It was too distinctive. He might as well leave his card at the scene. He cursed his stupid, petty desire for revenge. It was dumb to be thinking like that, and it could get him in trouble.

Another woman was loading up on ice cream. She stacked three cartons in her trolley and walked guiltily on. Cyrus smiled. Everybody has their dirty little secrets, he thought. He pulled himself together. There was no point in backing out now. He walked slowly back down the aisle, his breathing tight. The *William Tell Overture* faded and instead, in his head, he heard Mozart's Great Mass in C. Now *there* was music for grand occasions.

He reached into his plastic shopping bag and felt the frozen limb. A piece of thigh. The boy's, he thought, though he wasn't sure. His gloved hand closed around it. He edged one strap of the shopping bag off his shoulder to help get the thing out.

Then he stopped. Oh God. A shop assistant was coming straight at him.

'Can I help you, ma'am?'

Cyrus froze. What was he supposed to do? He hadn't anticipated having to speak to anyone. What should he say?

'Need help finding something?' The assistant had a lilting Spanish accent.

Cyrus cleared his throat, kept his head down. The stupid little man was still standing there. Why wouldn't he go away? He couldn't think of anything to say. All he could think of was ice cream, and that wasn't good.

He didn't want to be associated with the frozen foods. It was all going hopelessly wrong.

'Apples,' he finally squeaked, in an unconvincing falsetto.

'Apples, sure. They're two aisles over to your right.' The assistant was looking at him as though he was crazy. Cyrus hobbled over to the apples, his shoes were giving him hell. How did women walk in them every day?

God, he'd really screwed up now. He might as well just go home. He was finished. A failure. Why did he have to say 'apples'? Why hadn't he just said 'no, thanks' like a normal person? He just didn't have the ability to think on his feet. He couldn't make decisions on the fly. Everything had to be planned. No wonder there was no spontaneity in his life.

He picked up a couple of apples, listlessly. Checked their skin for flaws before he remembered he wasn't there to buy apples.

Fuck it, he was just going to do it. To hell with the consequences. There was no one looking at him. The annoying little assistant was now sweeping the floor up front. The clerk was filing her nails. Remembering to keep his head down so the wig covered his face, he marched up to the freezer, opened it and put the frozen leg inside. The door shut with a sucking hiss and a spume of cold air escaped. Cyrus walked calmly towards the door. The staff paid him no further mind.

He had done it.

# PART TWO

# Chapter Thirty-Four

Catrina Vermont was putting on her make-up in the women's toilets at five in the morning, wondering what amount of pancake was going to disguise her chronic lack of sleep, when the night editor barged in and started pulling her towards the door.

Catrina's first response was to elbow him in the jaw. But she didn't, because she was nearly forty-five and needed the job, even the shitty early morning job that barely covered her exorbitant Upper East Side rent. She had more or less shelved her dreams of network stardom but that didn't make the incompetence of this tinpot place any easier to bear, especially when they treated her like a geriatric joke: poor Cat, no husband.

In fact, Catrina did have a personal life but she chose not to share it with her colleagues. Not that she was ashamed of her preference for girls; she just liked to keep her private life away from prying office busybodies. And if she ever did make it to the network . . . she crushed the thought. It wasn't going to happen now, not with the next birthday being the big four-six. She looked good for forty-five; on a good day she looked great. But in television it made no difference because there were thousands of twenty-seven year olds streaming out of universities and journalism schools who were quite happy to leave the heel marks of their Manolo Blahniks in the back of her head as they walked over her to get an on-air job.

Cat knew this because she had been one once herself.

She could have plastic surgery. She'd seriously thought about it, even went to visit a doctor. She'd come away horrified by the thought of having her face cut open. And when she'd mentioned it to her girl-friend Renee, she had threatened never to speak to her again. No. She wasn't going to the network. That was it, end of story.

'Live truck's waiting,' Max the editor said, pushing her towards the elevator. 'Get down there. Need a five thirty hit.'

Catrina still had her uncapped mascara wand in her hand. She put it under Max's eye.

'Max. I'm a professional. I don't go out without a notebook, tape recorder or my jacket. I especially do not go out without lipstick. Now let me go or you get this right in your baby blues.'

'But, but—'

'Max. I mean it.'

'The story—'

'What have I told you about taking diet pills to keep you awake? It's not good for your nervous system.'

'Body parts,' Max said, finally loosening his grip on her arm.

'Those either. Now, what's the story? Is there any wire copy?'

'No. Just broke. Police scanner. Found a body part. In a refrigerator.'

'Not at the morgue I'm guessing.'

'At Food Phantasmagoria.'

Catrina swiped her eyelashes with the mascara wand. 'A new dining sensation for jaded palettes. White or dark meat?'

Max didn't get it. The pills were keeping him awake but that was all they were doing, Catrina thought. He hadn't always been like this, but she remembered a time when she had been a sharper blade as well.

'What are the cops saying?'

Max shook his head. 'Not saying.'

Catrina capped her mascara and threw it into her handbag. 'Right,' she said. 'Let's go find out.'

The live truck drove at life-threatening speed down Sixth Avenue while Catrina finished putting on her make-up. She could do it perfectly now in any conditions, in any weather – force ten gales, prison riots, sales at Macy's. She could even do it with WKLP's engineers behind the wheel, that curious breed of professional who seemed to be chosen specifically for their cavalier attitude towards the rules of the road.

Cat sat in silence beside her producer, Peter Ratch. Although they worked together they rarely spoke more than about two words a day. Peter Ratch made no secret of his contempt for her and he did no work. Cat had tried everything from bullying to buddying up. She'd failed. Now when they went on a shoot or a live shot, Peter sat in the car and talked on his cellphone and Cat did her job. She actually preferred it that way.

Trying to break down his sullen resistance was more than she had the energy for.

It was nearly five fifteen when they got to Food Phantasmagoria and the sun was not yet up. The air smelt fresh and the day seemed filled with promise. Wrong on both scores, thought Catrina as she leapt out of the truck and went in search of a cop.


Cyrus didn't normally watch television, especially in the mornings, but he was up at six that day with a cup of coffee and the TV remote. The networks were salivating over him! Grotesque, hideous, heinous. Fabulous words, all applied to him. He had the city enthralled. He felt quietly satisfied as he watched reporter after reporter standing outside the supermarket speculating about his identity and his motives. Some stupid people even thought it was a terrorist attack. Imbeciles! They did not even begin to understand his work.


Quinn was buying his morning coffee when he noticed a large crowd on Sixth Avenue. Police cars, TV news trucks, the fire brigade. He joined the rubberneckers clustered at the police barrier, straining to hear what was going on. He could only catch the odd word. He turned back, he didn't have time for such things, he had to start organizing his move, getting his stuff out of storage. There was a lot to be done. He felt happier than he had in days. At last his life was moving on.

Rhonda and Mal could pork themselves stupid and he wouldn't be around to hear it.

Tye had waited a few days to return to Juliana's apartment. She had a clutch of messages from people who were willing to sell somebody near and dear for the apartment. The day before she called them all back and arranged for afternoon viewings. She wanted to be out of the place by early evening because she had a date with Dickie. It was funny how a few thousand miles changed your attitude to people, she thought. In London, she and Dickie would have exchanged a few polite words at a cocktail party and moved on. Now they were suddenly old friends. Tye didn't like to admit it, because she wasn't one for hanging about in ex-pat huddles complaining about the locals, but she missed the conversation of the English. Americans lacked bite; there was no nuance or subtlety in their social behaviour and their habit of getting directly to the point was simply appalling. She was looking forward to seeing Dickie.

Catrina filed live reports throughout the morning, every half hour. It was more of a conjuring than a reporting job because there was no information to go on. The cops were saying *nada*, the supermarket owners even less. The body part had been removed by forensics, that was it. All morning she had anchors with lower IQs than their hair spray asking her inane questions, such as, 'can you tell me what the atmosphere's like down there?' as if she were reporting on a ball game or a parade. Then again, it might as well have been a parade the way people hung around. Women with kids in strollers, dog walkers, shoppers. Didn't these people have anything more important to do? One guy with his arm in a cast had actually winked at her while she was preparing for a stand-up. She'd given him her 'not in a million years' freeze-stare. He'd shrugged his shoulders as if to say 'your loss'. Men! What was with them? Did they think every single woman was available? If you were ambulatory and breathing – hey, great! Let's do it!

Her cellphone rang. It was Eric Atlas, in the office and making trouble. Catrina sighed. God how she wished it had been Atlas in that freezer.

'Hey, babe.'

'I'm not your babe, babe.' Catrina emphasized the last word carefully and smothered the irritation that arose when she even thought about Eric Atlas.

'Whatever. Listen. We've got a lead on this story. It's a hot lead. An animal liberation group has phoned in saying they planted the meat. It's a protest against the zoo.'

Catrina squeezed the web of skin between her thumb and forefinger. She could feel the headache crashing down on her. 'What kind of meat?'

'Hey babe, what was that? God, it's noisy in here. Will everybody SHUT THE FUCK UP! Sorry babe.'

'What kind of meat, Eric. Badger? Polecat? Wolverine?'

'Ah . . . they didn't say.'

'And what's their beef with the supermarket?'

'They said it was just like a general statement.' Eric didn't pick up on Cat's pun. She pressed her hand more tightly, even though she knew her headache was more of an Advil problem.

'They've claimed responsibility,' Eric said. 'And I want you to put that in at the top of the hour.'

'Sure, right,' Catrina said and hung up. She went to see if the engineer had any over-the-counter drugs.

# Chapter Thirty-Five

Marion slept badly and woke with an even more acute sense of dread than she'd grown accustomed to. For solace, she called her friend Jonie in Michigan and spoke to the twins, who were staying there. She told them the truth, even though she hated to do it over the phone.

The girls were subdued. He'd turn up, they both said. Don't worry, Mom.

They were good kids really, she thought. They'd turn out all right.

'How ya doing?' Jonie asked when she came back on. Marion told her about her conversation with Chuck.

Jonie said nothing. Everything that was possible to say about Chuck had already passed between the two women.

'I'll get the money.'

'How?'

'I'll think of something. You just leave it to me, okay? Maybe you should offer a reward or something. Put up some posters.'

Marion went to an art supply store and bought some white paper. Then she went to a copy shop and had Gus and Susie's wedding photo blown up. She made up fifty posters that day and pinned them on telephone poles around the Village and Chelsea. Afterwards she felt a little better – at least she was doing something.


Tye was back in her hotel room at six with a pile of ATM receipts. She had deposited today's cheques at her various banks on the way. The first lot would clear by tomorrow. If all went well, she would be fully paid up on her hotel bill and then have some fun money left over. She turned on the television as she got ready for her date. The news was on, being mouthed by a woman who'd had so much plastic surgery her lips were permanently pulled back in a smile that looked like a grimace.

'Shoppers got more than they bargained for at a fancy New York supermarket this morning. Cops say the unidentified package left at a Food Phantasmagoria overnight is human flesh.' The anchor paused and raised one eyebrow before continuing. 'A thigh bone to be exact. Forensic tests show . . .'

Tye turned it off. What was the matter with these people?


Russian rabbits, Marion thought as she watched the evening news on the small black-and-white television that Jim and Mike kept behind the desk at the hostel. Her legs were burning. At the hip joint, the knee, the ankle. And her arms too, wrists, elbow, shoulder. She was on fire with pain.

'You okay, Marion?' Mike asked, 'you look pale.'

'Gus!' Marion moaned as she fell on the floor in the dead faint.


Cyrus ate popcorn as he watched the security video of himself on the news. This had worked out a lot better than he'd imagined. The outline was him, all right, but nobody would be able to tell. His bangs and glasses covered the top of his face and he was careful never to look up, so they hadn't got a decent shot of him. He could have been anybody. He was lead story on every newscast except PBS – and who cared about them, anyway?

He'd done all right.

He took his mother's dress back upstairs, the seams hanging open. Good thing it never fitted her.


Renee was waiting with a Martini and a kiss when Catrina got home. Larry, the fox terrier, was leaping up and down at her side like a toy on a spring.

'Tough day?' she murmured as she attacked the knots in Catrina's shoulders. The television was on but the sound was down. The black-and-white security pictures from the supermarket showed a figure in a dress moving forward in five-second jerks.

'The worst. They went hysterical. Anyone would have thought it was the President in the freezer. They've put us all on standby because they think he's going to strike again. I probably shouldn't even have this drink. They'll be pulling me in again in a few hours.'

'Have it,' Renee said. 'We should drink a farewell toast to the poor bastard whose leg it is.' They raised their glasses. 'And the impeccable dress sense of the sicko freak who put him there.'

'Yeah, he's real class.' Cat took a grateful gulp from her Martini and waited for it to work its unravelling magic.

'No, I mean it.'

'So do I.' Cat waved her arm at the screen as if to banish it. God, she was so tired. If only she could think straight. If only she wasn't in a perma-bitch mood.

Renee put her glass down. She took the remote control and pointed it at the television. The security camera picture froze. 'I recorded it, see? Because of the dress.'

'Have you thought of joining Designers Anonymous?' The Martini was smoothing out the rough corners. 'Not everything has to do with clothes, you know.' Cat smiled a little extra to show she was kidding, because she and Renee had been having a few problems lately, their banter wasn't as rough and tumble as it used to be.

'It's a designer number, honey. Antique. I'll bet you anything you like.'

'How can you tell? The picture's so fuzzy.'

'I know.' Renee crossed to the television where the image was frozen. 'Look at the line. You can tell the quality even from these pictures.' She squatted by the television. 'And that embroidery on the shoulders?'

She pointed to what looked to Cat like a bunch of squiggly lines. 'I've seen that pattern before. That is one expensive dress. Besides, I've got goose bumps. Only pre-sixties couture does that to me.' Renee held up her arm. 'See?'

'I'm sure they were ripping off designers, even when that dress was made.' Cat secretly felt a bit sorry for her girlfriend for working in an industry that was even more frivolous than television news.

'I'm right,' Renee said, sing-song. 'And you know what? Couture is easy to trace.'

Cat had her eyes closed, wondering how long she would need to sleep before she felt even remotely human again, when Renee's words sank in. She opened one eye. 'What are you saying?'

'You know. Not that many of them. Only a few women can afford it. And they tend to be photographed a lot. No point in having a viciously expensive dress if nobody sees you in it.'

Cat opened her other eye. She felt a tiny stirring of something she hadn't experienced in a long time: enthusiasm. She shot out of her chair, bounced across the room, kissed Renee hard. 'This is the reason I love you,' she said before grabbing her coat and her bag.

'Cat, where're you going? You just got here.'

'My sweet, I'm going to the network.'

Cyrus realized too late that he'd screwed up. He should have spent the whole of last night distributing parts, because now every supermarket in the city would be on the alert. Now he would have to lie low for a while.

There was nothing he could do for at least a week, probably more. There was not enough room in his refrigerator.

But that was okay. No point in rushing things. He had time. Besides, he had to get on with his life. He'd been thinking of joining a reading group. He'd got some names from his local bookstore and planned to check a couple of them out. He'd also looked into learning an instrument. He'd always liked the cello, but when it came down to it, he couldn't decide between that and the French horn. He intended to visit a music shop to look at instruments and see how he felt about each of them while he held them in his hands. He would take up the one that spoke to him the most clearly.

But first there was dinner. He'd found a hip Belgian place down by Chelsea Market and made a reservation. He showered and dressed and hummed to himself as he fastened his tie in the mirror. It was a silk tie, although the design was a little less conservative than one he would normally have chosen. It was from a young, trendy designer whose work was pretty expensive. Cyrus tweaked the knot and smoothed it into place. The tie made the whole outfit, he decided. He studied his reflection, trying out different expressions, just to see how they looked – in case he ran into anyone, or somebody started a conversation with him. He'd read the paper and a couple of magazines, so he was sufficiently up on the affairs of the city and the world. If somebody asked him about a baseball team, for example, he had an answer ready. He could even start a conversation if the right opportunity presented itself – why not? Tonight he was going to go out and be a regular guy.

Jim and Mike revived Marion with a wet facecloth and then made her take a sip of brandy. The alcohol burned and Marion felt sick. She ran outside and threw up, retching painfully till her guts had no more to give. Mike brought her back inside gently and sat her down.

'It's him. I know it's him,' Marion moaned, over and over. 'Oh, God, Gus. My Gus.'

'You don't know that, Marion,' Mike said gently. 'You're worked up, that's all. The last few days have been tough.'

Marion shook her head. She knew. Just like that Russian mother rabbit in the experiment had known when her babies met their deaths in the black depths of an icy northern ocean. She knew. The thought of what had happened to her son made her want to throw up again but she couldn't, she realized miserably. She had nothing left inside her.

'It's a nice theory, Marion,' said John Abruzzo after she managed to get through to him on the phone. 'But what are the chances?'

'Just have them do the test, John.'

'They've got enough on their plate. The mayor, the media, the whole fucking city is screaming bloody murder.'

'I'll give you the name of my doctor. He did Gus's blood test. He just got married, you see. They both did . . .' Marion trailed off. 'Please, John. I have to know.'

'It's some homeless guy somebody found on a park bench,' John said.

'It's my son, John. I know it.'

John Abruzzo didn't have the heart to tell Marion how many people had called precinct houses all over the city that day, claiming that damn piece of meat as their own. 'Okay,' he said. 'Give me the doc's number.'


Catrina was fumbling for her car keys when Renee slunk up behind her and put a cool hand on the back of her neck. 'Levink so soon darlink?' she said in her Marlene Deitrich accent. 'Ven ve haf only just begun?'

'I've got to go to the office.'

'And I can't come?'

'You know why.'

'Sure, I know why.' Renee waggled her eyebrows and did her Groucho Marx. 'You wouldn't want to belong to a club that has me as a member.'

'Your Groucho and Marlene sound too much alike.'

'So sue me.'

'I've gotta make some calls.'

'Cat, what do you know about dresses? I buy your clothes. Hell, I make your clothes. Well, okay, a nice Hungarian woman does. And it's a good thing too, otherwise you wouldn't look like a chic woman of the world. You'd look like a cross-dressing lumberjack who's just been released from a loony bin.'

'So?'

'So where you gonna start?'

'I'm just going to the newsroom.'

'To do what? Tell them you've got a hot lead they

can piss away? No, no, no, my girl. That's the wrong way.'

Catrina found the key and unlocked her car. Renee was inside in a flash, feet up on the dashboard.

'The world of fashion, my dear, is like a secret society. These people are more hierarchical that the Hapsburgs. You have to know the passwords to get in. You've got to know the handshakes, the right asses to kiss. You're not going to get that with a couple of phone calls to PR flacks. You're gonna get zip. Oh well, too bad. Nice lead you had there. Then Atlas has you interviewing the Hoboken branch manager of Gap – a blue cocktail dress is a blue cocktail dress, am I right? – and someone else has the story. Bye, bye network. I'm really sorry, Mr Brokaw. Not this year.'

Catrina put her fingers to her temples. The damn headache was back. She turned to face her girlfriend. 'What are you saying? 'Cause I'm not in the mood for riddles right now.'

Renee flinched from her harsh tone and Cat instantly regretted what she had said. 'I'm sorry, Renee. You're right. I'm not thinking. I'm so tired.'

'Knew you'd see it my way.' Renee whistled short and sharp. Larry bounded around the corner, Renee opened the door and he leapt onto her lap, panting.

Renee grinned. 'Just like Nick and Nora Charles. Except for the queer thing, of course. Now let's go out for dinner.'


It was a costume party. Tye and Dickie had decided what to wear over the phone and he'd picked up the costumes from a contact in the movie business. Ted O'Reilly was the host – he was throwing a late Halloween party in celebration of his movie deal.

'Last worn by Uma Thurman,' Dickie shouted into the bathroom where Tye was changing.

The suit was gorgeous. Butter-soft leather, it was a struggle to get into but it fitted. And how.

'Oh, my,' Dickie said when she came out. Tye smiled.

'Ready, Mr Steed?'

'As I'll ever be, Mrs Peel.' Dickie twirled his umbrella.

They took a taxi to Williamsburg. Tye gazed at the lit city and felt happy. She had money, she was making contacts. Things were working out.

'Great you could make it.' Ted was dressed as Hillary Clinton. He was wearing support hose and he'd padded his calves with foam. He placed a firm hand on Tye's elbow and guided her into the room. It was a young crowd. Men in white tuxedo jackets and Bermuda shorts distributed drinks.

'Just moved in,' Ted shouted over the music. 'Thought I'd better have all my messy pals over before I got furniture.' Ted whistled down a waiter and grabbed two glasses of champagne. Somehow they'd lost Dickie, which she suspected had been Ted's intention.

'To your eyes.' Ted raised his glass.

'I hope you don't put lines like that in your screenplays.'

'There are no women like you in my screenplays.'

'There you are, chaps.' Dickie had squeezed his

way through the crowd. He was holding two glasses of champagne and had his brolly hooked over one arm. A party streamer draped from his bowler hat. When he saw that Tye had a glass he downed his spare in one.

'Smile.' Tinkerbell had a camera. Dickie and Tye posed. Dickie tipped his bowler hat. Tye held his umbrella at a jaunty angle. The flash blinded her temporarily but when the spots had faded from her eyes, she thought she saw somebody she recognized. But it was gone. Imagination, she thought. She didn't know anybody in New York.

'Come and look at the view.' Ted, feeling bolder, put his arm around her shoulders. Tye looked in Dickie's direction, but he had wandered off and was deep in discussion with Frankenstein. She felt light and carefree for the first time in weeks.

'Sure,' she said.


Quinn had only decided at the last minute to come to Ted's party. He was feeling better about his place in the world now that he had an apartment lined up. It seemed to be a symbol that things were going to improve. He'd even tried to lull himself into thinking he could feel happy for Ted. He wasn't such a bad chap, he'd told himself as he got ready, and the party was bound to be good. He was determined to have a great time. Maybe even get laid. He wondered if Ted had a virgin sister he thought the world of who'd be there. But no, that wasn't right. He tried to think of Ted in a kinder light. He'd done nothing to him, really, except be everything he wasn't. And he'd asked him to a party, which meant an evening of free booze. It'd be mindless fun. He'd enjoy it.

How wrong he'd been.

Ten minutes after arriving, it became clear that Ted had organized the whole evening just to torture him. He was now going to have to kill Ted, and knowing his luck, get caught and do life on Riker's Island.

Quinn had grabbed a Guinness from a waiter and was strolling, checking out the female half of the crowd. No real talent yet, but that didn't matter, he was patient. Women always looked different after a couple of beers. He might even get a sympathy vote, having his arm in a cast. He sipped from his can, tapping a foot idly to the music. It was bad – some indie rock band who were obscure for a very good reason.

Then he saw her. Not clearly, a glimpse. But it was enough.

She was tall, slender and utterly perfect in face and figure. To top it off, she was wearing leather. 'Jesus. Thank you God,' Quinn murmured as he inched his way through the party throng. He had to find out who this person was and tell her she was the answer to his dreams. Even the ones he hadn't had yet.

It seemed to take forever, traversing Ted's cavernous space. Too many people. And it were as though he were in a trance. His heart was beating fast, he felt sweaty, his hands were shaking. Who was this vision and how had she turned up at Ted's?

He was near enough to reach out and touch her when she turned away and put her arm around Ted.

*Ted!* And allowed him to guide her to the balcony. She laid her head lightly on his shoulder – Ted was whispering something in her ear and sliding his arm lower, down towards her perfect, leather-clad ass.

It was now official. Ted had absolutely everything and Quinn had nothing. Not only that, Quinn would have traded all the nothing he didn't have for that one thing he really wanted of Ted's. God, he was a wretched miserable excuse for a human being.

The Pope offered him a joint. He took it and breathed deep. He needed a little altered consciousness right now . . . reality was just too fucking dismal.

Tye couldn't believe her monstrous bad luck. Of all the parties in New York she had to show up at the same one as one of her marks. Good God, it was enough to frighten a person into going straight. And now here he was, coming towards her. She turned her back and grabbed the first thing to hand, which was Ted.

'Let's go and take in that view again,' she said, trying to appear calm and light-hearted. He couldn't be coming after her, there was no way he would recognize her, especially dressed like this. But still, she couldn't afford to take that chance.

Quinn smoked most of the joint and another one besides. Then he danced a few times with a woman dressed as a Playboy bunny. Then he sank a couple of shots of tequila. Then he wondered what the hell he was doing messing around with the Playboy girl when the real Aphrodite was feet away. Fuck Ted anyway, what right did he have to claim the best of everything? Life wasn't a zero sum game. There was enough for everybody.

It was while holding this thought that he decided to go up to the goddess and introduce himself. What did he have to lose? He might never see her again. Besides, she might fall madly in love with him, just as he had with her. It was possible, anything was. This was God-damned America.

Out of the corner of her eye, Tye spied him and panicked. He was making his way towards her again, that meant he must recognize her. Ted and Dickie had disappeared, there was nobody nearby to help her – just Zorro chatting up Tinkerbell.

She tried to pretend she wasn't looking at him, but she could see him, shouldering his way through. Tye cast about for escape routes, but she was stuck in a corner. If she went anywhere, it would be straight towards him.

She drew a deep breath. There was nothing she could do. Zorro and Tinkerbell moved off, giggling. They were pissed or stoned or both. Goddamn it, where was Dickie when she needed him? She took a deep draught from her champagne glass. Perhaps he'd stop, get waylaid.

No. He was coming through. She turned quickly, trying to think and bumped into Zorro, who was clearly drunk, his cape and mask had come astray.

He was right behind her now, she could tell. She turned slowly, to delay the inevitable moment.

# Chapter Thirty-Six

'Mrs Peel, I've always admired your work.'

Tye turned to face him, fastening Zorro's mask in place. 'It's Batgirl, actually,' she said in the 'screw-you' English accent her parents had paid a fortune for her to acquire.

'My mistake.' Quinn bowed slightly from the waist. The voice was a shock. He'd been expecting an American. He felt formal, and awkward. He tried to remember a few things his mother had said about being respectful to women, but all he could think of was that he wanted to seize her.

Tye's fingernails were digging into her palms. She searched his face for signs of recognition, willing herself to be cool. He didn't appear to recognize her and she told herself firmly that there was no reason why he should. In her experience, recognition was mostly about context and it was unlikely that he would connect the dowdy, bespectacled American redhead with a British leather vamp. She reached up to make sure the mask was fastened securely. He was cute. Perhaps she could even enjoy it a little.

'And you are?'

'Deeply jealous of Ted.'

'Really?'

'Sure. He holds a party and superheroes turn up.'

'I'm a mere mortal.'

'I bet you leap tall mortals with a single bound.'

'Come, Mr—' Shit, she nearly said Quinn. She nearly said his name. She recovered and he didn't appear to notice. 'Mr . . . ?'

'Call me Quinn. And you?'

The crowd pressed around them. He took the opportunity and moved in a little closer. They were maybe ten inches apart. She could see his chest rising and falling underneath his cotton shirt. She realized she was holding her breath and it wasn't just nerves. She felt a little dizzy. Good God, she hadn't felt this foolish since Hugh Hadley in the sixth form.

'It's Tye,' she blurted out.

'As in old school?'

'As in tie me up.' What was she doing? What was she saying? She knew she should get the hell out of here and fast. But she couldn't move. He has mesmerized me, she thought, the colour rising in her face. She couldn't move. She wanted to but she couldn't. And now she'd stolen all his money.

'Thought you'd never ask.' Quinn lifted his beer can and touched Tye's glass gently. 'Let's drink to the ties that bind.'

'Dear girl, would you come and advise me.' Dickie burst into their circle, drawing Tye away. 'Do excuse us,' he said to Quinn. 'Now my dear, I really do need your expert opinion.'

Dickie pulled Tye gently and she felt relief as the connection to Quinn snapped.

'Thank you.'

'For what, dear girl?'

'Oh, for . . . bringing me. This is a nice party.' Tye put her glass to her forehead to cool her down.

'Absolutely my pleasure,' Dickie said. 'Dear girl, I wondered . . .'

Quinn watched them go. He felt suddenly happy for his brother and Rhonda. What did an over-aerobicized bunny matter to him when there was an actual goddess walking the streets of New York City?


'See, an haute couture dress is like a member of the aristocracy,' Renee said to Catrina as they ate dinner at their favourite place in Chelsea. 'It has a lineage. Some of them end up in museums and collections. But most women won't part with haute couture. So they tend to stay with a single owner for a long time, like, until they die.' Renee did a quick sketch of the sunburst on her paper napkin. 'And now when they change hands, it's at the big auction houses. At least that's how it's been done for the last ten years or so.'

'And what if it was before that?' Cat's euphoria was starting to wear off. There was no way she was getting a scoop from such a flimsy lead.

'I'm going to find it, don't worry,' Renee said confidently.

# Chapter Thirty-Seven

The next day, Tye wrapped Juliana's keys in a padded bag and mailed them to her next-door neighbour. That way, when Juliana got back from her holiday she wouldn't be locked out of her own apartment. Tye had cleaned the place yesterday, dusted all the surfaces and made sure it looked exactly as it had when she left it. She took the answering-machine cassette and replaced it with the original. It had been a profitable relationship, her and East 88th Street, but it was time to move on. An important rule that should never be broken – don't dip in the well too many times.

She thought about the Irishman called Quinn as she went through her tasks. A man hadn't had this effect on her, ever.

You've stolen his money, she told herself. Get over it.


Not even seeing Rhonda emerge from Mal's bedroom fuzzy from lack of sleep could dent Quinn's good humour. He distributed cheerful good mornings, offered home-brewed coffee and bagels and assurances that he'd soon be out of their hair.

'Young love.' He sighed as they shut the door. It warmed his heart. He decided to call Kathleen about the new apartment. She'd rung him late yesterday and left a message firming up the moving-in date. He hadn't yet called her back.

He dialled the number but the voice didn't sound like hers. He double-checked the number, dialled again. Same machine. Perhaps he was getting a crossed line. He drank the rest of his coffee and dialled a third time. Same person. Someone called Juliana, not Kathleen. He called his bank. His cheque had been cashed.

His head was a little thick from the alcohol of the night before so it took him longer than it should have done to realize that he had just thrown several thousand dollars away. He would never see that money or Kathleen again.

He threw his coffee cup across the room. It left a dent in Malcolm's carefully distressed wall.

John Abruzzo picked Marion up at the hostel. They drove slowly through the early morning traffic, not speaking. Marion watched people out the window, walking to work, hailing taxis, sipping coffee and wondered what it would be like to rejoin normal society. Not that she ever could. She could never go back. She would always be marked.

'Another kid's been reported missing,' John said finally. 'A foreign student from NYU. Parents are flying in today from Germany.'

'Oh, God,' Marion said, stifling a sob. She was always on the verge of tears these days. She couldn't see most of the time. Her eyes were swollen and sore. She had taken to wearing her sunglasses all the time, even indoors. She closed her eyes but all she could see were baby rabbits trapped in big metal cylinders sinking under the sea.

Renee got up early to watch Cat on television. She and Larry the terrier sat on the sofa. She ate oatmeal and drank coffee. There was no news to report. The body part had not been identified. There were no new leads. That was good as far as Renee was concerned; nobody was onto the dress angle yet. She finished her third cup of coffee, then dressed and went to the library at the Fashion Institute of Technology.

It didn't take her long to find the dress. It was part of the New Look collection shown by Christian Dior in 1947. She made a photocopy of it and a more detailed sketch of the sunburst. Then she checked with the big auction houses. None had sold it. She called all the museums with costume collections to see if any of the curators had seen it, but none had.

She called Mandell, a former college pal who knew everybody in New York fashion.

'You want what?' Mandell's throaty voice sometimes had people thinking she was a man on the phone. 'What for?'

'Favour for a friend.'

'Oh, right, how is Madame Cronkite?' Mandell and Cat didn't get on. The only thing they had in common was Renee.

'Please, Manny.'

There was a sigh and a suck on the other end of the phone. Mandell lived on French cigarettes and bagels. 'All right, darling. Since it's you . . . let me see. Try Joan Hamilton Richwright. She's an old lady who kept track of who bought what in Paris back then.'

Anger was not a state of mind that Quinn was used to. He found it easy to forgive and move on. It was his nature to do so. The very act of anger, the energy it required, was something that didn't suit his temperament.

Now though, he could feel it. It surged through his body like static electricity. It burned him as he rode the subway to the Upper East Side. It was so strong it made him squirm. He stood outside the apartment, looking up. He rang the bell a few times. He phoned the number again. Same answering machine. Then he buzzed the neighbour who told him what he'd expected to hear – that a woman called Juliana lived in the apartment and that she was away on vacation.

He'd been well and truly had. His money, his nest egg was gone.

He wondered how Malcolm was going to take the news.

Mrs Hamilton Richwright reminded Renee of a bird. She was extremely old, slender and tiny with very small hands and feet. She was dressed in a purple suit. Sixties Givenchy, Renee guessed, and with it wore a rope of very large pearls and black pumps. Her huge Fifth Avenue apartment with its Danish modern furniture and abstract paintings was flooded with sunshine. The view of Central Park was picturebook.

A butler brought tea things on a silver tray.

'Who is your couturier?' Mrs Hamilton Richwright asked.

'I am, Mrs Hamilton Richwright.' Renee smoothed her suit. The old lady straightened her spectacles to get a better look. 'Please call me Joan. Very nice,' she said. 'Very modern. It's so important to be modern. India or China tea, my dear?'

'China, please.'

The butler poured the tea and placed it on a side table. Mrs Hamilton Richwright's hands shook as she raised the thin cup to her thin mouth. Beside her was the photocopy of the dress and Renee's sketch of the sunburst.

'I take it you're a designer, and I'm terribly sorry that I haven't heard of you. I used to keep up, you know. But it's more of an effort these days. There are so many new ones and I regret to say I've become a little set in my ways. I wasn't like that forty years ago, of course.'

'I'm new,' Renee said. 'I've just started on my own.'

'Then I hope you have a very rich husband.'

Renee smiled and turned her hands out.

'But of course you don't. It's not the way any more, is it?'

'You could say that.'

'So,' Mrs Hamilton Richwright placed her cup

carefully down, 'you wanted to know about a dress.' She picked up a pair of dainty gold-rimmed spectacles and perched them on the end of her nose.

It was just a matter of going through the motions, Marion thought, as she drank cup after cup of bad cop coffee. Waiting to hear what the results of the DNA test would be. She didn't need the stupid test. She knew.

The precinct house was awash with people. Crooks, cops – uniformed and plainclothes. Marion counted guns. Almost everybody was wearing one. They were so strange when you saw them for real. On the movies or on TV they always had a toy-like quality. Up close, she was surprised at how substantial they looked. She wondered if Gus and Susie had seen a gun before they died. How had this person they didn't know forced them to do his bidding? Gus wasn't exactly a weakling and Susie had done karate for years. She was strong and fit and could kick like a mule, Gus had always told her proudly.

'Dear Peg Mayhorn,' Joan Hamilton Richwright said. 'She was terribly rich, but no amount of money could make up for the fact that she was . . . well . . .' The old lady held her hands wide to indicate plumpness. 'Even for those days she was corpulent. She couldn't help it, the poor thing. She tried everything. Fat farms, diets. Her parents took her to Paris twice a year for the shows. She bought up large, as it were.' Joan smiled faintly at her own joke. 'Those dresses were beautiful but the best stitching in the world could not address the basic problem. Society is so cruel to women. It doesn't matter so much now, of course . . . for most people . . . but then, a young woman's face was almost all she had. A college degree was all very well but marriage was the ultimate aim. To marry well, I mean.'

The sunlight in its slow arc touched the Persian rug and the butler appeared and adjusted the blinds. Then he quietly refilled Renee's cup.

'What happened to Peg?' she asked.

'My dear, it was an utter catastrophe,' Joan said, pausing dramatically.

'Why?'

'She fell in love.'

Detective Sergeant Tom Sweeney of Homicide ushered Marion into his office. The sun slanted through a set of dusty blinds and fell on the clutter on his desk. Half-empty coffee cups, a bagel with a bite taken out. The sergeant was skinny with rumpled hair. He looked about Marion's age.

John Abruzzo shut the door and the ambient office noise died away. He guided Marion into a chair and sat beside her. She gripped the arms, afraid.

'Mrs Neidermeyer,' the sergeant began. 'I'm very sorry . . .'

Over the humming in her ears Marion thought she heard someone screaming. Probably one of the prostitutes or drug dealers in the outside office. It sounded muted, as though it was coming from two or three rooms away. It went on and on like the yell of somebody falling over a cliff. It went on so long that she began to get annoyed by it. Couldn't they shut that person up? There were enough cops around. Why weren't they doing something?

Then she realized it was coming from her. She was the one making that God-awful sound. Anything to block out the noise, the terrible words that Tom Sweeney was saying.

# Chapter Thirty-Eight

'A lobsterman, my dear,' Joan said, putting her cup aside. 'Peg Mayhorn fell in love with a fisherman. It was a scandal. The family had always had a summer home in Bar Harbor. They went up every year. One year Peg was driving around the island and her car broke down and a little local man stopped to help her. He gave her a lift back to her house and that was it. Next thing, they'd run off and got married in Nova Scotia and were living in his shack and having babies. The family refused to speak to her, never met her children.'

'So she renounced her fortune?'

'Oh no, dear, she wasn't that stupid. A lot of the money was hers anyway, handed down from a grand-father, nothing the parents could do about it however much they disapproved of the match. But we never saw her in New York again. Never saw her in Maine, for that matter. The set she married into weren't known for their parties.'

'What happened to the dresses?'

'Her parents sold them at a charity auction to raise money for the Red Cross. It was a strange thing to do, I always thought. It was as if they wanted to renounce her in the most public way possible. They really did treat the poor girl as though she was dead. Sold off everything. Cleaned out her room, cut her out of the family portraits.'

'And did she live happily ever after?' Renee could picture an ample, happy woman standing outside a white cottage surrounded by children

'Who knows, my dear? I believe they stayed married, if that's what you mean.'


Tom Sweeney was stringing together lots of words that Marion couldn't make sense of: murder investigation, autopsy, top priority. A doctor had given her something to calm her down but she wasn't used to taking tablets and they had left her feeling fuzzy and disconnected. She was in shock. There were so many things to do now and she didn't know where to begin. She had to tell the twins and Jonie. She had to protect them too, somehow. How was she going to do that? She felt as though her body was shrinking with the weight of all the demands she had to meet.

'We'll find out what happened to Gus and Susie,' Sweeney was saying. Marion tried to focus on his words. My son is dead, was all she could think. But it couldn't be. She had seen him just two weeks ago. He was so healthy, so solid. So happy. He had a life and he was looking forward to the future. Now someone had taken his life and thrown it away, as though he were not a human being but a soda can or a cardboard plate.

As these thoughts rushed through her head Marion

wondered how she would get through this thing that faced her. It seemed impenetrable looking at it – as though she were standing in front of a sheer cliff and had been told to climb it.

'I'm just an ordinary person,' she said.

Sweeney's mouth twisted in a wry expression of sympathy, as though he'd had to tell too many people too much bad news.

'I'll take you back to the hotel,' John Abruzzo said.


Renee turned on the little television set she kept at her studio to see if there was any more news. She knew better than to call Cat when she was out in the field. She was doing a live shot from the precinct house in the Village saying that the body part had been identi-fied as belonging to a young male from Michigan. Nothing so far on the dress. Good. She took the vellum paper that Joan Hamilton Richwright had given her out of her bag, unfolded it carefully and dialled the number.


'I want to report a real-estate fraud,' Quinn told the bored desk officer at the precinct house on the Upper East Side.

'Go ahead,' said the cop, not looking up from his crossword puzzle.

'I gave someone three months advance rent on a sublet and they've absconded with my money.'

'What's a seven letter word starting with "h" that means terrible?'

'Heinous.'

'Was it a legal sublet?'

'No.'

'How about this one then . . . eight letters, ending in "ry" meaning alone.'

'Solitary. Look, a crime has been committed against me. This person took all my money and just . . . vanished.'

'Sublet, eh?' The cop put his pen down and leaned over to get a better view of Quinn.

'Six letters, starts with "s". I had no choice. I was desperate. Do you have any idea how difficult it is to find an apartment in this city?'

'Giving your money to complete strangers is asking for trouble,' the cop said. 'I'm telling you that for free.'

'Like I said –'

'Everybody wants to live in goddamned Manhattan,' the cop went on. 'You move to Queens, you wouldn't have this problem.'

'What can I do to get my money back?'

'You know where this person lives? Send around a big pal with a baseball bat, although you didn't hear that from me.'

'And if I don't know?'

'Eat it.' The cop shrugged. 'You got taken.'


Quinn called Molly in Las Vegas.

'Me darling boy,' she shouted over the roar of the one-armed bandits.

'Hey, Molly, bad news I'm afraid.'

'What's bad? The sun is shining. I'm working on my tan.'

'Don't work on your tan, Moll, you're gonna die of skin cancer.'

'Cancer, schmancer, I want to look good. I bought a gold lamé pantsuit. It needs a tan to set it off.'

'The Irish don't tan, it's against our religion.'

'Then when are you coming down to visit me, boy? We'll go out on the town and have a few laughs.'

The last time Quinn went out with Molly, the evening had turned into a marathon bar crawl and brain-cell massacre. They had ended up in Times Square where his grandmother tipsily tap danced her rendition of 'Thoroughly Modern Millie' in front of a bunch of bemused tourists from Reykjavik. He still shuddered at the memory.

'Moll, I lost your money.'

'Blackjack or roulette.' Molly was under the impression that Quinn gambled, which was one of the reasons she sent him money. Quinn, who didn't want to disappoint her, had let her believe it.

'I was conned.'

There was silence on the end of the line. 'Conned?' Molly repeated, puzzled. Let down.

'It was clever con,' Quinn said defensively.

'Well, that's what happens when you go to university.' Molly distrusted universities, she saw them as the enemies of common sense.

'Moll, I wouldn't ask if I weren't desperate . . .'

'You want me to arrange somebody to go to this person and collect?' Molly asked eagerly.

'You know someone who could do that?'

'Sure. It's a very mixed community here and hoodlums have to retire too, you know.'

'Don't worry, the money's long gone. But I'm kinda short now . . . I'm staying with Malcolm and he wants me out of the picture. There's a girl – it's a long story.'

'Malcolm has a girlfriend?' Molly's tone was curt with disbelief. Quinn debated whether to tell her it was Rhonda. Decided no. Molly already thought he was an idiot.

'Yeah, he's very happy and not interested in having me hanging about.'

'I wish you'd called me yesterday,' Molly said. 'I just spent a grand on the lamé trouser suit.'

'You what?'

'Everybody's wearing them. This is Vegas, you look outta place if you don't glitter a little. And then I dropped a couple a G's at the tables last night. Don't know what happened, I don't usually lose so much, I think it was the pink squirrels. Anyway I'm a bit strapped for the rest of the week. Johnny's gone to LA to look at some project. I don't have anything lying around, I'm afraid.'

'It's okay,' Quinn said. 'It was nice talking to you.' He suddenly had an image of how pathetic this picture was – a grown man trying to borrow from his grandmother. It was time he grew up. Took responsibility for his own life. He hung up the phone.


Mal and Rhonda were either practising Tae Bo or having noisy sex when Quinn returned that evening.

He tried to turn on the television to drown out their ecstatic cries but it was impossible. He watched a few minutes of the news very loud. He recognized the reporter from the crowd gathered on Sixth Avenue. Jesus, he thought, body parts in supermarkets. What will they think of next?

# Chapter Thirty-Nine

Lucretia DeSalle was an Englishwoman with a mid-Atlantic accent who described herself as a fashion historian. She was probably in her sixties, Renee estimated. She was dressed entirely in purple and green and wore a French hunting hat with a two-foot-long feather arching proudly from the top. Her office was the top floor of a loft in the meat-packing district and was decorated in brocade- and velvet-covered furniture, oversized and overstuffed. It looked like a Wild West bordello, except for the treadmill in the corner upon which Lucretia was striding briskly. Even her running shoes were purple.

'The Americans were the only ones with the money after the war, darling. Europe was on its knees, but the Americans bounded over to the Parisian salons and bought everything.'

'This dress was sold in 1961,' Renee said. 'It showed in 1947.' She handed Lucretia the photocopy and the sketch. Lucretia pulled her glasses from a voluminous fold in her shirt and inspected the page, her face lighting up in recognition.

'Gorgeous, isn't it?' she murmured. 'These days designers try to shock with tricky effects and see-through designs, and people are so bored, they've seen everything. But that! One of the most shocking statements ever made in fashion and only because of the sheer amount of material used. Twenty-five metres, some of them were. An outrage after what everybody had gone through. Women even picketed on the streets.'

'Do you know what happened to it?'

'The notion of collecting couture didn't really exist then like it does today. But I read about that auction once. I think – I'm almost certain in fact – that Nathan Reynolds bought them all. He had a shop.'

'Where can I find him?'

'He's dead, darling. AIDS. One of the first to go. But he passed the business onto his son, Sean. He still runs a shop out in the Hamptons. Begin Again, it's called. The most exquisite antique couture.'

Renee called directory enquiries when she got back to her studio and dialled the number they gave her for Begin Again. There was no reply. She put it aside. She had work to get on with. Cat's career wasn't the only one that mattered.


Cyrus couldn't resist watching a couple of hours of television, even though he had promised himself that he would crack his new book. He'd bought *Remembrance of Things Past*. He'd always meant to read it. He'd opened it to page one, but the lure of the remote control had proved too strong.

He made coffee while he watched.

The kettle boiled and he poured water over his

coffee grounds, sniffing them as he did so. He loved the smell of coffee, it was more seductive than any French fragrance. But, as he sniffed, he discovered another note, stickier. He left the coffee and moved around the apartment. The smell seemed to get stronger in the bedroom. He went through to the back rooms. It was in here. It hit him like a heat wave. Sick and sweet, like meat gone bad.

He knew what had happened. He crossed to the big freezer and opened the door. The smell of death came rushing out, almost pushing him off his feet.

Now he knew how it was possible to go from the heights of elation to the depths of despair in seconds. Cyrus wailed and banged his fist on the freezer. He didn't care that he was acting like a spoilt kid, it was how he felt. His perfect plans had been ruined by a stupid door. He hadn't shut the door properly because the freezer had been too full. And because he hadn't been back there in a while, he hadn't noticed it was standing open.

Now he had to ditch the stuff and fast – how the hell was he going to do that? He had no idea. He needed time to think, and time was the one luxury now denied him.

He kicked the freezer. Betrayed by an appliance. Of all the dumb, stupid luck.


Tye went for a swim and massage at an expensive club on Madison Avenue. She had always loved water – some of her fondest childhood memories were from family holidays on the Costa del Sol. Tye's father would discuss business in the hotel with men with thick East End accents while she frolicked in the pool or at the beach – the pampered child.

She swam evenly up and down the pool for nearly an hour. When she got out her limbs were tired and heavy but her mind felt fresh. She suddenly thought of Adrian and wondered how he was getting on. On impulse she used the poolside phone to call a surgical supply company and have twelve surgical trusses sent to his apartment.

'Miss Fisher? Are you ready for your massage?' A young man in grey held up a towelling robe, making sure he looked at her eyes and not her legs.

'Why, yes, thank you. I believe I am.' Tye smiled sweetly and gathered up her things. She had a date with Dickie tonight. She was going to hold him to his suggestion of a screen test, or whatever it was one did to get into the movies these days. Life was budding with opportunities.


Catrina Vermont had a long and frustrating day. The cops weren't giving out any information about the identity of the victim until the next of kin had been notified so she was faced with another morning of doing live shots in which she and the anchors traded banalities. It was not riveting television, she knew that. But it was face time. Maybe somebody was watching. An emissary from another galaxy perhaps. One with intelligent life.

'If you can hear me on the planet Zortaan,' she said as the sound man tested the IFB. 'Come down right now. There'll never be a better time.' Peter Ratch, hearing her, curled his lip as though her humour was too puerile for words. Another reason she was in a bad mood all the time, Cat thought. She was surrounded by enemies.

Of course, there were rumours about the body part – Satanic sacrifice, paedophile rings, Islamic fundamentalists, white slavery, although how anybody could be sold into slavery without their leg Cat wasn't quite sure. She resisted each and every attempt by Eric Atlas to include hearsay in her reports. Things were bad enough without her spouting half-heard rumours like they were fact. The man really was an idiot, she thought angrily. Some days she could laugh at him but not today – she'd had too little sleep. She'd tried to call Renee a couple of times but she wasn't at the office. Out pursuing her hot lead, no doubt. Cat shook her head. Now that she'd thought about it, it really did seem like wishful thinking. Renee thought everything could be explained by clothes. At first Cat had assumed this was a defence she'd built against waking up one day and discovering – shock – she'd devoted her professional life to something that didn't matter. But then she realized that to Renee it mattered very much. Renee routinely read *Women's Wear Daily* before the *Times*, she devoured all the fashion mags, even the ones written in languages she didn't read. The only places she ever wanted to go on vacation were Milan and Paris. She had a wardrobe the size of Arizona. No, Cat wasn't going to say anything to Renee, but she was convinced the dress angle would not come to anything, even if she were right about its origins. It was just too long a shot.

Her phone rang.

'It's Atlas.' Automatically Cat reached for the spot between her finger and thumb. Pressed it hard.

'What?' she snapped. 'I'm on air in two minutes.'

'Cops are going to ID the guy, want you to throw live to the press conference.' He slammed the phone down.

'Thanks for the heads-up,' Cat said wearily. She'd have to wing it again, like she always did. No information, no facts. Blithely spouting ignorance to an ignorant public. God, was this any way to earn a living?

Cyrus taped the door shut. The bodies would be frozen again in a matter of hours, but he had to get rid of them. The smell was terrible. He opened the windows and got some disinfectant from the kitchen and scrubbed the floors. They weren't dirty, but the smell of bleach helped to disguise the odour of decomposing meat. The work slowed his racing mind down. By the time he'd finished, he had the answer.

He dialled the garage where his father kept his car, told them to have it ready for him that evening.

# Chapter Forty

The Tribeca restaurant that Dickie took Tye to was striving for the French effect with maps of the Paris Metro on the wall and tourist pictures of the Eiffel Tower. Dickie waved to several people as he guided Tye to her seat. 'Movie types,' he said in her ear.

It was bog standard bistro fare, the prices high. Tye shrugged. Dickie would probably pay and even if he didn't, tonight she could afford it. She decided to have a steak. Swimming had made her hungry. Dickie ordered a bottle of Krug, leant back and lit a cigarette. 'You really are made for the camera,' he said idly, surveying her through cigarette smoke.

Tye smiled, tilting her chin slightly. She was wearing a black low-cut sheath dress with a jet necklace. Her hair was piled up on top of her head. She'd taken more care with her make-up than normal, and she was glowing from her swim and massage. Tonight, she wanted Dickie to see her at her best.

'Are you ever out in LA?'

'I could be,' Tye murmured. She hoped she sounded non-committal.

'You must try and make it. Meet some casting directors. Did you say you were taking acting lessons?'

Tye shrugged. She hadn't, but she practised deception every day, just not in the way that Dickie thought.

'Not that it matters in this country. Hollywood is not exactly the RSC.' Dickie drank his champagne, eyes scanning the room. 'This project that I'm working on at the moment – there might be a part . . .' he trailed off.

Tye matched his casual manner although her heart was beating faster.

'Really?' she said after a suitable pause.

'It's small . . . but a good part. You'd be noticed.'

'It's always nice to be noticed.'

The waiter came to take their orders. Tye chatted with him, barely able to conceal her elation. She realized this was what she'd been preparing for all her life. The chance to act. Acting – even the sound of the word thrilled her. She was made for it. She loved to dress up and pretend she was somebody else. Wasn't that just what acting was? She loved to get paid vast sums of money for very little work. She could see herself with a bungalow in Malibu, cool colours and sharp design. Perhaps a cook and a pool. Driving to the studio in her convertible. Why not? Why not her?

'There's just one thing,' Dickie said as he refilled their glasses. 'A small favour I'd like to ask in return.'

Cyrus put most of the body parts in garbage bags, packed ice around them and sealed them inside another bag, then put them in the trunk of his father's Mercedes. He drove out of the city. All the news radio stations were talking about him, which made him happy. He had done it. He'd become the person he wanted to be, and without the help of some sicko shrink. He'd done it all by himself.

The big vehicle made almost no noise as he drove through the Bronx. The cream 1965 Mercedes sports car was his father's real child. It was much-admired but seldom driven – if his father wanted to make a long trip he took a rental, which seemed stupid to Cyrus. It had a big engine, why not drive it? But his father was fussy. Actually, his father was fussy to the point of being deranged, but that was another story. No concern of Cyrus's any more. He was free of all their mind games.

The drive took a little over an hour. It was dark when he arrived at his destination and there was nobody else around. He unloaded the bags, a shovel and a flashlight, and walked into the wood. It was hard work, the bags heavy and awkward. He had to stop every few yards to rest.

The air smelt of pine. He breathed deeply as he walked. Listening for someone but knowing really that he was quite alone. He found the spot he was searching for by following the clearly laid-out trail markers. He'd done this walk a couple of times before, years ago, but nothing much had changed. The trail followed a river, but it peeled off along the side of a steep hill. There was a bank maybe thirty feet high. Cyrus threw the bags down the bank and then slid after them. It was a rough fall; he was bruised and scratched when he reached the bottom and the bags were ripped in places, but nothing had fallen out – and the spot was perfect. Nobody would come down here.

He put the flashlight up on a tree stump and started digging.

The earth was hard and Cyrus quickly worked up a sweat. He didn't intend to dig too deep – a couple of feet or so at most. Winter and wild animals would take care of the rest.

When all of the body parts were below ground except for one, he scrambled back up the steep hill. He drove home stopping just once to leave off the last of the contents of the bag. That would give the jackals of the news media a metaphor to fight over.


'Twenty grand?' Tye said, wondering if she'd heard it correctly.

'Don't bother about it, dear girl, if it's going to put you in a spot.' Dickie smoked a cigarette while Tye pretended to contemplate her steak. Actually she was doing sums in her head. Twenty thousand dollars. Could she afford to lend that sum to Dickie? Why was he even asking, when he was loaded?

'It's just till Friday, when pater's cheque arrives,' Dickie said. 'I need it to clinch a deal – a very hot script that is going to make my name. I've been sweet-talking the writer for a week. Thought we had agreed on the price, but he's gone and stiffed me. A bidding war has developed – well, more of a bidding skirmish but I have to up my price if I'm going to stay in the game.'

'Can't the writer wait?'

'He wants it yesterday,' Dickie said. 'And the other company is prepared to step in with the readies. I'm

really in a bind, dear girl. Otherwise I wouldn't ask.'
Dickie took a drink of champagne. 'I know, why don't
I pay you for the loan – how does a producer credit
sound? You can even leave some money in, if you like
the sound of the project.'

It sounded good to Tye.

'If it's just till Friday.' She smiled. Dickie smiled
lazily back. 'Midday, dear girl. Not one second later.
Pater's very reliable, God bless him.'


Martin Brookner was driving home from work on the
Taconic Parkway dreading the dinner party he and his
wife were hosting. The Marches were dull people: he
was a belligerent bore who talked constantly about his
investments, and she drank too much. The two things
were probably related, Martin reflected as he edged his
Lexus over the speed limit. More than ten minutes
with the guy and he usually wanted to hit himself over
the head with a whisky bottle – anything to stop the
incessant stream of words that flowed from March's
self-satisfied mouth. If it were up to Martin he would
have crossed the street to avoid them. But they were
neighbours and his wife, who was from Texas, had old-
fashioned ideas about hospitality. Three months ago
the Marches had invited them over to a room filled
with smug new money. Martin had vowed never again,
but Karol had talked him around. They're neighbours,
she said. It's one night of the year.

That night was tonight.

Martin was so deep in thought that he didn't notice
the obstacle on the road until it was too late to avoid it.

He swerved but nicked the side of it. There was an ominous thump and the car skidded. What looked like a log was lying right there. Shaken, Martin pulled over onto the shoulder. His collision with whatever it was had pushed it further out into the lane. He ought to move it, or there'd be an accident. He walked back towards it. Traffic streamed past, glaring and noisy. Martin checked his watch. He was now officially late. Ted March would be sitting in his living room, clutching his low-cal beer yammering about hedge funds and Latvian high-yield bonds. Karol would be smiling, poised and charming, distributing tricky little canapés. Ted March would be casting sly, lustful glances at Karol. Perhaps that was the reason he didn't like Ted, Martin thought. Maybe it was just one of those instinctive things you feel when you know another man has mentally undressed your wife.

He checked to see there was no traffic about to mow him down and then reached out to move the branch from the road and realized it wasn't a branch. He prodded it with his foot. It was soft to the touch. He flipped it over, bent closer to look and then stepped back in horror.

The 'branch' was a human thigh. He could see the femur protruding from one end. The flesh had been gnawed at, or perhaps that was where Martin had hit it. The phosphorescent lights gave it a green pallor. And it smelt terrible.

'Jesus Christ!' The bile rose in his throat.

Martin sprinted back to the car to get his cellphone.

# Chapter Forty-One

Catrina was thanking God for under-eye concealer cream when Max the editor barged in.

'How many times have I told you?' she said gently, taking him by the shoulders. 'This is the little girls' room. That means girls, not boys. Not even strung-out ones.'

'Another piece of meat,' Max said.

'No, Max. You're much more than that to me.'

'The Meat Man, he's put a thigh on the highway.'

Catrina involuntarily rubbed her eye, smudging her mascara. 'Shit,' she said. 'Where?'

'The Taconic. Press conference, this morning.' Three years of night shifts had robbed Max of the ability to speak in complete sentences.

The bathroom door opened and a gazelle-like young woman stepped tentatively in. She stopped when she saw Max and Cat. 'Oh, sorry,' she said.

'It's okay. This is what passes for the morning meeting on the graveyard shift,' Cat said, smiling at her. She didn't recognize her, but interns came and went pretty quickly.

'Angie, new intern,' Max said. Cat shook her hand. Angie's was sweating. 'Angie's with you today.'

Cat punched Max on the arm. 'You used a complete sentence. Well done, Max.'

'Smartass,' Max said. 'Get out there.'

'And another. Is there no end to this man's accomplishments?' Cat snapped her make-up bag closed. 'Welcome to oblivion,' she said to Angie.

'The body part found on the Taconic has been identified as that of James George Neidermeyer, twenty-four years old from Lansing, Michigan,' said the Police Commissioner, reading from a prepared statement. 'His wife, twenty-four-year-old Susan Jordan Neidermeyer, is still missing. Also missing is Anna Kinkel, from Frankfurt, Germany. We are pursuing every avenue of investigation.' There was an explosion of flash bulbs and a wall of shouted questions. Cat scribbled some notes for her live shot. Angie scampered along beside her, breathless and impressed.

'Eric hired me,' she said.

'I can tell, honey.'

'How?'

'We only get the babes now. No offence or anything.'

'Well, I – I kinda blew it.'

'Why? You wouldn't put out?'

'Well . . .' Angie blushed again.

'Kid, you wanna know something for free?'

'Ah . . . sure.'

'This is a shitty way to earn a living. Do something else. Do anything else, but not television news. It's demeaning, much too hard on your social life

275

and these days it's just plain stupid. You're clever, right?'

'I guess.'

'Then run far, run fast. Now I gotta go. Live shots wait for no man and very few women.'

'But I—'

'See you out front.'


'James and Susan Neidermeyer came to New York in search of work. He was killed just days after they arrived. Police fear that his young wife may also be dead, along with a German student Anna Kinkel. The apparently motiveless crimes have shocked the city and led to a huge drop in frozen food sales. Back to you in the studio, Ken.'

For once, there were no stupid questions to answer. Cat breathed deeply. No matter how many live shots she did, they always made her nervous. People, passers by, always stared and she hated that. Angie was hanging around, clutching a clipboard, trying to look like she belonged. Cat went to the truck and took a sip of cold coffee from her cup which was perched on the dashboard. Her producer, as usual, was nowhere to be found. Angie came scampering up.

'I got in trouble with Eric last week,' she said. Cat closed her eyes for a moment. She didn't want to hear about this child's problems. She had more than enough of her own. She worked in television and she was getting old.

'Don't worry about it, everybody does.' Cat forced a cheerful smile.

'But I need at least three internships on my résumé and now I'm worried he won't give me a good reference.'

'Eric Atlas has the attention span of a table lamp. Whatever you did, he's already forgotten, trust me.' This wasn't true; the vindictive little slimebag never forgot a slight, no matter how small, but Angie didn't need to know.

'The thing is, I didn't know what I was supposed to do. This woman came to the office and I thought she was there to see him. So I brought her into the newsroom. And she wasn't there to see him. He got mad.'

Cat pinched her hand. Her perpetual headache was getting harder to ignore.

'Look, I'd love to discuss this now but . . .'

'It's such an unusual name, don't you think?'

'Excuse me?' Cat wondered if Max had slipped Angie some of his stay-awake pills.

'Neidermeyer. That's why I remembered it.'

Somehow, the penny started to drop through the early morning caffeine fog.

'You . . . ?'

'She came to the office last week. She said she had a news story. Eric bawled me out for bringing her into the newsroom and then he talked to her but we didn't do a story. Her name was Marion Neidermeyer.'

'And Eric passed on it?'

'I guess. He took her into his office but she didn't stay long. I guess she was his mother – is his mother. That dead guy's mother.'

Angie was twisting her ice-blonde hair, nervously stepping from foot to foot.

'Not much good, I guess. We don't know how to get hold of her or anything.'

'No we don't,' Cat said, 'but we can find out.'

The door bell rang annoyingly. Quinn had just sat down at his computer. He'd written a few phrases several times, rearranged the words of a single sentence but was no closer to inspiration. He decided to ignore the bell. He wanted to make a serious attempt to concentrate on his work. He drew a deep breath to calm himself, open himself up to the creative flow. He started to type.

Bzzzz.

He was going to ignore it. This was his time. He had decided to set aside some gold-plated writing time every day. If he was going to get anything out of this apartment disaster, at least it would inform his work.

He erased the words he'd written. That first sentence was so important. He had to get it right.

Bzzzzz, bzzzz.

Quinn decided to change from the first person to the third. Give himself a little space. He erased the first sentence and started again.

Bzzzz, bzzz, bzzzz.

'All right.' Quinn jumped up. 'Jesus Mary, is it not possible to get any work done around here?'

He looked in the monitor. Squinted, looked again. Could it really be her? With a sinking heart he pressed the button to allow his guest in.

# Chapter Forty-Two

A doctor had given Marion sedatives to go. A whole bottle of them. She had taken the prescribed number. She was sedate now, she supposed.

She had returned to her room at the hostel, that unfamiliar place that had become part of her life, because she didn't have the strength to think yet about going back home. Or what she should do about arranging a funeral.

John Abruzzo had visited her that morning and told her what the cops were doing. She could do a press conference if she wanted; sometimes it helped. She shook her head. What did it matter? It wouldn't bring her Gus back.

John nodded. It wasn't necessary, he said. Some people did it, some didn't. He sat on the side of the bed with her, asked her if she was okay and she'd told him yes. She couldn't share this time. She didn't know what to do with it, but she knew she couldn't share it.

Now, an hour or so later, she was still in the position he had left her in. Shoes off, sitting on the side of her carefully made bed. Back straight, shoulders back. Hands clasped in her lap. Contained. Wondering when this state of mind would end and what she would do when it did.

She had put the bottle of pills on the bureau, next to the photo of Gus and Susie.

Marion had worn blue. She had worn blue as she walked down the aisle on her son's wedding day. There had been blue in the flowers, in the cornflowers and irises that dotted the church, and in her son's tie. They'd taken so much care to get every little detail right. It hadn't been easy on a tight budget, but friends pitched in. It was a rite of passage, for her as well as for Gus and Susie. Everybody had wanted it to go well.

The sky had been blue, too. A sunny day. A good omen. And all her friends and her children's friends had come. Everybody except Charles, who had phoned the day before with a mumbled excuse. They were secretly glad about that because they knew he'd only bring his trashy wife, get tight and say something offensive.

The one thing that had marred the day was Marion finding out that, against her specific orders, the twins had had their navels pierced. She noticed the silver rings through the thin fabric of their summer dresses just as they were about to leave for the church. She'd been furious, they'd been surly. But Gus had laughed and teased them until they couldn't be angry at each other. Gus the peacemaker. The go-between. Always smoothing the way between the prickly female members of the family. What would happen to them now that he wasn't there?

The pills had a careful warning about not exceeding

the prescribed dose, and staying away from heavy machinery. Even though she didn't have her glasses on Marion could read the label by squinting and guessing what the shapes of the words meant. She tried to focus on it, tried to think the worst thing that could happen to her now would be to be caught drugged out and driving a forklift.

But it was no use. The sharp pain of her grief pierced her pharmaceutical haze. Made her brutally lucid. Showed her things about herself she had kept carefully hidden.

She went to the bathroom and ran the faucet. The water smelled of chlorine. She splashed her face, then patted it dry with a paper tissue.

She got out the bottle of vodka she had bought that morning.

She was thinking clearly. Scarily so. All of the superfluous clutter had sloughed off and she saw herself in a stark, new light.

Mothers don't have favourites, everybody knows. Love isn't divisible. Good moms love their kids individually and equally.

But if that were true, why did she feel as though her life had ended? And why did she now see down into the fetid depths of her grimy little soul and know that she wished it was any of her kids except Gus? How could she even think those vile, vile thoughts?

'The heart is deceitful above all things and desperately wicked – who can know it?' Marion said the words of the Old Testament prophet out loud as she studied her reflection in the speckled mirror. Her father – Gus's granddad – had been a fire-and-brimstone preacher. She knew a lot of verses from the Bible.

Who can know it? But she knew it, for sure. And she wished she didn't. Her father liked to preach about how God demanded sacrifices – how Abraham would have killed his son, Isaac, except God stayed his hand. Marion knew what she would have told God if He'd demanded such a stupid thing – nothing doing, Buster. I'll fry in Hell for eternity – gladly – before I give up my child. Take somebody else's. Take anybody but my boy.

Perhaps she was being punished for loving him too much. Perhaps there was a nasty, mean-spirited little God who really did think like that.

Marion went back to the bed and sat down. She opened the child-proof cap on the pill bottle and screwed the top off the vodka and sniffed it gingerly, even though she knew it had no smell.

She hadn't touched hard liquor for years, not since one drunken binge at college. She'd thrown up afterwards and had felt as though her stomach would never recover. But it didn't need to recover this time.

She took a quick swig of the vodka, her mouth pursed in distaste. Then she shook a handful of the pills into her palm. She took a bigger swig of vodka, held it in her mouth before swallowing. It was worse than mouthwash.

She hated taking pills. Usually she preferred to crunch them up, take them in honey or something, but that wouldn't work. The object was to get as many down as quickly as possible.

Besides, no one ever said killing yourself was supposed to be fun.

She popped five of the pills and washed them down with the liquor. She felt like crying. She squeezed a couple of tears out as she took six pills this time. The vodka part was getting easier. Her head felt light, as though she was coming down with the flu.

She tipped more pills into her hand, spilling some this time because she was half crying and shaking. They scattered on the floor. But she couldn't stop to pick them up. She had to get the rest down fast. She jammed a whole bunch in her mouth. The taste was acrid. She pushed them in with her hands and swilled more vodka.

Who would find her? She realized she didn't even know what happened when you died from pills. Did you throw up? Or lose control of your bowels? Would they find her in her own vomit? She hoped there wouldn't be a mess. She didn't want someone to have to clean up after her.

Too late to stop now. She forced some more pills down. Some were stuck in her throat. She was near the end of the bottle and the room was shimmering and spinning.

Only five pills to go. She crunched them and washed them down. Then she lay back on the bed, her head on the pillow.

Not long now.

# Chapter Forty-Three

'Molly.' Quinn stooped to kiss his grandmother on both cheeks. She was five feet tall in high heels. 'So good to see you. What did I do to deserve this honour?'

'Don't be a flaming eedjit, you know what you did,' his grandmother said. 'Make me a cuppa. I'm parched.'

She threw her handbags on the sofa and rearranged the folds of her dress before sitting down, wiping her forehead dramatically.

'What happened to Vegas?' Quinn asked as he sorted cups, tea and rustled around in the cupboard for cookies. Molly had the appetite of a linebacker.

'You're in trouble. I'm here to sort it out.'

'I'm not in trouble.'

'So my money just disappeared all by itself?' Molly glared at her grandson. 'Now tell me exactly what happened.'


Molly had drunk three cups of tea by the time Quinn had finished. She'd also taken copious notes on a stenographer's notepad and her blue eyes had narrowed to slits. Her hair was dyed candy pink which gave her the look of a malevolent doll.

'I'm sorry, Moll,' he said.

'Too late for sorry.' She snorted, got up and paced the room. 'It's time for revenge. There's the family honour to think about.'

'We're not the Mafia, Molly. We don't have any family honour.'

'We do now. And I'm here to protect it.'

Quinn laughed. He thought she was joking. But Molly silenced him with a wave of her hand.

'We're going to find the woman who robbed you,' she said. 'And then we're going to make her pay you back. If she refuses, we're gonna send around some friends to rearrange her bone structure.'

Quinn had always been proud of Molly's mental acuity, but now he feared that she was losing it. 'Moll, none of our friends would know how to do that,' he said gently.

'Speak for yourself,' Molly said tartly. 'I got contacts.'

'Do you think it's wise to—'

Molly crossed the room in a trice, grabbed Quinn by the chin and forced him to look up at her. 'Have some pride. Have some passion!' she commanded roughly. 'Remember, the Irish never forget!'

'And look where it's got us.'

'Don't argue with me, boy. I'm right on this one. Old Molly's going to teach you a lesson about life.'

Quinn very much doubted that. He made a note to call Molly's husband and ask if she was on any medication that might be toying with her sanity.

'How would that be, Moll?'

'First things first. We're gonna find this vixen. And we're gonna deal her a lesson.'

Quinn sighed. What Molly was really doing was wasting his work time. Maybe this morning he could have written something. A page at least. He couldn't stay blocked all his life. It was going to end any day now, it had to. 'The money's gone, Moll. I'm sorry. I'll pay you back.'

'How?'

'I'm going to get a job.'

Molly acted like she hadn't heard him. 'We're gonna find her,' she repeated. 'And I know exactly how we're gonna do it. Now shut up and listen.'

Cyrus had a calendar from the Museum of Modern Art and was marking off the exhibits he planned to catch in the next couple of months. He'd just become a member, which meant he could go to the museum whenever he wanted for free – and that included movies and special lectures. He hadn't been to a museum for years, there were lots of things he'd missed out on.

The television was on while he looked over the schedule and, of course, they were talking about him. Every so often he would hear an adjective that he liked and he'd write it in the margin of his calendar. Sometimes he was able to match them alphabetically so there was ruthless next to Rothko, killer next to Klee, brutal next to Braque and so on. He studied it closely when he'd finished. It was kind of cool and it set him to thinking: how had the great artists found their inspiration? Probably not the same way he had, but then you never knew. Maybe it was the big secret of the art world – in order to create, one first had to destroy – like a yin and yang kind of thing. Well, why not?

He pinned the calendar on the corkboard in the kitchen and stepped back to admire it. He must have been really concentrating on what he was doing, because he didn't hear the sirens and the alarms. It wasn't until the knock on his door that he realized anything was out of the ordinary.

Normally Cat didn't bother to try and get Peter Ratch to do his job because it was more hassle than it was worth. Peter Ratch was a protégé of Eric Atlas. He was putting in his obligatory six months on the early shift before being elevated to a job where he didn't need three alarm clocks to get him up in the morning. But Peter had better contacts with the cops than she did, mainly because he'd slept with so many of them. And she knew that if she appealed to his self-interest, she could get what she wanted. So she went and dug him out of the corner where he was making personal calls, which was how he spent most of his time on the job. He finished the conversation, making her wait.

'What's up?' He didn't bother to look apologetic.

Cat had written Marion's name on a piece of paper. She handed it to Peter. 'Here's your ticket off the graveyard shift. She's in New York.'

\*

Peter could move fast when it suited him. In half an hour he had the name of a hostel in Chelsea. Cat took a crew and drove over.

'Park around the corner,' Cat said. 'I'll go in first.'

'I'm coming too,' Peter insisted.

'No. She's already had one bad experience with our station, in the form of our glorious leader. I'm going to have to repair a few bridges.' Cat stared him down. He shrugged and sat back in his seat.

'You're coming, though,' Cat said to Angie.

'Why her?' Peter Ratch whined.

'Familiar face.'

'Fucking ball-buster,' he muttered under his breath, but he was already getting out his cellphone.

'I'm here to see Marion Neidermeyer,' Cat told the man on the front desk. Angie looked nervously around. 'Can you tell me what room she's in?'

'Sure, but I don't think she's receiving visitors.'

'Can I call her?'

Mike Schwab regarded the glamorous pair standing in front of him. It wasn't every day women like that came in here. The older one – he recognized her from the TV but couldn't remember her name – looked like she was used to getting what she wanted, but Mike had seen too much of life to be impressed by people like that.

'I'll call her.' He dialled Marion's room.

The phone rang and rang. The two women waited patiently. The younger, skinny one shifted from foot to foot, her big-heeled shoes making a hollow sound on the stone floor.

'Is she in?' Cat asked. Mike nodded.

'Maybe she's asleep.'

'That phone would wake the dead,' he said.

Jim came back from getting coffee.

'I'm going up to check on Marion.' Mike grabbed the master keys. Cat and Angie followed him to the elevator.

# Chapter Forty-Four

J. J. found the severed hand in the trash outside a nail salon on Madison. He was in the habit of swinging by each night after the salon closed and sorting patiently through the plastic sacks to find the soda cans. There were usually ten or twelve; the girls at the salon sure did like their cola. The number of cans made J. J. wonder if they bathed in it, like Cleopatra. Or perhaps they were using it in one of their beauty treatments. Who knew what these rich white ladies got up to?

J. J. had had a good week. He'd found a place to stay just in time for winter. No more freezing in a doorway like last year. He had shelter and a place to eat. And he made a little extra cash collecting cans.

At first, he thought the hand was one of those plastic gloves. It sure felt like it at first, the rubbery texture. But this was stiff and cold. He drew away instinctively, not wanting to know, even though after you'd sorted through folks' trash you got to where there wasn't much that could surprise you. J. J. had learnt a lot of things the years he'd been on the street. But this was different. It felt bad – it had a creepy vibe. J. J.'s instinct was to bundle his stuff up and walk away fast. He collected up his cans and shuffled off down the street. But before he got half a block, he stopped. Turned. Went back. He felt constricted in his chest, like he was about to burst out crying. He slowly untied the neck of the sack and the feeling got strong. He could hardly breathe. He had a stick that he sometimes used to poke things around, so as he wouldn't have to touch them. He got it out of the side pocket of his pants, removing the masking tape that kept it and his broken side-seams in place.

He gently lay the sack down on its side and teased the contents out. Coffee cups, half-eaten sandwiches, tissues, empty bottles of nail polish. Junk.

The thing was last. J. J. had to reach in to get it. It was heavy, the dowling rod bent and almost broke when he tried to pry it out. But it came, eventually. J. J. stared at it for a long time, wondering. He'd seen a lot of bad things in his time – he was fifty-five, at least as far as he could remember – but this hand, black at the edges, was different. It looked like a woman's hand. There was a slender gold ring on the wedding finger, and the nails were varnished.

J. J. was wondering what to do next when a cop car pulled up. A fat guy behind the wheel rolled down the window and yelled, 'Take a hike.' J. J. sat there mutely.

'You heard me, buddy. Clean up your shit and go.'

Still J. J. didn't reply. There were words, he knew, for this situation. To alert the cops to what he had found. But he couldn't think what they were and even if he could, his vocal chords were paralysed.

The cop turned off his engine and he and his partner, a young woman, got out. J. J., who was sitting on the pavement, scuttled backwards. Over the years he'd learned to move fast from any position. The cops hadn't noticed the hand yet; they were looking at J. J. They were seeing a poor guy who hadn't washed in weeks sitting surrounded by trash. On Madison. It violated the natural order. New York didn't stand for this now that it was cleaned up. Give me your poor, huddled masses and we'll drive them out of town.

'Buddy, move it.' The fat cop's hand hovered near his night stick. J. J. inched back a couple more inches. He was jammed up against the store shutters, nowhere else for him to go. The cops were on the sidewalk. The woman slightly behind the guy. Any minute now they were going to step on it because they weren't watching where they were going. J. J. lifted his arms, an instinctive gesture of surrender.

'Jones.' It was the woman. She'd seen it. Mouth popping open. 'Oh, my God, look!'


Mike Schwab didn't need his key for Marion's room. It was unlocked. He went in gingerly after he'd knocked and called her name.

Marion was lying on the bed, hands folded. Her shoes were off but she was fully dressed. Her skin was a white and dense and her eyes were closed.

The woman got past him somehow. Reached for Marion's pulse in her neck and wrist. Couldn't find it in either place.

Angie dropped to the floor. 'Look at these.' She held up a couple of pills and an empty bottle.

Cat found her compact and held it up to Marion's

face. There was a faint tracing of condensation on the mirror. 'Call an ambulance.'

Mike bolted out the door.

'What do we do?' Angie said.

'We wait.'

'Shouldn't we like try to wake her up or give her coffee or something?'

Cat searched Marion's neck for a pulse. She found it, but it was feeble. She was angry with herself for not knowing what to do.

'My father's a doctor,' Angie said.

'Do you know what to do?'

'No, he only, like, told me that if somebody falls down dead in front of you, then you, like, bang them hard on the chest to get their heart started. Other times he says it's best just to wait for like the experts.'

'Then that's what we'll do.' Cat gripped Marion's hand as if by doing so she could pull her back from wherever she was.

At last, she heard the sound of running and shouting.

Help was on its way.


'It's the only way we're going to find her.' Molly had the *Village Voice* spread out on her knees, and was marking ads with a large red pen. 'She's going to strike again. You won't be the only one.'

Quinn had called the *Voice* to report the fraud but had got a bored, indifferent employee who had told him that they were not responsible for anything, ever. The city was in league against him. Perhaps it was time to move to Austin, Texas. A number of his college classmates already had.

But Molly made him persevere. He had arranged to see three sublets that day.

'She's out there,' Molly said, after they'd visited them all. 'I can smell her.'

'She's probably resting,' Quinn said, weary. Desperate for a beer.

'She's greedy, she'll try again. I know her type.'

Quinn was about to ask how, but stopped. Best not go down that road.

'I won't even recognize her,' he said. 'She must use a disguise.'

'Trust your gut, boy.' Molly rapped him sharply in the stomach. 'Haven't I taught you anything? University. Huh!'

Quinn had an idea. He dialled Juliana Franklin's number again.


'Thank God, you—' Cat stopped. It wasn't the cavalry. It was Peter Ratch followed by the film crew. And the camera's record light was on.

'Spray the room,' Peter told the cameraman.

'What the hell are you doing?'

'The guy on the desk told me what was going on.' Peter was knotting a tie around his neck. 'So this is the mother, right?'

'You have no right to do this.'

But Peter and the crew ignored her. Cat's headache, her old friend, came pounding back. Where the fuck were the paramedics?

The cameraman knelt down by the bed and was taping Marion.

'You moron,' Cat hissed. 'This isn't going to help your career.'

The guy lifted one eye away from the lens and shrugged.

On the bed, Marion moaned and moved slightly.

'Go find out what's going on, Angie,' Cat said. 'Find out where they are.' Angie took off.

'Can you get out of the shot?' Peter said. 'I'm going to do a stand-up.'

'Go fuck yourself.'

'Suit yourself.' Peter Ratch's vulpine features creased into a smile.

Marion moaned again. 'You get that?' Peter said to the camera operator. He nodded.

'If you think you're going to sell this to one of those real-life cops and 'copter shows, I'll personally make sure you get fired,' Cat said.

'And that would work how, exactly?' Peter gave a final look at his tie. 'Okay, I'm ready.' He manoeuvred himself in front of Marion, crouching so that her unconscious face could be seen behind him. 'There's good depth in that shot, right?'

'Sure,' said the cameraman. Marion mumbled and stirred again. Cat bent over her.

'In this seedy New York hotel room –' Peter began and then stopped. 'That wasn't right. Pick up.' He cleared his throat, started again, his voice deeper. 'In this cheap New York hotel room, the next chapter in the drama –' he stopped again. 'Did I say cheap? I meant to say seedy.'

'The only thing cheap and seedy about this is you,' Cat said. Fuck it, where was the ambulance?

'Just shut up and stay out of the shot, will you?' Peter said. He checked his reflection in the mirror and straightened his jacket. 'Okay, third and final take. In this seedy New York hotel room, the mother of a murder victim lies unconscious by her own hand – Jesus fucking Christ!!'

When Cat told this story later, which she did many, many times, she always commented on how perfect Marion's timing was. Even though she was unconscious, she hit her mark like a Broadway pro. About half a second after Peter Ratch said 'mother' Marion Neidermeyer sat up, groaned and vomited all over him. Again and again. Disgusting, projectile vomit.

It hit the back of his head like a tidal wave. It oozed down his neck and into his clothes. It was the colour of old cream and smelt of stale alcohol.

Peter Ratch danced around the room retching and swearing and telling the cameraman to stop rolling, which wasn't going to happen in a million years, because everybody in the news business knows a Christmas reel moment when it threw up over a pushy producer – that tape was destined to be played at television parties until it wore out.

The paramedics arrived about sixty seconds later.

# Chapter Forty-Five

At midday on Friday, Tye ordered lunch in her room and waited for Dickie to call. The hour became one and then two. She read the paper, then a couple of magazines. She sorted through her clothes, did a little hand washing.

A four o'clock she finally forced herself to admit he wasn't going to call. If she wanted her money, she was going to have to go looking for him.

She had no doubt he'd checked out of the Metropolitan, where he was staying. She tried his number, just in case. One sometimes got lucky. Dickie was long gone, checked out earlier that day. He had not left a forwarding address. She called information in Los Angeles and asked for the number for Coronet Films. The operator told her there was no such number.

Tye supposed she should have been angry with him but she was more angry at herself. She had allowed herself to be taken like a stupid neophyte. She was getting soft.

The thing that upset her the most was not the money, but that there would now be no acting career.

*

Cat was almost glad of a little peace at the start of her shift the next day. The suits upstairs had whipped themselves into a frenzy over the Marion Neidermeyer suicide attempt. The station's PR flacks had wanted to put out a press release giving an almost truthful account of how WKLP's news crew had saved a woman's life. Cat put her foot down. The unvarnished truth will get out, she said, and we'll be a laughing stock. Oddly, Eric Atlas had been her ally. He knew that having turned down the story in the first place, it was going to come back and bite him. He wanted Marion Neidermeyer to go away as soon as possible.

Angie the intern was perched on the edge of the washbasin, sucking down cappuccino. Cat's was untouched, even though she desperately needed it. That morning she had to report live from Madison Avenue, where a hand had been found in the trash. The city was hysterical and it was her job to feed their hysteria. To make matters worse, Renee had become fixated on finding the imaginary dress. She spent days on the phone trying to track down some guy who owned a shop in the Hamptons. He'd taken off to Milan for the winter, but Renee wasn't deterred. She'd called every hotel in the city, asking in her tourist Italian for Signore Reynolds. The girl had missed her calling, Cat reflected, with persistence like that she really should have gone into television.

Just why she was going to all this trouble on Cat's behalf was a matter that neither of them chose to dwell on. It lay between them ticking, like a package from a terrorist.

One of Renee's old girlfriends had breezed into

town about a month ago. A Venezuelan dancer called Mercedes who now lived in Miami. Renee had wanted to go out with her, and Cat hadn't objected. She wasn't a jealous person. It was pointless, they'd both been around. Who didn't have a history? But one night out stretched to two and then three and on the third night, Renee hadn't come home at all. Cat sat up with Larry the terrier, drinking coffee and frozen with fear. When she left for work at four, she was buzzing from anger and caffeine and Renee still wasn't home.

The fight had lasted for days. An extended screaming match punctuated by bouts of throwing. Cat had cried until she thought her insides would implode. Renee had begged her forgiveness.

Somehow they'd managed to find their way back to each other. That's what being a grown-up was about, she supposed. Compromise. Picking your way through the minefield of hurt and recrimination. Side-stepping the bullet of revenge. Finding a place where she could calm herself, concentrate on what was important.

'Get out there, girl.' Max had slipped in. He patted her kindly on the arm. Cat didn't confide about her life to Max, but sometimes she felt he knew more than he let on.

'Another complete sentence,' she murmured. 'You shouldn't have.' She grabbed her make-up bag and the cooling coffee.


Molly talked her way into Juliana Franklin's apartment. Juliana was tearful and defensive, refusing at first to let them in. Molly eventually got her to open the door. Once inside, she made Juliana tea and calmed her down.

Quinn was surprised to find the apartment exactly the same as he'd first seen it.

'How many people have called?' he asked Juliana.

'The phone rings off the hook. Every single one of them abusive. They've threatened to sue.'

'They can't sue,' Molly said.

'Sure they can. This is America,' Quinn said. Molly shrugged. Urged more tea on Juliana. Quinn walked around the kitchen. There was something different, what was it? He prodded his memory.

'I was so centred after my trip,' Juliana moaned. 'And now this.' She resumed weeping into a patchouli-scented handkerchief.

'We're gonna find out who did this and beat the crap out of them,' Molly said reassuringly.

'Grandmother!' Quinn cautioned from the kitchen.

'We are! Lucky owes me.'

'Who's Lucky?' Juliana asked.

'Don't go there,' Quinn said. 'She's an old woman and her medication needs adjusting.'

'Don't be takin' any notice of him,' Molly said. 'He spent too long at university.'

Juliana glanced at Molly, taking in afresh her pink hair, her flamboyant clothing. She clutched her handkerchief tightly. 'I think you'd better go now,' she said. 'I need some time . . .'

'Of course, dear. We understand. You call us if you need anything. And don't you worry. We're gonna find this tart, you see if we don't.' Molly gathered up her bags. She never went anywhere without at least two.

Quinn was looking around the kitchen. There was something different . . . he looked around, willing his memory. It'd been quite good once.

'Quinn, come on.'

Refrigerator, stove, microwave. Corkboard. Shelves with vegetarian cookery books. 'Coming, Moll,' he said absently. Fridge magnets advertising takeaway places in the neighbourhood. What was it? What was different?

Corkboard. Hanging behind the bookcase. There'd been a photo of her on there, he remembered. One of those cheap sets that makes you look like a drug runner or child killer. Quinn peered at it closely. As he leant over he noticed something wedged down between the bookcase and the wall. He pried it out gently. Jackpot.

'Well, well,' he said, feeling pleased with himself. Evidence.

# Chapter Forty-Six

Tye was so angry with herself for being taken by Dickie that she went to Aveda and ordered a gift basket of shampoos and other expensive creams and then onto Rite Aid where she bought a jumbo bottle of depilatory. She tipped the conditioner out and replaced it with depilatory, tipped in some lavender oil to disguise the smell and sent the whole lot gift-wrapped to Adrian. He was the pig who'd got her into this mess, and she didn't intend to let him forget. He hadn't suffered nearly enough.

She'd have to go back to work sooner than she'd planned. She went to a cafe, got out her notebook and tried to think.

Perhaps the writer – what was his name? Ted? – knew where Dickie was. Unlikely, but worth a try.

God, she felt like an idiot. Of all the stupid things to fall for. She sighed, got up, left her cappuccino half drunk. There was lots of work to be done.

Sean Reynolds, the dress-shop owner, had left Milan to be the houseguest of an American family in Lucca. His hotel didn't know how to reach him there, but the desk clerk said he would leave a message for Sean to contact Renee if he checked in. He didn't know when that would be. Renee banged her fist in frustration as she hung up the phone. Her phone bill was going to be enormous, and she hadn't found out anything that could help Cat. Not only that, but Cat seemed increasingly sceptical of what she was doing. Why bother, she thought in a sudden spurt of anger. It wasn't as if Cat cared. She'd made that clear. Renee's belief was eroding as well. Even if she did track down the right dress and get Cat an amazing scoop, there was no guarantee that it would repair the damage to their relationship.

She bit the first knuckle of her index finger, thinking of another way around the problem. If she could get hold of the Lucca phone directory she could call every English name listed and find him that way. It was worth a shot. How big could Lucca be, anyway?

'I don't see as it's going to help us,' Molly said. 'She's a master of disguise, an arch-fiend.'

'It's a sign,' Quinn said, holding the snapshots out in front of him. 'God is on our side.'

'He never is, or the bastard Cromwell would have lost. Taxi!' Molly pushed a businessman with a briefcase out of the way and snagged the only available cab on Third Avenue. Quinn mouthed 'sorry' at the bewildered guy who raised a finger in response. Ah, New York. Bastion of civility, Quinn thought. He studied the photo as the cab lurched downtown. She looked familiar, this girl, almost like he knew her. But he couldn't think how. His brain really was going downhill. Soon he was going to have to hire someone to do his remembering for him.

'Ah, fuck you! You fucking eedjit.' Molly was remonstrating with another car driver who had cut them up. Quinn laid a hand on her arm. 'Don't worry about that, Moll. That's what we pay the driver for.'

Molly sank into her seat, a smile on her face. She loved New York, although she never admitted it. Perhaps that was really why she had come, Quinn thought, not to help him but to dose up on aggression. She needed to yell at people like a vampire needed virgin blood.

'I'll drop you at your hotel,' Quinn said, hoping she'd give him the money for the fare. He was really short.

'You've got three other places to see today,' Molly said when the cab stopped outside her hotel.

'I know.'

'You're gonna go and see them.'

'Promise.'

''Cos y'know I'll rip you limb from limb if you don't.'

'I know.'

'Bye, then.' She handed him a twenty. And then another.

'Thanks. Bye.'

The hotel doorman lingered as Molly struggled to get out of the cab's no-spring seats. She irritably waved away his offer of help, stalking into the hotel, swatting at the other staff who tried to assist her. Quinn smiled.

She could be an aggravating old bird at times, but she was truly herself.

Tye found Ted O'Reilly's card at the bottom of her handbag – a stroke of luck. She decided to visit him at home in Williamsburg rather than call. Perhaps Dickie might even be there. Perhaps Ted and he were in the game together. Then she could snap his teeth out of his head, one by one, till he gave her twenty grand back.

Ted was in, that was a good sign. That meant the party hadn't been a set-up. His eyes lit up when he saw his unexpected guest. He offered Tye a beer, which she accepted.

'Seen Dickie lately?' she asked casually. Furniture had arrived since she'd been here last. Nice stuff. He had taste. He had money, too, she seemed to recall. A screenplay. She examined the idea, dismissed it. Ted and Quinn were friends. She'd be running into him on a regular basis – there was no way to justify that kind of risk.

Ted shook his head. 'I thought he was . . .'

'No.'

'Ah.' Ted's expression was solicitous. 'Problems?'

'No, I'm fine thanks. Just a silly misunderstanding.'

'Do you need help?'

Here was the funny thing: a personable, solvent man was finally offering her the thing she'd been searching for. Shit.

She regarded Ted, and a bemused smile tugged at

the corners of her mouth. Then she nearly burst out laughing.

'What's the matter?'

Tye shook her head. 'Nothing, really. You're very kind.'

Ted shrugged. He wasn't so bad, Tye thought. Quite bearable, in fact. No, the thing that had struck her as funny was that her first, uncensored response to his question had been: But I don't love you.

Tye put her beer down. Strange how things turned out. 'I'd better go,' she said. 'Thanks for the offer, though.'

'Can I give you a lift somewhere?'

Tye shook her head. 'I'll take the subway, thanks.'

'Sure? I'm heading into Manhattan.'

The doorbell rang. Ted buzzed whoever it was in. 'My day for visitors. One of my deadbeat pals hitting me up for a loan, no doubt.' He grinned. 'There's usually a line out the door.'

Tye put the half-finished beer down. She didn't want to talk to anyone else. Ted followed her to the elevator.

'Are you sure you're okay?' There was concern in his voice.

'I'm fine, really. Thanks for the—'

The bell dinged, the doors opened and he stepped into the room. Quinn. His eyes angry, staring straight at her.

God, he knows! Tye thought. She fell to the floor in a dead faint.

Quinn and Ted picked her up and carried her to the couch. There was something elemental about this woman. Even unconscious, Quinn could feel himself being drawn into her orbit.

They laid her down gently. Ted brought a glass of water, tried to get close to her, but Quinn wouldn't let him. He put an arm around her neck, felt her pulse, strong and steady. His fingers lingered on her delicate wrists and hands. The flesh on her inner arms was translucent, streaked by tiny blue-black veins. No rings. No jewellery of any kind. Quinn wanted to go on touching her, but she was coming round. She shakily apologized. Put her hand to her head. Accepted the glass of water and drank. Quinn watched her throat as she did. It was as smooth and white as her wrists. God, he felt horny and something else too. He couldn't identify the other, more elusive feeling.

'I'm terribly sorry.'

'Don't be.' Ted and Quinn said the words together. Ted elbowed Quinn neatly out of the way as he laid a solicitous hand on Tye's forehead. 'I really don't think you should leave.'

'I'll be okay, honestly.' She began pushing herself off the couch. Ted and Quinn parted reluctantly as she sat up.

'Are you sure, now?'

'Absolutely, thanks.'

But she wasn't. She felt light-headed still. The two men stood waiting, expecting her to say something. The next thing she knew she was spilling it all.

'It's kind of a pathetic story. Dickie, that's my, er, friend. Well, he's gone off with something of mine, and I . . .'

'Something . . . like what?' Quinn asked.

Tye winced. 'Something big. Like money.' She gritted her teeth. Don't show me any sympathy, she thought. I can't stand it.

'Aye, there's a lot of it about.' Quinn nodded. 'Live and learn, eh?'

Tye couldn't look him in the eye. She felt shame.

'I've got a number for him.' Ted crossed to his palm-top computer. Punched the numbers into his phone. Put it on speaker.

'The number you are calling is no longer in service.'

'I met him in LA a couple of times. He said he had his own production company. Seemed on the level. Mind you, it was LA,' Ted said.

'I made some calls, you know, back home,' Tye said. 'His father's cut him off. He's gambled millions and drunk almost as much. That's why he's over here. The tabloid press have been hounding him in Britain. He totalled his father's Bentley when he was pissed and nearly killed his sister. Only just missed out on prison. What a wally I was. I didn't check.'

Quinn squeezed her hand. It was supposed to be a friendly gesture, at least that's what he told himself, but their touching skin seared. He withdrew his hand. This woman should come with a fire warning.

'I should be going,' Tye said.

'Let me take you.' Quinn stood up. 'Make sure you get home safe.' Tye looked at him for what seemed like a very long time. She was falling, flailing.

'Okay,' she said. Silencing the choir of common sense that was advising the complete opposite.

# Chapter Forty-Seven

Quinn kept his hand lightly between her shoulders as they stepped into the lift. He smiled serenely at Ted who shrugged, gave up and punched Quinn on the shoulder. Good old Ted, Quinn thought. More gracious in defeat than victory. Maybe not such a bad guy after all. Quinn could begin to see a time when they might be friends instead of just point-scoring drinking buddies.

The air was popping with tension by the time the elevator reached the ground floor. Quinn took his arm off her shoulders. It felt numb and useless lying by his side. He wished he'd taken more care shaving that morning. Wished he'd worn something more arresting than Nikes and jeans. Wished he could think of something to say. Suddenly all his usual lines of approach seemed facile. He was in uncharted territory – the place where they draw monsters on maps.

'Taxi or subway?'

'Subway's fine.'

They walked through the quiet afternoon streets, pace matching. Quinn thought of fifteen different topics of conversation. Discarded them all. He'd never been tongue-tied in his life.

In a way the silence was nice. It gave him time to concentrate on the sensations of the moment as opposed to his usual m.o. – always racing ahead, trying to come up with something witty and dazzling to say. He realized he felt great just walking with her.

Tye was jittery as a cat and deeply confused. Men didn't normally make her feel this way. Usually she could sum them up in a couple of minutes and map out how she would behave according to what she wanted from them. This one was different and, she was starting to admit to herself, it wasn't just about her having stolen his money. It was that she saw him as an equal. It was a scary thought and its implications were even scarier. Best not to think about them. Best to concentrate on the now. Trouble was, she couldn't concentrate. If only he'd say something.

He said nothing.

The autumn sun was warm on her neck. She felt a little dizzy from passing out. She tried to think of a light, general topic of conversation that would disperse her tension. There was nothing to say, she realized. Her predicament had gone way beyond anything that could be addressed with words.

They caught the subway into the Village and went to a bar. Quinn ordered Guinness and she did too. He forgot about his appointments to view apartments.

As he invited her to tell him something about herself, Tye wondered for the first time ever, 'Why not the truth?' But not for long. As she considered the question, she knew what she wanted from this man. But she could not have it, and it was her own fault. She couldn't give him back his money either because she had lost it. What a balls-up.

Tye did not believe in God or karma or any of the other things that social conscience is dressed up as, but she had begun to think: if there was such a being, he or she must have one hell of a sense of humour.

So they didn't talk about much. But somehow one drink became two and then dinner. What they ate, neither registered. Then they walked. Blindly. Trading small talk, telling jokes. Outdoing each other with bons mots, not saying what was on their minds.

Finally they reached South Street Seaport and the wet sea air acted like a wake-up call. Tye stopped and turned to face him. Took a small step back because, as usual, he was generating some sort of crazy force field that was turning her organs to mush.

'I've got to go.'

'Don't.' He caught her hand. She slipped free of his grasp.

'I must.'

'Give me your number, then.'

'I can't do that.'

'Sure you can. It's easy. Write it on this.' He held out his cast.

'Thanks for a nice evening, I had fun.' Tye turned, looking for a taxi.

'You can't.' He was behind her. Got hold of her arm again.

'Goodbye, Quinn.'

'It's not goodbye. C'mon. I promise not to spit in your soup next time.'

She smiled. He saw his advantage and moved in.

He put both hands on her shoulders, holding her loosely. 'Hey,' he said. 'I'm not that hideous, am I?'

Tye shook her head.

'So what's the problem?'

He smelt so good. 'It's too complicated to get into here.'

'So come back to my place. I'll make coffee and you can tell me all about it.'

Tye shook her head. 'I must go. I really must.' She twisted out of his grip. She'd already strayed way too far. Time to get out before the search and rescue party found only her remains.

'I won't see you again? That's what you're saying? You're not saying that, tell me you're not.' The civilized part of Quinn was urging him to get out while he still had his pride. The uncivilized part, which was clearly in the driver's seat, didn't give a damn.

'It's not possible.' Goddamnit, where were all the taxis?

'Why not? You're not married are you?'

'I have to go, okay?'

'Don't do this. You'll regret it, I promise.' Think, Quinn, think. Say something, anything to keep her here. Don't let her out of your sight. Something magical and lyrical that would capture her heart.

'Please . . . ?' Bloody brilliant.

'I had a nice time. You're a nice man.'

'No, I'm not,' Quinn wailed. 'I'm a complete bastard, everybody says so. I'm a loser, I use women, I've never done a day's work in my life. My grandmother supports me, I hardly even thank her. Worse, I throw the money away like a moron and then lie about paying her back.'

A taxi pulled up and Tye grabbed the door open and got in. Quinn scribbled his own number on the back of an old subway ticket, tossed it in the cab after her. 'Here, call me. If you want coffee, dinner, someone to do your heavy lifting . . . clean your floors . . . anything.'

She waved her hand, stiffly like the Queen. She was going. And there was nothing he could do.

The cab pulled out into traffic. Quinn watched the tail lights until the cab turned a corner. It was chilly now, and dark. He walked home, morose.

The apartment was empty. Quinn sat down heavily. He felt disgusted. How could he have screwed it up so badly? Why hadn't he thrown himself in front of the cab?

He had never before even considered the idea that he could be happy with one woman and the idea had a compelling novelty. She was the one, he was sure of it. And although one side of him felt weird to be thinking like that, the other side wanted to dive gleefully in – the house, the kids, the white picket fence. Even a goddamned golden retriever if she wanted.

But that wasn't going to happen because he'd screwed things up. Something he'd said or done had driven her away. He slammed his fist down, cursing with pain when it struck the edge of his laptop, which he'd left sitting out. Out of habit he turned the screen on. The empty document he'd left open was still there. White and accusing.

He pulled the computer around to face him, placed his hand on the keys. Then he began to write.

Tye felt as though she had a hangover when she woke the next day. Her head was heavy, her limbs shook slightly as she guided them through her morning ablutions. She had to arrange another apartment, but although she still had the list she'd stolen from the travel agent, she felt as though she didn't have the energy to pursue the leads.

Damn it, she should have slept with him. That would have got him out of her system.

Half of her expected that he would be waiting when she left the hotel. She looked up and down Wooster Street, but he wasn't there. She ignored the disappointment. Ignored the dull, feverish feeling in her bones. She consulted her list. She had work to do.

# Chapter Forty-Eight

The alarm at Cyrus's parents' house was faulty and kept going off at odd times. An army of men from the alarm company would come over, tinker with it and go away. Then it'd go off again and they'd come back. Cyrus rang his mother to tell her about this latest incident and didn't bother to hide from her how irritated he was by it – but in a calm, assertive way. Normally he avoided conflict with his mother because she was one scary bird when she didn't get her own way. He'd only just begun to admit this, but his mom frightened the bejeezus out of him, even when she wasn't around. For years he had not faced this issue because it seemed, well, unnatural. You were supposed to love your mom. She was supposed to be a kind, unselfish person who was your biggest fan. He knew other people had moms like that. But lately, with the Master helping him to re-evaluate his life he had begun to edge around and finally address this problem. It was a tough one, not getting on with your nearest and dearest. Society seemed to demand it, which was why Cyrus figured that he hadn't faced it sooner. Nobody wanted to think of themselves as a freak.

And his new, assertive yet neutral manner seemed

to work. His mother told him someone was coming over to the house to deliver some things, so he might as well turn the alarm off. And it wasn't as if Cyrus ever went out much – the jobless implication was pointed though unspoken – so there was somebody around to make sure she didn't get burgled.

Cyrus climbed the steps to his parents' house and did as his mother had asked.

When he got back to his apartment he turned on the television to find that the heart of a young woman who had been identified as Susan Neidermeyer had turned up in a box at City Hall. It was in bad shape, having been frozen, thawed and re-frozen. The parcel had been addressed to the mayor, but had been opened by the guys in the mail room. Cops came and took the parcel away, inspected it for fingerprints and other incriminating clues, but found there were none. Cyrus knew there was no evidence leading to him; he'd been careful. He didn't intend to get caught. That wasn't one of the habits of successful people.

There was loads of space in his freezer now. Time to start laying in stock for the winter.


Tye came back to the hotel, footsore and weary from a morning checking out apartments. None had been entirely suitable, but she was going to have to choose one and make the best of it. Many times she thought she should just get on the next plane to London before it all came crashing down, but it felt as though she was no longer in control; events were driving her. It wasn't an unpleasant feeling. It was comforting in a way, like going home to sleep in your childhood bedroom at your parents' house and finding it just the same as when you left it.

The hotel lobby was quiet. Enrico, the concierge carried a fistful of shopping bags to the elevator for another guest.

It was the older woman Tye remembered seeing check in a few nights ago. She was immaculately and expensively clad in a dark-grey suit. Her hair was almost the same colour and stiff waves of silver and grey framed her face. Tye smiled at the woman who looked frostily back. She was standing in a garden of designer bags sprouting tissue paper and blooming bows, clutching her Christian Dior handbag and a tip for Enrico.

'I can take it from here,' she said in a raspy, surprisingly deep voice, handing over the note. It was a fifty. 'You'll help me send the rest over?'

'Yes, Mrs Tower.'

'Wow,' Tye said after the woman had disappeared in the elevator. 'Nice work, Enrico. Does she need any staff, do you think? A companion perhaps?'

Enrico grinned, slipping the note in his breast pocket. 'She will leave soon. And I am poor again.'

'But she'll be back.'

'And my children will eat and wear shoes.' Enrico laughed. 'My children love American dollars. My wife, also.' He picked up the shopping bags that remained. 'I must go now – take these to her home.' Enrico tapped his forehead as if to indicate these crazy rich Americans.

'Her apartment? She lives near?'

'*Si.*'

'Why does she stay here?'

Enrico shrugged. He didn't know and as long as those fifty dollar tips kept coming, he didn't care.

An idea started to dawn on Tye. A brilliant idea. One that would solve all her problems. Impulsively, she kissed Enrico, who blushed. 'Here's to food and shoes,' she said before skipping up the stairs, delighted as a child.


Quinn wrote far into the night and got up early the next day and started again. Mal, puzzled at this burst of activity from his brother, silently placed a bagel and a cup of coffee in front of him before leaving for work. Quinn raised his good hand, said, 'Thanks, man,' in a distracted voice and clattered over the keyboard. His cast made it difficult, but not impossible. Anything could be achieved, once you set your mind to it.

Molly called at ten. Quinn emerged from his work as if coming up from under water. Molly had brought her tattered copy of the *Voice* and low-fat muffins. She was on a diet.

'Jesus,' she said, looking at Quinn: computer open, books spread around him. 'He's finally done it.'

'I've met the one, Moll.' Quinn said, eating a muffin. He was hungry, felt as though he hadn't eaten for days. 'She's the breath in my lungs. I'm writing . . . look at this, will you? I'm writing.'

Molly cast a cursory glance at the computer. 'What about my money?'

'What does money matter when we have art . . . and love?'

Molly's lip curled. 'Sometimes I wonder if you weren't a changeling. You're certainly no Quinn.'

Quinn beamed. Molly pushed him out of the way and sat down at the computer. 'Well, if you won't follow this thing through, I will. I didn't fly all this way to help you out so you could sing songs of love and moonshine. Get a grip, boy.' She closed Quinn's document and placed the *Village Voice* in front of him. 'Let's keep looking.'

# Chapter Forty-Nine

Tye watched Mrs Tower for a couple of days. The older woman did not seem to welcome overtures of friendship, but she had a schedule you could run a train network on. Tye 'happened' to run into her taking tea on the hotel roof garden one afternoon which she invariably did after spending the morning shopping. To her surprise she was invited to sit down. They exchanged names and pleasantries. Tye didn't rush anything. She didn't ask any direct questions. She noticed that Mrs Tower seemed less guarded today, her face older.

'This is a pleasant hotel,' Tye said eventually.

'Yes. I've been coming here for many years now. It's always exactly the same. Comforting, don't you find?'

'It's been a lifesaver for me. I split up with my boyfriend.' Tye hoped that one confession might engender another. Such as why she chose to stay in a hotel when her apartment was nearby.

'It is nice to have a back-up. A sanctuary.' Mrs Tower's gaze appeared to be locked onto a rhododendron at the far side of the garden.

'Are you staying in New York long?'

'Till they take me out in a box.' Mrs Tower smiled faintly. 'I live here. These days I never leave it if I can help it. It was different when I was younger, of course. I travelled constantly with my husband. Not now. What can I find in the rest of the world that I can't find here?'

'It must be comforting to think that,' Tye said truthfully. 'I like to move around, which is good, I suppose. But it also means I'm never happy wherever I am. I'm always looking to the next experience.'

'You'll grow out of that.' The woman's arrogant sense of superiority annoyed Tye, but she pressed on.

'Are your family in New York?'

'Unfortunately. We live much too close for my liking.'

Tye was shocked. Family was sacrosanct to her. It was the only thing you could count on, providing of course that they weren't in jail.

'I do my best.' Mrs Tower sighed. 'But sometimes it just isn't good enough. Nature dictates some kind of bond, I suppose. But if it wasn't for the blood tie – well . . .' She clicked her fingers.

Glad she's not my mother, Tye thought. 'How long are you staying?'

'Another few days. Till my husband returns. He's in California. Dreadful place. Wanted me to go with him. Imagine!'

'I think California sounds kind of nice.'

'You would. You Brits will do anything for sunshine.' A flash of contempt showed on her face.

And how would you know? Tye didn't say it. She got up, smiled politely and left. This was going to be much easier than she thought.

The next morning she waited till Mrs Tower left on her shopping trip and then went to the front desk and chatted with the receptionist, lifting the key to Mrs Tower's room while the woman ducked out for a quick cigarette.

The old woman's room was neat and smelt of freesias. Her keys, on a distinctive Gucci keyring were lying in the top right-hand drawer of her bureau. It took Tye only a few minutes to find them. She looked in the address book lying next to the phone. Eugenia Tower had written her name and address on the front page, in old-fashioned copperplate handwriting. Sixty-five Baxter Street. She flicked through the book.

Tye ran downstairs and replaced the room key just as the receptionist was guiltily returning.

Then she went to an internet cafe where she logged on and found a website which promised to find out about anyone for $23.95. She asked for the birth dates of Dr and Mrs Tower and that of their son. She also got their wedding anniversary. It took much less time than she imagined. She wrote the numbers down, careful to put the month first, the American way. If there was an alarm, she was betting the combination was a date that Mrs Tower would find easy to remember. She charged the computer rental and the $23.95 to Adrian's American Express card.

Mrs Tower's address was an elegant Italianate townhouse with a sweeping stoop. The windows were tall and narrow and the roof was trimmed in black iron trim. A creeper clung to one side of the building. Tye approached the front door. There was just one door-bell, which meant Mrs Tower occupied the whole house. Tye cursed. A house was no good to her. The people who rented this type of place could afford to do it legally and properly, through an estate agent, not some fly-by-night ad in the *Village Voice*. And she should have realized, a woman who can afford to stay at a posh hotel was going to have a nice place.

There were four keys on the ring. She stared at them in her hand. They were shiny and new. 'Why not just have a look?' a stubborn, wilful voice said. She'd come this far.

She chose one of the keys and inserted it. The lock wouldn't yield. She tried the second one. It didn't fit either. But there were only two locks on the front door. Why then were there four keys?

She noticed the basement. It was so close to the street that the stoop hid the front door. But when she went down to check, she saw there was a separate front door.

She looked in the window and couldn't see any furniture. The lights were off. The first key fitted and so did the second.

It was completely empty. Perfectly so. A little confined, but that was because there was only light from one source and since it was below street level, there wasn't much of it. It made the place feel un-balanced, but otherwise, it was fine. A small kitchen, with a few cupboards. A living room with a sofa, a lamp and a table. The bedroom had a nice bookshelf and a fair amount of closet space. A selling point in this town. An entirely separate, uninhabited space that she could flog off for more than two grand a month, easy.

Mrs Tower obviously wasn't using it, so no reason why she couldn't move in for a few hours.

Cyrus was surprised to see a woman coming out of his apartment when he returned. An emissary from his mother, perhaps? A spy? He had been meaning to get his locks changed, just to spite his mother, who seemed to consider it her right to be able to get into his apartment if she wanted to, but with everything that had been going on, he hadn't had the time. Now he knew that it had been part of the plan.

He wasn't concerned that a woman had been in there. In fact, it seemed right. After all, there was nothing to see in the front apartment, not since he'd moved his belongings into the back to get more peace and to spend more time with the Master. He'd made the decision a couple of days ago. Something big was brewing. He could feel it, and he wanted to be prepared. The next stage was near.

And now this woman. Turning up out of nowhere. She was a sign of something important, Cyrus realized. He didn't have to go looking any more – his work came to him. It was beautiful the way that happened – the minute you stopped striving, the universe worked with you.

The only drawback was that she didn't have blonde hair, but that probably didn't matter now. Perhaps the change of hair colour was also a sign that he was moving in a new direction.

There was no doubt that she was beautiful. She was slender and tall with dark hair. Well dressed in black pants and a black leather jacket with a silk scarf knotted casually around her neck. She looked a little like his mother, now that he thought about it. His mom thirty years ago. Her hair had been dark, too.

Yeah, it felt right to just go with this one.

He didn't follow her. He knew she'd be back. It was all clicking into place.

# Chapter Fifty

Marion Neidermeyer was officially 'under observation', in case she tried to kill herself again. Well, they didn't need to worry because she wasn't going to. There was no need. She was dead already. Whoever had killed Gus and Susie had got a three-for-two deal. A real bargain.

Marion studied her hand as it lay on the outside of the thin hospital blanket. She had a plastic bracelet around her wrist, and she was wearing a regulation hospital gown. The staff had been kind to her. Firm, but kind.

Marion was ashamed of what had happened. Everybody knew her story. It had gotten on the TV somehow and a couple of the papers had followed it up. Suddenly she was newsworthy. Marion thought back to her meeting with that pugnacious journalist in his office, the one that had been so rude to her because she didn't have pictures. How things had changed.

The reporter had been nice though, the one that found her. She'd come to visit, without a camera crew, just to see how Marion was. Marion had lain there awkwardly, wondering if she should thank this woman for saving her life. Not that she cared, but it seemed polite to do so. But the reporter, Catrina Vermont – even her name was glamorous – said there was no need to say anything. She'd sat with Marion for a bit and chatted about inconsequential things. And she'd brought flowers. Some lovely, sweet-smelling lilies. After she left, the blooms and Catrina Vermont's perfume had vied for supremacy in Marion's tiny room.

John Abruzzo visited too. He came every day and sat by her bed. Sometimes he brought something for her to read, like a decorating magazine or a best-selling novel. For his sake, Marion had tried to concentrate on them, but even the pictures seemed to make no sense. She would read about how so-and-so had hired such-and-such an architect or designer to rearrange the furniture and she would think; what does this have to do with reality? John Abruzzo thought so, too, because he would read the articles out loud to her in funny voices.

'You're not like the New York cops you see on television,' she said one day. In reply he formed his fingers into a pistol, pointed them at Catrina Vermont's lilies and said, 'Freeze, motherfucker,' in a heavy Bronx accent.

For the first time in days, Marion laughed.


All Quinn had been able to do was think about Tye. Although Molly had hustled him around town looking at sublets, he didn't really care whether he found the woman who robbed him or not. It didn't bother him that people thought it odd that he was looking at apartments with his grandmother. He'd gone through the mechanics as though he were heavily sedated, which wasn't too far from the mark. He felt drowsy and heavy with the sense of her. The only time he was the old sharp Quinn was early in the mornings when he wrote – those precious hours that went by as fast as a jump cut.

There were times when he thought maybe she hadn't been real. That she'd come and gone like a gift from God, or like a faery. But when he'd broached this with Molly, who was usually the first one lining up for pseudo-Celtic mystic twaddle, she said, 'Don't talk such bollocks, boy. This is New York City.'

There were other times when he allowed himself to think that it didn't matter if he never saw her again, that it was enough for him that she had allowed him to work. But mostly he yearned for another glance, another meeting. He would give anything for that.

Tye bought another wig and some coloured contact lenses. They hurt her eyes. She went to a Goodwill shop in the East Village and picked out an outfit. She got the keys to the basement apartment copied.

She tried not to think about Quinn as she did all these things, but it was becoming increasingly difficult not to. She kept imagining she saw him in the streets. She'd spot someone with his swaggering walk and her stomach would plunge. She even fantasized about getting the money from this job and then sending him a cheque. Then they could start again – Quinn, Tye and Tye's clean conscience.

Dream on.

A passer-by banged into Tye, scattering her belongings on the sidewalk. Didn't apologize or help her pick them up. She knelt, half crying, trying to gather her things. This was madness; she was a wreck. She hadn't done her homework, she should be running away. Stealing took time, research, planning. Think of everything that can go wrong and then think of a few more things besides. Then be aware that you'll probably screw up in another way entirely. That's what her father said.

Oh, God. Oh, God. What was she doing? She was falling apart. Get on the next plane, girl. Right now.

'Let me help you with that.'

'Quinn?' She looked up eagerly.

'Joe.' The black guy in a smart suit smiled. 'Sorry.' He noticed her red eyes. 'Everything okay?'

'Thanks. Yes. New lenses.'

Joe nodded, pointed at his specs. 'Know what that's like. I gave up on them. Sometimes honourable retreat is the only way.'

'Yeah,' Tye said. Oh, God. Oh, God. Perhaps the universe was trying to tell her something.


Renee had called fifteen numbers in Lucca. She called Sean Reynolds's Milan hotel three times a day. The staff were unfailingly polite but Renee could sense they thought she was one slice short of a pizza.

They weren't the only ones. Cat was voicing her doubts too.

'You know, reporters only solve crimes on TV,' she said. 'In real life we let the cops – with their vastly superior resources and training – handle it. In real life reporters have much more important things to concentrate on, like office politics.' Cat had meant it to be jokey, but she was so tense it came out wrong and sounded snippy.

The trouble was that Cat had so much to worry about at work that she didn't have time to sit down with Renee and explain properly what was going on. Each time she did, it came out like she was making an excuse for her short temper.

And Renee was still fixated on the dress, even though she was getting nowhere with it. Maybe she was using it as a shield, an excuse to insulate herself from the truth – that as a couple, they were just about washed up.

'Fancy a Martini?' she asked Renee.

'Sure. I've got two more calls to make.' Renee waved the photocopied pages of the phone book. Cat sighed, went to the kitchen. Just thinking about Eric Atlas made her want to finish the bottle. Maybe he *would* drive her to drink. That would be his final, ironic victory. Jobless and alcohol dependent. Gee, that'd really make her loveable in this town.

Cat could hear Renee speaking in her tourist Italian. The conversations were both short. When she finished, Cat was standing at her elbow with a Martini. 'No luck? Consolation prize,' she said, putting her hand on Renee's shoulder. She wanted to do more but she felt there was too much distance between them.

'I'm going to find that dress,' Renee said, taking the glass and, as she always did, digging the olive out first with her fingers.

# Chapter Fifty-One

There's no such thing as easy money. Her father had drummed it into her over the years. It was practically emblazoned on the family crest. But now Tye was going to break the habit of a lifetime and go for the fast buck. She couldn't shake off her dread as she went through the motions of setting up the plan. She felt sleepy, but when she slept she had anxiety dreams, the sort she used to have before exams. And trying not to think about Quinn made her brain hurt.

She nearly gave up about fifteen times that day. Nearly called Quinn. A couple of times she even went to the phone. She'd call him, no harm in that. Just one little date. Where was the problem? She could fake it, she'd been doing that all her life. Or maybe they could live together in poverty. They had each other. They'd be happy. Sex and sunshine.

But fortunately these fantasies never lasted long. She was a modern girl, and she needed money. She had to do what had to be done. And she would get sick of Quinn, that was inevitable. No matter what kind of gods they seemed to be at the beginning of a relationship, men always emerged as mere mortals.

No, she was doing the right thing – leaving her care and well-being to the only person who really knew how to do the job – herself.

She called the *Village Voice* and placed the ad, leaving the number of her newly hired cellphone.


'This is it!' Molly punched her hand in the air. 'I can smell it. Sunny, spacious West Village apartment. One bedroom, closet space. Six months to one year sublet. We've got her, me boy!'

Quinn was sprawled on the sofa drinking tea and eating chocolate chip cookies wondering why his granny didn't crochet or live in Florida like other oldsters who knew their place. She was exhausting. He'd seen so many apartments in the last few days that they'd all blurred. Too bad he didn't have the money for a deposit. There were a couple he'd seen that he quite liked. Ah, well. He had his work. If only his muse weren't so elusive, all would be perfect.

'Are you listenin' to me, boy?' Molly put herself in Quinn's line of vision. Her pink hair looked even crazier with the green pantsuit. Also striking were the diamanté choker and Tyrolean tweed hat.

'Sure.' Quinn sat up.

'Here's the number, now call it.' Molly thrust a shred of paper at her grandson.

There was no arguing. Just one more time, he promised himself as he shuffled to the phone. Then this was absolutely, definitely the last one. He'd get the old bird on a plane back to Vegas if he had to hire professional muscle to do it.


Sean Reynolds called in the middle of the afternoon. Renee was at the studio, staring at a blank piece of paper. She was having trouble concentrating these days, doubting the strength of her commitment to finding the blue dress, perhaps even her commitment to Cat, who hadn't shown any gratitude. Hadn't shown much of anything lately. Maybe she was beating a dead reporter, Renee thought crossly. Maybe she should just get on with her own career. What did it matter anyway? Even if she did trace the dress, it could have been stolen or lost or given away. Anything. No guarantees – nothing was for sure. And even if she got Cat the biggest scoop of her career, she couldn't say they'd still be together in a year from now. Or six months. Perhaps it was time to admit defeat and walk away, find somebody new.

Then the optimistic side of her nature sprang back. No use thinking like that. It was defeatist. They'd made a commitment to each other, they'd made promises. Sure, they'd sealed them with plastic rings from K-mart, but that didn't cheapen the sentiment.

She picked up a pencil. She didn't have the luxury of thinking about Cat right now. She had to think about the season after next and the one after that.

So when the call came and the person on the other end spoke the magic words, Renee was almost dismissive with him, partly from surprise.

'Oh, hi,' she said. 'Oh hi,' repeating herself stupidly.

'Ms Smith? I have a number of messages for me to call you,' Sean's deep voice boomed down a startlingly clear phone line. 'Thirty-five in all. And I can't even begin to wonder what this is about. Do I know you?'

'Oh, no. Not at all. Sorry I was a bit of a pest,' Renee said. She did a little jig. She'd found him, she'd found him! Larry the terrier looked up from his bed, noted Renee in a bored way before closing his eyes again.

'Is there something you're looking for? I'm assuming there must be – thirty-five messages.'

'Yes,' Renee said. 'Yes. As a matter of fact, there is.'


'We need to talk.' Eric Atlas shut the door to his office, motioning Cat to the least advantageous seat in the enormous room. She had a cubicle in which the air conditioning didn't work, and which she shared with a man who ate nothing but greasy food. Atlas had a view of midtown and an office the size of a tennis court.

She looked around for signs of human habitation but there weren't any. Even though Atlas had a wife and two kids lurking somewhere in Jersey, he didn't advertise them. Not one snapshot or bold crayon scribble. Maybe the man lived for his work, Cat thought generously. She smiled at Atlas as he seated himself. No sense in getting him riled up right off the bat.

'We got some issues to address here.' Atlas leaned back in his chair, legs spread wide. She wondered if that sophisticated move worked on the interns. Show 'em your business end, just like a dog. 'I want to take issue with your . . .' he searched for the word, 'your unprofessional attitude.' He smiled a condescending smile.

'Really,' she said flatly.

'It isn't up to scratch.'

'Says who?' Cat snapped.

'Says me.'

'I'm busting my chops out there, Atlas. Every single day.'

'Really.'

'Every single day.' A slight narrowing of her eyes was the only sign that Cat was displeased. Still, her tone was light. Light and bright. Might get away with it. Might not.

'Well, I wish it showed more on air.'

'What's that supposed to mean?'

'What it sounds like.'

'Let's be frank, Atlas. This is personal. You don't like me. It's okay to admit that. But don't question my professionalism. I professionally get out of bed at three thirty every goddamned day for this network. And I do a good job.' Reflexively, Cat massaged her hands. 'We can only discuss this if you admit it's personal.'

'Alright. It *is* personal. It's your personal attitude. It's sloppy and you're a bad influence on the rest of the staff.'

'*The rest of the staff!* This isn't high school, Atlas. I can't "influence" anyone. We're all grown-ups.'

'You're off the Meat Man story,' he said.

'I don't fucking believe this. What have I done?'

'You've been fighting me every step of the way on

this, and I'm tired of it. Peter Ratch is on and you are off.'

Cat gripped her chair with both hands. She was so angry she didn't trust herself not to grab Atlas by the throat. When she spoke, her voice was very low.

'You're the one that turned the mother away. We could've had the story days before anybody else.'

Atlas looked at his computer screen. He didn't even have the grace to blush. 'It wasn't a story then. And you don't have the experience to criticize me. You're the weakest link in our on-air chain.'

'I know a story when I see one. Two missing white kids. That's a story, Eric.' But as she read the expression on his face, she understood: she was being punished for his mistake.

'Well, babe. When you sit in this chair, you can make the decisions. In the meantime, I have the support of the President.'

He was right Cat thought, and it depressed her suddenly. It wasn't about how you did your job, it was about how many suits would go to bat for you.

She stood up, walked slowly out of his office and closed the door quietly and precisely. There would be no histrionics. She wouldn't give him the pleasure.

She went to the ladies' room and was going to bang her fist on the glass when the sound of someone crying in one of the cubicles distracted her.

She knocked tentatively on the door.


Adrian didn't consider himself a vain man but when chunks of his hair started coming out in the shower, he knew it was time to find Tye and remind her forcefully that she'd gone too far. He was thinking about all the ways he would enjoy doing this. Then his American Express bill arrived.

Fortunately, his wife had returned to France by the time he discovered just how much of a sorry turn things had taken. She would not have been amused. Her daring experiment in living with her husband had not been a success. She hadn't found New York remotely like the place she'd seen in the Hollywood movies she professed to despise but nonetheless watched avariciously. It seemed too flat. She had made several trips to Fifth Avenue in a vain attempt to blunt the edge of her dissatisfaction, but found it a short-term palliative. Regretfully, she had booked her Concorde ticket and departed several weeks short of the time she had planned. She would not return to New York. In future, if Adrian wished to see her, he would have to set foot on French soil.

Adrian had thought the Aveda package was a thank-you gift from his recently departed wife – a way of acknowledging their unwritten understanding that their marriage could only survive if they saw each other no more than once or twice a year. But that was before he saw his hair disappearing down the drain.

Now he was set on revenge.

He reckoned that Tye must still be in New York. She had no reason, as far as he could tell, to go anywhere else. He didn't think it would be too difficult to find her. Tye was a sybarite. She would have found a wealthy friend or crashed at a hotel.

A couple of hours on the phone ruled out the friend

option. No one had seen her since the party at the Glick gallery. That only left hotels. Even that didn't daunt Adrian, because he knew Tye had very particular tastes. She would not stay in a place with flounces of chintz or patterned carpet. Her taste was sleek and modern, like the woman herself. Treacherous bitch.

Adrian made a list on a sketch pad with blue marker. It wasn't that long. A patient man would find her soon enough. And he was going to make her pay. She would be very, very sorry that she ever decided to take Adrian for a fool. He smiled as he dialled the number at the top of his list. The smile turned to a frown as another lock of hair flopped on the page. Oh, yes. She would be sorry.

# Chapter Fifty-Two

Cat knocked on the door of the wash room cubicle. 'Is everything okay?'

'No.' A snuffling sound from within. The woman blew her nose hard.

'Are you sick?'

'No.' Another big nose blow followed by a gasping sob.

'Why don't you come out and we'll talk about it,' Cat said in a soothing yet no-nonsense voice.

'I can't.'

'Why not?'

'I'm too ashamed.'

'There's nothing to be ashamed of.'

'Yes, there is.'

'Why don't you come out, anyway.'

Cat heard the rattle of the toilet roll holder and another loud blow. Then the person in the cubicle emerged. She was red-faced, clutching a handbag. She wore a pencil skirt and a tight, blue angora sweater.

'I'm Catrina,' she said, offering the girl a fresh tissue.

'Thanks.' The girl took it. 'I'm Freya. Freya Leith.'

\*

Renee had hit the jackpot with Sean Reynolds. He gave her the number of his father's former assistant. She had remembered the couture dress and the woman who'd bought it without any difficulty. Renee found the customer's phone number in the book. She lived in the Village, not too far from Renee's office. She decided to swing by.

She desperately wanted something solid to present to Cat, and soon. This whole thing had gotten out of hand. Cat was so preoccupied and short-tempered that she seemed to assume Renee's hunt for the dress was some kind of aggressive act, designed to prove her wrong. Renee felt as though her motives had been misrepresented, which made her nervous. She was sure that Cat had begun to regret her decision to stay in their relationship and that her bad mood was the set-up to the 'It's not you, it's me' speech. Renee did not want to hear that speech from Cat.

The house was closed up. Renee rang the bell a couple of times and then stood on the street, staring up at the windows until she was convinced there was nobody inside. She would have stayed longer except some weird guy came along and stared at her. She moved quickly along. No matter what the spin doctors of the new Manhattan said, it was still a science lab of lunacy.

What was with his parents' house all of a sudden? Cyrus wondered as he watched the petite blonde woman lean on the doorbell and then go to the other side of the street. This one was more to his taste than

the one with dark hair, but he'd made up his mind
about the other one now and it was his new policy that
once he'd decided on something, that was it. Prevari-
cation was for losers who didn't have long-term goals.

Still, he did enjoy watching her. She had a nice
figure and was dressed in very fashionable clothes that
fit her extremely well. He also liked her big earrings.
He smiled at her indulgently when she spotted him.
He even thought about going up and introducing himself – just like that. Maybe asking her out for a coffee
or something. But she had given him such a look of
contempt. Cyrus shrugged it off. Normally something
like that would have made him angry but now that he
was more mellow, it was kind of funny. Hey, *he* wasn't
the one hanging around outside complete strangers'
houses.

Although he prided himself on his artistic temperament,
Adrian was extremely methodical when he needed to
be. He bought a couple of New York City guidebooks
and read through the hotel listings thoroughly, deciding
from their descriptions which ones would suit Tye. This
helped him to narrow down his list.

He now thoroughly regretted ever meeting her. It
was only because his wife was an old-fashioned Catholic that she hadn't divorced him after the Victoria's
Secret lingerie – if you could call it that – had arrived
at the apartment. She was so horrified that she had had
to lie down while he held a cold cloth to her head. It
had taken some quick work on Adrian's part to persuade her not to leave him.

It never crossed Adrian's mind to wonder what he had done to get such a sweet deal. He had a highly successful wife whose responsibilities for the family export business kept them apart for months at a time. She also gave him a generous allowance, which let him paint and pursue his other interests. It had worked well up till now and he didn't want it to end. He loved his life. He would buy his Marie an expensive present, he decided. Something with diamonds. Maybe even spend a week or two in Lyon. It was perfectly bearable for short periods of time. He had spent a year there as a student, which was how he met Marie. She'd been different then, or maybe it was just because his French hadn't been very good. But he didn't regret marrying her, not for an instant.

He moved methodically down the list, ripping the pages out of the guidebooks as he did so.


'So what's up, Freya?' Cat asked kindly. The kid was no more than twenty-three or so.

Freya spent a few seconds assessing whether Catrina Vermont could be useful to her.

'Can we talk someplace private?' Freya asked, sniffling into her Kleenex.

'Sure. Let's go to my office.'

Freya sat in the only spare seat and drew a deep, shuddering breath.

'I guess you know I'm an intern here,' she said. 'I've only been here about a month but things have been going pretty well. I'm learning a lot. A lot more, I guess, than if I went to journalism school. I don't really feel like going back to college.

'So I'm trying to do everything I can. I know I'm going to have to spend some time, you know, some-place like a small-market station to get the kind of wide-ranging experience I need. I don't want to just have to work in the city, I think it's really important to get out there . . . in the real America . . . and work my way up.'

Cat smiled dryly and looked at Freya's kitten-heeled mules with the faux-leopard trim. They were going to come in really handy in the 'real' America.

'So what's the problem?'

Freya plucked at her handbag, one fingernail scraping the tiny black label on the front. She looked up at Cat and her blue eyes filled with tears. 'It's Eric Atlas,' she said softly. 'He's . . . he's . . . sexually . . .' her voice dropped away to a whisper, she cleared her throat. 'He's sexually harassing me.'

Even though Cat despised Eric Atlas, she did not believe for one minute that Freya was the innocent victim. She had 'vamp' written all over her and there had been whispers among the staff about one of the interns. Besides, the business about working her way up sounded a little too earnest to be true.

'That's a very serious allegation.'

'I don't say it lightly.' Freya's eyes glinted. She had expected more sympathy. Maybe she'd misjudged Catrina. But then the old bat had probably forgotten what sex was like. Assuming she'd ever known.

Cat had the internal phone directory pasted to the

wall beside her desk. She ran her finger down it until she came to Human Resources. She wrote the name and number of the woman who ran the department on a Post-it and handed it to Freya. Still, she felt obliged to warn her.

'Y'know I've worked with Eric for six years,' she said. 'When he's cornered, he's like a wounded bull elephant. He really doesn't care who he hurts.'

Freya lifted her shoulders and her mouth, a tiny mouth that seemed to draw her face down to a thin 'v', tightened. Cat could see what she was thinking. 'You're over the hill, but I'm young and beautiful, so the rules don't apply.' Freya got out her Filofax and carefully stuck the Post-it to a page decorated with hearts and bunny rabbits.

'I want to thank you for your help,' she said. 'I'll let you know how it goes.'

# Chapter Fifty-Three

I'm screwed, was Tye's first thought when she woke the next morning. She dragged herself out of bed. Stumbled through her morning routine. She ordered room-service coffee while she showered and dressed. She'd wear her normal clothes to the apartment and change once she got there.

She had scheduled five appointments, starting at midday. She tried to think of the personality and the accent she would assume. She tried a few half-heartedly and then discarded them. She'd just have to wing it.

Her father would have been appalled. His whole professional life he'd never deviated from his high principles and here she was, diving into the pond without even checking the depth of the water.

'I have no choice, Pop,' she said as she studied her reflection in the mirror. Pinching her cheeks. She was way too pale, like she was sickening for something.

She put on her make-up, applying a little more than usual. It had to work, that's all there was to it. She'd make it work.

*

Cyrus got up early and went out for breakfast. He took his sacred book to read while he ate a bagel with low-fat cream cheese. Even though he knew it practically by heart, he was always nourished by the wisdom he found on the pages. There was always a new way of looking at something. A little gem that lay previously undiscovered. Life was a lot like that, he thought, surprised at his clarity of thought at this hour of the day. Life was full of pleasant little surprises and they always came out of left field.

'I *love* that book,' the waitress said. She peered over his shoulder, pretty rudely, Cyrus thought. 'I musta read it fifty times.'

'Really?' he said coolly. He didn't welcome the intrusion.

'Sure. Looks like you have, too.' The waitress pointed at the book's torn spine. 'Isn't it the greatest? It must be hard to find someone in this town who hasn't read it, after all those weeks on the best-seller list.'

Cyrus had no idea it was on the best-seller list. He put his bagel down, uneaten.

'Sure. You musta seen Dr Finkelziz on the TV. He's always on. *Oprah*, *Ricki Lake*. He's got an ad in the subway.'

'I haven't seen him.'

'Gee, that's too bad, he's a real inspiration. Ya didn't see the show where they went to his house? The gold taps? The three Rolls Royces?'

'No.'

'Ya know he's got statues in his bedrooms, real

marble. Marble on the floor . . . everywhere. I saw it in *People* magazine.'

Cyrus was starting to feel he'd heard enough. He turned back to the book. The waitress didn't seem to notice.

'I only bought it in the first place because of the title. Made me wanna pick it right up off that shelf.'

Cyrus sipped his coffee, wondered if he should just tell her to go away. He didn't want to share the Master with this vulgar creature. It wasn't about material possessions, he knew that. It was about something far more profound. She might have read the book but she didn't get its real message.

'. . . and *Climbing the Mountain of Me* really says it all, dontcha think?'

'I never thought much about the title,' Cyrus said. He turned to the cover – what kind of title was that anyway?

'I always thought those self-help books were all the same,' the waitress said, and swept his plate away. 'And let me tell you, I've read a few – but *Climbing* is the only one that's helped me. Do you know that people who've read it get together to discuss it? They call themselves Social Climbers. Cute, dontcha think?'

Cyrus barely heard her. He had to put his coffee cup down. His hand was shaking that much.

'But this isn't a self-help book,' he said. 'It's a philosophical treatise.'

The waitress shrugged. 'Call it what you like.'

Cyrus sat stunned. Self-help? His precious, luminous work was a self-help book? For the first time in ages a horrible, debilitating word had re-entered his lexicon. Doubt.

Quinn had been up since six, writing. A stunned Malcolm and Rhonda had left at eight, slipping out in silence. Malcolm even came back from Starbucks with a latte, which he placed by Quinn's computer like an offering. Quinn hardly even stopped typing to thank him and wish his brother a cheery good day.

These words! He was surrounded by them. They vibrated around him like radio waves. Crouched over his laptop, words spitting out, he was suspended where time and place had no meaning. His reality was bounded by a ten-inch screen. By the smooth feel of his fingertips on the keys.

He would have forgotten his apartment-viewing appointment if Molly hadn't showed up and made him get dressed. She hassled him like an old fishwife. She even made him put on one of Malcolm's ties, for God's sake. Like he was going to meet the bank manager instead of some slick con woman.

When Quinn came out of Mal's bedroom, tie in place, Molly was studying the photo of the woman with a magnifying glass that she never admitted needing. 'We've got you this time,' she murmured. 'Your goose is cooked, me girl.'

Quinn shook his head. He really hoped he didn't end up like that.

*

Marion's hospital room got sun for about twenty-five minutes every morning. A pale yellow trapezoid shape would come to rest on the wall, edge across to her bed and then slip away.

It was a trick of reflection. Marion couldn't see the sun from her window because her room faced north. What she got was the second-hand sun from the glass tower on the opposite street. She watched it solemnly every day. She even came to look forward to it. It was like a tiny vacation. It became the time when she gave herself permission to blank her mind and not deal with the pain that threatened to crush her. She was sure Gus would understand that she could not grieve for him twenty-four hours a day. Not if she was going to find her way out of this.

Marion barely slept at night so the doctors gave her a light sedative. She had to prove to the nurse that she'd swallowed it and was not storing up a bunch to try to kill herself again. She told them she wouldn't, but they didn't believe her. Most suicides tried again, she supposed. If at first you don't succeed and all that.

There was a knock. John Abruzzo put his head around the door, grinning.

'Brought something for you,' he said.

'You shouldn't have. It's my last day.'

'This one you can take away with you.'

John Abruzzo looked down the hallway, beckoning. 'C'mon. You can come in.'

Marion sat up straighter in bed. What had he done now?

'Mommy!' Antonia and Grace threw themselves at her, knocking the breath from her lungs.


When Cat got up, Renee was in the kitchen and the apartment smelt of fresh coffee. One good thing about being off the story was that she could get up at a reasonable hour.

'Hey, babe.' Renee handed her a mug. 'What does a girl have to do to get a date around here?'

'Sorry. I fell asleep early last night. I was exhausted.'

'I have news that'll put the pep back in your stand-up.' Renee paused expectantly.

'Can it wait? I have to shower.' Cat headed for the bathroom.

'We used to shower together.' Renee followed her.

'This isn't the time to pick a fight,' Cat said. 'I have enough on my mind, okay?'

Renee was ready with a snippy reply but bit her tongue. 'Okay.' She waited until Cat was out of the shower and tried again. Cat was blow-drying her hair.

'I've found the woman who owns the dress,' she said casually. 'You might want to follow it up.'

'I can't. I've got too much other stuff to think about.'

'At least talk to this woman,' Renee said. 'You never know. It could lead somewhere. At least try.'

Cat put her brush down slowly. 'You're not listen-ing to me! I'm in deep trouble here. I can't think about stories. I have to think about saving my sweet ass. If it's not already too late.

'But . . .'

'Just . . . butt out, will you?'

Renee backed off. 'What did you say?'

Cat picked up the hairbrush. 'Please. I'm late. This isn't the time.'

'Yeah. Job first. That's always the way it is with you. You'd take that stupid place over me any day of the week, and they don't even like you there.' Renee could feel the blood rushing to her head. All that time and effort for nothing. She was shouting now. 'You have no idea about anything . . . you're so dumb. You just don't get it. This is about us. It's always been about us. Don't you see that?'

Cat flicked the blow-dryer on and aimed it at her head like a gun.

'Why don't you at least try? Why are you giving up? You never used to be like this. The woman I knew had some fire.'

Cat put the dryer down, turned on Renee, furious. 'Sermon over? Cause I gotta go.' She pushed past her, grabbed her coat and bag. Renee stumbled along behind.

'Cat, I didn't mean . . .'

'Don't you dare lecture me!'

'So I'm supposed to go on paying, is that it? For ever and ever? What happened to forgive and forget?'

But she was gone, slamming the door. Renee sat down in the middle of the floor. Larry the terrier saw his chance and licked her face. She scratched behind his ears. She'd only tried to help. Tried too hard, maybe. One of her old girlfriends had accused her of that. She always plunged into things without thinking.

Her tears ran. Larry, sensing salt, licked them

away, putting his paws on her shoulders to get a better angle. Renee pushed him off. 'You're the only action I'm getting these days,' she told his happy doggy face. He didn't seem upset at the rejection but settled at her feet.

That reminded her how tired she was. She hadn't slept properly in days. She stretched out on the floor next to Larry and fell asleep.

# Chapter Fifty-Four

Cat held onto her anger in the taxi to work. Renee had no right to interfere. She knew nothing about the politics of news. Shit. And to pull that stunt on this day of all days, when she needed her wits about her. She wasn't going to feel guilty. She would not. She had to keep herself together, focus on her career, because if she didn't, she could be damn sure nobody else was going to.

She had to talk to her boss, Gerald Long, immediately and find out what her position was. If it was a worst-case scenario, and Atlas was marshalling his argument to have her sacked, maybe she'd start working on her resumé, call up a couple of contacts at one of the networks. They were tenuous contacts but this wasn't the time to be squeamish. Maybe this was the opportunity she'd been waiting for. She'd been talking for years about getting another job, but had been too apathetic to get out there and network. Now was definitely the time. She still had a good few years left in her.

'Here you are, miss. Have a nice day.' The cab drew up outside the building.

'Thanks, but I very much doubt it.' Cat paid the

driver and ignored the feeling of dread she had as she walked through her employer's doors.

The contact lenses tinted Tye's eyes a startling shade of purple and they hurt like crazy. She brushed away the tears as she walked over to the apartment. She was figuratively and literally blind. Great, just fucking great.

She got to the apartment in good time, but realized she'd left her mobile phone back at the hotel. Double damn. She pulled her key out of the lock. She'd have to go back. She needed that phone.

Cyrus heard the key in the lock and his heart leapt. She was here and she would help him make it all right. His confidence had been jolted by that stupid waitress, with her talk about marble floors and gold taps. At first he had thought she was right, that the guy who had written his book – who had introduced him to the Master – was another charlatan who only cared about the bottom line. But after thinking about it for a while he had realized that it was just another test. His reality was what he made it.

He felt tense, a little nervous – clammy hands, dry mouth, that sort of thing. The nerves you feel before a big, important day. The ones that disappear once you're in the middle of things and the adrenaline is surging. He couldn't wait to dive in and smother his doubts completely. A self-help guru. What a joke!

She was coming. He could hear the key rattling in the lock, but then nothing. The key was removed. He went cautiously to the window. She was gone, disappearing fast up the steps to the street.

His first instinct was to run after her and pull her back but that, he knew, would be wrong. Instead, he took deep breaths to control his panic and anger. It was just another test, that was all it was. She was coming back. There was a psychic connection between them. She belonged to him now.


Marion was surprised how weak she felt. How different the outside world looked, how grown-up the twins seemed. They were serious, not fighting. Concerned about her. But it hadn't been that long since she'd seen them, so why did everything seemed so changed?

Antonia and Grace had helped her pack her things and check out of the hospital. They walked on either side of her down the long hospital corridors, their tall young bodies ramrod straight, as though they were providing her with an official escort. John Abruzzo lumbered along behind with the lilies, which were still in full bloom and smelling glorious. It was funny how life went on. She hadn't expected flowers to still smell.

The twins watched gravely as Marion went through the check-out procedure. They asked the doctor intelligent questions. He didn't look much older than they did. Another bottle of sedatives was handed over and Grace put it in her bag. The two girls exchanged a glance.

'Ready, Momma?' Antonia asked.

Marion nodded. 'Is my hair okay?' she said suddenly, surprised by the irrelevancy of her concerns.

'You look great.' Grace smiled, and hooked her arm through her mother's. Antonia did the same on the other side.

'Wait!' Marion twisted out of their grip. Turned to study each of them. She touched their blonde hair, searched their green eyes.

'I –' Marion looked at each of her girls in turn. How would she begin to apologize for the terrible thing she had done to them?

'We'll talk about it later,' Grace said. 'When you're ready.' She put a jacket around her mother's shoulders to protect her from the thin wind that sliced up the avenue.


Although she was no intellectual, Freya Leith had profited enormously from the twenty-one years she had spent being expensively educated. And the most important thing she had learned in that time was how to get her own way.

Eric Atlas had lied to her. He'd promised her a job and he'd reneged on that promise. He had to pay, simple as that.

Freya was not stupid. She knew that her complaint against Eric Atlas wouldn't do the damage she wanted. Eric would counter-attack. Maybe even say that she had harassed him, or get the Human Resources people to believe that their affair had been consensual. Somehow, he'd get out of it. Freya knew that, no matter how many politically correct platitudes the company code listed, there was always a discrepancy between the rule book and the way things actually worked. Eric's career might go through a rough patch for a couple of years but he would survive it. Boys always stuck together. Freya would be labelled a bimbo, her career would be dead before it had even started and Eric Atlas would rise as steadily as a helium balloon. She couldn't let that happen.

She pulled her phone out of her handbag and carefully punched in a New Jersey number. The phone rang six times – she counted – before a woman's voice answered.

'Mrs Atlas?'

'This is she.'

'Hello, my name is Freya Leith. Do you have a minute?'


Cyrus found it hard to focus on being positive while he waited in the apartment for the woman to come back. He was hungry. He wanted more coffee and bagels and cream cheese. He wanted satisfaction, closure, love, self-respect. Everything! Everything he'd been denied through his miserable life.

He pulled himself up short. Self-pity. He couldn't let himself fall into that trap. The road was mined. He really would fall apart if he went there. No. He had to remain disciplined. Everything that happened was part of the plan. His plan. He was in control. He paced and paced. Then he stopped. He had to force himself to be calm. To be still and to concentrate on the moment.

He was concentrating so hard that he almost didn't hear the scraping of key in the lock again.

She'd come back!

# Chapter Fifty-Five

Renee made a very strong cup of coffee at her studio. She'd felt so lousy when she woke up that she hadn't even put make-up on before she left for work, which was something she normally never let slide. She contemplated her white face in the mirror of the washroom and grimaced. She was thirty-six. Make-up was no longer an optional extra.

Larry bumped against her shins.

'We're going to miss her,' she said to the dog. 'In spite of it all.'

Her tiny work space, which usually never failed to make her happy, felt grim this morning. She noticed the plaster was chipped, that the windows needed washing and pads of dust had collected under the radiators. She'd let so much slide lately, that even the battery in her cellphone had run down. She'd put her whole life on hold for that ungrateful shrew of a girlfriend. Well no more.

Renee sat at her drawing table and took out the piece of note paper on which she'd written down the address of Mrs Tower, the dress owner. She neatly ripped it into quarters then eighths and threw it in the trash.

'You'd never let me down, would you?' she said to Larry as he settled down to sleep on his mangy rug.

Success came easily to Adrian. He hadn't had to endure the struggles and setbacks of so many artists and so over the years had slipped into a sense of complacency that on some level he believed to be self-fulfilling.

This morning, for instance, he'd gone to SoHo to check a couple of hotels. At the same time he was awaiting confirmation that a fashionable SoHo gallery would mount a one-man retrospective of his work. Adrian thought it auspicious that the two things were happening in the same part of town.

He found Tye at a hotel on Wooster Street.

He waited outside until Tye came out about an hour later, carrying a small bag. She didn't see him. She walked west on Spring and kept putting her hand to her eyes as though she was crying. Good. The bitch. He hoped she was really fucking miserable.

Still, he was surprised at the lust he felt as he followed her. She had good bones, a good arse and tits. Perhaps now that his wife had gone, he should invite her back. Pretend nothing had ever happened. He fantasized about grabbing her and pulling her into an alley somewhere – really giving it to her. But it didn't last long – he caught his reflection in a window. He was almost completely bald, which would not have been so bad except that he'd always imagined himself to have good bones, and the lack of hair had shown him quite brutally that this was not true. His face looked puzzled and slightly squashed, like a just-born baby's. He would need to buy a baseball cap. No, that was much too plebeian. A fedora, perhaps.

Adrian followed Tye to the West Village. She stopped at a basement apartment, unlocked the door and went inside. He was about to follow her down the steps when his pager went off. He checked the number. It was his dealer calling about the retrospective. He looked up and down the street but couldn't see a payphone. Shit.

He needed to know about the exhibition. Tye would have to wait. He went to find a phone.


'Cat, what's up?' Gerald Long smiled as his glasses slipped down his nose.

Gerald's corner office had a view of downtown. His desk was covered in photos of his wife and kids. Smiling faces at the beach, in the park. Vacations on Cape Cod. Cat looked at them and back at her boss. Her kind, affable, supportive boss who, if the office rumour mill contained any truth, was on the way out. A new senior executive had been bought in – a business-school graduate who wanted to make his mark. Gerald wouldn't have that downtown view for long. Soon a cigar-chomping hotshot would be practising his putting on the worn carpet and bragging about the price of his five iron.

Cat said good morning, and noticed, as she always did, a framed quote that hung behind Gerald's desk. 'Three things in human life are important. The first is to be kind. The second is to be kind. The third is to be kind.' It was attributed to Henry James. Cat remembered that the first time she'd read it, she'd felt a stab of contempt for Gerald. How outdated. How non-news, she'd thought. Why was he displaying his weakness on the wall like that? But now she felt differently.

Renee. She covered her eyes in shame. What had she done?

'Is everything OK?'

She nodded. She couldn't speak just yet. She'd cry.

'Atlas?'

'Sort of,' she said, muffled. Gerald came out from behind his desk and dangled a box of Kleenex in front of her. She took one. Blew her nose briskly. 'He's taken me off the story.'

Gerald knew. He pointed to the television. The sound was turned down and Peter Ratch was doing a standup outside Police Plaza. He looked as relaxed as a wooden clothes pin.

'Freya Leith has filed a complaint,' Gerald said. 'It'll grind through the usual channels.'

'I tried to talk her out of it,' Cat said.

Gerald shook his head. 'Which ever way it goes it can only end badly – for her.'

'That's what I told her.' Cat looked at the Henry James quote again. What did that tight-assed Victorian know anyway? The man had never been near a newsroom. She wondered what Eric Atlas's framed quote would be. Something pithy from Vlad the Impaler, probably.

Gerald took off his glasses and squinted at her. 'You know there's not much I can do. For you, I mean.'

Cat nodded slowly. Her eye kept returning to the photos. The gracious, smiling wife, the happy kids. She wondered if they all had fun when they got together.

Did they genuinely enjoy being with each other or were the smiles just a polite lie for the camera?

It's about priorities, she thought suddenly. Gerald had it right. Renee had it right. People first. She took a breath.

'I've got a lead on the story. I need a crew.'

'What kind of lead?'

'It's about the dress in the security video.'

Gerald raised his eyebrows.

'The dress is extremely rare.'

'Cops tell you?'

'No.' Cat paused. Gerald seemed to be expecting an answer. 'A designer. My girlfriend. My girlfriend's a designer. She's found the person who owns the dress.'

Cat had expected Gerald, who was old-school WASP, to be shocked by her confession, but he took the news calmly.

'Well, that's good enough for me,' he said. 'Why don't I distract Atlas while you take a crew?'

How did he ever get into news? Cat wondered. His manners were a huge disadvantage in an industry where only bull-headed ruthlessness got you anywhere.

'It might not—' Cat started to say, but stopped. What did it matter if it didn't add up to anything? It was all falling apart anyway and this might be her last chance to stick it to Atlas. Why not just go with it?

Cat arranged to meet the crew downstairs. She felt better than she had in weeks.


Tye didn't remember the apartment being so dark. She turned on all the lights, but it didn't make much difference. A couple of bulbs had blown. She tried to open a window to get some fresh air, but it had been painted shut and wouldn't budge. She fiddled with the air-conditioning switch and the system came on with a loud shudder, making her jump.

It was eleven forty. Perhaps there was time to nip to the store and buy some light bulbs and a bunch of flowers to brighten the place up a bit. She grabbed her handbag, checking to make sure she had the keys, and went out.

Cyrus had the closet door open a little but he couldn't see what she was up to, so the sound of the air conditioning made him yelp in surprise. What on earth was she doing? Why didn't she just come into the bedroom, like he'd visualized?

Then he heard the door closing. Oh, man. She couldn't be leaving already. What on earth was happening?

He stayed in the closet for a couple of minutes taking deep breaths to control his anxiety – and to double-check that it wasn't a trap of some sort – before pushing the door open gently and stepping out.

'Will someone tell me what the hell is going on?' he said out loud to himself when he discovered his apartment was, once again, empty.

Cyrus glanced around. What was he supposed to make of this? Reflexively, he switched the lights off. He hated wasting energy.

Then he saw the bag.

It was a green canvas bag with brown leather trim. Cyrus's first thought was that he shouldn't touch it because it didn't belong to him. But that was stupid.

This woman had entered his apartment illegally. He could do what he wanted with her stuff.

Besides, he couldn't shake the feeling that the bag contained a message.

He upzipped it carefully. The zipper was stiff, so he had to tug it in a couple of places. He was a bit nervous, to be honest. He felt as though there ought to be a drum roll or something.

He peeled back the zipper. There was a chiffon scarf underneath. Tentatively, he pulled it away.

Human hair!

'Ohmigod,' Cyrus breathed, staring at it. His heart was racing. He felt hot all over. Human hair. 'Ohmigod,' he said again and wiped his hand on his pants leg. He was reaching out to touch it when he heard the rattle of the key in the lock. Quickly he pushed the scarf back in, closed the bag and darted back in the closet. He stood in the dark, hands pressed against the wall, breathing, breathing.

Human hair! That changed everything.


Tye sniffed. There was definitely a strange odour in the place. She put the light bulbs on the breakfast bar. There was one wooden chair in the corner. She pulled it over to the lights so she could reach them. The central chandelier had five bulbs and two were dead. The extra light will make all the difference, Tye thought, as she freed the bulbs from their cardboard wrapping. Although God knew in the West Village an apartment could come with its own unwashed religious hermit and still rent for three grand a month.

She reached up to take the dead bulb out when she remembered she'd left the lights on. But now they were off. Had the power gone out? She jumped off the chair and flipped the switch. The lights went on.

She felt as though she had been doused in ice water.


Human hair.

Cyrus could not believe that his deepest yearning had been answered. A soulmate. Someone to share his work, his vision. He had no idea how she'd found him, or why. But he knew she was the woman for him – the hair proved that – so he put those other questions aside. He was going to accept this gift humbly and gratefully. There would be plenty of time later – when they were comfortable with each other to tease out the 'how comes' and the 'what ifs'. He imagined them taking long, winter walks around Manhattan, all bundled up against the cold, laughing at private jokes and marvelling as all lovers do, he felt sure, at the miracle of having found each other.

'Hello?' Tye forced her voice not to tremble as she peered around the door to the bedroom. She was furiously thinking of ways to salvage the situation. 'Hello?'

The bedroom was empty. Tye let out a breath. Everything was okay. She must have imagined leaving the lights on. She leaned against the door jamb. Her nerves were shot and the first apartment viewer was coming in a few minutes. She had to change and get her shit together.

Cyrus watched her through a crack in the closet door. She was very beautiful. She could have been a model or an actress. Maybe a little thin for his personal taste, but he knew that's the way women liked to be these days. And she'd probably put on a little weight once he started taking her to his favourite restaurants.

The reason he was still in the closet, that he hadn't just stepped right out and introduced himself, was that he wanted to make a really great first impression but he couldn't decide what his opening words should be. Although one part of him thought it didn't even matter if they were meant for each other, the other side, his creative side, wanted to say or do something really classy that she would remember for years later – maybe even tell their kids. Or when they were out at night with new friends and they asked, as people usually did, 'how did you meet?' she'd glance fondly at Cyrus and say: 'Oh, he just walked up and asked me to marry him.' Or something like that.

So there he was, waiting for inspiration. Besides, what was another couple of minutes when they had the rest of their lives together?

Cat called Renee at home and at work and got an answering machine both times. She tried her cellphone but a robotic-voiced woman informed her it wasn't available. Damn. They'd just have to drive over to Renee's studio. She'd probably just gone out for coffee or something. Or wasn't answering because she was pissed at Cat. I'm sorry, she thought, willing Renee to hear her telepathically. I am a bitch. You're right and I'm wrong. Call me, please. But her phone remained stubbornly silent.

The crew car inched through traffic. The President was visiting and the whole city was gridlocked. Cat leaned back in her seat and closed her eyes. She and Renee needed to go away and spend some time together. They hadn't had a decent vacation for over a year. She imagined a lovely country inn with blazing fires and hand-stitched quilts. She'd talk to Renee about it once this awful day was over.

Quinn had finally shaken Molly off. It was so simple that he was annoyed at himself for not having thought of it sooner.

'Have you heard of Century 21?' he asked casually. They were getting ready to go to the apartment viewing.

'What's that?'

'A department store. Designer clothes at knock-down prices. I'm surprised you don't know about it.' Quinn inspected a fingernail.

'Where?'

'Downtown,' Quinn said airily. 'Maybe we can go there after the apartment, although it's best to get there early . . . the bargains and everything. Gucci . . . Prada . . .'

How an Irish octogenarian peasant woman had developed a lust for flashy European designers was going to have to remain one of life's subtler mysteries Quinn thought. Only clothes could put such a glint in Molly's eyes. Nothing else on earth gave her the same pleasure. Not her family. Not even winning at blackjack.

'Early, you say?'

'The earlier the better. It's probably already too late –'

Molly considered, 'I don't know why I'm doing this. You don't need me.'

'Are you sure?' Quinn said innocently.

'Course. I'll jump in a cab.'

'But what about the apartment? The con woman?'

'Deal with her the way I told you.'

Quinn went downstairs with Molly and put her in a cab. The haste with which she left was almost indecent. He was tempted to go indoors and start writing, but he'd already put in a couple of hours of solid work that day and he felt like a walk. Besides, he still needed an apartment and who knew? If this one worked out maybe he could persuade Molly to stump up for the deposit.

Tye opened the bag and saw that it wasn't the way she had left it. She felt strangely calm as she closed it again. She stood up slowly and crossed the living room to get her handbag. Time to get the fuck out of this place.

He was standing behind her when she turned. Blocking her exit. A tall guy dressed all in black. Long, straggly hair. A thin face with dark brows and a wide, lopsided mouth. His hands were in his pockets and he seemed keyed up, maybe even high.

She stood still, gripping her bags, one looped over her forearm making her feel like the Queen Mother.

'Hi,' he said, 'I'm Cyrus.'

# Chapter Fifty-Six

It took fifty-three minutes to get from the television station in mid-town to Tribeca. Cat was humming with frustration by the time they arrived. She pressed the buzzer for Renee's loft and waited.

'Hello?' Renee's voice sounded tinny and suspicious.

'It's me. Can I come up?'

'Sorry, but I'm busy.' Renee broke the connection. Cat pushed the buzzer again.

'Two minutes.'

'I don't want to talk to you right now.'

'I want to apologize,' Cat said. 'I've been acting like an idiot and I'm really sorry. I'm so tired, you know. And the pressure . . .' Jose, the cameraman and Johnny the soundman were staring at her from the car, which was double-parked. A queue had formed behind them and a quartet of angry horns sounded.

'Go around the block,' Cat said. Jose took off. She hit the buzzer again. 'Please, Renee. I promise – two minutes.'

Renee buzzed her in. Ignoring the elevator, Cat ran up three flights of stairs.

Renee was standing in the doorway, her face

pinched and white. Cat had rehearsed a speech, but when she saw Renee, she forgot it. Instead she threw herself into her girlfriend's arms.

When Jose came back, there was another woman with Cat and a small fox terrier. They all climbed in the back.

'Jose, Johnny, this is my girlfriend, Renee. The hairy one is Larry the terrier. Are you sure we couldn't just leave Larry in your studio?'

'He gets really nervous when he's left alone – he was abandoned as a puppy,' Renee explained to the two men. 'He'll sit in the car and not bother anybody.' Larry leapt onto Cat's lap and licked her face. She pushed him away and picked the dog hairs off her black suit. Renee looked at her, hurt. Cat had always politely ignored the dog, but now perhaps she should try harder, tentatively she scratched behind Larry's ears. The dog belched and grinned. Cat smiled weakly.

'Hey, Renee, nice to meet you. Where to next, Cat?' Jose asked.

Renee spread the ripped-up pieces of paper on the back seat and pieced them together. 'The West Village,' she said. 'I'll have the exact address in a minute.'

'No hurry,' Jose said. 'In this traffic nobody's getting anyplace fast.'


'Hi, Cyrus,' Tye automatically slipped into an American accent. 'I'm Penny.'

Cyrus pointed at the bag. 'I see you know the Master.' He took a step towards her. Tye took a half step back.

'I don't know what you mean,' she said carefully.

'Yeah you do. I saw what you have in your bag,' he said. Damn, it wasn't coming out right. He wanted to be light and chatty and here was this whine creeping into his voice, like a petulant kid. He smiled, hoping that'd get things back on a flirtatious note. Trouble was, he wasn't much good at flirting.

'My bag? Oh, that.' Tye began assessing possible weak spots. Knees, eyes, throat, instep. Perhaps she should go for his eyes with the keys. 'It's just clothes and stuff.'

'Yeah, and stuff.' He was aiming for a light, debonair laugh but somehow it came out as a snicker. God, he was really messing this up. They wouldn't have any happy first memories as a couple if he didn't get his act together pretty damn quick.

He noticed she was wearing a lot of make-up. He'd have to have a word with her about that later – not now of course. But in the next couple of months he'd let her know, very gently, that he thought she was beautiful as she was and didn't need a lot of war paint to make her look better.

'I'm going now,' Tye said. She started towards the door.

'But you just got here.'

'I have a busy day.'

'Penny is a pretty name. Is it short for Penelope?' He moved squarely in front of the door.

Tye couldn't decide whether to keep him talking or to be firm and just try and leave. Perhaps talking was the best. Keep him from thinking about other things. 'Ah . . . yes it is. Penelope Ann. Listen, I'd love to stay and talk but I'm real late for another appointment. Please excuse me.'

Cyrus put his hand over the doorknob. 'But I want you to stay.'

'That's not possible—' Tye started to stay. He stopped her.

She was surprised at his strength. He grabbed her, turned her round and held her firmly off balance. She thrashed and kicked but hit nothing that would make him loosen his grip. Tye was choking. The pressure on her throat and the smell of the guy made her gag.

He dragged her into the bedroom. Oh, dear God, Tye thought. He was grunting. His horrible, greasy hair flicked in her face. She thought irrelevantly of how she hated long hair on men.

It was dark. He reached out with his foot and kicked the skirting boards. Tye kept trying to twist in his grip. Why the hell was he kicking the skirting boards? Then the bookcase swung open and he was dragging her into another room, one she hadn't seen before. This one was clinical. A large steel cabinet. A futon. There were no windows and it smelt rotten.

Tye knew then that she was going to die.

Quinn didn't have any trouble finding the apartment. He was a few minutes late because he'd stopped for a coffee and the line had been long, but he didn't think it would pose a problem. He descended the stairs, double-checked he'd got the right apartment, then rang the bell. Nobody came to the door. He rang the bell again. Waited. A third ring. Nothing. He walked up the stoop and checked the bell up there, but that one was clearly a whole house and therefore not the right one.

He thought maybe he'd misread Molly's spidery scrawl. He checked the address again. It corresponded with the number on the door. Damn. Probably Molly had copied it down wrong.

Oh well, nothing really lost. He'd had a pleasant walk. He was eager to get back to his work.

'Now you sit here, missy.' Cyrus had forgotten all about making a dazzling first impression. He was a little piqued because she didn't seem to get that they were supposed to be together. So he figured he had to do the caveman thing at first. Just to get her attention. He'd had to get the razor out of his pocket to let her know he meant business which wasn't the most ideal thing, but she would understand at least that he was committed to making this thing work.

'You stay there, okay?' He pushed her into the chair and backed towards the metal cabinet where he had stored some things to tie her up with. He didn't intend to hurt her, but he wanted to keep her in one place while they got to know each other. So what if she had to come around to loving him because of the Stockholm syndrome? That wouldn't make her feelings any less valid. Besides, he'd heard that women really went for guys who took charge.

He searched frantically through the cupboards. He was sure there was masking tape in here someplace.

He only took his eyes off her for a second, so he was surprised when the chair came crashing down on his head.

Freya Leith finished talking to Mindy Atlas and hung up with a prim smile. Eric's wife hadn't been too eager to talk to her in the beginning, but Freya was good at holding an audience. Besides, no woman can resist hearing what her husband does in bed with someone else. Not that they'd actually done it in bed ever – or even lying down, for that matter. Freya had spared Mindy most of the details, instead she had played the abused youngster card to the max. She'd done tears. She'd done the 'He promised to marry me' line, her voice quivering as though she were deeply upset, when actually she could barely stop herself from bursting out laughing. Mindy had listened with a silence so frigid that a couple of times Freya wondered if she was still there. Eventually, Mrs Atlas had said, 'I have to go now,' and had hung up the phone.

Freya wiped the tears of laughter from her eyes. She was reasonably confident that if she hadn't killed the Atlas marriage she had at least dealt it a maiming blow. But that didn't mean she had finished with him, not by a long shot.

Eric Atlas's fatal mistake had been to lose his temper. He had shrieked at her. He'd called her a fucking cunt, which Freya Leith considered really unacceptable. He had changed the rules of the game with that one crude remark, and he had altered his own fate. There was only going to be one person left standing at the end of this little war and Freya Leith was calmly determined that it would be her.

She opened her Filofax and extracted a photocopied list that she had stolen from Eric's office. It contained the names and phone numbers of twenty or so former interns. After all, one complaint of sexual misconduct was one thing – but two or three was quite another.

Marking the female interns carefully in purple ink, she began making her way down the list.

# Chapter Fifty-Seven

Adrian was pissed off and shocked in equal degrees. The gallery had turned him down. And not only that, they'd chosen instead some bastard whose work Adrian considered far inferior to his – a Hispanic artist from East Harlem who was flavour of the month. Bloody Yanks, always choosing the fucking PC option. The way things were going the white male middle-class artist was going to be a fucking endangered species. And he'd be swept away by the tidal wave of talentless pricks who talked a good yarn about how fucking hard their lives had been struggling against the establishment. What was so wrong with being white, male and middle class anyway? Just because a bunch of learning-impaired lefties didn't fucking like it.

Fuck Tye. This was all her fault. The mood he was in, when he found her, he'd fucking strangle the bitch.

Quinn was walking back down the street, thinking of perhaps another cappuccino when a mad-looking guy in paint-stained jeans barged past, pushing him to one side.

'Hey, buddy, can't you see I'm in a cast?' Quinn yelled. The guy took no notice. Quinn nursed his shoulder, shooting daggers at the guy's back – what right did he have just to thump into somebody without apologizing? He decided to go after him, have it out.

The guy was striding fast. Quinn had to half run to keep up. Then he stopped. The paint-stained guy was going to the apartment Quinn had just left. He jumped down the stairs and banged on the door.

Quinn edged up to the railing. The guy was banging the door so hard it was shaking. Yelling something Quinn couldn't catch. Quinn hung back. Maybe Molly had been right and this was the con woman at work again. He decided to hang around. Things could get interesting.

Tye had half expected the chair to break when she hit the lunatic, because chairs did that in movies. Most other times they stayed whole, which wasn't a lot of use to her. The lunatic was baying, and Tye realized the chair was too heavy for her to use quickly in a second strike without the advantage of surprise.

She had done some damage, though. She'd given him a crack on the head and there was blood pouring from his hand, probably from the razor he'd been holding. Trouble was, his injuries seemed to have made things worse.

Tye tried to focus on keeping the chair between them while she assessed her options and came up with some kind of plan, but the guy was nimble. He made a couple of attempts to grab her. She feinted, trying to remember the shadow-boxing lessons her dad had given her.

Where was the door? It had closed flush with the wall, and she couldn't make it out in the dim light. There didn't appear to be any windows either. She didn't know how much longer she could keep this up. She was shaking so hard, she thought she would fall apart if this guy didn't slice her apart first.

He sprang at her, razor outstretched. She dodged to one side but went over on her ankle. The chair tumbled down on top of her and Cyrus grabbed it, turned it round so the legs had her pinned to the ground.

'Gotcha,' he said. Blood from his hand dripped onto Tye's face.


The crew car was crawling up Sixth Avenue when Eric Atlas got on the two-way radio.

'Crew Twelve, call the desk. Do you copy me?'

Jose picked up the receiver and pressed the button. 'Copy. But we're not done with this job. Over.'

'Copy. Just come back to the bureau.'

Jose turned to Cat and shrugged.

'Give me that.' Jose handed the receiver to Cat.

'Eric, this is Catrina. I have the crew and I'm keeping them. Do you copy?'

'No copy, darling, you can't play Lois Lane today. We need the crew for real news. Over.'

'This is real news, you asshole.'

'Either return to the bureau or lose your jobs. Copy?'

'We copy,' Jose said. He replaced the receiver in its cradle. 'Sorry, Cat.'

'Pull over,' she said. 'I'm getting out.'

The terrier was delighted with the unexpected walk. He frisked up Seventh Avenue with Renee struggling to keep up in her dominatrix-style shoes. Cat dialled Eric's number on her cellphone.

'Atlas? Catrina. I'm not coming back to the bureau. I'm chasing this story. I've got a real lead here and it's going to bury you when it gets out that you tried to stop me.'

Renee heard what sounded like barking on the other end of the line. Cat held the receiver away from her ear. 'I'm giving you fair warning, that's all. Be on guard, you asshole, because you are going down.' She jammed the aerial down and closed the phone.

'Is that true?' Renee asked.

Cat shrugged. 'Who knows? I just felt like shouting at him. Now where is this place? Maybe the woman will invite us in for coffee and cake.'


He had to tie the girl up, but he couldn't find anything to do it with, and his hand was bleeding where he had accidentally cut himself with the razor. And now there was somebody banging at the door. Who was that banging coming from? Cyrus thought, annoyed, as he tried to find something to staunch the blood. There was shouting now, too. Soon he was going to get really angry. Was it too much to ask for people to just leave him in peace?

'You don't have a Kleenex or anything?' asked the woman, who was still pinned by the chair. If he was going to tie her up, he'd have to take his hands off the chair and then she'd undoubtedly try another trick. What to do?

Damn. What would the Master do? He couldn't think clearly. Who on earth was banging on the door? He wasn't expecting any guests.

The idea came in a flash, and it was simple and beautiful. He didn't need to tie her up. He would put her somewhere while he dealt with whoever was at the door. He lifted the chair off of her and pulled her to her feet. Dragged her towards the other room.

Tye couldn't see much. They went through another door – God, what sort of lair had he built here? They were at the back of the apartment now, she figured; the windows were covered in blackout cloth, but there were faint lines of light where they didn't sit flush.

There was a large steel-cased refrigerator. Panting, Cyrus dragged Tye up to the door, wrenched it open. Icy fumes curled out.

'Please, no. I'm claustrophobic.'

'It isn't what I want either, you know,' Cyrus said as he pushed her inside and shut the door.

So this is how it will end, she thought, as the cold slapped her skin and the rough air scraped her throat.

It was funny how the smallest injury could hurt like hell. And the blood – there was so much of it. Cyrus needed something to wrap around his wound. He went out to the front, where the guy was still thumping at the door. He saw the bag with the hair sticking out and he remembered the scarf. That must still be in there.

He reached in and grabbed the hair instead, by accident. He went to put it back, but his blood was all
sticky and the hair somehow got embedded in the
wound. He didn't want to make things worse, so he
wrapped it all up tightly. He'd deal with it when he'd
told the guy at the door to go away. This guy was
getting on his wick. He was losing his train of thought
– he really needed silence to be able to concentrate.
He cleared his throat, straightened his shoulders, put
the razor in his pocket and opened the door.

# Chapter Fifty-Eight

'I know she's in there!' Adrian yelled. 'I want to speak to you, Tye.'

'Tye?' Quinn thought. He'd moved closer to find out what was going on. His Tye?

'Tye, we have to talk. I mean it. You've gone too far.'

Quinn edged closer still. The guy took no notice of him.

'Tye, come on out and deal with me.'

Quinn stayed, rapt. Who was this guy? An old lover? A new lover? That was probably why she hadn't wanted to take up with him. Perhaps they were married. Oh, God, he hoped not. Quinn went down the stairs. It was a miracle. He'd found her again.

The door opened so suddenly that Adrian was not prepared. On the other side was someone with blood in his hair and on his hands, and holding what looked like a scalp. Adrian fainted dead away leaving Quinn and Cyrus staring at each other.

'Hey,' Quinn said, stepping over his body. 'Is Tye here?'

Cyrus glared at the guy. The nerve of it – just waltzing in without asking.

'That looks like a nasty cut,' Quinn said. 'You oughta get that looked at. I got blood poisoning once, when I was a kid. Nearly died from it. I'm lucky to be alive. Can you tell Tye I'm here? She's expecting me. William Quinn.'

'I don't know anybody called Tye.' Cyrus wanted to try and match this guy's insouciant tone, but he had too much else on his mind.

'Nice place you got here. Must be expensive,' Quinn said. 'What do you pay? Two, three grand?' Quinn strolled around the living room, trying to get the measure of the place. Not very big, so not much room to hide anybody. 'View's not much, but that's good in a way – it gives you privacy.' Quinn leaned against the windowsill. What the hell was going on here? Should he leave and call the cops? Was Tye in some kind of danger? Perhaps if he could keep him talking, somebody would come by. Or maybe the lump by the door would wake up. 'Mind if I look around?' he said. 'I'm in the market for an apartment.'

'Be my guest.' Cyrus held out his good hand in an effort to imitate Quinn's natural ease.

Tye's vital functions had slowed down, which at least gave her some way to control her panic. Her breathing was shallow and her heart had slowed. Her extremities felt as though they might snap off. She struggled to get her keys out of her jeans' pocket, but her fingers would barely do what she told them, and there was very little room to manoeuvre. She couldn't even stand upright, her knees were bent and her thigh muscles were aching from being held in an unnatural position. She had tried pushing the door open, but couldn't move it. By probing with her fingers she had discovered the door hinges. If only she could get the keys out she could at least try to use them to loosen the screws, if there were screws. She couldn't tell in the dark and her fingers were too cold to get her any accurate information.

It was difficult to keep her mind on the task. Her fingers felt as though they were falling asleep. They were inside her pocket but she couldn't get a proper grip. She was reduced to nudging them up.

Finally, she worked them halfway out. She plucked at them with her left hand, which she had been holding under her armpit in a feeble attempt to keep it warm. The keys came loose but she couldn't keep her fingers curled in even an approximation of a grip. They dropped. Tye was wedged in so tightly, she could not reach down to pick them up.

She began crying quietly. She was entombed in a domestic appliance and no one was coming to save her.


'So this is like a sublet?' Quinn said as he stood in the bedroom. Place smelt off, like the garbage hadn't been taken out.

'What?' Cyrus said.

'You're what? Going away? Moving in with your girlfriend perhaps?' Quinn inspected the cupboard. Tye wasn't here, so time to get the hell out. In the smoothest possible way of course. The loon looked like any sudden movement would send him off the edge. He was going straight to the cops when he got out the door, this guy was Grade A Bellevue material if ever he'd seen it.

Girlfriend! Cyrus clapped his hand to his forehead. Oh God, no! What had he done? She'd been in the freezer too long. If he didn't get back to her she'd die and then he'd be all alone again. Why was he so stupid? That was no way to treat a lady.

Cyrus moved fast. While Quinn was looking in the wardrobe, he took the razor out of his pocket and put it close to Quinn's jugular vein. 'I'm going to have to ask you to stay in here,' he said. 'I have something I need to take care of.'

Quinn stepped into the closet and the door closed behind him. He waited exactly ten seconds before he began slamming against the door with all his might.


Adrian's first thought when he came round was to get out of that madhouse fast. He picked himself up, looked to see if the weird guy was hiding somewhere and ran up the stairs and out onto the street.

He didn't look back. Fuck Tye. Whatever happened would serve her right.


Tye was in the foothills of unconsciousness when she saw light. Through the icy air she made out a shape, come to her rescue. She instructed her foot to step out of her hideous frozen coffin but it would not move. Maybe this, then, was hell. Where you are shown the way to escape but can't summon the means.

Two hands reached in. Grasped her gently by the shoulders and pulled her. She stumbled and started to cry, to form words of thanks. Then she saw the hands that held her. One was covered in blood. Then she saw the face of the madman. She screamed.


Quinn tried, but couldn't batter the closet door down. Just my luck, he thought. In a city awash with cheap and shoddy woodwork I get locked in the one place that was built by a craftsman. He really wished he hadn't sent Molly shopping. She would have sent the maniac with the razor packing.

He'd tried yelling, in case the guy out front had come round, but no luck. He was massaging his bruised shoulder when he thought he heard a woman screaming. He put his ear to the crack in the door. Definitely screaming, but where was it coming from? Not the apartment, it was too muffled. Upstairs perhaps?

Ignoring the pain he heaved himself against the door one more time and was rewarded with the sound of splintering wood.

Quinn was certain it was Tye screaming. He ran out to the living room to see if the other guy was still there. He'd gone. Quinn looked around for a phone but couldn't find one. He went back to the bedroom; the screaming was definitely louder there. Where the hell was she?

Then Quinn noticed the blood on the carpet. A trail

of splodges led towards the bookcase. Right up to the bookcase, in fact.

Down on his knees, Quinn could see that the lowest shelf of the bookcase wasn't resting on the floor but had maybe half an inch clearance. So it was a door of some kind. Clever. He began to inspect it more closely.

Cyrus could not believe that his day, which had started so promisingly, was going so badly wrong. How the hell was he going to get rid of the guy in the closet? He'd just have to kill him, he supposed. Although he didn't really feel like it right now. He wanted to concentrate on Penny, who looked like she needed his care.

'I'm really sorry,' he said. 'I wasn't thinking, you know? I get a bit like that – panicked. I'm not good in emergencies. I'm working on that, but you'll have to be patient with me because I guess it's going to take a while.' Cyrus had decided it was important to be honest and open with this woman. Not in the way he had done in the past, in a cringing feel-sorry-for-me way, but in an up-front, manly manner. It was okay to admit your failings. It was a cool, brave thing to do.

Tye looked at him hollowly. Her eyes darted about the room for a potential weapon. There was nothing she could see, even if she did have the strength to use it. It was taking all her strength to stand upright. Cyrus tried to put a blanket around her shoulders but she shrugged him off. He brushed his hand down the side of her face. She was so cold, she couldn't feel it.

'I would love to use this time for us – to get to

know each other – but this other thing has come up, so I'm just going to leave you here. It's not what I want, but it has to be that way for the moment, okay?'

Tye didn't respond.

Cyrus moved tentatively towards her. 'I can tell you're a very special person and I know this is our first meeting and everything, and I hope you won't think I'm too forward, but would you mind if I gave you a kiss?'

Tye stood rigidly. Bloody terrific, she thought. Jeffrey Dahmer meets Pepe Le Pew. She cleared her throat, wondering if her voice would work. 'Okay,' she croaked.

Cyrus paused about a foot away from her face, partly because he wanted to savour the moment and partly because he couldn't decide which side of her face he would kiss, or if he should do both, like the Europeans. Her vivid purple eyes stared back at him, expressionless.

Might as well go for the right side, he thought and closing his eyes he placed his lips on her cheek.

'Jesus Christ,' he shrieked as she bit off a piece of his ear.

# Chapter Fifty-Nine

Cyrus stared in surprise at her. Tye stared back. Then she kicked him in the balls. Cyrus bent over and retched. The pain was exquisite. And not just the physical pain, either but the emotional pain. He didn't understand why, when she knew about the Master and everything.

She was trying to find the door.

His vision cleared. The kick did it. She really wasn't playing ball, which meant he'd just have to put the relationship issues to one side while he concentrated on the problem at hand. He simply couldn't deal with both right now. He grabbed Penny firmly by the back of the neck and smashed her face into the wall. With a small moan she collapsed. Cyrus dragged her to the futon and lay her on it, pulling the cover up so that she wouldn't get cold. Then he went next door to take care of that other asshole.

'These shoes aren't meant for walking,' Renee said as she stopped to massage her feet. Larry lunged at a piece of bread on the sidewalk. 'Larry, no! God, you are such a scavenger,' she said to the dog as he gulped his illicit snack.

'Not far to go now,' Cat said.

'You sure you want to keep going? With no crew or anything?'

'We're seeing this baby to the bitter end.' Cat punched Gerald Long's number into her cellphone. She was going to get the crew back if she had to rip teeth out to do it.

The bookshelf opened so fast it nearly knocked Quinn off his feet. He scrambled backwards. Cyrus saw that the closet door was open. He turned on Quinn, holding the razor like a fencing foil. Blocking his escape route. Quinn put his hands up.

'Hey, buddy. Let's talk about this, shall we?'

The blade came closer. Cyrus's hair fell into his face. He flicked it away and realized he'd used the razor to do so. A lock of hair fell on the carpet.

'Now look what you've made me do! I'm really running out of patience here.'

Quinn shrunk back into the corner, using the cast to protect his face. He said a Hail Mary just for the hell of it and wished again that he hadn't sent Molly away.

Tye dragged herself off the bed. The bump on her head hadn't knocked her out the way the lunatic thought. She watched him go through the door by pressing some kind of lever or button on the wall. She rolled off the bed and crawled to the door. Pressed the walls but couldn't work out how to open it.

There had to be a way. She wasn't going to die like this in a smelly back room. She had plans for her life.

She picked up the blanket, wrapped herself in it. Wondered who the person was out in the other room and what was happening to them.

Think!


Cyrus jabbed with the razor. Quinn tried to dive out of his way but the razor stuck fast in his cast. Quinn punched with his good hand. Cyrus grabbed Quinn's broken arm and banged it against the closet. Quinn grabbed a hunk of Cyrus's greasy hair and yanked hard. The lunatic remained stuck to him.

Quinn, who'd always thought that violence was a refuge for people who couldn't express themselves verbally, was surprised at how alive he felt, how clearly his thoughts were coming. It's him or me, he thought. It doesn't get more basic than this.


Tye's eyes had grown accustomed to the gloom and she roamed around the room. There wasn't much. A bed, a cabinet. She couldn't get back to the room with the freezer – and windows – in it. The maniac had locked it.

The metal cabinet might have something she could use though. If only she could get into it. Trouble was, the room was bare of tools. Tye ran her hands through her hair.

Her earrings. She twisted them out of her ears.

They were cheap, dangly things made from African beads and bought at a street market. Tye began to unbend the wire. She'd been a good lockpick in her day.

Quinn couldn't get another grip on the guy's hair. It was too matted with blood. He was pinned now. The guy was shoving him against the wall again and again. The only good thing was that he didn't have the razor, which was still stuck in his cast.

'Please,' he said. But the guy was in a frenzy. His lips were drawn back in a snarl and blood ran down his face from the cut on his head. It looked as though his ear was bleeding too. The adrenaline euphoria left Quinn and he felt useless and tired. He was going to die anyway, so why not just get it over with?

The metal cabinet contained piles of Ziploc plastic bags. Tye picked up a couple. One had human hair in it. Another had what looked like underwear and a diary. A third had a pager and sneakers. Tye shuddered and threw them down.

She had to force herself to keep looking through the neatly stacked shelves. Somewhere in these horrid piles was something that would help her.

Then she saw the most blessed of sights. A small battery-operated saw.

*

The sound coming from the next room distracted Cyrus. And he knew what it was. She was trying to get out, and she was wrecking his expensive door to do it.

'No!' he yelled. He dragged Quinn towards the door. The bookcase began to shake from the force of the pressure being applied on the other side.

Cyrus kicked the catch, the door swung open. Quinn felt the cold prick of the razor once more against his throat.

The first thing Tye saw was Quinn.

'Oh,' she said. 'It's you.'

'Hey. Is this how come you haven't called?'

Is this how come you haven't called? Cyrus sneered inwardly. Who did this guy darn well think he was, Cary Grant? How dare he be so cool when Cyrus was running the show. Cyrus suddenly saw the situation clearly. They were obviously an item and he'd made a mistake, a huge, embarrassing mistake. He was filled with shame at the way he'd misread the signals. Just because she had that hair in her bag didn't mean she was with the Master.

He'd just have to kill them both now. It didn't matter – there'd be other girls. It wasn't like this one was anything special. He jerked Quinn closer to him. 'Put down the saw, Penelope,' he said the name deliberately so that she would know he knew it wasn't her real name. 'Step in here and shut that door properly.'

The house was empty. Cat rang the door bell several times. Renee had peered over the stoop into the front window. It was dark. Renee flopped down on the steps. 'Oh well,' she said. 'Nothing ventured, nothing gained.'

'All's well that ends well,' Cat said, sitting down beside her and slipping into their old game.

'A penny saved is a penny earned.' Renee massaged her tortured feet. 'The early bird catches the worm.'

'How do you feel about living with a former television journalist?' Cat changed the subject.

'I say we move to Albuquerque and start a commune,' Renee suggested brightly. 'I've always wanted to design with feathers.'

'Somehow I don't think it'll be far enough away.' Cat pulled out her phone and dialled Gerald to tell him not to bother about the crew, the story was dead. She couldn't reach him. Maybe there was a crew steaming towards her at this very minute, Cat thought. If there was, what the hell. She'd buy them all a drink.

Renee wriggled her toes and Larry the terrier shot off, dragging his lead. 'Larry, come back,' she called. But Larry had scampered down the steps, sniffing. 'I swear that mutt can smell food at a hundred paces,' Renee complained. 'Don't go in the street, Larry.'

'Yeah, like he can really understand what you're saying,' Cat teased. She was surprised how relaxed she felt. Her career had tanked yet sitting on a step in the sun with Renee, she found she didn't really care. 'Larry, what's the atomic weight of oxygen?' she called, mock serious. 'What's your opinion on repayment conditions of Third World debt?'

Larry had his doggy nose down and his tail up. Both were quivering. 'Larry, come back.' Renee padded down the steps in her bare feet. 'I better get him, there's probably a dead rat down there.'

Larry daintily took the steps to the basement apartment.

'Chuck me my shoes, will you?'

Cat threw them down to Renee who caught them in one hand and slid them on and followed her wiry milk-and-coffee-coloured pet.

'Perhaps I should just be a kept woman.' Cat leant back on the step, turning her face to the sun. It was warm in this sheltered spot. 'Maybe we could take your company public and I could orchestrate the media campaign. Or I could be your muse. You know, loll around the studio eating grapes and reading obscure Russian novels. Giving interviews to *Vogue* about how my natural vitality keeps me thin.'

'Cat!'

'Oh, I forgot. I'm the cross-dressing lumberjack. Still there must be some place for me in your organization. Give it a think, is all I'm saying.'

'Cat! Get over here,' Renee shouted.

Cat's eyes flew open. She stood up and went to the stoop and looked over. Renee was standing at the bottom of the stairs holding Larry the terrier. His paws and nose were covered in blood. 'Look.' Renee pointed to the blood at her feet. 'Call 911. For God's sake, hurry.'

# Chapter Sixty

'I'm going to cut this throat while you watch,' Cyrus said to Tye. 'And then I'm going to cut yours. See? And it's your fault. You had your chance to be nice to me and you darn well muffed it, missy.'

'That's not a very good idea,' Tye said, keeping her American accent. 'Because someone is expected here any minute.' She swallowed carefully, although there was no saliva in her throat. 'So it's best if you just let us go. Killing us isn't going to make things any better for you.'

It was the same woman, Quinn realized. He recognized the voice. Tye was the woman who'd duped him out of his sublet. He should have seen it before, but he hadn't been able to get past the leather cat suit.

'I remember you.' He said the words levelly, without anger.

'I'm sorry,' Tye said. She sounded as though she meant it. Not that it mattered now. He felt sad. For him, for her. For his unfinished but highly promising novel.

Cyrus tightened his grip on Quinn. He hefted the razor in his bloodied hand.

'Say goodbye to your boyfriend,' he said the words with a sneer.


Cat and Renee stared at the door. Cat pushed it gingerly. It was unlatched. 'We have to go in.'

'He cuts people up into pieces!' Renee hissed. Larry wriggled in her arms.

'He's got somebody in there. We might be able to save them.'

'Or get ourselves killed!'

Cat walked in.

'I think I'm going to puke,' Renee said as she followed.


'What the fuck?'

Cyrus blinked. There was a television reporter in his apartment. The one he'd seen reporting on him from outside the supermarket. He realized then he'd have to get an agent. He wouldn't be able to deal with all of the interview requests. He'd have to pick and choose. He wouldn't ask for money, that would be wrong. But perhaps he would establish a charitable foundation. Either way, an agent was the necessary first step.

Cat stared aghast at the scene in front of her: a woman; a guy who had the mad glare of a Rasputin with an arm hooked around the throat of another guy as well as holding a razor to his throat. Nobody moved – it was like a gothic tableau.

Quinn knew he was hallucinating. There was no

oxygen going to his brain so it was making up stories – TV reporters were walking into his fantasies. The pressure on his throat was becoming intolerable. I hope I get out of this, he thought. I can write about this. I can use this.

'Oh, my God.' Renee pushed past Cat, who seemed rooted to the spot. The guy being strangled was going blue. Renee gave Larry to Cat. Somebody had to do something.

'Don't let him near that blood.' She slipped off one of her five-hundred-dollar shoes – they were heavier than they looked which was what made them so damn uncomfortable – and aimed the spike heel at the strangler's head. Then she pitched as hard as she could.

The shoe struck Cyrus sharply in the forehead. Stunned, he stepped back and dropped the razor. Tye dived for it. Furious and panicked, she lunged at Cyrus, who tried to put Quinn between himself and Tye. But Quinn wriggled out of his grasp. The blade connected with soft flesh. Warm blood bubbled and plopped out of Cyrus's back like a red dorsal fin. He turned towards Tye, looked puzzled for a second or two before flopping down face first.

Quinn stared around the room. There was blood on the walls and even more on the floor. Place looked like a slaughter house, except for the two well-dressed women who were picking their way towards them. Tye sank to her knees, stunned by what she'd just done. Feeling sick from the blood and the smell of it. Quinn knelt beside her, put his arm around her, exhilarated. He hugged her tight and stroked her hair. From now on he wasn't letting her out of his sight.

'See what happens when you run away from me?' he murmured. 'People get hurt.'

Cat went outside to wait for the camera crew. Renee fetched water for Tye and Quinn. Larry barked loudly at the unconscious Cyrus.

None of them noticed a very determined-looking young woman with a firm, set jaw and an old-fashioned perm, wearing a camel overcoat and sports sneakers go down the stairs and step carefully around the pool of blood at the door. Having knocked and received no reply, she realized the door was open and went in. She appeared not to notice the blood in the living room. She walked through to the bedroom, first checking to see whether the kitchen contained a gas cooker and a decent-sized icebox.

In the bedroom she stepped briskly over a prostrate body and surveyed the room. A couple hugging and half crying. A woman wearing one shoe and telling a terrier to be quiet. The closet space.

'This is the sublet?' she asked, clearly and firmly because her therapist was working with her about overcoming her timid manner.

Tye nodded dumbly.

'Twenty-two hundred a month, right?' The woman pulled her chequebook out of her fawn Coach shoulderbag.

Tye nodded again.

'Great. Three months' deposit okay?'

# Chapter Sixty-One

'Police arrested Cyrus Frederick Tower and charged him with a triple murder this afternoon. Tower, who was injured by one of his intended victims, is in a stable but serious condition at St Vincent's Hospital. A search for bodies is under way in the Clarence Fahnestock State Park.

'Tower, who wore one of his mother's couture dresses when he allegedly deposited some of the parts of people he'd killed in a supermarket freezer, was also expected to undergo a psychiatric examination. WKLP has exclusive footage of the crime scene.'

Cat paused, while back in the studio the pictures the cameraman had shot in the apartment played on air.

'Cops say that Cyrus Tower allegedly used a popular self-help book as his guide, giving these brutal murders, which have shocked New York, a further bizarre twist.'

'Cat, any word on the condition of the two people who were in the apartment?' the anchor asked.

'Well, Chad, quite a turnaround for those two. Writer, William Quinn and British actress, Tye Fisher had a narrow escape . . .'

'Due in no small part to you.' Chad chuckled. He

was an oleaginous twerp, Cat thought, for about the hundredth time that day.

'. . . escaped without serious injuries, Chad, and are now negotiating with top Hollywood agents to sell the rights to their story. One of the movie directors who's expressed particular interest in the project is Todd Rachenbach, who as we know had such incredible success last year with his film, *Dogs Don't Die*. It'll be interesting to see what comes out of this, Chad.'

'Thanks Cat. And we're just gonna take another look at those exclusive pictures of the crime scene. Some viewers might be offended by this . . .'

It was a media fiesta on Baxter Street and Cat had the best position. She also had the best pictures. The camera crew had arrived minutes after the cops and shot interiors, some good stuff of the arrest and the victims. Cat knew she hadn't seen all there was to see yet. She hadn't been able to get into the back room, but a senior cop had hinted at its dark secrets and promised her first look. It was day two and she still owned this story. She took a sip from her Evian water. As she put it down she noticed a woman standing nearby clutching a bunch of irises. Behind her were twin girls and to one side was a big guy who looked every inch a cop.

She went over to her. 'Marion? Hi.'

'Hi,' Marion Neidermeyer said. 'I was hoping you'd be here. These are my daughters, Antonia and Grace, and this is John Abruzzo.'

Cat shook the hands of each girl and the cop.

'I – we – wanted to thank you for finding him. And for, you know, everything.'

'I had help,' Cat said. 'And don't mention it.' She smiled. Marion looked very well indeed, considering. Colour in her cheeks, a lightness to her manner.

'Not that horrible Eric Atlas.' Marion smiled back.

Cat shook her head. 'He's taken a leave of absence to deal with some personal problems.'

'We came to say goodbye to Gus and Susie.' Marion held up the flowers.

Cat nodded. She knew if she were a proper journalist she would ask this woman if she wanted to give an interview, but she had never been very good at sticking a microphone in the faces of people who'd just suffered a horrendous tragedy and asking how it felt.

'You can film us if you like,' Marion said.

'If you're sure?'

'I'm – we're – sure,' Marion said. 'The girls and I talked it over and we decided that it's important for people to know that Gus and Susie – and the other girl, Anna – were human beings, not just victims. They had families and people who –' she stopped, swallowed hard a couple of times – 'people who cared about them.' Marion lifted her chin and smiled.

Cat signalled to Jose who hoisted the camera from its tripod to his shoulders. 'Not too close,' she said.

Marion gripped Antonia's hand tightly as she walked up to the iron railing that surrounded the house. She took the bright-blue flowers out of their store wrapping. Grace crouched down and poured bottled water into a glass vase. Marion slid the flowers into the vase. 'Goodbye,' she whispered softly. The girls helped her up. They walked slowly away. Cat noticed that the policeman followed.

# Epilogue

He should have been dead, so that was something to be grateful for. The razor had missed his lung by a shaving of an inch. And the morphine took the edge off things. There was pain, but it was manageable. It was there, but standing back politely as if it didn't want to bother him. He was free to focus on his thoughts. He couldn't pin things down so well, but he was enjoying the big ideas that floated by. He studied them as you would clouds on a hazy August day, appreciating them for their inconstancy.

Did he regret any of it? He guessed that would be the first question the talk-show host would ask him – that was how these things usually went. Something off-beat to get into the meat of the story right away. Would you have done any of it differently if you had to do it again, Cyrus?

He knew how he'd respond. He'd chuckle ruefully, maybe roll his eyes a little in a 'Like, hello?' kind of way. That would cut out the interviewer and get him on the side of the audience. They would understand his non-verbal language. Everybody in the goddamned world has regrets and if they said they didn't they were liars. Of course he had regrets, of course he did. That was part of the whole thing called living. You paid your money and you took your chance.

Yes, he'd made a couple of errors of judgement that had been, on reflection, pretty dumb. But they were understandable mistakes that flowed out of his enthusiasm and inexperience. Next time, for instance, he'd have been much cooler about the woman and the way he felt about her. He'd have been more subtle, he'd banter, like he'd seen that other guy do, so she wouldn't be frightened. And he wouldn't take a clue like the hair so much for granted. He'd question someone more closely about something important like that. So there was room for improvement, for sure. But even so he reckoned the good – what he had learned – had outweighed the bad by a long shot.

Why? They'd have to ask him that. There was no way an interviewer could leave that statement just hanging there – I mean, he was going to prison! (Or maybe he'd give the interview after he'd come out of prison and was telling everybody how sorry he was and how much he'd changed.) If he were honest, the thought of prison was kind of depressing. But then he remembered how women write to men inside, and some even marry them, and the thought that his social life might actually improve cheered him up.

So why did he think, despite everything, that he was still ahead? – the interviewer would press the point – it was important.

Simple. (Maybe he'd turn to his wife here, if it was after prison, and squeeze her hand and smile at her.) He'd realized something significant through all the craziness and the striving. It had hit him after he'd come round, after he found that he should have been dead but he wasn't. The very next thought had been this: You can't have it all. That was what struck him. You can't have it all. It's a lie. Sure, you can *try*. You can give it your damn best shot, but that's all. And when the winning and the fame and the riches don't roll in, well, that's when you have to think about the kind of person you are and how you will deal with it. That's called character.

And there's a kind of a victory in it. Any fool can deal with success but deciding to live nobly among your broken dreams, that takes something extra. Nobody ever talked about this stuff, it was kind of anti-American, but it was an arithmetical fact. Not everybody can be President. Not every little girl can become a prima ballerina. Not everybody can be Ted Bundy. There are just too many of us.

So how do you deal with it? That's what the interviewer would ask. Because he or she would be listening carefully to what Cyrus was saying and not merely thinking ahead to the next question or fretting about how much longer to the commercial break.

It was very important not to be bitter, he would say. More people needed to know it. Bitterness was poison and succumbing to it was the real defeat. He imagined people – the audience who'd waited for hours outside the television studio to get seats – really knowing about that, deep down. Someone else always got the things you wanted and deserved. Always. Everybody felt this, no matter how successful their lives were. No matter how many things you owned, there was always room for jealousy. But it was false. Sometimes success came down to one simple thing: changing how you saw your situation.

Take space as an example. He would lean forward in his chair as he said this part, that way people would know he was passionate about it, and that he wasn't some schmoe who never read a book. Space was a good example because Earth seems so stable and safe and still, but isn't. What's actually happening is that we're hurtling through space. Every two hours we travel a million miles and we're spinning on top of that. And the chunk of rock that we're spinning on, at its centre, is on fire! There's no such thing as safe and steady, it's just something you choose to believe. So what's your reality?

He'd chuck that rhetorical thing out at the end. Finish strong. Give 'em something simple to take away.

What's Your Reality? Maybe that'd be the title of his book. It had a nice resonance to it. Challenging. Make you want to pick it right up off the shelf.

Yeah.